EVERY SCAR tells a STORY

RAYNA YORK

ALSO BY RAYNA YORK

The Right Kind of Unexpected

When Life Gives You Lemons Instead of Lattes

Everything I Knew to be True

EVERY SCAR tells a STORY

RAYNA YORK

Toad Tree
PRESS

Published by Toad Tree Press

167 Terrace View NE

Medicine Hat Alberta TIC-OA4

Publishers Note

This book is a work of fiction. Names, characters, places, and incidents are derived from the

authors imagination and therefore fictitious. Any resemblance to actual persons, living or

dead, business establishments, events or locales is entirely coincidental.

ISBN 978-1-9990951–6-1 (paperback)

ISBN 978-1-9990951-7-8 (ebook)

Cover design by Rocio Martin Osuna

I dedicate this novel to my readers. Without your curiosity and love for stories, these characters would remain silent and their tales untold. Thank you for giving them a voice.

CHAPTER 1

SERENA

It always hits me like a slap in the face—a sudden awareness so powerful, it's like *wham*, what was I thinking?

I study Hayden's profile and wonder where the sudden realization came from. We've been together five months, a personal record. He's everything I thought I wanted—attentive, thoughtful, attractive, and we hang out in the same friend group. It should be a perfect match.

Hayden casually slings an arm over my shoulder and kisses the side of my head. "Hey, babe. Do you want to get out of here?"

"Sure. Let's go. I have a ton of homework anyway." His idea of 'getting out of here' is code for *let's go fool around*, but in the state my mind is in? Not a chance. Also, with finals looming and the valedictorian title at stake, I can't afford to slip. Especially with Rebecca Motts hot on my heels.

"School, work, homework," he sighs, nuzzling the side of my neck. "You're always busy. Take the night off."

"Football, wrestling... I'm not the only one with a busy schedule."

He sits back, shrugging dismissively like his shit is more important than mine.

Seriously? What the hell?

"We're gonna go," I announce to our friends, nudging Hayden out of the booth.

"See you at school tomorrow," Rowan says, her dark sculpted eyebrows pumping like Hayden and I are about to go rip each other's clothes off.

She knows better.

My friends call me fickle. Others might use a different word. But contrary to popular belief, I don't sleep around. Yes, I've had lots of boyfriends, but I've only had sex with one guy, and so far, there's been no desire to try it again.

It's close to nine on a Tuesday as we step outside. The sky is deep in twilight, and a spring chill lingers in the air, making me long for warmer weather. Here, at the base of the Colorado Rockies, summer can take its sweet time.

Summer... I can't help but smile. This one will be like no other. High school will be over, and I'll be heading off to college in the fall. I'm so ready to leave this small town behind.

It's not a bad place to live, but I'm psyched to move to an actual city where the downtown is larger than a four-block radius. *And* I'm eager to get my career started. Working probably isn't what gets most eighteen-year-olds jacked up, but I know the direction I want to go, and I'm motivated to get there.

Hayden walks ahead of me without a backward glance,

unlocking his early graduation gift—a shiny, new black Mustang. The jackass is sulking.

Reaching for the handle, I happen to look left and catch sight of a herculean figure walking on the sidewalk toward me. His head is down, face mysteriously shadowed by a hooded sweatshirt pulled low over his eyes. Somehow, he must sense me staring because he stops and snaps his head up, then looks around like I'm blocking his path and isn't sure what to do about it.

"Are you coming?" Hayden says over the roof of his car with a tinge of annoyance.

"Yeah, sorry." After opening my door, I glance back. The stranger is walking at a brisk pace across the street.

After we're both seated in the car, he says, "Do you know that guy?"

"No, but I think I startled him." I pull the seatbelt across my chest and secure it.

"Well, it *seems* like you did." He starts the car with a *vroom*. "Is there something I should know about?"

"No." My heart races at the aggressive sound of the engine. "I've never seen him before." I'm still plagued with nightmares and struggle with other people driving, all because of the accident I was in with my father when I was thirteen. Hayden knows this.

The drive to my house is silent, and I wonder about the sudden awareness I had back at the restaurant. *Am I really going to break up with him?* I doubt he's ever been dumped before. The guy is high school royalty. And it's going to mess up our friend group, not to mention our plans for prom in two months. Maybe I'm being too hasty this time. I mean, aside from occasional insensitivity, the escalating moodiness, and the increase in his drinking, what's really wrong with him?

Yeah, aside from all that, my brain shouts back at me.

We arrive at my house and Hayden parks along the curb. "I'll see you tomorrow," I say, leaning in and giving him a peck on the cheek before reaching to open my door.

He catches my hand before I can climb out. "What's going on with you?"

"Nothing. What's going on with you?" *Damn. Are we doing this now?*

"Honestly?" He releases his seatbelt and turns, leaning his back against the door to face me. "You never have time for me." He holds up a hand. "Don't get me wrong, I understand. You love school and working at the old folks' home—and both are important to you—but I feel like I'm only getting the scraps left over."

He reaches forward and takes my hand in his. "You're the only good thing I've got going, but I feel like you're holding back."

I am? "I'm not sure what to say... wait, is this because I won't have sex with you?" *Because it better not be.*

"No, well... maybe a little." He straightens in his seat, his head down. "Partly." There's a pause, then his eyes lift to mine. "Yes." I'm not sure if it's the glare on my face or my silence, but he drops my gaze to stare out over the steering wheel. "I can't help wanting more. But it's more than that," he quickly adds, facing me once again. "I feel like I'm only getting part of you—the small pieces you allow me to see. It's like you're afraid to open up or something—to get close."

Maybe I'm a little cautious since all my other relationships have turned out to be crap. "If I'm guarded, it's not intentional, but I won't be pressured into—"

"Who's pressuring?" his voice elevates slightly.

Without a word, I climb out of the car, slam the door behind me, and walk to my front door.

"Serena." I hear Hayden call out.

Ignoring him, I keep walking, then hear his car door shut and his running footsteps coming up behind me.

He takes hold of my arm, stopping me. "Why are you so mad?"

I whirl around to face him. "If you have to ask that? Then... screw you."

"Hey..." He gently pulls me forward, locking me into an embrace. "I really care about you, and I want you to trust me enough to let me in." He presses a light kiss to my lips—his words filling me with a tenderness that catches me off guard. "How can I show you what you mean to me?"

We've never shared this level of honesty before. "I'm not sure. I just..." My words fade into silence. My mind is spinning and I have no idea how to answer him.

Disappointment clouds his features. "I didn't mean for any of this to happen, and I definitely wasn't trying to pressure you." His arms fall away. "I'll see you at school."

"I heard everything you said, okay? I just need time to process."

"Sure." He nods and turns away.

Watching him walk back to his car, I wonder if tonight's sudden revelation has nothing to do with Hayden and everything to do with me. Sure, our entire conversation was convoluted, but overall, did *I* cause the disconnect between us?

I fish my keys out of the bag that's slung across my shoulder. Have I always been too quick to end my relationships?

If I sensed they weren't working, I didn't wait around for them to get ugly. I got out. What would have been the point of sticking around? I've witnessed enough crap between my parents to know it isn't worth it.

But what if I'm about to blow up a relationship that's truly worthwhile?

Sliding my key into the lock, I glance at the darkened house next door and an image of the tall, hooded figure from outside the restaurant fills my mind. I'd guess he's close to my age—the way he was dressed, his movements.

And that moment, when his head snapped up and he stared at me, there was something. It wasn't like I could see his eyes, or make out his face in anyway, there was just this odd feeling.

I shake my head, trying to clear the memory as I step inside my house. I'm probably making more of it than it was. He was just some random guy crossing the street. It didn't mean anything.

CHAPTER 2

SERENA

"Hello, ladies." I walk up to a table of seniors playing rummy in the common room at work. I'm sure Bertha and Agnes are kicking butt. They always do.

"You still seeing that putz, Hayden?" Bertha asks, her filter gone along with her youth.

"Yes. Same as when you asked me yesterday *and* the day before. And he's not a putz." I'm not sure where her dislike comes from. I haven't shared much about him, and he's only ever visited here once.

"You hear that smart mouth of hers?" Bertha complains to the others before a small, appreciative grin lifts the corners of her mouth. "He's not good enough for you. I don't know why you bother."

"Were you *wearing* your glasses when you saw him?" I joke.

She scoffs. "Looks fade, my dear, then what are you left with?"

Agnes and Bertha are my favorite seniors at the Sunnyvale Retirement Home. This place offers assisted living and long-term nursing care. I work here every day after school until seven and all day Saturday, offering an extra pair of hands wherever needed.

Laying three kings in front of her, Agnes says, "Pull up a chair, honey. Sit with us."

"I can't right now. I've got work to do."

"Isn't keeping us occupied part of your job description?" Bertha grouches—her standard demeanor.

"Leave the poor girl alone, Bertha," Agnes says, coming to my aid as she often does. She's the peacemaker of the two.

"Yes," I say. "It's one of my duties, but I have somewhere else to be at the moment." They nod in understanding.

Stuart arrived with an aggressive form of dementia. We had an instant connection... like my favorite grandpa suddenly came back into my life. Sadly, his rapid decline had him bedridden within four months. His wife and son are gone, and the remaining son never visits.

If my father was dying, I'd definitely be there to say goodbye. As much as I resent him, I couldn't bear the regret of missing that chance.

"Hi, Stuart," I say, entering his room. "My name is Serena. I came to read to you today. Would that be okay?" He nods his head tentatively, then points a shaky index finger toward his empty cup that's sitting on his bedside table. "Do you want me to get you some water?"

"Yes, please," his voice cracks. He coughs to clear it.

I give him a big smile and take his spill-proof cup into the bathroom, rinse it out, and fill it. "Here you go." I hand it to him.

Stuart takes several sips before handing the cup back to me.

After setting it on his side table, I pick up the novel next to it. "Is it okay if I read this to you?" I turn the title over so he can see it. It's the same book I read every visit, but he never remembers.

"That looks like a good one." He gives a slight smile.

"Can I turn down the TV so you can hear me better?"

"Okay."

I reach for the remote before starting at the beginning.

"Do I know you?" he asks politely.

"No. I'm just helping out today."

Treating each visit as if it's our first keeps him from feeling confused or inadequate. I learned the importance of this the hard way. When I first met Stuart, he told me he was an avid reader. Not long after, it became too difficult for him to do on his own, so I helped out by reading to him. Two months ago, I picked up where we'd left off the day before, and he asked what I was reading. I laughed, saying, "It's the same as yesterday, don't you remember?" From his confused expression, I realized how thoughtless my statement was, and I felt terrible.

Twenty minutes after I start reading, Stuart falls asleep. He sleeps a lot. Joan, the resident manager, or the Witch, as I like to call her, doesn't like me spending too much time with any one patient. But I don't give a crap. She can chastise me all she wants. I just nod, smile politely, then do it anyway. The other workers know of my affection toward Stuart and steer her away when they know I'm in his room.

Back in the common room, I attempt to get an exercise class started. I researched—as I do with most things—and wrote out an appropriate exercise plan, then got the program approved by the resident physician. I even compiled a playlist of old-time big-band music, swing, and early rock and roll. *Who doesn't like Elvis?*

"Bertha, Agnes, come on. Help me out here," I say. "If you two get up and try it, the rest will follow."

"Do you know how old we are?" Bertha grouches.

"You're only as old as you feel," I retort.

"Then I'm closing in on a hundred and thirty."

"You're just being lazy," I taunt. "I've seen how you move when you want to. Think chocolate cake with rich fudgy sprinkles."

Agnes rises slowly from her chair. "You know her too well. Get your fat ass off that chair, Bert."

"Who are you calling fat?" Bertha steadies her balance before standing. "And don't call me that ridiculous name, *Aggie*," she throws back.

Watching these two interact is always the highlight of my day.

Once work is finished, I change out of my scrubs into street clothes, slide on my jean jacket, and pull my backpack-slash-lifeline over my shoulder. I wave goodbye to a few seniors still lingering around before stepping outside.

Realizing I forgot to get my car key out of my bag, I swing my pack to the front of my body and feel through the outer pocket. As I do, my eyes catch sight of a hooded figure sitting comfortably on the bus stop bench across the street. His broad shoulders take up a large portion of the space as he reads from a book in his lap. It looks like the same guy I saw walking toward me when I was with Hayden last week.

Just as he lifts his head, the bus arrives, blocking him from view. Though I couldn't catch sight of his eyes, I swear I felt them on me, and my heart is racing from that split-second connection.

He makes his way down the bus's center aisle and takes a seat on the far side, his head turned away from me. I wait for him to lower his hood in hopes he'll turn my way, but he doesn't, and the bus pulls away.

It takes the entire ride home for my heart rate to return to normal, and I spend every minute of it wondering why.

"Hey, Mom," I call out as I set my backpack in the hallway.

"Dinner's ready," she responds.

I walk through the living room to our small kitchen. "What are we eating?"

"I picked up Thai food on my way home from work."

"Nice. My favorite."

My mother gets off work around the same time I do, and since neither of us like to cook, we eat a lot of takeout.

I help her set the cartons on the table, inhaling the fragrant scents of ginger and garlic as I open the first box. "*Mmm.* So good. Did you get wonton soup as well?"

"Of course."

"Spring rolls?"

She glances over her shoulder at me and laughs. "Have I ever forgotten them?"

"Not yet, but you *are* getting older."

She stops divvying up the soup. "Just for that, I get the extra wonton."

I chuckle, sliding into my chair. "Anything exciting happen at work today?" Mom works as an emergency room nurse at the hospital.

"A kid came in with a Lego stuck up his nose. The usual. How about you?" She places a soup-filled bowl at each of our place settings, then sits across from me.

"Same as always."

"Your dad called."

My hand pauses. "Really?" He almost never calls my mom, *or* me, because he sucks. "Did he say what he wanted?" I try to sound indifferent, continuing to fork noodles onto my plate. I hate that I can't stop caring.

"He said he tried calling you a couple of times but you haven't answered your phone or responded to his messages. He wanted to know how you were doing."

"Yeah, right," I scoff. "He probably wanted to inform me that another child was on the way."

"Why don't you call back to find out?"

I shrug. "I'm not interested."

"He's your dad."

"Was. He's been demoted to sperm donor."

"That's a bit harsh, isn't it?"

"So was cheating on you and starting a new family with barely a backward glance." His years of neglect still sting. A lot changed after the car accident. The move. The divorce. His new job. His new wife. Then the twins. I kept getting shoved further and further down the relevancy pole.

"Fine. I don't have the energy to argue about it, anyway."

I shove my food around on my plate. Conversations about my father always twist my stomach into knots.

"Hey," Mom says, pointing her chopsticks at me. "*Never* let anyone be the measuring stick by which you determine your worth."

I lift my head and sit a little taller as her words sink in. "I know, but thanks for the reminder." Honestly? It's easier on my self-esteem to just pretend he doesn't exist.

My phone rings beside me. I flip it over to see Hayden's calling. For a second, I debate whether to answer, then relent in the interest of keeping the peace. Swallowing a mouthful, I answer.

"What are you doing?" he asks.

"Eating. You?"

"Just finished my assigned reading for the night."

"When did you become Mr. Organized?" I tease.

"Since my new tutor told me if I didn't get my shit in order, he wouldn't work with me. It makes sense, though, to map out what needs to be done. I feel less overwhelmed."

"Good to hear."

"Are you up for some ice cream at Swirls? They just opened for the season, and I have a wicked craving for Moose Mash."

I check the clock on the microwave. It's close to eight and I have a quiz tomorrow, but he'll be disappointed if I say no. It's give-and-take, right? My life won't fall apart if I get a few less hours of sleep tonight. Besides, it's ice cream.

"Let me finish eating and I'll text you."

CHAPTER 3

SERENA

"Are you listening to me?" Rowan grips me by the shoulder, stopping me in the middle of the hallway as students continue around us like water around a boulder.

"What did you say?" I'm only half listening because my mind is racing through all the things I need to get done after I finish work today. Her mouth falls open. "*Kidding*," I say. "I'm kidding. I don't have an opinion either way."

"But you have to," she says half-hysterically, throwing her hands in the air. "It's prom! The theme is everything. And I just think 'A Night Under the Stars' is absurdly unoriginal. They should have had a vote with the entire school, not just the student council. They're all a bunch of geeks, anyway."

I scrunch up my face in distaste. "*No*, they're not."

"She didn't mean it like that." Tish gives Rowan a dirty look, concerned for everyone's feelings, as usual.

"Yes. She did," I snap. "Just because someone is intelligent or doesn't conform to social norms doesn't make them a geek. And why are you just commenting about this now? They announced it months ago."

Rowan shrugs, the messy top knot of black coils bobbing on top of her head as she does. "I just noticed the posters."

"A student vote would have been better," Tish throws out, probably to stop an argument from unfolding. "The student council could have picked four theme ideas, and the students could have voted."

At the ridiculousness of this conversation, I roll my eyes away from her and see an unmistakable figure in a dark-hooded sweatshirt and jeans walking past us. Seeing him this close, I realize the guy is not only huge but seriously muscular.

"It's him!" I smack Rowan's arm several times in excitement.

"*Ow.*" She bats my hand away, annoyed. "Why are you hitting me? It's who?"

"The guy."

"What guy?" Tish follows my line of sight.

"I'll be right back." I can't believe he goes to our school and I've never seen him before. Maybe he's new to town. It would explain why he suddenly appeared on my radar.

Why do I even care? He's just another guy with his head downcast, hands jammed into his front pockets, trying to be invisible.

No, there's something vaguely familiar about him, which doesn't make sense. I've never even seen his face.

"Hey," I say, coming up beside him.

He doesn't respond. Just continues walking.

Maybe he's shy?

He could have impaired hearing.

I try again, this time, gripping his forearm. "Have you been following me?" I tease, thinking he'd recognize me from the other day. When he stops short and glacier-blue eyes bore into mine, I quickly realize my mistake and drop my hand immediately. "Sorry," I say, my heart beating double time.

A loud noise causes both our heads to turn down the hall. Two guys are pushing each other—a fight is ready to explode. When I turn back, the guy has disappeared into the crowd.

Iceman. The name pops into my head, describing him perfectly.

Man, what's with the hostility? All I wanted to do was say hi and find out more about him. You'd think I destroyed one of his family members from the look he gave me.

"Who was that?" Tish asks, coming up beside me, Rowan stopping next to her, texting.

"Some guy stalking me." The words sound shaky coming out of my mouth.

"What?" Rowan snaps to attention.

Shaking my head, I turn to face them. "Just kidding. I've seen him around a lot lately, and I was curious."

She slaps a hand to her chest. "Don't scare me like that. There are a whole lot of crazies out there." Rowan may be a bitch fifty percent of the time, but she's protective and loyal as hell.

"It's fine," I say, feeling anything but. "Did either of you recognize him?"

"I didn't see his face," Tish says.

"Yeah. No clue," Rowan adds.

"His eyes..." I pause as a mashup of thoughts and feelings tangle in a fight for recognition. "Blue icebergs. There was this article in *National Geographic*—"

"Ugh!" Rowan goes back to texting.

"It was an interesting article," I protest. "During

compression, air bubbles are squeezed out, causing the ice crystals to enlarge. That's what makes the icebergs a light blue color."

"I could go without a science lesson." Rowan stops her texting and looks me over with a wry smile. "*Girl*, you've got the hots for your stalker?"

A shiver runs up my spine. I've never felt anger like that directed at me. "I do not. I—"

"Does Hayden know about this guy?" She elbows me, grinning now.

"There's nothing to know."

"I hope he's not going to be another one of your charity projects."

I cross my arms over my chest. "What's *that* supposed to mean?"

"You like to fix people—help people," she clarifies. "I mean, you work at a nursing home."

"So?" I snap defensively.

Tish reaches forward, gently resting her hand on my upper arm, a cascade of long dark hair falling over one eye. "Row just means you seem to—"

"Wyatt." Rowan throws the name at me.

"What about him?" I ask.

She shoots me a knowing glance. "He was manipulative and has a drug problem."

"He had strong convictions, and I didn't know about the drug problem until later on."

"Steven." Rowan raises a perfectly shaped eyebrow. "He was a pathological liar, and you were the only one who couldn't see it."

"He was sweet and—"

"Teagan," Rowan cuts me off. "Ben, Dustin... the list goes on, my friend." She stares down at her nails with a bored expression.

"Ease up, Row," Tish whispers out of the side of her mouth.

So, I've had to kiss more frogs than some people. Big deal. How else am I going to find my proverbial prince?

"Don't worry about it, Tish. Rowan is having one of her I-like-to-think-I-know-everything moments." I rub my middle finger against my cheek, giving Rowan a pointed look. "Remind me why I like you again?"

She extends her middle finger in the air as she turns and saunters through the stream of students, making her own path. We've been friends since kindergarten. Some relationships stand the test of time, regardless of how personalities develop.

CHAPTER 4

SERENA

Hayden is wasted and being a total jerk. When he's not leaning on me with his arm draped over my shoulder, he's groping me in ways that aren't *meant* for public display. I can't stand crude behavior—never could, never will. And with each beer he chugs, it just gets worse.

Why is he acting like this? I figured after our heart-to-heart, we'd kind of shifted onto better ground. Apparently not.

"I'm outta here," I tell Hayden after coming back from saying my goodbyes to Rowan and Tish.

He lifts his gaze from his seat on the couch, surrounded by his friends and a few girls who have been inching their way toward him all night. He has the kind of magnetism that only popularity brings, and the girls are like vultures waiting for their chance to get a piece of him.

I'm so over this high school bullshit.

"Why?" he protests. "You just got here."

"Actually. I've been here for over two hours." *But you've been too busy getting shitfaced to know the difference.* "I'll talk to you tomorrow."

Just as I pivot away, he tells me to hold up. Stupidly, I do as he says and watch as he gets himself up off the couch. Stumbling to the side, he knocks a guy's beer onto his arm.

"Watch it!" Hayden throws a fake punch, making the poor guy cringe.

"You're such a dick!" I spin away and head toward the exit. I'm over his obnoxious, drunk-ass behavior. *Seriously, why?*

As I near my car, I hear Hayden holler, "Wait up, babe. I want a kiss goodbye."

Wonderful. That's the *last* thing I want to give him. *Man, just get me out of here.* Was I a fool to be sucked in by his kind words the other night? Was it all bullshit?

When he reaches me, I set my hands on his shoulder and stretch up, giving him a quick, hopefully appeasing kiss on the lips and move to turn away. But he grabs a hold of my arm and yanks my body up against his.

"That wasn't a kiss," he slurs and grinds up against me.

"Gross." I push away, but he locks me into the embrace with his arms barred around my waist. I push against him harder, and when he doesn't budge, I yell at him to get off.

"But you feel so good." He slides his hand up the front of my shirt and grabs my boob.

"Hayden. Stop." I try to pull his hand away, but he's too strong. "What the hell is wrong with you?" I shove him as hard as I can, attempting to break free, but once again, don't get anywhere.

"Why can't you ever just chill and have fun?" His mouth

finds my neck and leaves a cold trail of beer-infused slobber in its wake.

"What is wrong with you? Get off me!" Lifting my knee, I try to reach his balls, but we're too close.

Out of nowhere, a massive arm snakes around his neck. The sudden attack weakens his hold on me, and Hayden is flung to the ground.

"What the hell?" he rages at a hooded figure standing over him.

It can't be, I think to myself as I stare at the scene in stunned silence.

Hayden kicks out, his foot connecting hard with Iceman's thigh, and sends him staggering backward. Drunk or not, Hayden is up on his feet lightning fast, charging full tilt. When they crash onto the ground, Hayden manages to land on top and throw the first punch with a sickening *thud*.

Iceman blocks the next blow, and the next, but why isn't he fighting back? He's got at least fifty pounds and several inches on Hayden. The next blow connects, followed by a torrent of raw fury as Hayden lashes out in rapid-fire succession, too fast to be blocked.

"Get him off," I yell to the crowd that's gathered to witness the drama. A guy standing beside me gives me a look like, *why?* I take a step forward to pull them apart myself, but Iceman bucks Hayden off, so I step back. When Iceman tries to stand, Hayden sweeps his legs as quickly as he would at any of his wrestling matches, and the pummeling begins again.

My stomach feels sick watching this, and I hate everyone cheering this nastiness on. *Screw this.* I step forward again, this time, gripping Hayden's arm and yelling at him to stop. When he throws me off, I fall backward and hit the ground, hard.

I scramble back to my feet and start shouting at Darius, who just appeared on the other side of the scene. "Stop the fight!" He barely glances in my direction, too busy enjoying his friend's brutal take-down.

Pushing my way through the crowd, I give Darius a solid shove. "The guy's not fighting back, you moron!" Kai shows up, his gaze bouncing between us and the fight like he's trying to process what's going on. "Get in there and stop Hayden before he actually kills him!" I yell at them.

I see the words finally penetrate their thick skulls, prompting them to act. Both grab one of Hayden's arms and drag him off, legs kicking and hurtling insults at Iceman.

I drop to my knees next to the guy. "Are you alright?" During the brawl, his hood fell away, revealing short, pale blond hair. His face is bloodied, his eyes are closed, and the swelling is already distorting his facial features. When he doesn't answer, I place a hand on his shoulder, but he shrugs it off and rolls onto all fours, spitting blood into the grass before slowly rising to his feet.

"What the hell?" I growl at Hayden, standing up.

"He came at *me*. You saw. The fucker got what he deserves." He wipes the sweat from his face with the back of his forearm. Blood all over his hand.

"I can't believe you!" I turn, my eyes scanning the area. Iceman seems to have vanished into the crowd gathering around us. "Make sure someone takes Hayden's keys," I snap at Darius. "He's hammered." Then push through the mass of people to look for the injured guy.

I reach the sidewalk and sweep my gaze up and down the street, but he's nowhere to be seen. He couldn't have gotten very far.

Did he go back inside the house? He must have been at the party, right?

I quickly check inside but then realize how stupid the idea was. I would have seen him if he'd been here earlier. The guy is hard to miss.

"What's going on?" Tish takes hold of my arm, stopping me on my way out. I hadn't seen her standing there.

"Hayden got in a fight. Did you see a big guy come in here with his face all bloody?" I'm not sure why I'm asking her this. I already know he hasn't been here.

"Oh my god." She covers her mouth, looking horrified. "What happened?"

"Never mind. I need to go." I turn away from her and rush out the front door.

"Serena," she hollers after me.

I'll explain it all to her later. Iceman is hurt. Really hurt, and all I know is that I need to find him.

Walking quickly to my car, I hear Hayden calling out my name but I ignore him, slide into the driver's seat, and start the car. As I pull away from the curb, I head straight, only to realize it's a cul-de-sac and have to turn around.

This situation—the entire night—has been a disaster. I weave through the neighborhood, eyes peeled for the guy, but he's nowhere to be found. Still determined, I cruise around aimlessly for a solid twenty minutes without catching sight of him.

It's getting late, and I should be getting home. Just as I'm about to call it quits, I spot him on the sidewalk, walking down the main street through town.

Parking the car, I jump out. I'm about to call out to him, but he turns the corner. When I get to the end of the street, he's already heading into an alley. I search both ways before crossing, then peer down the narrow, dark road in time to see him disappear around the side of a beat-up detached garage. I debate the intelligence of my plan for a few seconds, then shake my head at myself and hurry after him. He's not a threat. He just saved me from being mauled by Hayden.

When I get to the structure, I peek around the corner and see him enter through a door on the second floor. Moving quickly to the stairs, I place my foot on the bottom step, testing its strength in the dim light of a streetlamp that's several houses away. The image of Iceman's bloody face pushes me onward, taking the rickety stairs one cautious step at a time until I'm gently knocking on the front door.

There's no response. I wait a few seconds, then knock a little harder. Wait again, then lean my ear toward the door, listening for any sounds. What if he passed out?

Now I'm pounding frantically with my fist.

Please be okay. Please be okay.

When the door whips open, I take a step back as a half-crazed, bruised and battered body fills up the doorway. "What are you doing here?" he growls, his voice deep and menacing.

I move out of his way as he steps out and casts a glance down the stairs. The mostly dried blood on his pale skin glows eerily in the shadowy light. "I—"

"Go home." He steps back inside and throws the door, attempting to close it.

My hand instinctively reaches out, blocking it. "I wanted to make sure you're okay." I'm sure I'll process the error of my ways later, but right now, making sure he's not going to die feels like the right thing to do.

He releases a deep sigh of irritation, folds an arm high on the door frame, and rests his forehead against it. "Don't worry about it."

"Too late. Are you alone here?"

"None of your business." He turns his head until his translucent blue eyes glare into mine.

"Why did you get involved? I'm not complaining. I just—"

"Momentary lack of judgment." He straightens, his face coming into full view as he begins to close the door again.

The whole left side of his face is bruised and swollen. There's a gash on his eyebrow, cheek, and bottom lip. "He's never done that before," I say, and the door pauses. His nose is swollen, but doesn't appear to be broken. I doubt he'll needs stitches. "You weren't at the party, were you?"

He leans a shoulder against the wood frame. "No. Just passing by."

Finishing my assessment of his wounds, my gaze settles back on his eyes and there's a look there like, *are we done?*

"You don't live near there," I say.

"Obviously."

"So, what were you doing out, walking so late?"

He stands up straighter. "You act like I was prowling."

"Were you?"

"*No.*" His defensiveness lets me know I'm way off base. "I couldn't sleep. Not that it's any of your business."

"That was a long way to walk."

"Whatever. I like the architecture of historic homes."

"Yeah?" That's the last thing I expected to come out of his mouth. "Me too." The adrenaline suddenly drains from my system. I'm not sure why it picks this moment, but it leaves me with a nasty feeling of vulnerability.

I refuse to fall apart, so I do what I do best. Deflect. "Did you know there is a kit home in town that came from Sears and Roebuck? It's unusual because—"

"That sounds really interesting," he cuts me off. "But it's late and I have a raging headache, so can I *please* shut the door now?"

"Okay. Right. Sorry." I turn to leave and take a few steps down. He's obviously fine, and I'm in the way. But what if he has a concussion? He shouldn't be alone. I stop and turn. "So, you're alright?" I check one last time. "You're not lightheaded, nauseous, or seeing double?"

"I'll survive," he says in a way that makes me believe he's dealt with a lot worse.

"Okay." As I turn and walk down the stairs, an outside light comes on. That was nice of him.

When I reach the bottom, I hear heavy footsteps on the stairs behind me and look up. "Where are you going?"

"I want to make sure you get to your car okay."

There's really no need. It's not like there's much crime in our little town, but I welcome the kindness, especially after tonight. "Thanks." I smile as he nears.

He pulls the hood back over his head, covering the bloody mess, and trails behind me as we walk into the alley.

Now, I feel guilty. He's hurting and should be looking after his wounds. Gravel crunches under my feet as I stop and turn to him. "It's okay. I'll be fine. There's no need to come with me." He holds out a hand, directing me to keep moving. "You don't have to walk behind me," I tell him. In two steps, his long legs have him at my side. "How do you like school?"

"It's okay."

An actual answer. "Do we have any classes together?"

"No."

"That's weird, isn't it?"

"Not really."

I wonder why that is, then remember I'm in all AP classes and feel kind of bad for asking. I've never had such a hard time talking to anyone before. We walk the rest of the way in silence. "Well, this is me." He eyes my tiny, pockmarked Fiat 500 I got for a bargain because of the hail damage. "This is Fred. Fred, meet, uh…" I hold out my hand in an *and your name* is gesture.

He shakes his head and turns to go

"Seriously? You can't give me your name?"

His eyes narrow with a tilt to his lips that might be a smile. "Anyone ever tell you that you're pushy?"

"No. That comment is usually reserved for my best friend, Rowan." I wait, then lift my brows like *I can stand here all night.*

He huffs out a breath. "Knox."

"Is that your first name or last?"

"Does it matter?" he says with an exasperated sigh.

I shrug a shoulder. "I guess not. I'm Serena, by the way."

He pinches the bridge of his nose. "I need something for the pain. Can I leave now?"

"Absolutely. Sorry. And be sure to get some ice on that eye."

"I was about to when you started banging on my door."

Weirdly, his surliness brings a smile to my face. "Thanks for walking me to my car."

He seems lucid. His eyes aren't dilated unevenly. He's sure-footed and hasn't gotten dizzy. I'm glad he came with me. I'm more confident about leaving him by himself.

"Sure," he says, walking away.

Nice talking to you, too, I laugh to myself. I can't blame his irritation. I would be too if I got the shit kicked out of me. Poor guy.

My phone is sitting on the passenger's seat when I slide into the car. Three missed calls from Mom and five texts from Hayden.

"Hey, sorry," I say as soon as Mom answers. "I had to take care of a friend who was in a fight at a party I was at."

"Do you need me to check them out?"

Man, I love her.

"No. I think he'll be okay." I'm hardly an expert, but I've taken several first-aid courses and picked up a lot from my mother.

"He?"

"Yeah, long story. I'll explain when I get home."

We end the call and I put my car in drive. What the hell was up with Hayden tonight? What I said to Knox is true. He's never acted like that before. A shiver races over my body. I don't want to think about any of this right now. All I want is a comforting bowl of ice cream and my soft, cushy bed. The rest will have to wait until the morning.

CHAPTER 5

KNOX

I shouldn't have gotten involved. But seeing her tell that asshole to stop while he continued to force himself on her... I just lost it.

The only reason I was out walking was because Rhett sent me to Boulder today to pick up a load of lumber, and I was edgy from being around so many damn people. I knew if I didn't work off some of the restlessness, I would never get to sleep. I wasn't in the mood for a run, so I figured losing myself in the dark, quiet streets would help release the tension. It was late and I thought I would be fine. Big fucking mistake.

I study my hideous reflection in the bathroom mirror. Clearly, I did a shitty job defending myself—not that I've had to in a long time. Since growing up, I was the one handling the beatings. I hated it, but it was my job. Never again—not after what happened in Denver. I lean toward the mirror and gently probe the swelling around my eye. Rhett is going to kill me. Fighting is a hard rule for him.

I blow out a heavy sigh and walk back to the kitchen. Pulling a clean rag out of the cupboard, I return to the bathroom, wet it, and get to work cleaning my wounds.

When the knock came at the door, I felt the usual panic but for a different reason. Figured that ass-wipe and his friends must have followed me home. I opened the door, ready for battle, only to be blindsided for a different reason. Because standing there, wide-eyed and braced for whatever came next, was the little redhead with the corkscrew curls I helped at the party. She didn't even flinch at the sight of me. Anyone else would have—all that blood and rage on my face.

The girl's got guts. If things were different, I'd definitely want to know her better.

I rinse the blood from the rag and wring it out. No one other than Rhett has ever come knocking. I feel bad for being such a jerk to her, but I was in pain, and I don't like the unexpected.

Besides, I lost the ability for normal social interaction a long time ago, and she asked too many damn questions. They made me uncomfortable. So did her light-brown eyes and cute freckles dotting her nose and cheeks.

Fuck, Knox. When did you start noticing that shit?

Leaving the cloth in the bathroom sink, I head to the kitchen and grab a bag of frozen peas from the freezer. Then I drag my tired ass to the bed, sit at the end, and fall onto my back. I can't believe this night.

I rest the bag against the most swollen part of my face—my eye—and wince. Man, that fucking hurts. As I absorb the throbbing ache with gritted teeth, my mind drifts to Serena again. There's no way she should be with that idiot. She seems nice enough. Came here to check up on me. Anyone that'd do that for a complete stranger deserves better. Hell, any girl deserves better than that dickweasel.

Whatever, not my problem.

CHAPTER 6

SERENA

The sun blasts me in the face, waking me up in one of the most annoying ways possible. Hoping for a second chance at sleep, I fumble over the edge of the bed, snag a t-shirt, and toss it over my eyes.

Sundays are usually my favorite because they're alarm-free, but last night I barely slept, and I feel like crap. Annoyed, I pummel my pillow into a comfortable shape, flop to my side, and adjust the shirt to cover my eyes again.

Thoughts of Knox sneak in, and I wonder if he's alright. It sucks that he got beat up because of me. Well, not *because* of me —not really. Still, the guilt is there eating away at my conscience.

I can't believe Hayden was so forceful last night. He needs to stop drinking. I've been down this road with my father. I know how ugly it can get.

I growl, fling the t-shirt to the floor, then flop onto my back like a starfish. So much for sleeping in. Reaching to the nightstand, I grab my phone. Seven missed calls from dickface and a literal avalanche of texts. My group text with Rowan and Tish has exploded, too, with them wanting details about what went down and if I was okay.

Firing off a quick text, I let my friends know I'm okay, and I'll fill in the details after food and caffeine. As for Hayden... I don't want to deal with him right now.

My stomach grumbles with a need to be fed.

Well, sleep isn't happening, so I might as well go eat.

Kicking at the sheets while trying to get up sends me crashing to the floor. Great friggin' start to the day.

Freeing my legs, I make my way to the bathroom and cringe at my reflection in the mirror. The frizzy explosion of hair, puffy eyes, and smeared eye makeup is horrifying. *Shit. I forgot to take my makeup off.* Heaving out a heavy sigh, I turn on the faucet.

Face clean, I leave the hair disaster and shuffle my way to the kitchen. Mom is at the table clutching her coffee, looking as ragged as I feel. "Sorry for making you worry and lose sleep."

"Your heart was in the right place, but don't risk your safety like that again, okay?"

"I'll do my best."

She shakes her head, her expression telling me she knows I'm just saying what she wants to hear. "What's on the agenda for today?"

"Homework." Usually, I take Sundays off, but I have a paper due tomorrow that needs an edit, and it counts for thirty percent of my grade.

"Serena, you work too hard."

I pour myself a coffee, add cream and a heap of sugar. "So do you."

"Yeah, but I'm the adult." She tucks her wavy, chocolate-brown hair behind her ear. "Let's get out of the house for some fresh air. Maybe go for a hike or a bike ride?"

I lean back against the counter and take a sip of coffee. "A hike sounds good if we go right after breakfast. I can work on my paper when we get back."

"Perfect. How about some eggs?" she asks, getting up. "I was just working up the energy to make a veggie scramble."

"Yes, *please*." There's a knock at the front door. Mom and I exchange puzzled glances. "I got it," I say grudgingly, setting my coffee down.

Looking through the peephole, I spy Hayden's profile. I'm tempted to walk away, but I know I'll have to deal with him at some point.

As soon as I open the door, he whips out a bouquet of roses from behind his back and holds them toward me. "I'm so sorry." He steps in, even though I'm blocking the entrance, and kisses the side of my head.

"Come in," I say acidly, taking the roses from him.

"I know you're pissed, and you have every right to be."

"Ya think?"

He takes my free hand. "I'm so sorry."

"You already said that." I yank free of his grasp, not liking the feel of his touch. "You forced yourself on me. It was disgusting."

"What are you talking about?" He looks struck.

I jerk my head in surprise. "That's why the guy tackled you! You were hurting me."

He runs a hand through his hair. "I-I didn't know."

"Then what the hell are you apologizing for?"

"The guys told me I knocked you down. It was an accident, of course. You should never get in the middle of a fight. You could have been seriously hurt."

With brows raised to what felt like my hairline, I give my head a shake. He's going to lecture me? After last night? "Leave, Hayden. Just go." I motion toward the door.

How can he not remember?

Even my father remembered every dumbass thing he did when he was drunk, and *he* was an alcoholic.

"Serena, please. I would never intentionally hurt you." His expression looks confused, almost pained.

I clench my hands. "Intentions don't matter. Actions do. You know... I'm not sure what's worse, you mauling me, or being too drunk to remember. Either way, it was *seriously* messed up."

"I know. Please." As he takes a step forward, I take an involuntary step back. "You *know* that's not me."

"No. I don't know that. Not anymore." Hayden's never been a mean person—it's the alcohol. But still. I thought he was different from the other guys I dated—that he had it together.

He reaches for me. When I take another step away, he lets his hand fall to his side. "Please don't do that—don't pull away like you're afraid of me." He drags a hand through his hair. "It kills me that you think I'd physically hurt you. I promise I won't ever drink again, okay?"

I've heard that more times than I can remember. "I can't be in a relationship with you anymore. We need to—"

"Don't say it." He stops me. "*Please.*" Closing the distance with a giant step, he cradles my face between his palms. "I need you." His lips touch softly to mine. "Please," he says, his voice desperate.

I twist out of his hold. "Don't touch me." The memory of last night mixed with the Hayden who's standing here looking like he's about to break is messing with my head. I need space to think and he keeps crowding me. "You beat the crap out of a guy."

"He tackled me!" He throws his hands in the air. "I just reacted."

"That was more than a reaction. You tried to beat the life out of someone for helping me. He did the right thing, Hayden."

"I *know* he did," he says, sounding frustrated and helpless all at once. "I'm screwing this all up. I'm just... surprised and confused by everything you've told me. I don't remember any of it, and I don't like that a stranger could come between us so easily."

"It wasn't the guy who came between us—it was the alcohol," I say, frustrated.

He shakes his head like he's trying to come to grips with the truth. "You're right. We were moving forward and I screwed it up. Please give me another chance. I can do so much better."

"Serena." Mom steps out of the kitchen. "Hayden." She acknowledges him with a tight-lipped smile.

He sighs, shoulders slumping. "Hi, Ms. McNeal."

"I think it's time you leave," she tells him, then turns to me. "Breakfast is ready."

"Okay. I'll be there in a minute."

"I'll wait until you see Hayden out."

"It's okay, Mom. I got this."

She pauses a moment as if debating the right course of action, then turns and leaves. As soon as she does, Hayden pulls me tight against his chest. The flowers dangle at my side. "You're okay, though, right?"

"Yeah," I say to his chest, angry that I crave physical contact so much.

He kisses the top of my head. "I'm trying to wrap my head

around what I did to you. I-I never—the thought of it makes me sick." He leans back, looking me over intently. "You mean so much to me." His words tug at the newly created wall I've added around my heart. "Please. I don't know if I can make it without you. You're everything to me."

I open my mouth to tell him no, but he adds, "Give me a little time to make it right. After that, if you still want out, I won't fight you." He cups the back of my neck in his hand. "Please, Serena." I drop my eyes to the space between us. "I can't lose you. Not like this. I need you in my life. You make it all bearable."

He nudges my chin, getting my attention. When I glance up, I see the honesty of his words in his expression. "I'm done drinking. I swear."

What could be so unbearable in his life? He's got it all—looks, friends, great family, comes from money, a full-ride football scholarship. Nothing with him makes sense these days. When I told Knox he's never been abusive before, I was honest. He's changing, and I don't understand why.

"Okay, but this is it. You won't get another chance to make it right, got it?"

I guess if staying together gets him to pull his head out of his ass and rethink his priorities, it can't be that bad. He's a good person and has always treated me with respect. I know he cares about me—he wouldn't have said all that stuff if he didn't. And if he stops drinking like he says he will, then everything should be fine. Prom, graduation, and then I'm out of here in the fall. Staying with him is the least stressful route anyway.

Relief washes over his face as a heavy exhale rushes past his lips. "You won't regret it. I promise." He releases me and steps back. "Sorry for keeping you from your meal. Your mom already wants my head on a stake. You should go eat. I'll see you tomorrow?" He kisses my cheek and walks to the door.

"You should tell that guy you're sorry," I say to his back.

He turns, looking remorseful. "I don't even know who he is."

"Well, if you see him." Would he even remember his face? Probably not.

"I will. We're cool, right?" His eyes search mine.

"Yeah." I nod, fingers wrapping around the doorknob.

"If you want to hang out later, let me know."

"Maybe. Mom and I are going to go for a hike, and I have a paper to finish."

"You're already the smartest kid in the school. Give your brain a break."

"Second smartest. Maybe," I correct with a smirk.

He grins. "That's debatable."

"Suck up."

He lifts my chin, leaning in to kiss me. "Anything for you." His words are barely a whisper against my lips.

Mom is buttering toast when I enter after saying goodbye to Hayden. "So? All's well in paradise." There's a bitter edge to her tone.

"Don't start. I already know what you're thinking. He's not like my father."

"Maybe not, but he's well on his way."

"He said he'd stop. I need to at *least* give him the chance."

"You don't *need* to give him anything. Why didn't you tell me what he did to you?"

"Because I didn't want you freaking out. I needed to handle it without you pressuring me like you are now."

"I'm not pressuring," her voice rises. "You just deserve better than"—she points toward the door—"that."

"It's not about being deserving, and you should have seen how devastated he was about what he did."

"I'm sure he was," she says, sarcasm lacing her words. "Action and regret are a shifty duo."

I cross my arms over my chest. "What's *that* supposed to mean?"

"It means that drinking and regret tend to go hand in hand. It's a slippery slope that never leads to anywhere good."

She would know. "Your metaphors are a bit much this early in the morning."

"It's ten," she deadpans, then eyes the flowers in my hand with distaste. "There's a vase... well, you know where they are."

I wonder how many bouquets of apology my father gave her. Judging by her expression, I'd say a lot.

I snip the ends off the roses before placing them in a large Mason jar from the cupboard, then sit at the table where a plate of food is waiting.

A silence settles over us as we eat. Both of us generally wake up starving, and with Hayden delaying breakfast, each mouthful becomes a focused event. That, and we're irritated with each other.

Mom takes a sip of coffee. "Did you get in touch with your dad?"

I set my fork down with a loud clang. "Not now, okay?"

"You're right. Bad timing."

"Look, I get that you think having a relationship with him is important. That I'm missing out on some big father-daughter bond. But believe me, I'm really not. You've always been there for me. I love you, trust you, and you're my closest friend. You are all I need, okay?"

Her eyes well with emotion. "I don't know how I got so lucky to have you for a daughter."

"I didn't mean to make you all teary-eyed."

She dismisses me with a wave of her hand. "They're happy tears. It's just important that you have a male figure in your life, you know? A father's love. A masculine influence."

I roll my eyes. "He hasn't given me either of those things since he left. I doubt he's going to morph back into super dad any time soon."

"Fine. I'll stay out of it."

"Good." I pick up my plate. "I'm tired. Maybe I'll take a short nap before we head out on our hike. You should too." I stand up with my dish, rinse it in the sink, and put it in the dishwasher.

"You're probably right," she says. "Serena, promise me... this thing with Hayden... be careful."

"I will. Leave in a couple of hours?"

"That should work."

I head upstairs to my room, my steps heavy from the late night and warring emotions, and crawl into bed. Staring up at the ceiling, Hayden's words—his apology—replay in my mind. I desperately want to believe him, but the sting of unkept promises and broken trust is all too familiar—my father having taught me well. As my eyes drift close and sleep finally begins to take hold, I wonder if this was a one-time mistake, or am I once again putting my faith in someone who doesn't deserve it?

CHAPTER 7

KNOX

Just as I expected, Rhett blew a gasket when he saw my battered face. He went on and on, lecturing me about getting into fights and not letting me get a word in to explain. When his rant petered out and I gave him my side of the story, he backed right off. Which was a relief because the last thing I wanted to do was let him down.

Even in his seventies, the man is tougher than most guys half his age. He makes his living as a contractor, managing big jobs and working the smaller ones with a handpicked crew. He's been teaching me the ins and outs of the building industry for the last two and a half years, and I owe him everything.

We do a lot of work in the mountains. There's a peacefulness up there I never knew existed. I breathe easier, think clearer, and even started dreaming about building a house of my own—one totally off the grid, maybe next to a stream. I could get a dog. I've always wanted one.

Saving money hasn't been an issue. Rhett doesn't charge me much for room and board, so most of my paycheck goes right into savings. At first, I was getting paid under the table, all cash, but when the job became more permanent, he put me on the payroll. I wasn't exactly thrilled about giving him my full name or explaining why I couldn't use it. I thought for sure he'd kick my ass to the curb, but he didn't. He just nodded and said I was a good person who got caught up in someone else's *bad* shit. Then he helped me legally change my name. He's a solid guy, and I would do anything for him.

"You gonna sit on your ass all day, boy? There's work to be done." He's also the hardest-working man I've ever known.

"Just finishing up my sandwich," I tell him. My first, actually. I usually go through three or four during a workday.

"It's only ten in the damn morning and it's hotter than hell out here." Rhett takes a blue bandana from his back pocket and wipes his brow. "Not right for this time of year. You drinking enough water?"

I shove the last bit of food in my mouth and stand up. "Had to piss often enough, so yeah."

"Alright then. We're raising that south-facing wall and could use that size and strength of yours. We lost Bob for the day. His kid got hurt in the schoolyard, horsing around or some such nonsense."

Best part of the job is feeling useful. "Okay. I'm ready." And there's something satisfying about working with your hands, seeing what you build take shape. Learning this trade has really changed things for me. It's not just the financial independence, but it gave me a purpose and maybe even a bit of pride.

CHAPTER 8

SERENA

It's been a little over a week since the fight at the party, and I haven't seen Knox at school or anywhere else. Nobody seems to know who he is.

What if he's worse off than I initially thought, and that's the reason he hasn't been at school?

"Have you two gotten your prom dress yet?" Rowan asks me and Tish at lunch.

Her question feels trivial compared to the real-life concerns taking over my thoughts, but she won't let up unless I answer. "I haven't had time."

"And *I* can't find one I like," Tish adds.

"Cutting it a bit close, don't ya think?" Rowan's eyes dart between us.

Tish leans forward, her forearms on the table. "I'm thinking of heading to Denver this weekend. There'll be a wider selection. Maybe we could all go together... make a day of it."

I planned to stop by the fancy dress shop downtown and grab the cheapest one I can find that isn't completely hideous, but a short road trip with my friends sounds like fun. "I won't be able to go unless they're open on Sundays."

Rowan pulls out her phone, types, and scrolls. "Yep. Two different locations. Both open from twelve to five."

"Sounds good." Who knows, maybe I'll get lucky and they'll have a clearance rack. "But not this Sunday. It'll have to be the following one."

"Again," Rowan says. "Cutting it close."

"Don't have a choice," I respond.

Hayden sits down, straddling the bench next to me, kissing my cheek. "So, what's the lunch topic today?"

He pulls out a brown paper lunch bag from his backpack and sets it in front of him.

"Prom dresses," Tish answers.

"Serena is dragging her feet." Rowan nudges my shoulder.

"How come, babe?"

That endearment is getting annoying. "I haven't had time."

"Well, you could wear a garbage bag and still look great," he says, sliding an arm around my waist and pulling me between his legs.

"Is that an option?" I joke, wiggling a short distance away. Hayden's crowding has triggered an overwhelming need for personal space. I thought everything was okay after he came to the house and apologized, but the cringy remnants of that awful night are still with me.

"No way in hell is that an option!" I flinch at Rowan's screech. She's obsessively fashion-conscious.

"Unnecessary," I mutter. "I already said I'd go."

"Trash bag," Rowan grumbles. "Ridiculous."

"I don't know. I think I could pull it off with a cool belt and pair of sparkly Converse high-tops." I nudge her with my elbow, which she returns with an exaggerated eye roll.

Kai arrives and sits down next to Tish, who suddenly becomes engrossed in her lunch. The poor girl has been crushing on him for years. "Hey," he says to the group. "What's up?"

"Nothing," Hayden responds, reaching for his sandwich. I use this opportunity to scoot even farther away. It's too hard to eat this close together, anyway.

"Where's Darius?" Rowan asks Kai.

"Not sure. He was still in the locker room when I left."

"I swear that boy takes longer to get ready than I do," she huffs, but I catch her sending a warning glare at Hayden not to comment.

"Hey, are we on for that party this Friday?" Kai asks, directing the question to Hayden.

Hayden raises his fist to Kai, who bumps it with a solid pound. "Of course. You comin'?" he questions with a tweak to my side.

"No. I work early on Saturday, like I do *every* Saturday." Bitchy, I know, but Hayden made a deal with me, and I assumed no drinking meant no parties. "Since the last party was *sooo* much fun..." I pause, letting the sarcasm sink. "I think I'll pass."

He leans in close, plants a kiss behind my ear, and whispers, "I told you... I'm done. No more alcohol."

The warm breath sends involuntary shivers down my spine, leaving me somewhere between wary and cautiously optimistic that maybe we'll be okay after all. "That's what you said, but I'm not up for a party again so soon. Besides, I work till seven on Friday, and then have to turn around and be back early in the morning." If the party was Saturday, it might be a different story, but that's a big 'if'.

He pulls his leg over the bench seat and sits facing forward, visibly irritated. Hayden's family is loaded. He doesn't understand the concept of work.

Just before the tension at the table becomes a thing, Darius slides in next to Rowan and kisses her cheek. "What did I miss?"

"Most of lunch," Rowan bites out. "Were you having trouble getting your hair to settle just right?"

He grips her chin and gives her a loud kiss on the mouth.

"*Ew*, gross." She wipes it off.

"Gross? Since when are my kisses gross?"

"Since they became wet and slobbery."

Darius gives her his smoldering look. We all laugh as Rowan leans in so he can give her a nice kiss. They've been dating for two years and already squabble like an old married couple.

I lean over to Hayden and lower my voice so only he can hear. "Have you seen the guy you beat up at the party so you can apologize?"

His look tells me I've picked the wrong time to bring it up. "No. Maybe he doesn't go to school here? He could have graduated."

Rowan glances up from her phone. "No. He goes here. Serena was talking to him."

Apparently, I wasn't quiet *enough*.

Hayden's eyebrows pinch together. "But you said you had no idea who he was."

"I don't." *Not in any real sense.* Damn Rowan and her big mouth. She wasn't even at the fight, but thanks to social media, she recognized Knox's face.

"He's her stalker," Rowan chimes in casually.

Seriously, Rowan?

"What the hell?" Hayden's voice booms across the cafeteria, attracting the attention of everyone within earshot.

Thanks a lot. I glare as she flashes me an innocent, apologetic smile. Meanwhile, the rest of our friends suddenly find their lunches extremely interesting.

"He's not a stalker," I tell Hayden. "He seemed lost. I thought maybe he was new, so I went to see if I could help. Not a big deal."

"You approaching some random guy is definitely a big deal," he bites back.

"So..." Kai interjects. "Football and wrestling is over and Coach is still kicking our ass. Isn't that right, Darius?"

Hayden shoots me a suspicious look before returning his attention to his lunch.

My thoughts circle back to my interaction with Knox in the hallway at school. Rowan totally blew it out of proportion. Okay, granted, I probably shouldn't have approached him, and it might have appeared a little suspicious, but it's not like I was trying to hit on him or anything.

The chatter swirls around us while Hayden and I remain silent. When the bell rings, signaling the end of lunch, our friends say their goodbyes, leaving us alone. "Why did you lie to me about knowing that guy?" he asks, sounding hurt.

"It's not the way Rowan made it sound. You know how dramatic she can be, and I was only joking with Rowan when I called him a stalker. The reason I kept quiet was because I didn't want to add to the dumpster fire that had already been started. Sorry."

His expression softens. "You were just being your usual, thoughtful self. I can't fault you for that, especially when it's one of the things I love about you." *Love? He just said love.* "But don't you think it's odd that he happened to be at the same party you were?"

"You're letting Rowan get in your head. It's a small town, and he's close to our age. It's not weird at all. And he wasn't at the party, he was just passing by."

"How would you know that?"

Shit, shit, shit. "I just assumed. I need to get to class."

We start down the hall. "Still seems weird," Hayden says. "If you come across him again or feel threatened in any way, you'll let me know, right?"

I was expecting more of his territorial bullshit. The fact that it didn't come is a welcome surprise. "Of course. But honestly, you don't need to worry."

He takes me by the wrist, stopping me. "I know, but I'm here for you if you need me."

That's the thoughtful, sweet guy I came to like in the beginning. I stretch up on my toes and press my lips to his.

"*Mmm.*" He grips my waist and hauls me up against him. "I miss you. A lot."

Nervousness churns in my stomach, prompting me to step out of his embrace. His hold brings back uncomfortable reminders of his drunken aggression.

A wave of confusion crosses his face, but it quickly disappears. "Maybe rethink coming to the party. It's senior year. You should get some playtime in before life gets too serious, you know?"

"No way I'm letting Rebecca take the distinction of valedictorian away from me." The words are a dodge, but they seem to have the desired effect.

"Fine, my little brainiac. Do you think you could schedule me in for some quality time soon?" He wriggles his eyebrows.

Despite my uneasy feeling about the whole intimacy thing, I laugh at his playful antics. I've always liked his cute, affectionate side. "I'll see what I can do, but I've got to go. I don't want to be late for class."

He plants a quick kiss on my cheek, then walks backward, pointing at me. "You're killing me, Serena." Then turns and disappears into the crowd of students.

By the end of work, thoughts of Knox have me worried to the point of heavy concern. I can't, in good conscience, not check on him, so I've decided to drive to his place and make sure he's okay. Unfortunately, I'm having a hard time remembering exactly where he lives. It was dark when I trailed him, and my mind was too overloaded with nervous energy to take in any details.

I park near the same spot I did before and follow the ghost of him from memory. Sunset has brought a coolness to the air. I'm glad I grabbed a jacket before attempting to retrace my steps.

I find the alley leading to Knox's apartment. Or, at least, I think it's the one. There are several dilapidated, detached garages lining the road, but only one with an upper level. Hopefully, this is it.

The building doesn't look as rundown as it did in the darkness that night. The siding is old, but there are three newer windows stretching across the top.

As I round the corner, I see a green truck and vaguely remember it being parked there before. When I reach the bottom of the rickety stairs, I know I'm in the right spot.

At the door, I pause. *Should I really be doing this?*

I press my ear to the cold wood and remind myself I'm here out of concern and nothing more. Hearing nothing, I lift my hand, knock, then peer over the ledge while I wait for him to answer.

I wonder if that truck is his.

Several seconds pass without a response.

I knock again in case he didn't hear the first time, but there's still no answer.

It's possible he isn't home, but then again, I saw lights in the windows of his apartment that overlook the alley.

He could just be ignoring the intrusion. Or maybe he's too hurt to answer.

Now, I'm pounding on the door in desperation.

After a full minute, it opens a crack, revealing half his face. "What do *you* want?" he snaps before opening it wider.

Once again, I'm struck by his size and the unusual lightness of his eyes. The pale color looking even more vibrant against the purple and green bruises marking his skin. His swelling is mostly gone and the natural angles of his face coming to rights. He has nice features—rugged and blocky but appealing somehow. I shake my head at myself.

His light shaggy hair is soaked. Wet spots dot the t-shirt clinging to his muscular chest. His blue jeans are unbuttoned, and his feet are bare. No wonder he looks pissed. I pulled him out of the shower. A sudden image of him naked and dripping wet has my mouth going dry.

Oh my god. Seriously? Get a grip, Serena. That's not why you're here! Realizing he's still waiting for a response, my brain fumbles for words. "I, uh... haven't seen you at school."

"That's because I don't go there." He continues to scowl.

"Oh... but I saw you in the hallway."

"I was on my way to the office. I'm in the distance learning program. I take my tests in one of their conference rooms." His words tumble out like a list of chores he's being forced to recite. It's clear he's appeasing me but would rather have me gone. Too bad for him, I'm not that easy to get rid of. "Why distance learning?"

He exhales a frustrated breath. "Because I work full-time and I don't like being around people." And to prove it, he begins to close the door.

"Hey!" I throw a hand out and the door stalls. "I never asked you to step in and go all white knight on Hayden's ass. The only reason I'm here is because you weren't at school, and I didn't want you hemorrhaging all alone in your apartment, or something equally awful."

His face softens and the corner of his mouth twitches like he might smile. "Well, as you can see, I'm alive and well." Heaven forbid he be a decent person for two damn seconds. "How do you know I live alone?"

"What?" I huff, a little breathless from standing my ground.

"You said, 'I didn't want you hemorrhaging all alone in your apartment.' How did you know I lived alone?"

That's all he took away from my rant? "What does it matter?"

"You're right." He shakes his head. "It doesn't."

I blow out a breath, releasing some of my agitation. I shouldn't have gotten so wound up. There's obviously something unique about his situation if he is living alone while still in high school. "Do you? Live alone?" The space above this garage can't be that big. There wouldn't be room for more than one person.

He doesn't answer, just stands there staring at me, making an already awkward conversation worse.

"You know," I start. "Too much time alone can be bad for your mental health." His eyebrow raises slightly. "It's true. Studies have shown that social isolation and loneliness can increase mortality by thirty percent."

If he's not with family... does he have any friends? "Maybe we could go for coffee or something?" The words pop out as an extension of my thoughts. *Coffee?* I roll my eyes to myself. *Really?*

"I'm not—I don't—" He drags a hand through his damp hair, making it stick up at odd angles.

"Or we could go for a walk," I interject, suddenly not wanting him to turn me down for some reason. "You mentioned that you liked checking out old houses. Maybe we could go some night after I finish work."

"You don't let up, do you?" he grumbles, which I return with a small raise of my shoulder. "*Fine.* Meet me at Greenbough Park. We can walk there. I'll meet you by the picnic tables near the amphitheater."

"I get off at seven most nights. I can be there shortly after."

"Fine."

"Is Thursday okay?"

He rolls his eyes upward and sighs. "Why won't you just leave me alone?" He doesn't sound angry—more resigned than anything.

I shrug my shoulders and tell him I'll see him on Thursday before walking down the stairs, asking myself the same damn question.

KNOX

I stare at the closed door. *What did I just agree to?*

I don't *do* social.

It's not a big deal, I reassure myself, even though my stomach is already twisting into a knot. All I need to do is show up and continue being a dick. She'll realize there's nothing interesting about me, then I can go back to being anonymous.

Hopefully that'll work. I should be able to make it to the park, and I'm good at turning people off. Maybe I'll get lucky and she won't show up at all.

No. She'll show. My feet begin to pace involuntarily. Too curious for her own good. And strong-willed. No one from my past would have dared to stand up to me that way. She has her mind set on something. I guess I'll have to show up and find out what it is, then deter her in any way I can.

Yeah, like going there to meet her is that easy. A sudden rush of adrenaline makes me lightheaded and my mouth uncomfortably dry. I fill a glass with water and knock it back in several huge gulps. It does nothing to quench the thirst, so I refill it. Then, leaning against the counter, I take slow sips while thoughts of Serena pound my brain. She's got that kind of impact.

Her hair was tied back today, exposing more of her face—all soft curves and smooth lines. *Man, I'm pathetic.*

Her eyes, though—a unique shade of light bronze that... I don't know. When they lock onto mine, it's unsettling, like I'm caught in a trap I never want to be free of. My palm lightly rubs back and forth over my heart. I don't know if I've ever come across anyone who made me wish my life was different, but she does, and that scares the hell out of me.

"Can I play too?" I ask, buzzing with the excitement of a small child. The little girl next door, with her fiery red hair, is busy in her sandbox, playing with her brand-new yellow dump truck.

"Okay," she says, looking up at me, her face lighting up with a wide smile.

She's my friend and has the coolest toys.

I climb into the box with her. She's just about to roll the truck over to me when a dark figure appears behind her and lifts her by the neck. Her little legs kick wildly in the air as she gasps for breath.

Desperate to help, I jump up. Her eyes lock onto mine, full of terror, but my legs are stuck in the sand. The man snaps her neck—the sound sickening. Her eyes go blank. Her life just... gone. The man throws her to the side, then takes a step toward me.

Soaked in sweat with a scream lodged in my throat, I bolt upright, gasping for air. I wrestle my legs free from the twisted covers, then swing my feet onto the floor.

That little girl and her family are a favorite memory of mine. Her house was an escape from my reality. She's never been in one of my nightmares. *Why now?*

Dropping my head in my hands, I squeeze my eyes shut as my gut churns. *Fuck,* that was a bad one. All those happy memories, ruined by the violence of one fucking dream.

As a little kid, I didn't understand neglect because it was all I knew. Then I met the family next door. The mother and father of the little girl were always doing fun stuff together, and when I came over, they included me. *My* father's specialty was yelling and beating the crap out of us, and my mother could barely drag herself out of bed most days.

I scrub my hands back and forth over my damp hair, lift myself onto my feet, and head to the shower.

The shock from the ice-cold water hits my body with the severity of a hundred needles jabbing me at once. I hate this almost as much as the nightmares, but it does a decent job of casting the demons out of my head.

Bracing one hand on the wall, I lean into the freezing spray, letting it roll down my back until I'm shivering uncontrollably. Usually, that's enough to clear my head, but the images have a grip on me like never before. So with my hair still damp and my body barely dry, I throw on sweats, a t-shirt, and lace up my running shoes.

It's going to take every bit of strength I have to shake this fucking nightmare loose. As I step out of the apartment, the sky is just coming alive with its deep shades of red and orange, working its way up into the dark blue. I take off at an easy speed, but the nightmarish images hound me, so I pick up my pace until I'm near sprinting.

Running aimlessly, I drive myself to the breaking point for

over an hour. The sun has risen and it's bright out. Time to get off the streets.

Heading back home, I find myself coming up on the house I lived in as a kid and slow to a walk.

Not sure why I would come this way.

Dark memories flash through my mind in snapshot images. Every one of them making me sick to my stomach.

How my mom survived with my father as long as she did is a miracle.

Shaking my head in disgust, I redirect my gaze to the house next door and wonder if the little girl and her family still live there.

When the door opens suddenly, I quicken my pace.

It's the curly red hair I see first. The sight just about knocks the wind out of me.

Can it be the same girl?

Her back is to me as she locks the door.

Not wanting to be seen, I break out into a run. That's when I see Fred, Serena's car, parked at the curb.

The realization hits me like a two-by-four to the head, making me stumble. The little girl from my past, from my dream... is Serena?

It has to be. Two redheads? Same house? The car? No way this is just a coincidence.

Holy fuck!

My adrenaline skyrockets. Add that to intense pounding of my heart after the run, and I start to feel lightheaded.

She's going to see you. Keep moving.

But part of me wants to ask if she remembers me—if she has similar childhood memories. My skin prickles at the idea of confronting her and I know there's no way I can do it. Not in the state I'm in.

Quickly, I round the corner and take off running again.

Now, meeting her at the park takes on a whole new purpose.

I can't believe it's her.

Coming back to this town, it never even crossed my mind that she would still live in the same house. My life has been so transient. The idea that she'd still be there wasn't even a consideration.

By the time I make it home, I'm past exhaustion and teetering on numbness. After that shitty nightmare, it's what I wanted, but wearing myself down before I've even started work isn't the brightest idea. In this case, I didn't have a choice. I had to erase that garbage from my head, but now, this thing with Serena...

I can't begin to wrap my head around it.

She's back in my life—a living, breathing piece of my memories.

The good ones.

There were so many that involved her. Warm cookies, playing catch with her dad.

Her family talked in soft voices. They laughed and were affectionate with each other, and sometimes that affection would spill over on to me. Neither of my parents touched me with soft hands, so I loved those times with them the most.

When my mother took me and ran, it was like being ripped in half, leaving a part of myself behind—the good part I never recovered. Because that family... that little girl... gave me the only happiness I'd ever known.

Sweaty and stiff from the run, I strip down and step under the spray. I opt for a hot shower this time. Dropping my head, I soak up the intense heat while running through the homework assignments I need to get done after work. My mind is on overload, and it's the first thing I can think of that doesn't involve Serena. So, I focus on the chemistry test I have in four days, followed by the essay due two days after that on Shakespeare's *The Taming the Shrew.*

If I had stayed in school, I'd have graduated a couple of years ago. But with all the turmoil, I couldn't keep up. Part of my agreement with Rhett is that I'd finish.

Rhett and his hard lines. I laugh to myself.

Finishing high school through distance learning allows me to continue working full-time. I don't know why Rhett was against me getting my GED. It would have been so much easier. *And* faster. Besides, it's not like I'll ever go to college. With all those people? No way in hell.

Dried and dressed for work, I slide on my steel-toed work boots. I wonder if Serena was on her way to school when I saw her.

Is she graduating this year or next? I have so many questions. Questions I'm not sure I'll ever get to ask. Because if I do, she'll pry as well, and that shit is just too dark to share.

CHAPTER 10

SERENA

"You got ants in your pants?" Bertha squints at me across the backgammon board.

"No," I say. "It's your turn."

"I know it's my turn. I'm thinking."

"Are you going to still be thinking an hour from now?"

She chuckles. "You kids are so impatient. I'm strategizing."

"*Uh-huh.*"

She finally moves her two pieces, so I roll the dice. "Ha! Double sixes."

She leans back in her chair and huffs. "You cheat."

"Yeah," I deadpan. "They're trick dice, and they only work for me."

"*Pfff.* You gonna move or what?"

"Now who's impatient?"

"Don't you have some other senior citizens to pester?"

"You love me, and you know it." I move my four pieces, leaving none uncovered.

"Yeah, well... I may like you a little bit." She cracks a smile and rolls her dice as I check the clock on the wall.

"You have somewhere else to be?"

"Just meeting a friend after work."

"Is this friend who has you all fidgety a boy?"

"Maybe."

"What does Hayden think of that?"

It's not like it's a date. Knox is just... a new friend I want to know more about. "He doesn't know." I study the board, suddenly feeling a little guilty. Hayden would lose his mind if he found out what I was doing. Too late to back out now. I can't not show up.

"Good for you." Bertha winks.

"It's not like that." I throw my dice.

"Whatever it is... he's got you in a dither."

"What the heck is a dither?"

"Don't you read?"

I scrunch up half my face. "You know I do."

"It means worked up."

"I'm not worked up." *Am I worked up?* Maybe. I'm going to meet a guy I barely know. But it's more than that. He took a beating for me and didn't fight back. I want to know why.

"*Ahhh*... so you couldn't charm him like all the others."

"What are you yammering about *now*?" I quote one of Bertha's favorite sayings. "I don't charm anyone."

"When Hayden stopped by to visit, I barely recognized you, the way you were acting. You shouldn't have to change for *anyone*."

"I *don't* change." She eyes me up and down. "Aren't most people different with whoever they're around?"

"Some, but you shouldn't have to act to impress. Always present yourself as you are, otherwise, how will you know if they like you for you?"

"I don't do it intentionally."

"I know." She softens. "It's a defense mechanism. But if you have to raise those defenses, then the person you're with isn't worth your time." She reaches over the board and gives my hand a squeeze. "Your personality shines as bright as the heavens. You don't need to go changing it."

I lean back in my seat. "Are you feeling okay?" I pause, eyeing her over. "Having a stroke or something?"

She cackles. "You are too much, Serena, my girl. Now take your damn turn."

After finishing our game, I decide it's time to do some *real* work. I fold towels and stack them where they need to go. I sweep the entryway and wipe down doors with disinfectant—just anything I can do to help the full-time staff out.

After emptying the garbage at the nurses' stations, I visit some of the residents who can't leave their beds. I like stopping in to say hi and get them whatever they might need. They have the best stories, even if they keep telling the same ones over and over. I visit Stuart last, wanting to spend as much time with him as possible.

"Hi, Stuart. I'm Serena."

"Hi." He glances at me, uncertainty in his eyes.

"I thought I would read to you today. Would you like that?" He nods in agreement, and then I notice a photo album on the table next to his bed. "Can I look at these pictures?"

"I guess so. I'm not sure whose they are."

I open the cover and realize immediately that they're pictures of Stuart and his family. I smile at him and wonder where the book came from. I've never seen it with his stuff before.

The photos begin when Stuart was a young man. There's one of him and his wife. Another with him and two young boys who I assume are his sons. They seemed to be an active family—the images show them involved in all kinds of outdoor activities.

"Do you want to have a look at the pictures too?" I ask, hoping something might spark his memories. "They seem like a happy family."

"Okay."

I set the book on his lap. He flips through the pages like someone perusing a magazine—for enjoyment, with no recognition of the images. He stops suddenly, puzzling for a moment, then continues until he reaches the end and hands it back to me. "You have a nice family," he says.

"Thank you. I'll just set the book on the table while we read." He won't question why I don't take it with me. He won't remember.

Picking up the novel, I start at the beginning like I always do, but he's asleep within ten minutes. I wish there was more I could do for him, but I know there isn't. This awful disease will take him, and that's the harsh reality of life.

I stop at the nurses' station on the way out. "Did Stuart have a visit from a family member?"

"Not that I'm aware of. Why?"

"There was a photo album on the table next to his bed. I've never seen it before."

"Oh. Laura mentioned he was asking for it the other day, so she dug it out of his closet. It's the first time he's been lucid in a while, so it was a big deal."

"Wow. I'm sorry I missed it. Why the change?"

"They added a new medication."

"But he didn't recognize the photos in the album just now."

"Today wasn't a good day."

While sitting on top of a picnic table with my feet resting on the bench below, I consider the stupidity of being out here alone in an empty, heavily wooded park that's getting colder and darker by the minute.

After thirty minutes, the heebie-jeebies have gotten the better of me, so I step down from the table.

I guess I'm not surprised he bailed.

"Hey," comes a deep voice from behind me.

I jump at least a foot in the air with arms flailing. As soon as I see the creeper is Knox, I slap a hand over my heart. "You scared the crap out of me! Give a girl a warning—footfalls, a cough... *anything*." His eyes are wide, startled even. "I was starting to think you weren't coming." I climb back on top of the table to sit.

He stays where he is and jams his hands into the front pockets of his jeans, looking uneasy. "I almost didn't, but leaving you here alone in the dark wasn't an option. Plus, the bus was late."

The hood of his sweatshirt shields his face when he turns his head away. As he stares off into the darkness, an awkward silence settles between us. I'm about to throw out the useless fact that a Pink Moon will be rising in a couple of hours when he faces me again and says, "You must have better things to do, so why am I here?"

"Because I asked you." The words come out flirty without

meaning to. His pale eyebrows narrow slightly, reminding me of Bertha's advice to be myself. *Do I even know who that is?*

I clear my throat. "Have you lived around here your whole life?"

"No."

"Do you have family nearby?"

"No."

"This isn't how conversations are supposed to go. I ask you a question, and you're supposed to expand on the answer."

"I should go. I'll walk you to your car." He turns and walks away.

I climb off the table. His giant steps force me to walk quickly just to catch up. "But you just got here," I say, speed-walking beside him.

"I told you. I didn't want to leave you out here alone."

"Okay. Well…" I pause. "Tell me *one* thing about you."

He gives me a side-eyed glare as we continue to my car.

"Fine. I'll tell you something about myself." I tap a finger to my lips, quickly shuffling through possibilities. "My father is a recovering alcoholic who moved Mom and me to Denver when I was fourteen for a fresh start, but then he cheated on her. So, Mom moved us back here to the *exciting* small town of Cedarvale two years later."

He looks genuinely shocked by my words. I'm not sure why. Maybe he wasn't expecting that much honesty. Me neither, if I'm honest. Geez, of all the things I could have shared, why did I pick that? "Your turn," I prompt him.

"Did you move back to the same house or a different one?" He stops at my car and stares at me like he's trying to puzzle something out.

"Same house. Maybe Mom always knew things wouldn't

work out with my father because as much as he pressured her into selling, she wouldn't agree to it. He even suggested renting it, but Mom kept dragging her feet. Good thing, huh?" He doesn't respond. "Still your turn. It doesn't have to be personal. What's your favorite food?" I smile up at him.

"Pizza." He pulls the corner of his lower lip through his teeth, pauses a few beats, then says, "Can I show you something?"

"Sure." I wait, expecting him to pull out his phone and show me a picture or something.

"You'll have to drive us there."

"Oh... okay." I unlock Fred's doors.

"Where to?" I ask as he squeezes himself in next to me, his broad shoulders touching mine. Nervous energy ping-pongs around in my stomach at the simple connection.

He clasps the seatbelt and catches me staring at him. "Are you okay? Your face is all red."

His body touches mine, and what... I instantly combust? "Just hot." As I start the car, my cheeks flame brighter. It's cold out.

"Did you know this car was commonly known in Italy as *Topolino*, which means little mouse?" I ask, my words coming a little too fast.

"No. I didn't." Knox reaches between his legs, releasing the lever to adjust his seat, and slides it all the way back to accommodate his legs. "If you go back toward town, I'll direct you from there."

"Sure." Still nervous, I ramble on. "In 1972, they fit fourteen business students into the original Fiat."

"*Hmmm.* Take a left and go about a mile."

"In the newer cars, an espresso machine is a special feature."

"Take this right." I do as he says, then he tells me to pull over.

As I park the car, I turn to him in confusion. "Why did you take me to my house? And how do you know where I live?"

"It's not what you think." He clenches his hands in his lap.

"How do you know what I'm thinking?"

"At school, you asked if I was following you. I'm not."

"It was meant as a joke. I went from never seeing you to seeing you everywhere. But you have to admit, this is a little weird."

He shifts his gaze from me to the passenger window. After a slight moment of silence, he says, "It looks nice painted that new color. And the yard is well kept."

"My house has always been this color."

"Not yours. The one next door."

Whaaat? "I'm confused."

He faces me and says, "We've met before," then pauses like he's waiting for a spark of recognition. "My family. We lived next door. The house on the right. We used to play together when we were little. My mother didn't leave the house much. You were close to my age, and your mom and dad were always friendly." He lifts a hand and rubs his palm over the left side of his chest as if soothing an old ache, then lets it fall to his lap.

"Why don't I remember you?" Puzzled, I study his features more closely. The dim dashboard light throws a shadowy red glow across his face, revealing faint white scars I hadn't noticed before.

"Age, I guess. I was close to six when we moved away. I think you were around four. After we left, and things got bad, which was a lot, I'd remember your house and all the kindness I found there."

"Why didn't you tell me this earlier?" I strain my memory,

desperately searching for any recollection of him, but come up empty.

"I didn't know you were *that* little girl until a few days ago. Even then, I wasn't a hundred percent sure." He lifts his eyes to mine, then drops them again while his large hands slide up and down his pant legs. He seems to realize what he's doing and stops.

"I struggle with nightmares," he continues. "The other night, I dreamt we—um, I mean the little girl and me—were playing in the backyard of your house. And..." He shakes his head, then turns his gaze on me. "It was bad. The dream, I mean. When I woke, I went for a run and ended up here. I saw you leaving the house and I thought, what are the odds of two redheads growing up in the same house?" Knox's leg bounces up and down while his hands twist together, clasping and unclasping in his lap. Instinctively, my hand reaches out, covering his. "Look, it's strange, and—" The nervous action stops, so do his words.

"It's okay," I tell him. "I get nightmares too." My mind jumps to the crash. The twisted metal. The pain.

I watch as his eyes drift closed like he's absorbing my touch. I'm captivated, and all thoughts of trauma suddenly disappear. But then his eyes flash open and find mine. The heat burning behind those icy blues radiates an intensity I've never experienced before.

In the split second it takes for me to acknowledge what I'm feeling, he breaks eye contact, slides his hand from underneath mine, and climbs out of the car without a word.

Did he? Was he? My brain stutters to formulate a coherent thought. My heart is pounding in my throat—my body vibrating. *I have no business feeling this way,* I tell myself as my gut whirls with a mix of guilt and the intense need to go after him.

I inhale a deep breath. *What was that?*

It's just... I didn't expect... And the look in his eyes. It made me feel so... I don't know how to describe it.

As Knox disappears around the street corner, I think about how I'm in *way* over my head. The guy's got more demons than *I* do. Besides, I have a lot going on with finals coming up, not to mention Hayden. So, whatever just happened between us, I have to let it go.

Even as I tell myself this, all I want to do is track him down and experience it all over again.

CHAPTER 11

KNOX

I didn't plan on bringing her to the house, but when she mentioned her father and what he put them through, I don't know... she trusted me—someone she knows nothing about. Maybe it made me think I could trust her, too. And this was Serena, the friend I lost a lifetime ago. Her memory became a safe place when my life got too difficult to handle.

Now everything is jumbled—the past—the present. I take long, quick strides, getting myself as far away as I can without running.

I've never wanted... *needed* someone. Ever.

How can the little girl from my past be the same as this beautiful, fiery... I groan at the memory of her touch. It felt safe, freeing, like every possibility in the world was open to me.

Turning the corner out of her view, I break into a run.

Stupid, so stupid, I mentally berate myself. Meeting up with Serena, telling her about our shared past was a mistake. I've connected us in more ways than a chance meeting of strangers. It was selfish of me. Now she'll be even *more* curious. With my past, it puts her at risk.

I need to stick with my original plan of getting rid of her. And next time—if there is a next time—I'll do whatever it takes to make her lose interest in me because, as much as I want to keep her, there's just too much at stake.

CHAPTER 12

Last week, when I got home from meeting Knox, I mentioned him to my mom. She told me she hadn't thought about him in a long time but always wondered what became of him. The name Knox wasn't familiar. She thought it was something like Garrett or Gabe.

She said he was a sweet little boy who was over almost daily, and that she and my father were suspicious he might have been suffering from neglect since he always seemed to be starving. But since he was a growing boy, they let it go.

When he stopped coming over, my father went over to check on him. The man who answered the door was in a drunken rage, ranting about how the mother took the kid and left.

I've thought a lot about Knox since the last time we met. Not just his rough edges and crappy social skills, but about how he made me feel and the almost obsessive need I've had to see him again.

I know it's crazy. But whatever we shared before he left so abruptly... was unique. And it's that messy detail I need to stop thinking about. As complicated as my relationship is with Hayden, I don't cheat.

Hayden shoulder-checks me playfully as we walk down the hall after the last bell. "How was your day?" he asks.

"It was like every other day, and I'm glad the school year is almost done." I'm so ready for something new. "Do you want to hang out later?" I ask, still trying to settle my mind around him.

He throws an arm over my shoulder and pulls me into his side. "I'd like to, but I have a tutoring session at the library."

"Right. I forgot." The feeling when he touches me hasn't changed. I still find myself wanting to pull away.

"Are you coming to my party this Friday?" Rowan asks, walking up beside us with Tish.

"You know I work early on Saturday," I remind her, feeling shitty about missing her big day.

"But it's my birthday!" Rowan complains. "When you said you had to work, I thought it was code for some sort of birthday surprise."

"Sorry." I wince apologetically. I'm sure I could make it work, but I'm leery of going to any party with Hayden. The stupidity of that thought hits me hard. I shouldn't be missing my best friend's birthday because of Hayden's issues. "Let's celebrate Sunday when we search for prom dresses." Even as I suggest the alternative, I consider the possibility of showing up for a little while.

She looks slightly appeased. "Fine. But we're going out for lunch, and I'm ordering whatever dessert has the most chocolate."

"Fine with me. Tish?"

Hayden stares straight ahead, clearly not happy. *Well, hell.*

"I'm in. You know me—any excuse for chocolate."

Pushing through the double door, we head outside. *Fresh air. Finally.*

After saying goodbye to my friends, Hayden walks me to my car. "You're being quiet," I tell him.

"I was really looking forward to Friday. I thought for sure you'd be there and we could hang out."

"Sorry. You know I need to make as much money as I can before college starts. I'd rather not work during the semester if I can help it." *And I refuse to ask my father for help.*

I really should go to Rowan's party. It's not like I have an important role at the senior home. I'm sure they'd let me take the day off.

When we stop beside my car, he surprises me by pulling me into an embrace. "It's okay. I get it. It's just I had the night all planned out."

"You did?" Uneasiness knots in my stomach.

"Are you sure you can't get off work on Saturday?" He slides his hands into the back pockets of my jeans, cupping my backside.

The familiar feeling of being violated is back. I release myself from him, saying, "No, I can't," and then kiss his cheek. I still might ask for the day off, but I'm not telling him that. I don't want to get his hopes up and then deal with his disappointment if I change my mind.

"Okay," he breathes out, disappointment lacing his tone.

Part of me misses the way things were before he became a drunk-assed jerk. Before Knox.

Things were good between us. They were simple. I was happy enough. Now it's all a big mess.

On the drive to work, I can't stop debating whether I should go to Rowan's party. At a stoplight, I let my eyes roam the intersection, then land on the shopping bag sitting on the seat beside me. Last weekend, I decided to purge some of my books with the intention of donating them to Goodwill. I remembered Knox reading at the bus stop and thought he might want them. They're still with me because the idea of seeing him again gets my stomach all fluttery.

I walk into work and see the "Spring Has Sprung" banner and lots of bustling going on. It's a yearly event with different themed activities scheduled throughout the day. "Oh, Serena." The Witch stops me. "I'm sorry. I should have called you, but we won't be needing you today. We have dueling pianists coming"— she glances at her watch—"in ten minutes, and several other events. I don't have anything for you to do."

"Oh. Okay." They've needed me every other year. *Is she pissed at me for some reason?* I wouldn't put it past her.

"I'll see you tomorrow?" she asks, her heels already tapping the floor as she walks away.

"Sure," I respond, but she's halfway down the hall.

I decide to say hi to The Ladies before I go. Walking into the common room, Agnes waves at me from her seat next to Bertha. "Serena, over here."

"Can you believe this garbage?" Bertha gripes when I reach the feisty pair. "Dueling pianos, *paleeease.*"

"It's giving you the opportunity to share in a cultural experience," I say, smiling.

"More like an opportunity to give me a raging headache," she returns, followed by an elbow to the ribs from Agnes.

"They broke the mold when they made you, Bertha."

"Damn right, they did. Who are you looking for?" she asks as she notices me scanning the room.

"Stuart. I was hoping they'd have brought him to watch."

"I haven't seen him," Agnes says.

"I'm going to ask if I can rescue him from his room for a while."

"You are a sweet girl," Agnes tells me.

"Thanks. If all goes well, I'll see you in a bit."

After Agnes and Bertha lift their crossed fingers, I walk from the assisted living area to the extended care unit.

"Serena, did you come to see Stuart?" Laura asks.

"Yeah. Is he coming to listen to the pianos?"

"We don't have anyone to spare."

"Could I bring him? There will be lots of staff around. I can take him in a wheelchair, and if anything goes wrong, I can get someone to help or bring him right back."

"What about your other duties? Won't that piss Joan off?"

"She said they don't need me today, so I'm officially off the clock."

"You should be off having fun with your friends."

"Stuart *is* my friend."

"I meant your non-geriatric ones?" she laughs.

"I think he might like it," I say with pleading eyes.

"Sure. Let's go and see how he's doing, then go from there."

"Perfect."

"Stuart," Laura says, entering his room. "How are you feeling today?"

"Oh, I'm doing okay, I guess."

"They're having an event in the common room. Do you feel like listening to some music for a little while?" Stuart looks at me without any recognition. "This is Serena. She's offered to take you in a wheelchair since that new medicine you're on makes you a little dizzy."

"Some music might be nice," I say. "What do you think, Stuart? Do you want to be my date?"

He chuckles. "I think you might be a little old for me," he jokes. "But if you behave yourself, I'd *love* to go." His words charm their way into my heart, filling it with an overwhelming sense of affection.

"I'll go and grab some wheels," Laura says, leaving the room.

"Let's sit you up and swing your legs around, then we'll wait for Laura to get you seated in a wheelchair."

"That sounds alright."

I have him in position when she comes back. Using a strap belt around his waist, she aids Stuart into the wheelchair.

"No speeding," he chuckles when I get him out into the hall.

"*Aw*, you're no fun," I return.

Stuart loves listening to the pianos. At one point, he leans over and tells me he once saw the New York Philharmonic perform at Carnegie Hall. I'm not sure if this is a true memory or not, but I pat his arm and tell him how lucky he was to experience the event. He places his hand over mine and gives me an affectionate squeeze.

Definitely a good day.

After taking Stuart back to his room and helping Laura get him situated, I grab my backpack and move toward the exit.

"What are you still doing here?" Joan asks with a pinched face as we cross paths in the hall.

"Don't worry. I'm off the clock." How did she not see me at the performance?

"That still doesn't answer my question."

The woman does not like me. "I took Stuart to the dueling

pianos. Laura mentioned they were short-staffed, so I offered to help."

Her shoulders tense. "I explicitly told you to go home."

Adrenaline kicks me in the stomach. I didn't think lending a hand while off the clock would be a big deal. "Sorry. I was just trying to be helpful."

"Next time, do as you're told."

"Okay." I stand there, dumbfounded, as she dismisses me with a nod and walks off. Holy crap, this woman has issues. You'd think she'd be happy—the event was a success.

CHAPTER 13

SERENA

Sliding into the front seat of my car, I catch sight of the bag of books once again, and my stomach does that flippy-rollie thing.

I don't want this added... *what, tension? This driving need to see him again?* I mentally throw my hands in the air, confused at my state of mind.

Whatever. I'll just drop them off at his door.

Satisfied with my decision, I put the car in drive and head over to his place. Halfway there, the nervous stomach turns into a heart-pounding adrenaline rush.

Get a friggin' grip, Serena. Just leave the books and go. It's not that big of a deal.

But what if he hears me on the stairs and opens the door?

Thoughts of his heated eyes locked onto mine have me clutching my stomach.

Parking, I'm out of the car before I can stress anymore and quietly make my way up the steps.

Outside his door, I glance down at the bag in my hand, then up at the sunny sky. What if it rains? They'll be ruined. A sudden downpour isn't out of the question this time of year.

"Can I help you?" a man calls from below, startling me.

"Oh, hi." An older man with dark skin and graying black hair stands behind a wooden gate and watches me as I walk down the stairs. "I was bringing these books over for a friend." I lift the sack.

"Really?" Surprise flashes in his eyes. "And how do you know Knox?"

"Oh, uh... he intervened when my boyfriend was acting in a way that he regretted once he sobered up."

"*Ah*," he says with recognition, his aged eyes crinkling at the corners. "The fight."

"Yeah," I say. "How did you—"

"Know?" he finishes for me. "The name's Rhett." He holds out a hand. "Knox works for me, and I rent the apartment to him."

"Nice to meet you. I'm Serena." I grip his hand, feeling thick callouses that come from working with your hands most of your life.

"I sent the boy on an errand. I was just about to grill some steaks." He opens the gate for me. "Come on in. You can wait for him if you like."

My belly gets all nervy again. "Oh. I was just going to leave these at his door."

Yeah? Then why didn't you? I think as I step into a beautifully manicured backyard. "Your flowers are beautiful, and your deck... *wow*. Did you build it yourself?"

"I did. The house too."

"You're a carpenter?"

"And a contractor."

"So, Knox builds houses with you?"

"He does." I set the books next to a patio chair as Rhett walks over and lifts the barbeque lid. "He should be back any minute. Would you like to stay for dinner? I have plenty."

"Oh, I don't know."

He stabs a massive cut of beef with a long fork and sets it on the grill. Instantly, it sizzles and smokes. "Well, you can think on it while you wait," he says, adding three more hunks of meat to the grill.

"How did you meet Knox?" I ask.

"Well, now. That's an intricate story, one that he should tell. But we've known each other for..." He stops to think. "Going on almost three years now." He flips the steaks. "Are you still in school?"

"Yes, sir. Senior year."

"Just call me Rhett. Sir was the title my father demanded, and he was a mean son-of-a-bitch. You going to college?"

"I am. I'm going to the University of Colorado in Denver on an academic scholarship."

"Good for you."

"Thanks." I smile at the praise. It always feels more genuine coming from a stranger.

"I'm surprised you and Knox are friends, being that he doesn't—"

"Serena!" The harsh, deep tone has my head snapping toward the patio door. "Why are you here?" Knox demands, coming toward me.

"Now is that any way to treat your new friend?" Rhett intervenes. Knox returns his comment with a scowl. "I invited her to stay for dinner after she was kind enough to drop some books off for you."

"Can I talk to you?" Knox takes me by the arm before I have a chance to respond, half-dragging me toward the back gate. Disappointment sits heavy on my shoulders. I thought we were past this defensive guard of his.

"Knox!" Rhett lashes the name out, anger mixed with concern. "You behave yourself. You hear me?"

Knox's eyes drop to his grip. He releases his hold like I've burned him, then unlatches the gate and forcefully pushes through.

"What is *wrong* with you?" I snap.

He whirls on me and throws a hand in the air. "You can't keep showing up here."

"I was getting rid of some books and thought you might like them. Big friggin' deal. Why are you being so hostile?" I fist a hand on my hip and glare up at him. "I thought maybe we could be friends, you know, get to know each other again for old time's sake, but clearly there's a reason you spend your time alone." The anger on his face falls away, but he doesn't respond. I shake my head and walk past him to my car.

"Dinner's almost ready." Rhett appears at the gate. "Knox. Go and get an extra plate for Serena," he commands in a tone that doesn't leave room for argument.

Knox's eyes drop to his feet as he grips the back of his neck and rubs, then steps back through the gate toward the house.

"Thank you for inviting me to dinner, but I'm going to go," I tell Rhett.

"Don't mind him." He nods in the direction of the house. "He's had a rough time of it and probably isn't too keen on bringing anyone else into his life." He leans toward me in a conspiratorial way and winks. "But I'm glad you came by. He could use a friend." I want to laugh because he needs a hell of a lot more than that. "It takes him a while to get comfortable with new things. Give him another chance? Have some dinner with us? I don't get to visit with people much either."

"I don't think that's a good idea. He *really* doesn't want me here."

"Want and need are two different things. You understand what I'm saying?"

"With Knox? No."

Rhett throws his head back and laughs. "Come on." He holds out an elbow to me. "Keep an old man company?"

Even though a part of me is shouting, *"Nope! Don't do it!"* I step toward him and loop my arm through his. "I'd love to," I say.

If all Rhett has for company is "Iceman" Knox, then hanging out with this sweet old man for the evening is the least I could do.

Back on the deck, he gives my arm a squeeze, releases it, and tells me to have a seat while motioning to a square glass table and chairs. "I better rescue those steaks before we're gnawin' on rubber tires."

Laughing, I pull out a chair.

Just as I sit, Knox comes out of the house with an extra plate, some utensils, and an empty glass. As he lays them out in front of me, I notice a network of scars crisscrossing his knuckles.

Before I can think more about it, a paper napkin flaps in front of my face. When I glance up, he mouths, "Sorry."

His expression isn't soft, but it's honest. Now I'm not sure what to make of this situation. I take the napkin with a nod and a small smile. He turns and walks back into the house, returning almost immediately with a pitcher. He fills my glass with lemonade, then Rhett's.

When he's done, he sets the pitcher on the table and goes to talk to Rhett. As I study his profile, I notice for the first time the bruises have almost completely faded. As if feeling my gaze, he shoots a look my way. Dropping my eyes to my plate, I busy myself rearranging the utensils in front of me.

"Let's eat," Rhett says, carrying over a platter loaded with steaks and foiled baked potatoes.

Knox follows behind him and sets a deep pot on the table. He lifts the lid. "Corn on the cob," he tells me, then sits on the chair to my right.

"This looks incredible," I say, eyeing all the food in front of us.

Oh, crap! "I forgot to text my mom to let her know I won't be home for dinner." I thumb in the direction of my car. "I'll be right back."

Jumping up out of my chair, I hurry out of the backyard, retrieve my phone, and fire off a quick text. After grabbing a light jacket from the backseat, I chuck my phone into my backpack and close the car door. I'm about to run back but pause, steeling a moment to catch a breath after this dizzying evening, and take in the colorful sunset.

Knox twists my emotions in every direction, making me feel unbalanced. It's like walking on a tightrope over fiery-red coals—one wrong step and I'm bound to get burned.

CHAPTER 14

KNOX

I can't believe I lost it when I found her talking to Rhett, but he was about to share something he had no business sharing. It caught me off guard, and I fucking grabbed her arm. The moment I realized what I was doing, flashbacks of my father's abuse tore through me. If I've bruised her, I'll never forgive myself. She isn't a threat—nosy, but not a threat. Still, she can't be here.

The silence that stretches on as we eat is uncomfortable. Rhett's generally not a talker. Neither am I. But with Serena's silence... it's so unlike her, and it's all my fault. I wish I knew how to fix the awkwardness, but communication isn't one of my strong points.

"Serena says she's going to the University of Denver in the fall," Rhett says.

Thank fuck.

"Nice." I return. "That's a good school." *There. That wasn't so hard.*

"She received an academic scholarship," he continues, sounding like a proud papa.

I eye him quizzically, then turn to Serena. "That's impressive. Congratulations." *She* looks at me like I've grown horns and sprouted a tail.

"What are you going to study?" Rhett asks her.

"I want to be a nurse like my mother, then join Nurses Without Borders for a year. After that, I'm not sure what specialty I'd like to veer toward. Maybe geriatrics. I work over at Sunnyvale Retirement Home and enjoy working with the seniors."

"Rhett's becoming one of those," I say, bringing a forkful of potatoes to my mouth. Serena coughs out a laugh. When I glance up, her smile is so big, I feel like I've died and seen my first angel.

"*Boy*, I could still *whoop* your ass." Rhett points his fork at me. "Don't you go carryin' on about me being no *damn* senior."

I roll my eyes and turn my attention to the small buzz of excitement in my chest. Suddenly, I'm not so sure of my resolve to get rid of her. "You'd need some serious backup to take me down, and you know it."

"*Puh*," Rhett forces the sound between his lips. "I could still do you some damage."

"Keep telling yourself that." I spear a chunk of steak and pop it into my mouth.

Light conversation continues through dinner, easing the tension in my chest. As the sky darkened and my words came easier, I found I didn't want the evening to end.

"Well." Rhett stands up. "I'm going to clean up here and

have a rest in front of the TV. You two go on. Maybe go for a walk or something."

"Let us help you," Serena says, getting up from her chair.

"No need. If you two could help me carry all this back inside, I'll do the rest."

"I've got it, Rhett. You cook. I clean. That's how it's done."

"Not tonight, my boy. I have to stay busy and work off this meal. I ate too damn much. Go have a visit with your friend."

He says it as if it's the most normal thing on the planet. Meanwhile, the knot is suddenly back in my chest and I'm wondering how to "have a visit" without him moving the conversation forward.

Maybe she'll just leave. I can't think of any reason she'd want to spend time alone with me. I haven't given her a reason to want to stay.

I sneak a peek and see she's gazing up at me with a questioning gaze.

Shit. What do I do? Asking her to stay is a bad idea, but I don't want her to go. My heart pounds as my nerves begin to fray. Ever since the realization we knew each other as kids, I haven't been able to get her out of my mind, but holding on to her is dangerous.

When my silence stretches on, she turns away and starts picking up the dishes. We bring everything in. I put as much away as I can before Rhett shoos us out the back door. As I follow Serena under the crisscross of string lights, my skin prickles at the next awkwardness about to unfold—saying goodbye.

Serena picks up a heavy bag that was next to her chair and holds it out to me. "Here."

"Thanks," I say, taking them from her and quickly looking inside. "Why did you bring them?"

"I saw you one day at the bus stop with a book in your hands."

"Oh-kay?" I draw out, a little confused, then remember catching sight of her across the street a while ago.

"Never mind," she snaps, making a grab for the books.

When I turn away from her reach, her body presses up against mine, and *holy fuck*! Then her hands are pressing against my chest as she steadies herself and heat pulses where it shouldn't.

Unnerved by the whole situation, I take a step back, causing her to stumble forward before she catches herself.

We stare at each other for several heartbeats. "I hope you, uh... like them," she says.

"What?"

"The books."

Realizing I'm staring at her mouth again, I quickly drop my gaze and look inside the bag. The titles range from suspense and thrillers to horror. Exactly what I like to read. "Do you want them back when I'm done?"

She's chewing on her bottom lip, eyeing me with an unreadable expression. "No," she pauses, then adds, "It was either give them to you or a second-hand store."

"Makes sense. So, is this what you like to read?"

"I read almost everything," she says, then we're both silent.

Shifting uneasily on my feet, I shuffle thoughts through my mind, trying to come up with what to say next.

"I like Rhett," she pushes the words forward.

"Yeah. He's something else." The smile that comes to my lips feels wooden and I hate it.

"Well…" She looks toward her car. "I guess I should get going," she says, making the move to turn away.

What if she never comes back? my inner voice screams. "Do you want to come up?" I blurt, instantly breaking out into a nervous sweat.

"*Sure,*" she draws the word out like she can't believe I made the offer.

No. Never mind. I take it back! my mind screams at me, but my feet lead us forward anyway.

At the top step, I glance at her over my shoulder, wondering what the hell I'm doing. She has a boyfriend. *Remember him, dumbass?*

I open the door. Not that she'd be into me—I just don't need him beating down my door if she decides to share that we spent time together.

"My mom remembers you," she says as we step inside.

"Really?" I respond with genuine surprise. I've felt like a ghost most of my life—in and out of foster homes, not really mattering to anyone. The idea of someone remembering me feels damn good.

"She thought your name was different, though," she says, to which I shrug. Knox is the only name she needs to know.

Her eyes widen when she takes in her surroundings.

"What?" I scan the room, trying to figure out what's got her attention.

"It's so… *nice.*"

"Were you expecting a dump?" I say, mildly insulted, while shutting the door behind us.

"I don't know. I pictured food containers or dishes in the sink, clothes everywhere, and crappy furniture. This looks like the Pinterest board I created for when I get my first apartment."

I turn toward the kitchen. I'm proud of what Rhett and I accomplished. The remodel was a lot of work, but I enjoyed every minute of it. He let me pick out the natural wood floors and warm white on the walls, then designed the rest, keeping with the neutral tones. It's only a studio apartment, but it has everything I need.

"I love the large windows and the exposed vaulted ceiling," she says. "It makes the small space feel bigger."

"That was the idea." The awe in her voice and expression fills me with a sense of pride.

Her hand sweeps across the smooth cement of the kitchen island I helped Rhett build from scratch. The hanging copper pendant lights were my idea. As for the wood-grained stools lining the counter underneath, Rhett found those at the local flea market.

I lean against the island, watching as she takes in the deep, smoky blue cupboards, then walks over to the raised bed we built under a wall of windows. I'm glad Rhett left enough room for me to recline against stacked pillows without leaning on the glass. It's my favorite place to read—my only place, really. There's no other comfortable furniture.

"You have plants." She glances at me over her shoulder, clearly impressed.

"I do."

"And they're living." When I let out a short laugh, she flashes me a bright smile. "I like that sound."

My brain instantly goes on the fritz. *She likes the sound of my laugh?*

Feeling unbalanced, I open the door to the refrigerator and stare inside to give myself a moment to recalibrate. When my eyes land on the water bottles, my mind snaps into focus. "Can I get you anything?"

"No, I'm fine." She's examining my bookshelf as I pull out one of the bottles.

Anxiously, I run the selection of books through my head, trying to remember if there's anything she would think was off. Now she's leaning over my nightstand.

"You have an eReader," she says, her tone somewhere between amazed and perplexed as she picks it up.

I crack open the water, then hip-check the door closed. "I'm not a cave dweller, and leave my shit alone," I say, sounding harsher than I mean to.

"Sorry," she sets it down, looking startled. "I've never known a guy who had one."

"You've been in lots of guys' rooms?" Her face pinches at the retort. "It's easier to download books than walk to the library," I quickly amend. *Shit. I'm screwing this up.*

I can't help it. She's making me nervous. Having her look at all my personal stuff is like having the inside of my brain examined, and I don't like feeling exposed.

"What's wrong with the library?"

"Nothing," I say, relieved she hasn't bolted toward the door. "I'm just busy." In reality, all those people milling around staring at me as I pass by, it's just too much. I shop online for everything.

I can't believe she's standing here in my space. No one's been in my apartment other than Rhett, and even that's rare.

"How do you know Rhett?" She comes over, pulls out a stool, and sits.

"He saved me," I admit without thinking. *Fuck.* I could have given any number of bullshit answers.

"How?"

No way. That shit's private. "Never mind. Figure of speech," I quickly deflect, hoping she'll drop it.

She studies me for a moment like she's gauging the honesty of my answer. "What are you afraid of?"

You, I want to say, surprising myself. *You being here. What that could mean. Me wanting to touch you, but knowing I can't.* I scrub a hand over my mouth and jaw. "Look... I'm not used to, uh... talking a lot. This isn't... I'm not comfortable being social." *That's* putting it mildly. My heart is slowly pounding its way out of my chest.

Her face softens. "You're doing fine. How did he save you? I'd like to hear the story, if you'll share it with me."

I shift uncomfortably. My chest tightens as panic begins to squeeze my throat. "Um... you should probably go." My hands clench by my sides as I fight for the air needed to fill my lungs. I know how this goes, and losing it in front of her would be devastating. "It's getting late."

"Oh... okay." Disappointment flashes across her face as she slides off the stool. Her eyes shift to the fisted hands at my side. With eyebrows pulled together in a curious frown, she reaches out, picks one up, and turns it over. My breath stalls as she slides her free hand down my wrist and under my clenched fingers, gently prying them open, then smoothing her palm against mine. "Is it stressful to talk about your past?" she asks as if her touching me is the most natural thing ever.

She has no idea the impact her simple kindness has on me. She couldn't. It makes me want to tell her everything, give her anything, be all I'm not capable of being. I inhale a lungful of air and step closer, drawn by a force out of my control, and link my fingers with hers. Wanting more of this—more of her, I drop my guard. "Rhett found me hiding out up here when it was a junk-filled space over the garage. I was lucky to come across it. Winter had already hit."

I was freezing and half-starved. Rhett thought he found a drug addict when he lifted the tarp with a shotgun and saw me all skin and bones shivering underneath.

"He took me in, fed me, told me I could stay if I help him fix up the space"—I look around my apartment—"make it livable. Shortly after starting the project, he gave me a job with his company."

Sympathy fills her eyes, and I find myself taking a step back, the charged undercurrents sputtering out.

"You... were living on the streets?" she asks.

I hate that expression. It's more than concern. It's an *oh, you poor broken thing.*

"I did as you asked. I gave you a piece of my story." I slide my hand from hers. This was a mistake. "I've still got some homework to do, so you should probably get going."

Confusion fills her eyes. I don't blame her. I've been hot and cold all night. The poor girl's head must be spinning. I know mine was, but it's clear now. That pitying look was the excuse I needed to remove myself from what was feeling way too good.

"I still have homework to do as well," she says. "Can I come back again sometime or maybe text you since you don't like surprise visits?" She gives my shoulder a playful shove.

"I don't have a phone." This has to end here.

"What about a landline?"

"Rhett has one, but I think it would be better for both of us if we didn't see each other again." The words taste like acid in my mouth. "You have a boyfriend who would *not* be happy you're here, and I've got a lot going on in my life right now."

Guilt washes over her features as she drops her gaze. "You're right."

Making her way toward the door, she adds, "Maybe I'll see you around town or whatever."

"Yeah, you never know."

You moron. You can't let it end like this.

No. It has to be this way, even though part of me is disappointed she didn't fight me on it. She's been pushy every other time.

Probably because of the guilt trip I laid on her.

I open the front door and switch on the porch light. "Be careful on the stairs."

"I will. Please thank Rhett again for dinner."

"Sure."

We say our final goodbyes. I watch until she gets to the bottom step before closing the door, already feeling like I lost something vitally important.

CHAPTER 15

Knox is right. I have a boyfriend. And as innocent as my initial actions were, my thoughts were drifting down a line I was not ready to cross, no matter *how* good he felt. It was the same as that night in my car.

I don't know what it is, but there's something about him that draws me in, and I can't seem to help myself. Everything about him affects me in ways I'm unprepared for.

Poor decisions and confusion aside, I'm glad he shared part of his story with me. But now I have even more questions. So many more.

"Hey, Mom," I call out as I drop my backpack at the front entrance.

"In here," she calls from the living room.

I find her curled up at the end of the couch, watching TV. "So, who did you have dinner with?"

I sit opposite her and pull my feet underneath me. "Knox and his landlord and friend, Rhett."

At her furrowed brow, I quickly explain how I ended up being invited, but leave out the part about going up to Knox's apartment.

"That's not like you to pursue another guy when you're in a relationship."

And this is why I left out being in his apartment. "*I wasn't.*" She eyes me skeptically. "I just... he likes to read, and I had books to unload. Knox and I knew each other at one point, and... he's not even my type," I throw out. *Then why did my heart skyrocket when he interlaced his fingers with mine?*

"I didn't know you had one—a type," she deadpans.

My mouth falls open. "Oh my god, *Mom*."

"I just think maybe you could work on being a little more discerning."

"As opposed to never dating anyone at all?" I retort.

"Ouch!"

"Yeah, tell me about it. I can't believe you slammed me like that." I stretch my legs out and nudge her with my foot. "So, my relationships haven't gone well in the past. That's no reason to go all monster bitch on me."

"You're right." She reaches out and squeezes my leg, looking apologetic. "I'm sorry. That was a horrible thing to say. That situation with Hayden upset me more than I realized."

"Do you want to talk about it?"

"That should be my line," she laughs. "I just don't understand why you're still with him."

Me either. "He's under a lot of pressure." I still don't know what's causing it, or why I haven't asked.

"Are you forgetting he attacked you?"

"It was a mistake that will never happen again. School's almost over, and he's got a lot riding on his scholarship." *That* I do know. He's always struggled in school. "I don't want to be responsible for him flunking out because of the drama I'd create by breaking up with him."

"That's a lot of pressure to put on yourself. His choices are his own responsibility. He's the one who put himself in this situation, not you."

"I know. Don't worry. We're working it out."

"Just please be careful. Keep your senses tuned in."

"Mom. It was one time! He's not Dad."

"Your father was never physically abusive when he drank."

"Mentally abusive doesn't count?"

Her face pinches in a scowl. "Wow! You know how to fight dirty."

"You started it," I snap back, regret quickly washing over me. "Sorry." I scramble over to her, drop my head on her shoulder, and snuggle into her side. "I guess both of us have our claws out tonight. Hayden was genuinely devastated by what he did." Lifting my head, I meet her gaze. "He's not going to drink anymore. You heard him." She raises an eyebrow. "Okay, so we heard that a lot from Dad, too, but I don't think Hayden is *that* guy. He's a serious athlete, and he's always treated me with respect. Honestly, Mom. He had one bad night." Unfortunately, it seems like that *bad* night has etched itself into me in a way I can't seem to get away from.

"I guess. Time will tell."

I lay my head back on her shoulder. "I don't like fighting with you. You're all I've got."

"I'm sorry for approaching the subject the way I did. Chalk it up to being overtired, overworked, and PMSing. It's a crappy excuse, but it is what it is."

"I know you only want what's best for me. But next time, could you think first before throwing your punches? The comment about my relationships stung."

"Yeah." She pats my legs. "That wasn't very motherly of me." She picks up the remote and switches the TV off. "How about I take you for ice cream and you fill me in on all those details you left out about Knox?"

I snort out a laugh. "I like that plan." She knows me too well, but I'm not sure how much I'm willing to share this time. Bouncing my thoughts off her has helped more times than I can count, but still. Tonight was the first time she'd ever thrown my decisions back in my face. I know it's because she's fearful of what Hayden is capable of. But I'm not. My eyes are wide open, and Hayden is nothing like my father.

CHAPTER 16

SERENA

I didn't have the guts to ask Joan for the day off, but I'm going to go to Rowan's birthday party after all. *So what* if I'm bagged at work tomorrow? As Rowan continually reminds me, I'm young, and we only live once.

By the time I get home, eat, get ready, it's around nine when I finally arrive at the party.

I can't believe her parents okayed this. There are a shit-ton of people here, and the music is booming. Their property is on an acre lot, so hopefully the distance from their neighbors will keep them from calling the police.

"You came!" Rowan drapes herself around me. She's well on her way to being hammered. "I'm so glad," she says, hugging me hard. "Come on. Let's get you a drink."

"Sure, why not?" I can stay the night and go home early in the morning to get ready for work.

"Be right back," she says, rushing off.

I hear someone squeal and turn to see Tish rushing toward me. "I can't believe you came!" She gives me a one-arm squeeze around my waist.

"I couldn't miss it," I holler over the noise. "Turning eighteen is a big deal. Hey, have you seen Hayden?"

"Not recently, but he's around. Come on." She pulls on my hand. "Dance with me."

"I will in a minute. Rowan went to get me a drink, and then I want to find Hayden. We can hang out after."

"*Ohhh-kay*," she says with an exaggerated groan. "I get it." She winks as she wiggles her fingers at me and then dances away.

Looks like she's been drinking as well.

Rowan hands me a beer-filled cup. "I'm going to track Hayden down," I tell her.

"Fine, but come right back. It's *my* night, not his."

"Spoiled much?" I tease.

She sticks her tongue out at me. "Where's Tish? I just saw her talking to you."

"She's dancing."

"Perfect." Moving past me, she hollers over her shoulder, "Hurry back."

I give her a thumbs up, then weave through the crowd, trying not to spill my drink in the process. I search the living room, the back terrace, around the pool, and the dining room where beer-pong is in full swing, but I can't find him anywhere. Screw it, I'll go dance with Tish and Rowan, but first, I need to use the restroom.

The hallway is crowded with people. I should have gone pee before I left. Now I'm going to have to wait in this long-ass line.

As it slowly inches forward, I take the phone out of my back pocket and text Hayden that I'm here, and ask where he is. I should just go upstairs and use Rowan's bathroom.

The door to the library is in front of me. It's my favorite room in the house with its dark wood, soft lighting, and comfy chairs. Deciding to take a peek and breathe in that heavenly book smell, I crack the door open,. A girl is straddling a guy's lap in my favorite chair, grinding on him like a stripper giving a lap dance. *Oops.* I begin my retreat, then stop suddenly when my eyes catch the familiar burnt-orange Converse. I step in farther to confirm whose face is hidden between the girl's boobs.

"You asshole!" I rush the couple and throw my beer at them —cup and all.

Hayden jumps out of the chair, sending the girl crashing to the floor, then stumbles. "Serena!" He wipes the beer from his face, then looks down and adjusts himself before zipping up his jeans.

"What the hell?" I holler at them.

The girl scrambles to her feet. Her button-down shirt is gaping open, revealing large breasts bursting out of a black-lace bra. She pulls her shirt closed and bolts for the door.

"I didn't think you were coming," he slurs and pulls me up against him.

"Gross. Are you kidding me? Let go of me!" I shove his chest. He immediately releases me, hands raised in surrender. *Smart move.*

His eyes are glassy and out of focus as he drops his head and runs a hand through his messy hair. "I didn't plan this. It just kind of happened."

I give a derisive snort, eyeing the dying bulge in his pants. "Yeah, this was totally out of your control."

His head snaps up. "Ya know what? Screw you. You're never

around, and it's not like I'm ever going to get any." He glares at me with contempt.

Without thinking, my hand comes up and *wham*. His head snaps to the side from the impact. Instantly, his teeth are bared. His hand fisted and cocked.

"Hayden!" a voice hollers from the doorway. It's Rowan. Clenched hand still raised, he glares at me, chest heaving. "Hayden, what the fuck?"

He lowers his arm and takes a step toward me while my heart rams double-time against my chest. Leaning close to my ear, he whispers, "I could have given you everything."

My body trembles with anger and disbelief. *How can he do this?* That speech about how important I am and how badly he needs me in his life. "The alcohol is twisting your reality."

"*Wrong*. It makes me see things more clearly." His eyes rake me over with distaste. "Because now I see what a mistake you were." Stepping forward, he shoves me out of his way—his strength throwing me off balance. My hands don't come up quick enough, and my head slams against the coffee table right above my cheekbone. Stars burst behind my left eye.

"Get the hell out of my house!" I hear Rowan shriek as I stare in shock and pain at the sparkling flecks of light dotting the floor.

"Screw *you*," Hayden bites back.

Rowan crouches down next to me. "Are you okay?"

I gently touch the side of my head. The pain from the light pressure making me feel like I'm going to pass out. I feel wetness and stare at my fingers. "Shit. I'm bleeding."

"He never even looked back," she says, disgusted.

"Too drunk to care." I close my eyes. I can't believe this is happening.

"Has he been abusive before? Has he hit you?"

"No." I try to stand up, but everything spins, so I sit back down. "Did everyone hear?"

She stands and rushes to the door, shutting and locking it behind her. "Not sure," she mutters upon returning. Her gaze sweeps over me, lips pressing into a thin line. "Fucker. I'll make him pay for this. Be right back." Spinning on her heels, she strides into the adjoining bath. The sound of her angry mumbling blends with the running water. She returns in less than minute, handing me a damp towel. "Oh, look at your eye. It's already swelling."

"Great," I mumble, then glance at the towel she's handed me. "This is too nice. I'm going to wreck it."

"Don't worry about it. It's not a big deal."

A week ago, he couldn't live without me. Now he friggin' knocks me to the floor without a second thought.

The coolness of the cloth helps the throbbing heat radiating from the wound. I sigh heavily and close my eyes. "I was on my way to the bathroom when I found them."

"That's where *I* was heading when I heard you shouting." She reaches down, hooks both hands under my arms, and lifts me to my feet. "Let's get you into the chair."

My vision darkens and the room begins to spin. "Not in *that* one." I point to my no-longer favorite reading chair while taking deep breaths to fight off the wave of nausea. "That's where they were."

"Who were?" She guides me on shaky legs over to a divan.

"Hayden and some girl." I slowly recline against the pillow. Thankfully, the spinning stops, and so does the nausea.

"Gross! I'm so sorry. He's the one who fucked up. Why was he so mad?"

"I slapped him."

"Good for you." She grins.

"Not so good. That's why this"—I gesture to my face—"happened. I'm so stupid. I knew things weren't right between us." But I fell for his bullshit and look what it got me.

She flicks her hand dismissively. "You were too good for him, anyway. He doesn't deserve you."

"No. He doesn't."

I'm glad she doesn't bring up yet another failed relationship. *Has he cheated on me before?*

"I'm going to get you some ice and pain medication, then I'm driving you home."

"No way. It's your birthday party. Besides, I'm fine, and you've been drinking."

"I'm sober *now*."

"I doubt it. I can drive. Come on. Help me up." When I swing my legs over to sit up, a rush of dizziness hits me, and I instantly regret it.

"No way. You're not fine. I should get you to the emergency room."

I lift a leg back up on the divan and lay back. "No. I just want to rest for a moment. Besides, Mom can check me over, and if she thinks I need to go to the ER, she can take me."

"You're shaking. Are you cold?"

"Probably a mixture of pain and rage." And a bit of shock.

She takes the blanket that's slung over the back of this fancy piece of furniture and lays it over me. "I'll be right back with ice and something for the pain."

"Rowan?"

"Yeah?"

"Thank you."

She tilts her head and smiles. "Of course. Be right back."

Hearing the door shut behind her, I close my eyes against a throbbing pain more excruciating than anything I've ever experienced.

Would Hayden have punched me if Rowan hadn't come in?

The thought is terrifying.

"Serena!" Tish barges into the room several minutes later. "Are you okay?" She comes to a halt beside me and swears *loudly*. I can't help laughing because it sounds ridiculous coming out of her mouth. She never uses foul language. *Frick!* The added movement makes the pain worse.

"Rowan will be right back with the ice." She sits beside me. "I can't believe Hayden did this," she says, disbelief written all over her face.

"He was drunk. I don't think he knew what he was doing."

"Don't make excuses for him," she snaps.

I hold up a hand in defense. "Calm down, teen avenger. I'm not."

"Good, because I don't give a shit if aliens invaded his body. There's no excuse for what he did."

"I know."

"Let me rinse this." She holds out her hand for the cloth. "And when I get back, you can explain exactly what happened. Rowan only gave me the vicious end. Just a second." She rushes off and comes back with the semi-clean, much cooler cloth, and sits next to me while I fill her in on the crappy details.

"Do I bring out the worst in every guy I date?" I ask. "Because they sure don't start off being pieces of shit."

"Of course not. They probably just show you their best side in the beginning. Aren't we always on our best behavior when we first meet people?"

"I guess. How is anyone supposed to know what they're getting into?"

"Don't rush into a relationship? Get to know them better first?"

Normally, she'd be right. "I've known Hayden for four years. Shouldn't I have seen it?"

"Stop blaming yourself. We all should have seen it. I don't know *what* happened to him. He's never been like this."

"He discovered alcohol," I snort. How did it get so out of control so fast? Maybe he's always had a problem and lost his ability to hide it.

Rowan is back and hands me her high-tech ice pack. "Tish was swearing," I tattle. It's too good to pass up.

"Don't look at me like that," Tish defends against Rowan's infamous *WTF* gaze. "I'm pissed! That piece of—he... then he—"

"Come on," Rowan goads. "*Say it.*"

"That no-good, piece-of-shit, cock-sucking, son-of-a-bitch, bastard cheated and hurt my best friend." She smacks a hand over her mouth, her eyes wide.

"Impressive." Rowan nods in appreciation, then hands me two pills and a glass of water.

Tish drops her hand. "That felt good," she says, ducking her head.

"There are even better forms of release you might want to try."

Tish smacks Rowan's leg. "Don't be crude."

"I think you get to take the trophy home on *that* today."

Tish snorts out a laugh.

After taking the pills Rowan gave me, I gently rest the ice

against my temple, instantly pulling it away. "Oh, hell no! It feels like someone just lodged a hatchet in the side of my head."

"Just give it a minute." Rowan guides the ice back slowly.

"You're already bruising," Tish says. "Can you even see out of your eye? It's so swollen."

Barely, I want to say, but instead tell them I can. I don't want to add to the worry already displayed on their faces. *He pushed me and never gave me another thought.* The realization hits me hard once again. I was wrong to believe the previous violence was a one-off. He's a mean drunk who needs some serious help.

The pain from the ice is making me nauseous again. "I feel a lot better," I tell them, taking the cold pack away and making a move to get up.

Tish stands and holds out a hand to me. "Are you sure? Maybe you should stay a while longer."

I swing my legs over the side and let her help me up. No dizziness this time. "See? I'm fine." I want out of this room. Visions of Hayden with that girl are everywhere in here.

My friends eye me warily.

"Really," I tell them. "I'm good. I can drive, no problem. If Mom's asleep when I get home, I'll wake her up so she can check me out."

"Why don't I call you a ride?" Rowan suggests.

"It'll take too long. It's a Friday night. I'm good. I promise." *Pound, pound, pound,* my head throbs against the lie. I need to get to my car fast.

"Text us when you get there, okay?" Tish says. "Where are your car keys?"

"In my pocket."

"Your phone?"

"Uh." I look around the floor. Tish finds it by the table I hit and hands it to me. "Hey, the door at the end of the hallway leads outside, right? I don't want anyone to see me like this." I hand Rowan the ice pack.

She pushes it back at me. "Take it with you, and yeah, the door will lead you out. There's a gate to the left that opens into the front yard.

"Thank you both for taking care of me."

"Absolutely." Tish leans forward and air-hugs me. "I'm afraid I'll hurt you."

"I'm fine. Really."

Rowan opens the library door a crack. "There's still a line to the bathroom."

Rowan and Tish do a great job of shielding me as we walk out. When we get to the end of the hall, Rowan unlocks the door and holds it open for me.

"Don't forget to text," she says as I step out into the cool night air.

"I won't." A censored spotlight shoots blinding white light into the darkness. I throw up a hand to block the intensity as it cuts into my brain like a thousand shards of glass. Sweat breaks out all over my body.

"Are you sure you're okay?" Tish asks.

"Yeah. That light's just super bright," I lie, heading to the gate. When I reach it, I flip the latch and toss a casual wave over my shoulder. "See you on Monday." I don't wait for a reply.

Once the gate is closed, I'm hunched over, hands on my thighs, taking deep breaths to fight off the pain that's threatening to take me out at the knees.

I feel like I'm going to puke.

After several minutes of deep breaths, I straighten up. Some people are staring at me. They probably think I'm sick from drinking too much. Let them think whatever they want as long as they don't see my face.

I pull my knotted-up hair free of its tie and let it fall to shield the damage, then walk quickly to my car. I can't believe this night. As soon as I'm seated, I recline the seat and close my eyes, needing a minute for the pounding to subside before starting the car. Thankfully, I'm parked far enough away from Rowan's house that I don't think anyone will notice me lying here.

As soon as the thought passes through, I hear voices coming my way. *Crap.* I lift my seat slowly, then start the car.

As I pull away from the curb, thoughts of my mother's *I-told-you-so* make me want to avoid her a little longer. I could sneak in—chances are she won't hear me—but she'll see the damage in the morning and lose her shit for not waking her.

I need somewhere to chill until these painkillers kick in. There's no way I can handle her freaking out in this state. And maybe with a bit more time, my face won't look as bad as my friends made it seem.

CHAPTER 17

SERENA

I'm not sure what makes me pull into the alley behind Knox's place.

Seeing his lights on, I wonder if he's lost in a book or zoning out to a movie.

I crack the window open for some fresh air and close my eyes, letting the cool breeze soothe my burning wound.

Crap. I was supposed to text my friends. Digging my phone out of my backpack, I quickly find our group chat, then text, *I'm safe and not to worry.* Hopefully, they'll take it to mean I'm home.

As soon as I turn to tuck my phone away, a knock at my window startles me, and my phone goes flying as I let loose a strangled scream.

"You scared the crap out of me!" I slap a hand over my heart. *Pound, pound, pound.* Each beat feels like a hammer against my head.

"What the hell happened to your face?" he shouts, his deep voice reverberating against the mostly closed glass.

"*Shhh.*" I glare up at him. "Do you want someone to call the police?"

He opens my door, looking ready to commit murder. "Did your boyfriend do that?" he shouts again, disregarding my warning.

Reaching forward, he takes a hold of my wrist and guides me up and out of the car with a gentleness I would never equate to him.

"*Ex*-boyfriend, and it was an—" I start to say accident, but stop myself. "He was drunk and pushed his way past me. I fell and hit my head on a table."

He glares down at me in a way that says there was nothing inadvertent about it. "Did you call the police?"

The shove may not have been an accident, but the force behind it was. "*No.* I instigated it by smacking his face. I'm not saying he had a right to retaliate. It's just what happened."

"*Good.* I'm glad you got a shot in." Knox reaches toward my face, causing me to flinch. His hand falls to his side with a frown and something a lot like sadness crosses his features.

"I know you would never hurt me. It's just that it hurts *really* bad, and I was afraid you were going to touch it." I trust him more than he realizes.

Tucking my hair behind my ear, I tilt my head to give him a better view. He holds my gaze for a moment before his eyes shift to inspect the injury.

"The bleeding seems to have stopped, but you should get that eye looked at—make sure there isn't any serious damage." He nods his head toward his apartment door. "Did you want to come inside? I could get you some ice."

"I tried that. It makes it worse."

"Do it anyway. It'll help. Why are you even here? You should be home."

"Honestly? Other than not dealing with my mom's rage against the injustice, I really can't say."

We stand in silence for two beats before he says, "Are you coming or going?"

"You know, you could be a little nicer under the circumstances," I snap.

The corner of his mouth lifts and a dimple dents the side of his cheek. *No way!*

"Hey, *you* came here," he says.

"Fine. I would *love* to put a frozen object on my battered face and soak up more of your *exemplary* bedside manner."

Knox makes a sound somewhere between a cough and a laugh, picks up my elbow, and leads me toward the stairs. I must look worse than I thought if he's helping me like an invalid.

When we reach the top of the steps, he opens the door for me, letting me enter first. The only light on is a bedside lamp that casts a warm glow on the inviting interior that *still* takes me by surprise. The bed is rumpled, and a book lay open on its pages. I recognize the cover as one of the ones I gave him.

"Sit," he orders, pulling out a stool from under the kitchen island. "Why are you smiling?"

As if I'd tell him his surly, yet sweet protective side is cute as hell. "No reason." I sit as directed and watch as he pulls a bag of frozen peas from the freezer. He wraps a paper towel around it, then hands it to me. I'm not sure why the fact that he's reading one of my books eases the sting of this brutal evening, but it does.

This time, when I place the ice on the side of my head, it

doesn't feel like it's going to explode. I'm relieved—so is my pain tolerance.

Facing me, Knox leans his hip against the end of the counter and crosses his arms over his chest. "You said ex, right? You're not gonna go back to him if he apologizes, are you?"

"*No*. I'm done."

He looks at me in a way that says he's not sure if he believes me. "Would you like some water? Are you hungry?"

"Water would be great. Thanks."

There is a lot more to him than his broody, anti-social behavior—so much more—and if I'm being honest with myself, maybe that's what brought me here. That, and I feel safe with him.

He pulls out a bottle from the fridge, cracks it open, and hands it to me. Long, thick fingers brush mine as we make the exchange, setting off a buzz of awareness—a heated reminder of the last time I was in this apartment.

There has to be something seriously wrong with me if I get brutalized by one guy, and the next insensitive jerk who comes along sparks my interest.

No... it's the "more to him" part, I remind myself.

"Where did you go after your mother took you away from here?" I ask, needing to get out of my head. I'm not ready to take a deep dive into my own thoughts.

"How'd you know my mother took me?"

"My father apparently confronted yours when you stopped coming over. Mom told me when I asked her about you."

"Oh." His eyes widen slightly, flashing a hint of vulnerability, like he's surprised someone would care enough to check on him. "We were in Fort Collins for a bit. She had a friend there, but she wore out her welcome and moved us to Denver."

As I search his pale, almost colorless blue eyes, I wonder if we ever crossed paths in Denver the same way we seem to do here.

"You're doing that thing with your face again," he almost growls. "Are you dizzy at all? Have a headache? Maybe you got a concussion."

"Do you have something against smiling?"

Okay. Maybe it's a little weird considering what I just went through.

"You need to keep up with that ice." He lifts my hand holding the peas and carefully guides it back to my face—his massive hand cups my jaw along with the bag, holding it in place. The gentleness has me closing my eyes and leaning into his touch. Who is this enigma standing in front of me?

He clears his throat and drops his hand.

"What happened to your mom?" Things must have been really shitty if he'd rather live on the streets than at home.

"Your mind bounces all over the place, doesn't it? She died when I was fifteen. My dad several years before."

"Oh, I'm sorry."

"Don't be."

"So, that's why you're on your own?"

"I don't want to talk about it."

"Did you go into foster care?"

He straightens. "Man, you don't quit. Let's just say it didn't work out. Look, it's late. You should probably get home and get some rest."

I stand up and set the frozen vegetables on the counter. I shouldn't have pushed. "What time is it?"

"Close to midnight, I think."

I start walking to the front door. "Sorry for keeping you up." But I'm not sorry for being here or learning more about him.

"It's fine," he says from behind me.

With my hand on the doorknob, I turn to him. "Thank you."

"For what?"

"I don't know. Letting me in?"

"I found you in your car," he deadpans.

"You're right. You did," I laugh, remembering my near-fatal heart attack. "But you also raged about the injustice, then showed kindness without pity. My friends did the same thing, but you don't know me. The unbiased version meant more."

A faint smile tugs at the corner of his mouth, flashing that dimple again. The sight has me wondering if he has a matching set, and if he'll ever smile big enough for me to find out.

"Mom wants you to come by sometime to say hi. Maybe for dinner?"

He stands up straighter, looking surprised. "We'll see. Keep up with the ice."

"Yeah. Okay." When he reaches around me to open the door, his scent—one that's becoming increasingly familiar—surrounds me.

"Doesn't look like there will be any scarring," he says.

Fresh air, wood, and... what did he just say? Oh, right, no scarring. "That's good." The ugly, jagged one along the right side of my torso I got in the crash is plenty.

He follows me down the stairs to my car. I should have moved it before going in. It's blocking half the alley.

"I guess I'll see you around," I say, feeling the first drop of rain as I open my car door.

"Sure. Maybe. You shouldn't leave your car unlocked."

He's right. I left my backpack and phone in there with the

window partway open. "Yeah. I wasn't thinking." He shuts my door when I get in.

"And you are now?" He looks a little worried.

"I'm good."

He nods and takes a step back. After starting the engine, I roll up my window, then drive forward.

Glancing in my rearview mirror, I see Knox standing with his legs slightly apart, arms folded across his chest, watching my car drive away.

I'd give anything to know what thoughts are running through his head right now.

It rains all the way home. Because it's so late, I decide to deal with my mother in the morning. My mind is clear, and I don't have a headache. She'll be mad, but there's nothing she can do that I haven't already done.

When I drift off to sleep, I dream of iridescent blue eyes staring into mine and warm lips feasting with a powerful need as we sink like stones, deeper and deeper into dark waters. There's love, contentment, and a strength in our bond, but suddenly, I can't breathe. Awareness hits me with a tidal wave of panic—he's stealing my air.

I struggle to get free, but I can't.

My eyes snap open and heave in a lungful of air.

Head throbbing, I sit up and lean forward to catch my breath.

In the silent darkness of my room, I struggle with the disturbing blend of desire and dread leftover from the dream. *Shit.* Slowly lowering my head back on the pillow, I replay the images and sensations and wonder how I'll ever get back to sleep.

CHAPTER 18

KNOX

Serena left five hours ago and I can't sleep. All I want to do is tear this town apart until I find her ex and make him pay for hurting her. Did he even check to see if she was okay? Feels like a big, fat fucking no. I should have asked for more details, because the images racing through my head... I want to make him regret ever being born.

I hope she means what she says and doesn't go back to him. I know about co-dependent relationships. My mother was an excellent teacher.

Frustrated at being wound up and unable to sleep, I throw off the covers and slip into a pair of sweats, a t-shirt, my running shoes, and I'm out the door.

Raindrops pelt my body with a sharp sting as my feet slap the wet pavement. I normally don't mind running in the rain, but the temperature has dropped since Serena left, and with the wind picking up, it's uncomfortably cold.

Steamy breaths come out in puffs as I focus on the rhythmic pounding of my shoes. Regardless of how hard I push myself, the image of Serena's abused face mixes with gruesome memories from my past—my mother's bruises, the broken bones, the drugs she used to numb it all...

Breathe in.

Step, step, step.

Breathe out

I know they're nothing alike. The situation is completely different, but the helplessness and anger I feel are the same. I swear, if he hurts her again, I don't know if I'll be able to control myself. Because I *will* find him, and I *will* make him pay.

Breathe in.

Step, step, step.

Breathe out

No. Serena is nothing like my mother. She's strong. Hell, she's put me in my place easily enough. Not that I'm *trying* to be difficult, it's just... I don't know how to handle myself when I'm around her. Maybe if she could stop digging into my past, we could—what? Be friends?

Not a chance. I thought maybe, but no. My life is too fucked up.

It's strange the way she knots me up but also manages to make me feel... normal—even calm sometimes. And there sure as hell is no explanation for the intense feelings I have, or this consuming need to be near her. We knew each other as kids, but she's a complete stranger to me now. Yet every fiber of my being wanted to wrap her in my arms tonight and let her know she's safe. That I'm here for her. That I would do anything to protect her.

Right. When have I been able to protect anyone?

More unwanted memories flood my mind, zapping the strength from my legs. I stop and brace my hands on my thighs as I heave crisp air in and out of my lungs. I'm so tired of feeling guilty, wondering if I could have helped my mother more. If I made more money. If I was nicer to her. If I'd done everything differently, could I have saved her? There are so many "ifs" and they torture me relentlessly. I know in my head it's not my fault —it's on her—but my mind can't seem to accept it that way.

The sky has shifted from its inky blackness to a deep blue. As the world around me lightens, I realize I'm only a block from Serena's house. As I start to walk toward it, her words replay in my head. "I know you'd never hurt me."

It was a simple statement, but the truth of it makes me feel like I'm more than the waste of space I was made to believe growing up.

When I reach her house, I look between hers and the miserable place I lived for six short years.

I remember which room is hers. Will she come down if I throw stones at her window?

What would I even say?

At the ridiculous train of thought, I start running again, slower this time, with my mind focusing on her soft pink lips, out-of-control red hair, and that smile. If thinking of her gives me peace and keeps me from going under, I'll take it. Because, most days, it feels like I'm barely keeping my head above water.

Breathe in.

Step, step, step.

Breathe out.

CHAPTER 19

SERENA

My mother was furious—full-on lost her shit—when she saw my eye all bruised and swollen shut. I thought about making up a story, but since I suck at lying, I told her everything. She wanted me to go to the police and file charges, but I flat-out refused. It's not like Hayden punched me in the face. He shoved me aside, and I stumbled and fell. If my balance wasn't so off, or the table had been somewhere else, my face wouldn't look like a mess right now. Not that I'm making excuses for his actions. The whole thing was seriously messed up. I just don't think going to the police makes sense, especially since I instigated it.

Considering everything that went down, I assumed Hayden would keep his distance. There was nothing from him the morning after the party. No texts. No calls. He didn't even stop by to grovel, which was fine with me—better, actually. A clean, easy break saves me the hassle of officially breaking up with his ass. So, imagine my surprise when I walk into school on Monday morning and find him leaning against my locker, waiting for me.

He wants to do this now?

Or maybe he doesn't remember any of it.

"What?" I snap, coming up next to him and turning the padlock dial. A violent image of me smashing the locker open against his head flashes through my mind.

"What the hell happened to your face?"

My hand stalls, my mouth hanging open as I gaze through my one good eye. *Seriously?* "I hit my head on the table after you pushed me."

"I didn't push you!"

"*Yes*, you did!" *How can he not remember?* "You insulted me, so I smacked you. You insulted me again, then shoved me out of your way so hard that I fell and hit my head."

"No way," he scoffs. "You're just pissed about that girl."

"Right. I beat my head against a table because you were screwing someone behind my back." I give him a flat stare.

"I wasn't screwing her."

"Oh, *that* you remember, but not the rest?"

"Okay. Some of the details are a little fuzzy."

"Funny how that happens when you drink to *excess*," I shout the last word at him. "Ask Rowan. She'll be happy to fill you in on the missing details. You're lucky she came in when she did, or you'd be facing battery charges."

He looks horrified. "What are you talking about? I would *never* hit you. I—"

"It doesn't matter." I cut him off, not wanting to hear any more excuses.

"The hell it doesn't. Especially if you're telling people I gave you a black eye."

"I haven't said anything to anyone. I'm not sure what information *Rowan* is spreading. That's her business," I snap.

I rework my lock and open the door, flinging it as I do. Unfortunately, he moves out of the way in time. From the corner of my good eye, I catch him examining the faces passing by. I guarantee he's gauging if the rumor has hit the ground running or not. "That's all you're worried about? What people think? Look at my face, Hayden."

"I said I don't remember, and I have a football scholarship to think about. If news like this got back to them, they'd probably ban me from the team."

"Oh my god! You're unbelievable." I pull out books from my backpack and shove them into my locker, exchanging them for the ones I need for my next class. "If you're so worried about your scholarship, you might want to rethink your priorities. Starting with your alcohol consumption."

"You're right." He shakes his head as if awareness has finally settled in. "I'm sorry. Are you okay? I never would have done any of that if I hadn't—"

"Been drinking?" I finish the statement for him. "No shit."

"I said I was sorry," he bites back.

"You realize we're over, right?"

"Yes." He picks up my hand. "I do care about you. I just want a girlfriend whose... around more."

I yank my hand out of his grasp. "You are such a dick." I slam my locker closed. "I need to get to class." Turning away, I walk with the crowd down the hall. I text Rowan and Tish and tell them not to tell anyone about what happened to my face, and that Hayden and I are officially over.

Tish: Glad you're free of him. Kai knows, but he won't say anything.

Rowan: I already told Darius, and he's not going to say anything either.

By the time lunch rolls around, I've had enough of everyone staring at me. At least no one is whispering as I pass.

"Holy shit! That looks awful," Rowan says when I sit down to lunch.

"Thanks." I glare, not needing the dramatic reminder.

"Sorry, but why didn't you use makeup to hide it?"

"I did!"

At least I can sort of see through my eye now. The swelling goes down the longer I'm vertical.

"Are you okay?" Tish asks. "You were radio silent over the weekend."

"Sorry. I didn't feel like talking to anyone."

"I guess this means our plans for prom are screwed," Rowan pouts.

"It's not like I wrecked my face on purpose just to ruin your life," I snap.

"She didn't mean it that way," Tish interjects.

"No," Rowan hastily adds. "Not at all. It just sucks. I wanted us all to be together. You dumping his ass was the right choice. Will you still go?"

"I haven't given it any thought, but probably not." I turn to Tish. "Sorry about ruining our trip to Denver yesterday."

"It's okay. I figured you wouldn't be up for it. Maybe we could go this Sunday instead. But if you're not sure you're going to prom..." She shrugs. "I can just go by myself."

"No way," I tell her. "We all go together. Right, Rowan?"

"You know *I'm* in. And you should come to prom with us anyway. Hayden isn't welcome in our group anymore."

"I don't know. I'll think about it."

"Think hard. Prom is a rite of passage, like graduation."

"Yeah, I guess, but I really don't want to spend all that money on a dress I'll only wear once."

"I bought two," Rowan says. "I couldn't decide which one I liked. We're the same size. You can wear my second choice."

"Thanks. I don't know... maybe. But honestly, sitting like a wallflower doesn't sound too appealing."

"You wouldn't be. You'll be with us"—she gestures a hand between Tish and herself—"but I'll also understand if you decide not to go."

"Thanks. That's big of you, Rowan," I tease.

"I know, right? And don't forget you owe me cake."

"Hey! I showed up to your party."

She dismisses me with a flick of her hand. "Numbnuts ruined our time together. It doesn't count."

A laugh bubbles up. "Your self-centeredness is truly off-putting. You know that, right?"

She leans over and kisses my cheek. "You love me."

Darius appears and sits on the other side of Rowan, with Kai settling next to Tish and kissing her cheek. I wonder what that's about.

Not about to embarrass Tish and call them out on the PDA, I let my eyes wander the cafeteria and wonder where Hayden will sit now that he's been ousted from the group. My stomach roils with queasiness when I see him on the other side of the room cozied up to the girl from the party.

"Asshat," Rowan says, following my line of sight. "That girl has slept with half the football team."

"How do you know?" I ask her.

Darius leans my way. "I told her. And before you lump me in there, I wasn't one of them. Neither was Kai."

At least Hayden got someone who would put out. I'm sure *that'll* make him happy. "Look. I don't want you all to feel like you need to pick sides. I have no problem eating by myself."

"Screw that," Rowan says. "We're friends. We hang out at lunch, and that's the way it is. Besides, that's the only time we get to see you—you're always so busy. If the guys want to go and sit with dickhead over there, that's their choice."

"Hey!" Darius protests.

I appreciate the moral support, but I don't think it's going to be that easy. Whatever comes next, at least I know I have my friends by my side.

CHAPTER 20

SERENA

There is a collective gasp when I walk into the community room at work. "What the hell happened to your eye?" Bertha shouts from her bridge group.

Agnes is across from her and turns in her seat. "Oh, honey. What happened?"

"I'm a klutz," I say, coming to stand by their table. Agnes reaches up when I get close enough, but drops her hand when she sees how bad it is. "It's fine," I tell her. "I was fooling around, fell, and my head hit a table." At least part of that was true.

"*Mmm-hmm.*" Bertha eyes me over speculatively.

"Did you know the odds of falling to your death are one in a hundred and nineteen?" I throw out, fidgeting under Bertha's scrutiny. "Odds of being hit by lightning are one in a hundred and fourteen thousand and something. Yep. You can look it up. Well, I'm going to go and sit with Stuart. I'll talk to you all later, okay?"

Bertha shakes her head at me, while the others nod and turn back to their game. She'll question me later when it's just her and Agnes. She knows me well enough that my nervous rant was meant to cover the true details.

"Hi, Stuart." I knock on his open door. "I'm Serena. Do you want me to come in and read to you?" I step into the room, hoping today will be another good day.

"What happened to your eye? Did they put those drops in? I don't like when they put them in *my* eye."

"I fell. But I'm okay." I sit in the chair next to his bed.

"I fell a couple of weeks back," he laughs. "Hurt like hell. Had bruises for a month. You know?" He regards me as if contemplating a thought. "You look a lot like my granddaughter, minus the shiner."

I laugh. "Oh, yeah?" He mentioned this when we first met, but I love hearing it again. I'm happy he's having a good day. It's exactly what I need.

"I'll show you. Hand me that photo album over there on the dresser, will ya?" I'm so excited that he's lucid, my hands are trembling when I hand the book to him. Once he has it open in his lap, I turn the chair for a better view and lean in. He flips through several pages, then stops and points. "See?"

The image is of a little girl dressed in loud pajamas with a yellow cape tied around her shoulders and a toilet plunger in the air, ready to defend. Her skin is pale. She has freckles across her nose and red curly hair just like mine. "She's adorable."

"Her eyes were blue instead of your golden ones, but you're both beautiful."

Warmth dances in my heart. "Aw. That's so sweet. Do you see her much?" Stupid question to ask someone with advanced dementia.

His eyes close briefly, the pain evident on his face. "She and my son died. Sarah was her name, and she was almost twelve when it happened."

I knew his son had passed away, but he never mentioned his granddaughter. "I'm so sorry. What happened?" The question is out before I check myself.

"A drunk driver hit them full-on."

It feels like someone stole all the air from my lungs as the sound of screeching tires, crunching metal, and glass shattering echoes through my mind. It doesn't happen often, but every once in a while, the thought hits—*it could have been me. I could have died that night in the car with my father.*

That beautiful girl. What a waste of a life.

"Honey, are you okay? Serena?" Hearing Stuart say my name snaps me out of the horror that has its grip on me.

"I'm so sorry," I say, recovering as best as I can.

Maybe in this case, a failing memory is a gift. He doesn't have to remember such a painful experience every day. I know I'd do anything not to have to keep reliving mine.

"Don't be sorry. I have wonderful memories. Douglas was a great father. It wasn't easy. He was a lawyer and worked a lot. *And* had to raise Sarah on his own. She was such an active child." His face lights up. "She was in dance, soccer, and took piano lessons. That girl had more energy than anyone knew what to do with. They were on their way to the store when they were hit. The policeman who had the unfortunate job of relaying the horrid news reassured me that they died on impact."

"I'm glad they didn't suffer." I swallow hard, fighting the tears that are threatening to spill. My father's selfish drinking could have easily killed someone's Sarah.

"Oh, hey," Stuart says, taking my hand in his. "I didn't mean to make you sad. It happened a long time ago."

"Sorry." I quickly clear my eyes. "I'm grateful that you shared your memories with me. It's just... it feels all too familiar. My father was driving the night we were in an accident. We both survived. It's just... it still haunts me sometimes."

"Oh, and I went and brought it up all over again. I'm so sorry." He squeezes my hand affectionately. "Well, at least he was there to help you through."

I wish. "Sorry. I should go." I stand up. Fortunately, Stuart won't remember any of this tomorrow. "Thank you for sharing Sarah and Douglas with me. I didn't mean to get so emotional."

"There is nothing wrong with hurting a little from time to time. I don't know your exact situation, but your expression gave quite a bit away. Here's a bit of advice... life is fleeting, don't let yourself be crippled by resentment and regrets. Talk to your father."

"Oh, I—"

He places a hand over mine. "For me."

How could he possibly know? *Am I really that transparent?*

"Age affords a certain perspective," he says, reading my mind once again. "Young folks can often see things clearer because they aren't worn down by life's disappointments. Older folks have clarity because they've lived through life's challenges and gained insight from experience. In other words, these ancient eyes have seen enough to recognize the signs."

"Thank you, Stuart. It's nice to have you back."

"It's nice to be back."

"Tell me more about Sarah and Douglas."

Stuart continues his way through the photo album, putting

names to images and sharing the stories that go with them. This moment is a gift for both of us.

Reaching the end, he closes the album. "I think I need to close my eyes for a while. Will you come back tomorrow?"

"Of course. Thank you for sharing all your stories and letting me vent. This was the best afternoon I've had in a long time."

He smiles, his blue eyes sparkling. "My pleasure, young lady, but if this is the best afternoon you've had in a while, you're not living right."

"That's probably true," I say, laughing. "But I wouldn't trade today for anything." I take the book from him and set it back in its place. When I turn back, he's already asleep.

"Serena," Eva says from the nurses' station. "Joan wants to see you."

"Crap. What does the Witch want now?"

Eva chuckles to herself. "I wouldn't say that too loud. It could catch on."

I give an indifferent shrug and head to the evil woman's office. When I knock on her door, she calls out, "Enter."

"You wanted to see me?"

"Yes. Please have a seat." I do as she says and wait while she finishes typing on her keyboard. "Yes, your eye *does* look bad. I'm thinking you should take a couple of days off until that heals. Take the week if you need to."

Alarm at the lost wages rushes through me. "Why? I can still do my job."

"I overheard concern from the staff about your... mishap. Now that I see the damage myself, I think it's best you take some time off. You look like you were in a bar brawl," she says with distaste. "It's not the image of professionalism we aspire to maintain."

"Haven't you had a clumsy moment?"

"That's neither here nor there. Now—"

"*Please.* I'm saving money for college." The thought of having to ask my father for help fills me with a mixture of anxiety and dread.

"Be that as it may, not only is it unprofessional, it isn't safe. You can barely see out of that eye. Should you even be driving?"

"I can see fine," I snap, not meaning to. "Stuart is expecting me tomorrow." The thought of not being there if he has another good day, of letting him down, fills me with a fear far heavier than the loss of money. "He was coherent today. Did you know his granddaughter had red hair and that he lost her and his son in a car accident?"

"Dementia patients will have lucid moments. I'm glad that you were there, but—" She shakes her head like she's gotten off-topic. "When the swelling goes down and you can open your eye fully, then you can come back to work. I think that is a fair compromise."

"But what about Stuart?" I ask, panicking.

"I will tell the day nurse to explain why you can't be there—if, in the unlikely event, Stuart asks for you."

"Can I at least finish my shift?"

"No. I don't think that's wise."

Standing, I walk toward the door.

"Serena."

I turn and meet her gaze. "I'm glad you had some quality time with Stuart. He is a kind man."

The woman does have a heart. Shocking. "Me too."

Stuart's words replay as I step out of Joan's office and head to the locker room to get my stuff. I know hanging on to regret and resentment is toxic, but how do I let it go?

I keep telling myself my father is irrelevant—that I've cut him from my life—but that's not completely true because it still hurts. And why should I be the one to fix things? He's the grown-up. Shouldn't this be on him?

I get that life's too short, but trying to talk to him about it? Yeah, not going to happen. He'll just deny there's a problem and discount my feelings, and that would hurt worse than if I never brought it up at all.

After changing into street clothes, I grab my backpack and head out of the building. It's weird being out of work this early. I'm not used to having time like this to myself. And having all these crappy thoughts isn't helping.

Until I figure out what to do with them, I'm kinda stuck, because every thought seems to circle right back to where I started.

CHAPTER 21

KNOX

"Mommy?" My voice echoes around me while I frantically look through an old, rundown house. The paint on the walls is peeling, the carpets dirty and torn. I fling open a door and freeze. Fletcher is on top of my mother, pumping himself into her. He turns, locking eyes with me, places a finger to his lips, and whispers, "Shhh." Blood drips from his hand, trailing down his arm as he sneers at me. My mother's eyes are empty, lifeless, and I scream, "What did you do?"

Fletcher lunges for me. My instinct kicks in, and I run to my secret hiding spot. I squeeze behind the clutter under the stairs and hold my breath, desperately hoping to go unnoticed. But the door bursts open. "Come here, you little shit." He grabs my ankle, dragging me out into the open, a bloody knife in his hand. Just as the blade descends, I jolt awake.

My head whips left and right, terror still clawing at me until I slowly realize I'm in my bed. School books are scattered around me as I flop backward and stare at the ceiling.

Twisted fucking nightmare.

I scrub my hands up and down my face. Last thing I remember before taking a nap was thinking that Serena hasn't been back—not that I expected her to return. We never made any plans. But damn, I miss her invading my space.

It's close to seven, I think. The sun is still up, but low in the sky.

I roll out of bed and walk to the kitchen for a drink. It's been nine days since she parked outside my apartment. Nine days of her being a constant whirl in my head. *Is she okay? Is her dickhead boyfr—ex-boyfriend hassling her? Will she be back? Do I want her here?* Thoughts of her smile, her touch.

I'm losing my fucking mind.

If I could just see her again—to know she's alright—my thoughts might settle.

But that means I'd have to seek her out. A band tightens around my chest at the thought of knocking on her door.

It's just Serena and her mother. Shouldn't be a big deal. Two people. There's more than that on the jobsite.

Yeah, but no one is paying attention to me there.

Get your shit together! It's just Serena and her mother, for fuck's sake.

Leaning against the kitchen counter, I close my eyes, take a deep breath, and visualize myself as a child at Serena's house. Large pine trees frame out the backyard. Bird feeders hanging from branches. Birds and the sounds they make. *Chickadee, robin, goldfinch, junco, blue jay.*

The tightness in my chest loosens from the grounding exercise. *Sand sifting through toys in the sandbox. Dump truck. Bulldozer.*

Like a flip of a switch, the calming imagery I've relied on for years suddenly morphs into the nightmare I had of the little girl —Serena—being brutalized by a big dark figure. In a snap, my hard-fought peace shatters.

I force myself to think of Serena's injured face and the need to make sure she's okay. I squeeze my eyes shut tight as images and thoughts of her scream threaten to take over my mind.

It's not real. The dream's not real. Curly red hair. Golden eyes. Soft pink lips. I focus on the sensation of her hand in mine and wanting to feel her touch again.

The calmness that comes from being around her is like nothing I've ever experienced before. At first, it was overshadowed by the need to isolate myself, but now it's what's motivating me to put my shoes on.

I can do this. It's—I look at the clock—seven-fifteen. By the time I ride the bus over there, it will be a little before eight. Chances are Serena and her mom will have eaten. I'll say hi, make sure she's okay, and then come back home.

The thought of knocking on her door, exposing myself that way, has me breaking out in a sweat. I'm so fucking sick of this feeling, but I force myself out the door anyway.

Despite my resistance to Serena's presence, there's no denying the difference she makes in my tortured world.

So, if I can just get there, feel her. I'll be fine.

I hope.

Making my way to the bus stop, I wait. When it arrives, I take the steps up and find a seat in the last row by the window. There's only one other person on the bus, so that's good.

When I realize we're half a mile from my stop, my heart starts beating so hard, I consider bailing on this whole stupid plan.

No. I can do this. *Breathe, damn it. In for four, hold for four, out for four, hold for four.* Box breathing. I continue this technique as I work to control my anxiety.

When the bus arrives at my stop, I'm still struggling to breathe, and exit feeling lightheaded. I sit on the bench to give myself some time, but after ten or so minutes, I decide, *screw it.* I'll just wait for the next bus to take me home.

Irritated at my weakness, I throw my head back and absorb the disappointment sitting heavy against my heart. Why does everything have to be so difficult?

As I watch the sun set and the sky explode with color, my breathing becomes easier. Then I think about the three short blocks it will take me to walk to her house.

Three short blocks.

I push my hands against the bench, force myself to stand, and my feet begin to move.

Two blocks.

One.

My body begins to tremble as I stare at the front door.

That's it. I can't do it. I need to get out of here. Defeated, I begin to turn.

Just then, the door whips open. Serena emerges with her head turned, talking to someone behind her.

And now I'm stuck.

CHAPTER 22

SERENA

I never would have thought dress shopping could be that much fun. Even the drive was a blast with us hollering deafly out-of-tune lyrics over the blaring music. We devoured lunch, ate desserts so sweet they were almost lethal, and laughed so hard, we could barely breathe. It was exactly what I needed—a whole day of letting loose with my friends.

I even got to hit up a bookstore while Rowan and Tish went hunting for the perfect dress accessories. On the way back to meet them, I came across an oddball gift shop that had candles with names like *Zero F*ucks* and *Fart Extinguisher*. When I found one that smelled like wood smoke, pine, and maybe vanilla, I instantly thought of Knox. The label read *Sex in the Forest*. I instantly bought it.

The ride home was just as fun, but I was exhausted by the time Rowan dropped me at my house. Dinner was ready and Mom and I just finished.

"I'll clean up," Mom says. "Can you take this out?" She hands me a bag of garbage from under the sink.

"On it. So, the patient refused treatment?" I continue the conversation, walking into the living room.

"Yeah, he said it wasn't broken and we were only after his money."

Trash in hand, I open the front door. "Seriously?" I say over my shoulder. "No way I'm—" I slam into something large and solid. "Ow!" I stumble backward, glaring up at the obstruction in front of me.

"Knox!" I drop the bag and throw my arms around his waist, thrilled to see him after a long, miserable week. "You're here. I never expected..."

It takes me a moment to notice the rigidness of his body. I drop my arms and move away, realizing I might have crossed some invisible line.

"Knox?" my mother says from behind me. "Look at you. You've gotten so big. Wow! It's so nice to see you again."

Knox takes a step back, his eyes darting left and right under the hood of his sweatshirt like a cornered animal needing to escape.

What the heck? Is it because I hugged him? Maybe he has a thing for public displays of affection.

"Please come in," Mom says.

"I'm—I'm going to go." He shoves his hands in the front pockets of his jeans and takes another step back.

"You just got here," Mom and I say at the same time.

"Sorry. I wanted"—his eyes flash to my mother, then back to me—"to... make sure you were okay after... after what happened."

His face is ashen and his lips are almost white as he struggles for air. "Did you run here?" He shakes his head. "Knox?" I reach forward and wrap my fingers around his forearm. His skin is soaked and he's trembling. "Did something happen on your way over?" He shakes his head again. Maybe he doesn't want to talk in front of my mom? "Let's go out back." I gently pull him toward me, but his hands stay jammed in his pockets and his feet locked in place. "I guess you haven't been in the backyard since you were little. It's changed a bit since you were here." I give a little tug on his arm. "Come on. I'll show you."

When his feet finally move, I guide him inside the door and throw my mom a *I have no idea what's going on* look as I pass her.

Knox is a force to be reckoned with, but right now, he looks like he's about to pass out.

I lead him through the kitchen to the side door. The moment we're outside, he breaks free from my grasp, hastily slides the hood back from his head, and leans a hand against the house. "Just... give me a minute," he manages to say, struggling for each breath. "I need... I need a minute."

Feeling helpless, I rub a hand slowly up and down his back. "Is Rhett okay?"

"Rhett's fine," he gasps out.

Anxiety knots in my stomach as Knox battles to regulate his breathing. Whatever the problem, it's severe, and my worry intensifies with every labored cycle. After his fifth exhale, he straightens up. His breathing seems to have evened out a bit.

"I shouldn't have come." He looks around like he's searching for an escape route.

"What? Why?" This is crazy. He can't just leave. Not after what I just witnessed.

"This was a mistake." When his gaze lands on the gate, he's on the move.

"I don't understand." I move quickly to keep up with him. "Something must have happened."

"Nothing happened. It's just me," he says without slowing down.

"I don't—did I do something wrong? Is it because I hugged you?"

"Hell no!" He whips around to face me, looking pained that I'd even suggest it.

At least the color is back on his face. "Then what?"

He squeezes his eyes shut like he's fighting for calm. "It's just... I'm sorry, but I need to go."

He's almost to the gate and reaching for the latch when I hustle forward and grip his bicep—my hand barely covering half of it. "Please. Whatever it is. I want to help."

Staring at his exit, he drops his head. "Then let me go and forget I ever existed."

"I can't do that," I whisper. "You came to me upset. You're here for a reason. Let me help you the way you helped me the night I was injured and didn't know where else to go."

Just when I think he isn't going to respond, he turns his body to face mine. With eyes glued to the ground between us, he grips my waist with one hand and holds me there with an expression that says he's warring with his next move.

The unexpected touch sends a tidal wave of heat rushing through my body, and I have to mentally shake myself. This isn't the time for romantic fantasies.

"Knox? Talk to me? What's wrong?"

He releases me and steps away. "I wanted to make sure you were okay after what your ex-boyfriend did."

"That's it? Then why are you so upset?"

He runs a hand down his face, pulling at his features as he

glances up at the mostly dark sky. "I wouldn't even know where to start."

"Anywhere is fine. Start anywhere."

As he silently takes in the backyard, I wonder if he's flashing back to a memory from our brief childhood friendship, or if he's trying to pull together the right words that brought him to this point. Either way, he seems reluctant to start.

"Did you have another nightmare?"

"Yes."

"Do you want to tell me about it," I ask carefully.

He shakes his head. "No."

Chances are, the dream was somehow related to his past, so I ask the first question that pops into my head. "How did your mother die?"

His eyebrows pinch together as if he's remembering something painful, but he doesn't answer right away. I'm about to ask another question when he says, "Drug overdose."

"That must have been difficult to live with."

"Yeah." He glances up at the gate. "It doesn't matter, and this shit is dark. I should—"

"It *does* matter if it's still affecting you, Knox." I frame his face in my hands. "What happened a moment ago?" His gaze shifts to mine and holds. His expression is heated, but with him, that could mean anything. "You can trust me."

In a swift motion, he yanks me against his chest and wraps his arms around me, completely engulfing my body with his. "God, I hope this is okay," he murmurs, his voice edged with hesitation and raw hope as I melt against him.

I circle my arms around his waist and pull him closer. "It's fine," I whisper to the solid wall of his chest. But it's *more* than fine. It's a monumental leap of faith and it sends my heart soaring.

As we cling to each other with his heart pounding against my ear, I wonder how we came to share this strange new relationship. All I know is that as bewildered as I've been since he arrived, I'd gladly stay like this all night because, one, it feels amazing, and two, if it would save him from whatever demons are torturing him right now, I'm all in.

When he adjusts his weight and pulls away slightly, a twinge of fear takes hold. Is he going to shift back into that distant, guarded place and lock me out again?

His hand lifts between us, then pauses a little, hesitant, before gently tucking a stray ringlet of hair behind my ear. The soft brush of his fingers sends my belly swooping at the promise of more. Nothing since he got here makes sense. But when I look up into his eyes and see fear, pain, and something deeper... longing, maybe, the reasons don't matter. All I want to do is tell him I'm here for him—that it's okay to need someone. His thumb brushes over my lower lip, heating my body and stealing my breath. My heart pounds in my ears to the rhythm of seconds passing as our eyes lock. Neither one of us moving.

Bu-bump.

Bu-bump.

When his mouth crashes into mine, he's not gentle, but my own hunger sparks an inferno inside me, and I instantly lose myself in the feel of him. Hands are everywhere all at once, and every previous thought I had—his panic, my confusion, the past, the present—disappears with a desperate need for more. I've never tasted passion like this. It's intense and raw. There's nothing calculated. It's almost feral, and I can't get enough.

Lightning fast, he grips my arms and sets us apart. I stumble backward from the forceful disconnect. "I'm sorry," he says, his eyes drop between us. "I should never have—I didn't mean to..."

When I clue in to his words and see the guilt shadowed in his eyes, I reach out to him in confusion. "Knox. You didn't do anything wrong." I giggle at the thought of being lightheaded from a kiss. "I was kind of enjoying myself."

"I just... you're so..." He grips the back of his neck and finally meets my eyes.

I shouldn't have laughed. "Knox. It's okay." *Why is he reacting like this?* "Seriously, that was—"

"Wrong." He finishes my sentence. "I should never have touched you."

The simple word pierces my euphoria. "Oh."

His eyes plead for understanding as he takes another step back. "I shouldn't have kissed you." Another step. "Trust me. You're better off." He turns, walks quickly to the gate, and lets himself out.

He's gone. I stare at the empty space he filled moments ago, utterly lost and confused. Needles prick deep in the back of my throat as it tightens. Everything that's happened since he got here. All the strain from the last couple of weeks. The pressure was bound to build up. Collapsing to the cold, hard ground, I let my emotions explode.

The sound of my mother calling my name snaps me to the present. Minutes could have passed, maybe hours since the crying started. "Be right in," I holler back, slowly lifting myself off the ground. I wipe my eyes, brush myself off, and head into the house. "Hey," I say when I open the screen door.

"In the living room," she calls out.

"I'll be there in a minute." I stop off in the bathroom and blow my nose, then splash cold water on my face, hoping she won't notice I've been crying. "Did you need something?" I ask, entering the living room.

She stands up from the couch when she sees me and asks what happened before folding me into a hug. "Where's Knox?" When I don't respond, she sets me away from her and looks me over. "Did he hurt you?"

"No. Nothing like that. It's complicated. He had to go." I try to sound indifferent, but my voice cracks.

"Honey, what's going on?"

"I. Don't. Know," I manage to choke out in between sobs. I seriously didn't think I had any tears left in me.

"Okay." She pulls me back in, holds me tight, and rocks me back and forth. "Can I do anything to help?"

"No," I sniff. "I feel all over the place... like nothing makes sense anymore."

"I think you're overwhelmed. You've got a lot going on."

"Yeah. I guess." I pull away and wipe my tears. "Do I attract broken people?"

"What do you mean?"

"The guys I date. Do I have a big-ass sign on my forehead saying, 'Therapist, open for business'?" I bark a laugh through the tears.

She wipes under my eyes. "I don't know. They could be drawn to your kindness—your need to help people."

I snort. "You know how pathetic that sounds?"

"It's not pathetic. Sympathetic, empathetic, thoughtful, caring. You have *good* intentions, and an even bigger heart. Don't ever doubt it or *lose* it. It's a gift."

"It doesn't feel like one. It feels like a curse because I always seem to attract losers." Even as I say it, I know it doesn't pertain to Knox. He has issues I can't begin to understand. Still, nothing makes sense. Not the way he acted when he showed up. Not the way he kissed me. And definitely not the way he left me standing in the dark.

CHAPTER 23

KNOX

My lungs burn as I sprint down a side street, but welcome the pain.

When I was leaving, she seemed so... hurt, almost rejected or some shit. Why would she look at me that way? I acted like a pig ripping into its next meal. She should have slapped me.

What was I thinking?

I wasn't—that's the problem. Everything happened so fast—my mind went blank and I lost control.

A wave of revulsion churns in my stomach. I'm no better than her douche of an ex-boyfriend. And when she adds that to how I acted before the kiss, she's going to realize how completely unstable I am.

By the time I reach the garage, I'm soaked in sweat and my legs are done. I trudge up the steps feeling heavier than usual, the loss and self-loathing weighing me down.

Slamming the door behind me, I strip off my clothes leaving

a trail to the bathroom. I turn the shower spray to scalding, step into the enclosure, and brace my hands against the wall, letting the burning heat trail down my back and legs.

An image of Serena's heated gaze as I brushed her full lower lip flashes behind my closed eyes. Groaning, I turn my body and crank the lever in the opposite direction, tensing when the icy water hits my chest.

Blowing out quick breaths against the shock, I stare up at the ceiling, goosebumps rising on my skin. Despite the arctic chill, it can't wash away the intense heat her hands left on my body or the memory of her lips pressed hungrily against mine.

Wait. She was into it?

Not possible. My mind is muddling the truth.

Shivering uncontrollably, I turn off the water, and dry off, then swipe away a steamy section of the mirror with my hand.

Instead of clearing it, it warps the reflection of the pale, scarred, ugly fucker staring back at me. I turn away, disgusted.

I must have been delusional to think she'd ever want anything to do with someone like me. Hopefully, I never see her again—like on the streets or whatever. Seeing her expression of disgust would kill me.

Why the hell did I kiss her?

Not bothering with clothes, I lie on the bed and pick up my book, but trying to focus is useless. I get up, grab my laptop off the kitchen counter, and take it back to bed. I open a movie app and scroll for one that's as dark as I feel.

CHAPTER 24

SERENA

My brain was buzzing for hours after Knox left, trying to process what happened—both before and after the kiss. Finally, when the frustration became too great, I grabbed my keys and drove to his house to confront him. But when I got there, I couldn't get myself to walk up the stairs. He was upset when he ran away, and I was drained from crying. I didn't have the energy to deal with whatever he'd surely throw at me for showing up late and unannounced. It could have also been the fear of rejection that kept my rear-end planted in the seat of my car. Whatever the reason, I couldn't face him.

Six days later, I'm still doing everything I can to keep my mind from jumbling all the images, questions, and sensations that want to go round and round like a dust devil.

"Serena." I turn to see Bertha patting the seat on the couch next to her. "You've been wiping that same spot on the counter for the last five minutes. What gives?"

"I was... processing something I learned in class today."

"Hogwash. I know you too well."

I walk over and plop down next to her. "I'm trying to deal with something."

"Maybe that's the problem. Time to stop trying and start doing. Now, what's going on?"

"I had a situation with a friend. He's dealing with something difficult, but I don't know what it is. He's fine—at least, I think he is—but I think he's isolated and alone. I want to help, but I don't know how."

"Did he ask for help?" My gaze drops to my lap and the rag I've been twisting in my hands. *No.* "Honey, you can't help someone who doesn't want it."

"He came to my house. Something serious was going on, and then things got..." I think about his warm body wrapped around mine. That kiss. "Well, they got tangled, and he left."

"*Hmmm,*" she says. "I see." And knowing *her*, she does. My cheeks heat. "I suppose that complicated things. What about Hayden?"

"We're done."

"Good girl. Especially after what he did to you." My mouth opens to object, but she waves me off. "I may be old, but I'm not blind. I've seen enough in my day to know what's what without anyone givin' me the details. Is this the same guy that had you all worked up a couple of weeks back? The one you were meeting?"

"Maybe," I hedge.

She chuckles. "Alright. My best advice is for you to concentrate on your friends, school, and stay away from relationships for a while—focus on you for a change." She arches a drawn-on eyebrow, then says, "I know you know what I mean, but it also wouldn't hurt for you to be the selfless friend I'm sure that boy needs. Whatever happened between you two scared the hell out of him—that I'm sure of. Chances are, his life was ordered, simple, and easy to control until Hurricane Serena came along. Most likely, you demolished his comfort zone. People build walls for a reason."

"Are you psychic?" I laugh.

"*Pfff.*" Her brows pinch together, telling me not to be an idiot. "You said he seemed alone and isolated. People handle their issues in different ways. Having control is one of them. That being said, he wouldn't have come to you if you hadn't created a bond of sorts."

"You make it all sound so logical."

"It's easy when you're seeing things from the outside looking in. Now you listen here. This isn't about you. It's something a whole lot bigger, so put away whatever fear is keeping you from helping that poor boy and go check on him. Everything else will fall into place as it's meant to."

"You think so?"

"Have I ever steered you wrong?"

"You've never steered me anywhere," I snort. "But thanks for the wisdom. You're a smart lady."

"Damn right I am. Now..." Bertha pauses, then pats my hand. "You're looking a bit peaked, and I don't want to catch what's ailing you, so you go on and tell Ms. Joan that you're sick, and then go and see to that *boy*. Life's short. You've been around here long enough to know that."

I kiss her wrinkled cheek. "You truly are a special person."

"Oh, get on. I hate mushy."

"Where's Agnes?" I laugh.

"Got a date by the pond with Ed."

"When did that start?"

"Oh, a couple of weeks ago. It's disgusting if you ask me. She's too old to be carrying on that way." She smiles to herself, then jerks her head toward the exit. "Go on. And be sure to let me know how it goes with the boy."

I give her a thumbs up. "But first, I need to check on Stuart." He didn't recognize me when I came back from Joan's exile. Maybe I'll get lucky with another one of his good days. I could use a little good.

CHAPTER 25

KNOX

I'm glad Rhett let me put gym equipment in the garage, because between work, the grueling weights, running, and cold showers, I've done a decent job of draining Serena from my thoughts.

Bullshit, I tell myself, remeasuring the same two-by-four for the second time.

After a week of replaying my visit to her house, I realize I warped the whole thing into something ugly. The panic attack was fucking embarrassing, but the kiss... the kiss was a surprise—a shock really. I didn't know it could feel like that. And I'm not a hundred percent sure, but I think she was okay with it. She did say something like she enjoyed herself. Maybe she was just being nice or whatever, but thinking back, her expression *seemed* honest enough.

Doesn't matter though. Like a dumbass, I ran away. Now I'm left with all this... turmoil I don't know what to do with. And it's not just physical. It's like she sees me in a way no one ever has.

There's more, but I'm trying not to dig deeper into it than I already have. All I know is that I need her in my life—however she'll have me.

Not that she's going to want anything to do with me now after the way I acted.

It's for the best anyway. If my past catches up to me, she should be as far from me as possible.

My thoughts wander to her full, rosy lips and how they felt... tasted.

Groaning, I drop the safety glasses over my eyes, line the saw with the penciled guide, and squeeze the handle, sending the blade into a loud metallic whir.

Would that prick come after me, even after all this time?

Finishing the cut, I catch sight of Rhett framing out the east wall of the house with two other workers. He asked about Serena the other day, wondering when he'd get to see her again. He likes her. No way was I going to tell him what happened, so I said I didn't know, and that she was probably busy with school and work. He responded with an "uh-huh" and looked a little sad. I'm not sure if the expression was for him or for me. We're both lonely, I suppose. I never realized it until Serena came into my life. I imagine it's the same for Rhett.

If I had a phone, I could have texted her to see if she was okay after... everything. Maybe I should get one.

With the board in my hand, I nod to our electrician as we pass each other. He must be confirming something with Rhett because we're nowhere close to running electrical wires. After making my way to the window I'm trying to frame out, I lay the board in place.

Shit! Too short.

This has to stop. I've been screwing up all week.

I look around me, hoping no one sees the mistake. It's not like anyone would get pissed, but they'd tease the hell out of me, which doesn't help the need to keep a low profile.

Walking to the scrap pile, I toss the useless board, then search for another one that might work in its place. When I find one, I carry it back and slam it on the workbench, remeasuring it.

Until I get this thing with Serena sorted out, I'm screwed.

I've got to face her and get all these emotions under control —if that's even possible.

How would I even go about seeing her? I can't go to her house. Her mother might be there, and after last time... yeah, that's not gonna happen. *If not there, then what? School? Work?*

Then I'd *really* be the stalker she jokingly accused me of.

Pressing the handle, the saw comes to life once more. If I screw this up again... I'm going to lose my fucking mind.

CHAPTER 26

I've been waiting at the base of Knox's stairs for over fifteen minutes. When I got here, rock music was blaring from the garage and I figured he had to be in there. I doubt Rhett listens to that kind of music cranked to that volume.

When the music shuts off, a door opens and closes. Moments later, Knox rounds the corner, shirtless, with gym shorts hanging low on his hips. A sheen of sweat covers his skin, highlighting every contour of his well-defined muscles. *Whoa*. Realizing my mouth is hanging open, I snap it closed.

He lifts his head and stops abruptly when he sees me.

Please don't let this be a mistake.

"Hi," I say, standing up, wiping dust off my butt.

"Uhhh... hi." He doesn't look mad, which is a better start than when I've shown up in the past.

I scour my mind for the words I'd prepared, but seeing him partially naked has muddled my brain.

"You know... you can't just run away every time things get hard," I blurt. *Crap.* That wasn't part of the planned monologue. *Okay, well, short, sweet, and to the point. That works too.* But when his eyebrows pinch together, my stomach bunches into knots.

I'm totally messing this up.

Staring at the ground, he shifts on his feet, and after a moment, says, "You're right."

Oh. Now I'm really at a loss for words. I thought I'd say my piece, and... leave? I hadn't thought far enough ahead. I guess I assumed he'd get mad and I'd go back home. "*Soooo*, we can be friends?" I ask, sounding hopeful. *That's all I want, right?*

If the kiss we shared is any indication, then I want a hell of a lot more.

"Sure. I'd like that. But..." His voice trails off.

Waiting for him to continue, I notice the numbers inked in a horizontal line over his heart—coordinates. My fingers itch to trace them and ask where they lead. I shake my head at the thought.

"But, what?" I ask, gently prodding.

"Nothing."

I sigh, deep and frustrated. If he could just open up a little. Not shut down every time things start to move forward.

Bertha's words fill my head—a reminder that this isn't about me. And forcing him to give me what *I* want isn't right. I need to let him control the narrative. "Okay," I say, attempting to hide my disappointment. "I guess I'll let you get back to whatever you're doing next." Then I turn away and take a step toward my car.

Knox's hand grasps onto my wrist, halting me. When I turn, he's staring at the connection like he's not sure how it happened.

It's clear he's torn, his mind and body in conflict with each other. I know *exactly* how he feels.

"Tell me what you want?" I ask, barely above a whisper.

Slowly, his eyes find mine. "This." He steps forward, cradles my face in his hands, and pulls me in, but then hesitates. Recognizing his silent plea for consent, I place my hands over his. "I want this," he says and presses our lips together. "I want you."

I sling my arms around his neck and kiss him back with a week's worth of pent-up need I hadn't realized I'd been holding. He lifts me by the back of my thighs and starts up the stairs without breaking the kiss.

Trailing heated kisses along his jaw, he opens the door. The moment it closes, he presses my back against it and captures my mouth in an achingly slow, sweet kiss. Absorbing the sensation, my fingers weave into his hair at the base of his neck, gripping tightly as I nip his lower lip.

He jerks back, surprise flashing in his eyes. "I'm sorr—" I start, but his mouth crashes hot and hard on mine, silencing me. My hands glide over his bare shoulders and down his back, desperately needing to feel more of him. Somehow, it all feels like it's too much, but yet not even close to enough. How is that possible?

His muscles vibrate under my touch. His skin is so hot. *Wait...* he's trembling. Concerned, my hands change direction and slide down between us, nudging him gently. He stops instantly. "Are you okay?" I ask.

He leans his forehead against mine, our breaths coming hard and fast in the space between us. "I am so many things right now, but okay?" He relaxes his hold on my legs until my feet touch the floor. "I'm not sure how to answer that." He reaches up and coils a lock of hair around his finger, inhales deep, then releases it slowly. "I've never—*ever* felt like this before, and my reasons for staying away seem to disintegrate whenever I'm around you." He angles his head back, pinning me with an intense gaze. "So, why am I shaking?" Slowly, he leans in so his mouth is right next to my ear. "I'm fucking terrified."

The admission sends a shiver racing down my spine. When Knox lets his barriers crumble, it's a powerful thing, and he just let them fall... for me.

He picks up my hand and plants a kiss on the underside of my wrist before linking our fingers together. "Let's sit."

"O-oh-kay," my words stutter as I follow behind him on wobbly legs. Talking is the right thing to do, but I'm burning up inside. I want—need more than that.

He leads me to the bed. "I have to grab a shirt."

"Oh, but do you really?" I sit at the end, letting my eyes rake appreciatively over his stunning form.

He snorts out a laugh as if the idea of being impressed by his body is ridiculous. Crouching down, he opens a drawer from under the bed and pulls out a t-shirt. He slides it over his head, then sits next to me.

Picking up my hands, he flattens them together in his lap and lines them up like he's measuring the differences. "Serena," he pauses. "I don't know how to do this."

"You seem pretty adept to me."

His cheeks flush red. "That's not what I mean. I don't know how to do *this*." He releases my hands and motions between us. "Intimacy. I want it. I *really* do, but this isn't something I know. I'm—I'm probably not what you're used to, and I don't know if I'm capable of having a normal relationship."

What does all that mean? I want to press for details, but he might shut me out if I push for more. That's what he usually does. "It's okay." We all have issues. His may be complicated in a way I don't understand—yet—but that's just a matter of getting to know each other. "We'll take it one day at a time. Let this evolve into whatever is comfortable for both of us."

He rubs his free hands up and down his legs—a familiar telltale sign that he's nervous.

Reaching over, I lift one of his hands and kiss the scars on his knuckles. "That being said, the only way this is going to work is if we talk stuff through. You can't shut me out every time things get complicated or difficult. Can you trust me enough to try?"

"I want to," he says, sounding unsure of himself.

"We don't need to have all the answers right now." I lay my head against his shoulder. "Let's not worry about what can or can't be. The details aren't important."

He surprises me by flopping backward onto the bed. As I watch, he crosses his arms over his eyes.

What's he hiding from now?

I curl up beside him, resting my head on one hand and gently prying his arms away from his face with the other. Turning his head toward me, his eyes search mine as if trying to find the answers that will make all of this okay for him.

"Hey." I rest a hand on his cheek. "You are the boss of you. *You* control what happens. *You* can choose to let your past control you or shake it loose and live in the moment. That's all there is, anyway. Right here. Right now. All that other stuff, *whatever* it is, is irrelevant. It has no bearing on you unless you let it."

He rolls onto his side, props his head in his hand. "So smart," he says, his lips tilting up in admiration.

"Thank you. It's easy to repeat words I've read, but if it helps, I'm glad."

"Do you remember everything you read?"

"Not all, but most."

"You said you wanted to be a nurse, but with how smart you are, why not go all the way?"

"Be a doctor?" He nods in confirmation. "I could, I guess, but it's never been a direction I wanted to go." Turning over his hand that's resting between us, I trace my fingers over the rough callouses. "Nurses are on the front line. They connect with the patient in ways doctors can't. Plus, I don't want to be in school that long, not to mention the debt I would come away with."

"Makes sense."

"Did your mother always have... issues?"

"I wouldn't survive five minutes in your mind—the way your thoughts jump all over. And weren't you just saying I need to shake the past and live in the moment?"

"I did, but there's a difference between sharing and dwelling. This is a time for sharing."

"You make this up as you go, don't you?"

"I work with what I have." I shove his shoulder playfully. "If you don't want to talk about it, that's okay. I'm just trying to get to know you better. Is that a problem?"

A crease forms between his eyebrows. "Not a problem, just difficult for me."

"Sorry. I don't mean to press. You don't have to give me anything you don't want to."

He clasps our fingers together. "She took me away from my father because he liked to hit—she took the brunt of it, though. She tried to be a good mother, but struggled with depression, and when it got bad, drugs were her escape of choice."

"Were you with her when she died?"

Releasing my hand, he rolls to his back. "If you're asking if I found her, then yes." His words have a bite, which he immediately apologizes for.

"You're still angry. It's understandable." I twist the bottom edge of his shirt around my finger, exposing the pale flesh above his shorts. Needing contact, I let my fingers trail from his hip, up his side, and over to his stomach. Goosebumps rise along his skin. "Can I ask you another question?"

"Keep doing that and I'll tell you anything you want to know." He wrangles an arm around my shoulders and draws me in so my head rests on his chest.

He does intimacy just fine.

"Are you trying to distract me with flattery?" I tease.

"You're the one doing the distracting. Ask your question. I'll do my best to focus."

It's hard to reconcile this affectionate side with the guy who growled at me every time I was near him. I swear, he throws me off at every turn. "Were you in foster care after your mother died? I asked before, but you never answered."

"Yeah, when she died and a few times before. The first time was short... when she was taken to jail for possession. The second time was when she got busted for prostitution. Third time I was twelve, and she accidentally killed a man for beating me up." My hand pauses on its way up to his chest. "Since it was in self-defense, she was given three years for the drug possession, and the manslaughter charge was reduced to aggravated assault. The final time was when she died. I was close to sixteen by then."

"Were your foster parents okay?"

"So many questions."

"Sorry. Forget it."

He takes a deep breath, lifting my head as his chest expands. Several minutes pass as I patiently wait.

"The first set, I barely remember," he starts, then pauses a beat. "The second were fine, as long as you were invisible. The third, I was one of three foster kids—me, another boy, and a girl named Annie, all within a couple of years of each other. The foster parents were good people with the right intentions. I was twelve when I caught my foster brother attempting to rape Annie, and I beat him near to death. He was removed from the house, charged, and sent to juvie. I was almost reassigned to another family—my temper always being an issue—but Annie wouldn't let me leave her side. Since the foster parents were concerned about her mental state, they let me stay. After that, Annie and I became even closer. I slept on her floor, or she on mine. We slept better when we were together. Like me, she's had a fucked-up childhood.

"The near rape wasn't the only thing she struggled with. She caught a lot of crap from the other girls at school—stupid stuff like making fun of her hair and clothes, the fact that she was shy and struggled with her words. I tried to protect her, but they were relentless when I wasn't around.

"One morning, I woke before the sun and was surprised to find Annie wasn't in my room. I went to look for her and found her on the kitchen floor, her back leaning against the stove with both her wrists slashed. I was too late."

The image grips me, and I squeeze him hard around the middle. "Knox. I'm so sorry."

I realize the world can be an awful place, but hearing it straight from someone I know hits harder than I could ever have imagined.

He smooths a hand up my arm. "You don't want any part of this shit. Trust me."

"You're wrong. It's important. Besides, it made you who you are."

"Damaged."

"No. Dimensional."

He lifts my chin, tilting my head back so his gaze meets mine. "Are you psychoanalyzing me?"

I laugh, "Hardly. It's just... your traumas gave you facets, you know? Layers of sharp angles all leading up to the center of who you really are. You're not damaged. You're just put together in a way that makes you unique."

"You make me sound like some Picasso painting, all distorted and ugly."

"Art is subjective, and there is *nothing* ugly about you."

He rolls me onto my back and smooths my hair away from my face. "Trust me, there's plenty of ugly."

"I know what's important. You're hardworking, loyal, and protect those who need it. You're smart and want more from life than the hand you've been dealt. *And* you're a great kisser." I wiggle my eyebrows.

He snorts. "You sure you got the right guy?"

"You said I was smart. Besides, actions speak louder than words, and they're harder to fake."

He leans down and softly presses his lips to mine. "So, you think I'm bright and sparkly, huh?"

"Yeah." I smile against his mouth. "Almost blinding."

We kiss and hold each other while we talk of kinder things.

Sometime in the night, I'm woken when Knox twitches and mumbles something.

What time is it? I rub my eyes. *Mom's going to kill me.* Knox's body jerks, and then begins to thrash as if he's in the grips of a nightmare. I sit up and smooth his hair back from his forehead. "*Shhh.* It's okay."

He seems to settle, his body relaxing, but then he yells and bolts upright. "Holy shit," I cry out, my heart sprinting the hundred-meter dash. "Knox. It's okay. You're safe."

His eyes, unfocused and manic, dart from one side of the room to the other. When they finally land on mine, he grips my chin and crashes his lips to mine so suddenly that my palms fly up to his chest in surprised defense. His hands are everywhere all at once, then he's pulling me across his body so that I'm straddling him. Concerns instantly disappear as a tidal wave of sensations crash over me. I breathe out his name, urging him on, needing more.

He tears his lips from mine so fast, you'd think I burned him. "I'm sorry," he says, breathing heavily. "Not like this."

Embarrassed—either for him or myself—I slide off his lap and sit on my knees beside him with arms wrapped around my middle. When I don't say anything, he places a lingering kiss on my forehead. "You didn't do anything wrong. I'm the one who lost control. Again."

"I think we both did," I say tentatively.

He releases a deep sigh. "I just... I didn't want our first time to come from the hellhole my mind was in. It's too dark. I want to be with you in the light—the place I live when I'm around you."

"I'm glad I take you there," I say, honored that he would think of me in that way.

He lies down. "Come here."

I let Knox snuggle me in, my back to his front, but as I lie here, insecurity creeps in. Maybe it's the lack of sleep. Maybe it's… I don't know. I really like Knox, but what if I'm not strong enough to be the kind of person he needs me to be? As much as I hate admitting it to myself, Hayden did a number on my confidence, and being with Knox is like riding a roller coaster backward and blindfolded.

SERENA

"Good morning," Mom says as she takes a sip of her coffee when I enter the kitchen. "I appreciate the text, but I'm not sure how I feel about you staying out all night."

Waking up early in the morning, I knew she'd be pissed, but there wasn't much I could do at that point. "Mom, I'm eighteen. You trust me, remember? Or has that changed?"

"Trust has nothing to do with it. You being my daughter does, and I don't feel comfortable with you sleeping over at a guy's apartment."

"Sorry. It wasn't intentional. We were talking, and both of us fell asleep. Then he had a nightmare, and I didn't want to leave him. Nothing happened—like we didn't have sex or anything."

She covers her ears. "Lalalalalala."

"Real mature, Mom." I quirk a smile. "I'm leaving for college soon, you know. I'll be on my own."

"I know, but could you be my little girl for just a little while longer?"

Aw, I gush. "Sure."

"You've been through a tough time lately," she hedges. "Should you really be starting another relationship after what Hayden put you through?"

"Please don't wreck my high. I never planned on this. It just happened, and now that it has, I don't want to let it go. Mom. Knox is... special."

The fears I fell asleep with last night haven't left. They probably drove me to sneak out early this morning. That, and the possibility of waking up to his angry, guarded expression—or worse, regret.

Weak, Serena. Weak.

Leaving that way was a mistake. I should have faced him. Now, I don't know what to expect—where we stand.

I fill my glass. Once the orange juice hits the back of my throat, I can't stop chugging until I'm almost out of air and it's gone.

"What made you decide to go over to see him? He left you quite emotional after his visit last week."

"Bertha and her amazing intuition. She thought I should check on him. Make sure he was okay."

"She's been a great friend to you over the years."

"So has Agnes. I'm going to miss seeing them every day when I leave for school. At least I can visit whenever I come home."

"I'm glad you decided to stick close. I'd miss you horribly otherwise. Now, back to Knox. I'm worried about you."

"Don't be. I'm just getting to know him. There's a connection and depth I've never experienced before." The words sound lame rolling off my tongue.

"Don't confuse depth with deep-seated issues."

Should have kept my mouth shut. "We *all* have issues, and I'm not confused."

Well, I am, but not over that.

"From what you've told me, your relationship with Knox has been nothing but turmoil. Addiction to drama is a real issue."

My body tenses. "I understand your concern, but that's not what this is. He's had a hard life and could have easily crashed and burned. Instead, he became this amazing person. He's finishing high school through distance learning and works as a carpenter full-time. He reads, runs, and works out—"

"That's great, but you like fixing people—to feel needed and useful. Don't confuse that with something else."

"I'm not—"

"I can see it in your eyes! You're halfway in love with that boy. Look, all I'm saying is that you should be aware of what is driving your emotions. Is it the need to have love returned? Does altruism feed your self-love?"

"Oh my god, Mom! Way too deep this early in the morning. You see love, but I see respect. What's wrong with me exploring where this relationship takes me?"

"Nothing, but Knox is carrying a lot of heavy baggage. Maybe what's inside makes him interesting, but do you really want to carry all that with you to college?"

"Why are you ruining this for me?"

"I'm trying to make you aware."

"Mistakes are going to happen. It's what I learn from them that matters. You taught me that."

"I'm glad to hear you've been listening, but the pain of heartbreak could be avoided with a little common sense."

"Mom! Back off."

"Just take it slow, okay? The fallout from this one could sting. I don't like seeing my baby hurt."

"Fine. I get it."

Setting my glass in the sink, I head upstairs to my room. *Why? Just why?* I love my mom, but *damn*. Why the harsh dose of reality?

I flop down on my bed, face-first. Five minutes—that's all I have before I need to shower and get ready for school. I shift on my side, bunching my pillow under my head. My weighted lids drift to the candle I picked up at the mall. Reaching out, I bring it up to my nose. It smells just like Knox.

As nervous as I am moving forward, I hope last night isn't the end.

The unknowns border on scary and hell—Mom's words emphasized all that—but my feelings for him are louder than all of it. It's screaming that he's worth the fear and uncertainty and urging me not to give up.

Please don't let him regret what we shared.

Please, please, please.

CHAPTER 28

KNOX

Standing outside, breathing in the crisp morning air, I can't help feeling a little restless. The rest of the snow will be gone from the mountains soon, and I can spend my weekends getting lost in the woods. Backcountry camping is the only place I feel completely free. The smells. The sounds. Everything is simple and untouched by the harsh realities that gnaw at me daily.

I'm not sure if Serena's into that kind of thing, but it would be awesome if she was. I'll have to ask her the next time I see her.

The house we're building is completely framed in, perfect timing with summer rolling in.

We're rushing to get the plywood up before the heat gets out of control. Most of the crew is on that today, but Rhett and I are tackling the staircase.

With the nail gun in hand, I start laying the boards Rhett cut. It's the kind of work you can do without extreme focus, which lets my mind drift back to Serena. It was weird I didn't hear her leave this morning—I'm a light sleeper.

I wonder why she didn't say goodbye.

Probably regretted being with you and snuck out.

The negative thought stirs up all kinds of shitty feelings. That nightmare really fucked me up, and seeing her there in the dark... it was like she was the only one that could pull me back, and I clung to her, nearly losing control.

Going over our time together, I can't help feeling anxious. I gave her pieces of myself I've never given anyone and she walked out without a word. I know I'm a mess—a lot for anyone to handle—but from what I know of her, I didn't expect her to leave like that.

Maybe she didn't want to wake me?

Or maybe you're a fucking idiot for thinking she'd want to stick around. Why did you tell her all that shit? Now she really knows what a fucked-up mess you are.

And she doesn't even know the half of it.

An image of her in my arms fills my mind. I groan at the memory of how good she felt. Chances are, I'll never get a second chance. At least this time I know it wasn't one-sided. She was as into it as I was.

Then why did she bail?

This is so confusing. I have zero experience with women on an emotional level. I've had my fair share of sex. As unattractive as I am, getting girls wasn't an issue. I was an important cog in a powerful man's operation. The problem was the cringy feeling of their touch and the guilt that followed. But Serena's touch was nothing like that. It soothed and ignited at the same time.

"You got it bad, son." Rhett walks by me, laughing. "It looks good on you, boy."

"She deserves better."

"She deserves to be happy, and so do you."

"I don't think I can do relationships."

"Let's have a seat. I could use a break anyhow." Rhett sits across from me on the ground, both of us stretching out while leaning against exposed two-by-fours. "You know you're getting old when getting down is just as difficult as getting up."

"You're not old, just weathered by time."

He laughs. "Right. About this garbage you keep telling yourself." He points a snarled index finger my way. "I know you've got some scars on you. Not just the ones I can see, but the ones in there—you know—on the inside." I frown, not liking where this conversation is going. "Don't give me that look. I was in two wars. I know what it looks like when people wear their trauma around their neck like a noose. But you remember, your difficult start in life made you into the solid man you've become. You understand what I'm saying?"

"Yeah, I hear you." I pull my knees up and ball my hands together in my lap.

"There is *no* reason you can't make that girl happy. That is up to *you* and has nothing to do with your past unless you let it."

"Bullshit. What if Fletcher finds me? I don't want her caught in the middle." A sickening memory floods my mind. I'm standing beside the bastard as he pulls the trigger, coldly shooting a man in the head over a grave—a grave I helped dig.

"It's been almost three years," Rhett says. "I think if he was searching for you, he would have found you by now. Let it go, son. Move on with your life."

Fletcher will never release me. I've seen too much. But I can't tell Rhett that.

"Even so, I can't do normal couple things like go on dates,

have barbeques with friends, or whatever. She deserves to live a full life."

"*Boy*, don't *tell* yourself what you *can* and *can't* do. You're putting those barriers on yourself. I've seen changes in you since you met Serena—all for the good. Don't give up before it even gets started."

"Everything you say makes sense, but I'm scared shitless."

"*Of course* you are. This is new, and opening yourself up to someone can be difficult and scary, especially for someone with your past. But I think you can trust her."

"Maybe, but she likes to dig."

"Yeah, so?"

"I don't want her in my head. What if she doesn't like what she finds? What if she can't handle it?"

"You have to decide for yourself if that's a risk worth taking, and if she can't handle it, then she's not the one for you."

"I had a nightmare when she was with me, and—"

"You *slept* with the girl?" he cuts me off, sitting up straighter. "You better be respecting her, or you and I are having words right now," he thunders.

"*Slept*, and absolutely, I will respect her."

"Alright then." He gives me a narrowed side eye as he settles.

"I just don't want to mess this up."

"You be thoughtful, honest, and loyal, and the rest will happen as it should. There are no guarantees, even under the best of circumstances. You just have to be strong enough to give it your best and let the chips fall where they may."

Strong enough being the key words. I'm not sure if I am.

"Thanks, Rhett."

"You bet. Now, help me up off this damn floor. I can't afford to sit on my butt all day."

. . .

After a long nap and a gargantuan coffee, I'm able to get my schoolwork done. Not sure how I pulled it off after a physical day of work and being sleep-deprived, but I did.

My computer reads that it's six-thirty-five. Serena will be getting off work soon.

Before I can stress over what I'm about to do, I close my laptop, pull my hoodie over my head, and am out the door. Better to find out she wants nothing more to do with me now, than stress myself over it and find out later.

On the bus ride to the retirement home, I count the seconds with taps of my foot to avoid the sinking anxiety. At every stop, I mentally describe each new person getting on the bus. When it pulls away from the curb, the counting starts all over again.

Exiting the bus across from her work, I look both ways and speed across the street. My hood is up over my head as I lean against a tree across from the building and wait. Only ten minutes to go. People are watching me as they pass. Despite how cool I was on the bus ride, being in the open is making my chest tight. I work on saying the alphabet backward, attempting to distract my mind from the downward spiral.

The distraction isn't working. I turn away, ready to bolt, when I hear the door to the building open. Just seeing her eases the pressure in my chest. She smiles at me but it doesn't light up her face like it usually does. *Shit. This was a mistake.*

"You're here," she says, sounding confused or amazed. I can't tell. She's hard to read.

"Sorry. I just... I shouldn't have shown up, surprising you like this."

"Just because *you* don't like surprises doesn't mean I don't." She bumps me with her shoulder.

"Are you sure?"

"Absolutely."

"Okay. Are you hungry?" My fingers tap nervously against my leg. It's hard to let go of the nervous agitation when it comes on, and now that exposed, itchy feeling of being watched is coming back. I need to get off the street.

"Yeah, starving."

"I thought maybe we could pick up a pre-made pizza from Tony's and take it back to my place?"

"I'd like that." She fishes her phone out of her backpack as we start walking. "I'll just text my mom and let her know."

"Sure. Do you mind driving?"

"Not at all."

After she slides her phone back into her backpack and zips it up in the outside pocket, I take it from her and slide it over my shoulder. "What the hell do you have in here? It weighs a ton."

"Pretty much everything I would ever need if there was an apocalypse."

"Then I hope I'm with you when it happens. With all the crap you have in here, we could hold out for at least a week."

When she laughs, my mood soars with the realization it was because of me. Still, something is off. It's possible it has nothing to do with me. Usually, I read expressions well. My survival depended on it. It saved me from several beatings from my father and my mother's piece-of-shit boyfriends. But with Serena, I don't have a clue.

She tells me about her day as we drive. Two ladies, named Bertha and Agnes, got into an argument about their card game— I guess cheating is a regular issue. I ask her about school. She says it was okay, but the pause tells me it was anything but. "What happened?" Maybe this is where her tension is coming from.

"Hayden decided to sit at our lunch table with his new girlfriend." My fists clench at the sound of his name. "It was an uncomfortable scene. Our group has been together since junior high. I know he has every right to be with his friends—it just hurt having my face shoved in his cheating-ass business."

"He's the one who fucked up. If he cared about his friends, he wouldn't put them in the middle."

"You would think. My friend, Rowan, ripped him a new one —she's good at that—then she and my other best friend, Tish, came outside with me to eat lunch."

"I'm glad you have them. They sound like good people."

When she finds a parking spot down the street from the pizza place, we both climb out. I chose this place because it's familiar, and with their ready-made pizzas, it's a quick in and out.

"What kind of pizza do you like? I'm buying," I say when we reach the counter, nervous as hell but managing. I lucked out. There's no one in the restaurant.

"I like everything, so you can pick."

I order my favorite, The Works. The description on the menu board reads: This pizza has everything but the kitchen sink and anchovies.

After the girl behind the counter rings us up, Serena stretches up on her toes and stage whispers, "Good choice."

I smile to myself, her approval bumping my confidence a notch above zero.

The worker disappears in the back, comes out a few minutes later, and hands me the pizza. "Thanks," I tell her, then face Serena. "Ready?"

"Yup."

Serena opens the door, looking over her shoulder at me with a smile, and almost crashes into a couple on their way in.

"Rowan, Darius... hey," Serena says to the couple.

Shit. That's one of her best friends. Instantly, I break out into a nervous sweat.

"Hey," the girl says to Serena. "You out on a school night?" She takes a step back and glances up into the night sky. "Are the pigs flying? Is it raining frogs?"

"Ha, ha. I'm starving," Serena says. "You know how I am when I get hangry."

When her friend spots me, her critical gaze makes my skin crawl with nerves.

"You're here with the stalker?" the girl questions, looking a little hostile.

What the hell?

Panic surges through my body and the trembling starts.

"He's not a stalker, Row. I was kidding, and you know it." Serena turns to me. "Knox, this is Rowan and Darius—friends from school."

I swallow over the dry, scratchy knot in my throat. "Nice to meet you."

Rowan turns to Serena with a *why are you with him* glare. My heart is pounding out of my chest, and I'm starting to feel lightheaded. I want to push past them all to get outside for some air, but I restrain myself.

"I'll call you later," Serena tells her as we move forward, finally on our way.

Darius looks me over as we pass like he's gauging if Rowan was joking about the stalking comment, and says, "Why don't you stay and have pizza with us?"

"Thanks," I say. "Maybe another time. Serena, I'll meet you at the car." I step around her.

"Have you been hiding him from me?" I hear Rowan say behind me, but I'm out of earshot by the time Serena answers. As soon as I reach the car, I place the pizza on the roof, followed by my hand, and lean over, fighting for oxygen. *Fuck!* I scream in my head. I thought I could manage a simple evening with Serena, and now that's all been blown to shit.

CHAPTER 29

KNOX

"Are you okay?" Serena asks, placing a hand on my back.

I stand up immediately, taking the pizza off the roof. "I'm fine. Can you unlock the door?" My words sound uneven and strained.

The locks click open. "You're not fine. All the color drained from your face."

I open the door, shove my body into her tiny fucking car, and shut it without answering.

"Please don't shut me out," she says, sliding in next to me.

"Can we leave, please?"

"Sure." She yanks the seatbelt across her body, then starts the car.

I knew this was a mistake. I should have stayed home and let this thing with her fizzle out. She would have walked away eventually.

It's a quick drive. As soon as she pulls into the parking spot next to Rhett's truck, I hand her the pizza and jump out, telling her I don't feel good and maybe I'll see her another time.

The engine shuts off and I hear her shout, "You don't get to do this."

"Do what?" I snap, not bothering to turn around as I start up the stairs. My chest is already loosening now that I'm home. "I told you I don't feel good."

Her footsteps are coming up fast behind me. "That's a load of crap." She grabs my hand, pulling me to a stop. "What the hell is going on? Your reactions are all over the place every time we're together."

"Leave me alone, Serena." I pull my hand loose and continue up the steps.

"No. I'm not letting you run away this time." She picks up my hand again. When I stop and turn, she's glaring at me defiantly. "We need be open for this to work. Remember?"

I take a deep breath, hold it, then release it slowly. Part of me is grateful that she's calling me out on my shit. The other part is terrified that when I tell her what's really going on with me, she'll walk away forever. Maybe that's for the best.

"Do whatever you feel you need to do," I tell her, and continue up to the apartment with her hand still latched onto mine. My response was dickish, but I'm exhausted from the adrenaline dump and can barely think straight.

When I go to unlock the door, she still has a death grip on me. "Can I have my hand back?"

"Yeah. Sorry," she says with the cutest little laugh.

I roll my eyes upward at the insane effect she has on me. I unlock the door, flip on the light switch, then step inside.

"Here," she says, handing me the pizza box, which I just now realize she brought up from the car. Yep—totally brain-dead.

Taking the box from her, I set it on the kitchen counter, and then find myself staring at it, too nervous to face her.

"Why don't we wait on the pizza?"

"But you're starving," I counter, wanting to avoid the relentless questions I know are coming.

"Knox." When no other words come, I turn my head in her direction. She lifts a hand, holding it out to me. "Come on. Let's talk."

Shit. I'm not ready for this. My mind is slow and muddled, and I can barely keep my eyes open. Serena leads me over to the bed, crawls to the center, crisscrosses her legs, then pats the space in front of her. "If we're going to continue what we started, I need to know what's going on with you. Like... what happened when you came to my house, and then tonight with my friends?"

If there was a remote chance of keeping her in my life without sharing my shit, I would, but I know that isn't an option.

Sitting on the end of the bed, I pull up a knee, turning my body to face her. "This isn't easy for me to talk about."

She nods, hands folded in her lap, and waits. As much as I fight myself, I want a chance with her, but opening myself up the rest of the way is terrifying. And what if I screw it all up? Even worse, what happens when Fletcher finds me? What if she gets hurt?

Rhett's words come back from earlier today, and I think, *Fuck it*. "The clinical diagnosis I got was that I suffer from a social anxiety disorder that borders on agoraphobia."

"A fear of spiders?"

Leave it to her to make an intense situation sound funny. "That's *arachno*phobia. My fear is leaving the house. Being around people causes severe anxiety and panic attacks."

I brace for her reaction, but she smiles. "It all makes sense now," she says, exhaling a loud sigh of relief. "Thanks for telling me. We'll just work around it."

Confused by her reaction, I narrow my eyes, waiting for the *"But...*

She laughs, looking confused. "We *can't* work around it?"

"Well, yeah, I guess. I'm just confused."

"Why? Were you expecting me to run away screaming, 'Oh, the horror?' *Come on*, Knox. Lots of people struggle with anxiety. It's not like it's a contagious disease. Yours may be severe and cause limitations, but it doesn't make me like you any less. If anything, I respect you more because I know how hard it must have been to let me into your life."

Moving to the center of the bed, I press my lips to hers, breathing her in. "You are..." I struggle for the right words.

"Annoying? Nosy?"

Chuckling quietly, I pull her across my lap, then hold her tightly against my chest. Never have I felt more grateful than I do in this moment. "I was thinking amazing, but it didn't seem like enough."

"I think the word you're searching for is understanding," she says, her voice muffled as she nuzzles herself in deeper. "Something we all need more of." The feel of her... there's nothing I won't give her. "I suppose what you're coping with— it's like any other disability in that you have limitations. You just need to lay them out for me so I don't make things more difficult for you. Have you always been this way?"

"No. It started in my teens and gradually got worse from there."

"Was there more you needed to tell me, or is that it?"

"Isn't that enough?"

She leans away from me, a sweet smile on her lips. "Thank you for sharing. Like you said, it isn't easy."

You're a dick, I tell myself, because there is *so* much more I should tell her. I'm just being selfish.

I plant a kiss on the top of her forehead. "Thank you for not politely exiting my apartment."

"What kind of person would I be if I did that?"

"True, but we're just getting to know each other, and nice people seem to be in short supply." I like that she makes my fears seem minimal without minimalizing them. "And I'm still trying to figure out how you're even here in my apartment, let alone snuggled up to me right now."

"What, you're too good-looking for me?" she says with a straight face.

I scoff. "Yeah, whatever. Girls like you don't look at guys like me."

"Girls like *me*? I'm no beauty queen. Have you seen my hair?" she laughs, her face pinched.

"I have." I tuck a coil of bright red behind her ear. "It's stunning." I scoop my arms under her legs and inch us toward the side of the bed. "You need to eat."

"Kiss me first."

Will that ever not be a shock? To hear someone wanting me? I stand up with her in my arms. "Food first."

When we get to the kitchen, I lift her by the waist and sit her on the counter. I turn the stove on, set the pizza on a circular metal pan, and slide it into the oven.

When I face her again, she crooks her finger at me. "Come here. I know exactly how we can kill some time."

CHAPTER 30

SERENA

I decide to brave the lunchroom because it's raining out. Rowan is already seated at our table when I get there.

"Hey." I sit down across from her and pull my lunch out of my backpack. "Where's Tish?" She shrugs in a way that says she's still pissed I didn't tell her about Knox. "It's been several days, Rowan. Get over it."

"You just got out of a traumatic situation with Hayden, and you're already with some other guy." She scrunches up her face in disgust. "He looks mean and scary."

"That's why I didn't tell you. I don't need you judging me. And stop being a snob."

"I'm not, but you're getting involved with something worse than Hayden."

Before I can respond to her bullshit comment, Kai, Tish, and Darius sit down, followed by Hayden. *What the hell?* I thought when Rowan lost her shit on him, he'd be anywhere else but here.

"So... what's new?" Kai asks with Tish by his side. Apparently, her and Kai finally hooked up at Rowan's party. I'm happy for her.

"Besides Serena's new boyfriend?" Rowan says under her breath but loud enough for everyone to hear.

Seriously? Why? I glare. Her eyes widen like she just realized she said the words out loud.

Hayden's eyes narrow into slits. "*What* new boyfriend?"

"None of your business." I pick up my lunch and slide my backpack over my shoulder.

"Oh my god." He covers his mouth with his fist and laughs. "Darius said he saw you with that loser I took down at that party. Man, Serena, I know you rebound quick, but I didn't think you were *that* desperate. You have issues. You know that, right?"

"I have issues?" I sputter. "You, you—"

"What? You don't think every guy in this school knows how you hop from one boyfriend to the next?"

"Hayden," Kai cuts in. "Enough."

"Were you seeing him while we were together? Is that why he jumped me—some jealous side-fling?"

"No! And he pushed you *away* because you were hurting me. And I don't cheat... that's your area of expertise, remember? I'm out of here." I turn to Rowan, "Thanks for that." Then I walk away, feeling betrayed by every single one of my friends.

Bertha leans toward me. "Hey, space cadet, you with us?"

I had just finished folding the towels when Bertha and Agnes tracked me down, insisting they needed a third player for their rummy game. They probably just needed a referee since their arguing has taken on new heights.

"I'm figuring out my move," I reply when, really, I'm thinking about Knox, the soon-to-be bright spot in my otherwise crappy day. He's been meeting me after work since the night of our first kiss. I worry it will be too much for him, but he seems to be managing. Then again, his experiences might have turned him into a master at hiding his emotions.

All that fear and uncertainty I had the first night we spent together seems to have dwindled into nothing. Being with him is... more than I thought possible.

Bertha slaps her cards down. "Alright, what's his name? No one has a smile like that unless there's a man involved."

"Bertha!" Agnes admonishes. "Leave the girl alone."

"I'm just sayin'."

I finally decide my next move, then discard. "Your turn."

Bertha picks up a card from the deck. "Is this the guy who was having a tough time?" She discards.

"Maybe Serena doesn't *want* to talk about this." Agnes gives Bertha a meaningful look.

"Well, that last guy was a waste, and she can't keep tossing them aside like last week's news."

"Oh my god! I'm not *that* bad."

Agnes places her hand over mine. "Don't mind her. She's just sour because I kicked her butt in dominoes last night."

"Bull crap." Bertha points a finger at her. "You cheated."

Agnes rolls her eyes.

Yes, starting another relationship is a mistake, but A: Knox sharing his mental struggles with me was a game changer. I get it now. And B: I'm not about to get into it with them. And C: Well... I don't know what C is.

"Can we just finish this game?" I gripe. "Stuart should be back by now, and I want to check on him." Four days ago, he was taken to the hospital, but because of patient confidentiality, no one could tell me why, and I've been worried ever since.

After finishing up our game of rummy, and basically preventing another argument between the scrappy ladies, I say my goodbyes and head to the extended care unit, where they have full-time specialized care. When I step into Stuart's room, the first thing I notice is how pale his skin is. This is the hard part of my job—dealing with the imminent loss of the people you care about.

"Hi, Stuart." He gazes up at me with zero recognition. "My name is Serena. I was wondering if you would like me to read to you today? I see you have a book there." I point to the novel on the table next to his bed. The photo album is gone. I look around, wondering where it went, but I don't see it.

"Sure." His voice is raspy.

"Would you like some water?"

"Okay."

I fill his spill-proof cup and pass it to him. His hand shakes as he tries to hold it to his lips, so I steady it with mine. "Thank you," he says when he finishes.

"I'll just set it here on the table. Let me know when you want some more." He nods, and I pick up the book, but he falls asleep before I get past the first page. Setting the book back on the table, I touch his hand briefly before leaving the room. "He's not looking good," I say to Eva at the nurses' station.

"No, he's not. I'm sorry, Serena. I know how attached you've become."

I nod—afraid to answer with the massive knot stuck in my

throat—and head to the locker room, needing a minute to calm the ache in my heart. This disease has taken him so fast.

Knox is waiting for me after work, dressed in his usual attire of jeans and a dark sweatshirt with the hood pulled over his head. Without even a hello, I rush into his arms and hold tight. After the shitstorm at school and seeing Stuart today, I'm grateful for the enveloping hug.

He leans me back, assessing me. "Did something happen?" He glances over my shoulder at the building. "Are you okay?"

"I just missed you." I drop my head back on his chest and breathe him in. "You always smell so good."

A quick rumble of laughter vibrates against my ear. "I'm glad you think so."

Knowing he'd feel more comfortable off the main street, I release him and pick up his hand, walking us toward my car. I tell him about my history class, where a student argued that the world was flat, and a kid in my science class accidentally started a fire that caught on his lab partner's shirt sleeve.

"Are you going to tell me why you were upset?" he says when we reach the car.

So much for leading him off-topic. "And ruin the good times? No way."

"Weren't you recently preaching about the importance of communication?"

"I wasn't preaching. I was giving my opinion."

Knox crosses his beefy arms over his wide chest. "Still waiting."

"Fine. Hayden was being a dick at school, my friends are jerks, and one of the residents I'm close to isn't doing well."

He takes me by the arms and pulls me against him. "I'm sorry."

"Do you think, maybe, you could get a phone?" I link my arms behind his back and snuggle my head into his chest. "It would be nice to have easy access to you."

"I'm not the booty-call type," he deadpans.

I laugh. "Was that a joke?"

"Maybe. Now, tell me what that dickhead, Hayden, did and why your friends are jerks."

I lean back in his arms. "I was being honest when I said I didn't want to ruin the moment. I like seeing you happy."

"Serena," he says with a frustrated exhale.

"*Fine*." I give him the condensed version.

He kisses the top of my head when I finish, giving me the warm fuzzies. "I'm sorry shit's complicated for you right now. School's almost over and you won't have to deal with Hayden anymore."

"True."

Knox's hand slides up and down my back. "You told Rowan about me?"

"I didn't tell her anything personal. She saw us together, remember?" I tug on the back of his sweatshirt.

"Us..." he lets the word hang. "That sounds so strange. I never thought of myself being a part of an *us*. It sounds so... normal."

I frown up at him. "That doesn't sound good."

"I didn't mean it that way. It's just unexpected. I always saw myself alone."

"*Sooo*... you're okay with the *mundane* idea of an *us*?" I ask, insecurity rearing its ugly head.

He releases a sharp laugh. "Stop. You and mundane don't even belong in the same sentence. This is about me. Nothing in my life has ever been, *uh*... conventional, so I never thought I could have relationships the way most people do. I'm still not sure, but with you, I want to try."

Pleased with his response, I rise on my toes and steal a quick kiss.

"Do you have lots of homework, or can you take a break?" he asks.

I pump my eyebrows. "What did you have in mind?"

His lips spread wide, flashing his dimples. *So, he does have a matching set.*

"Not that. As appealing as the idea is, I was thinking of a short drive and some stargazing. Soon, it'll be dark enough."

"Sounds perfect." Exactly what I need to reset my day. "Do you have a place in mind?"

"If you drive up Sunshine Canyon, I'll show you where to park." He slides the hood from his sweatshirt off his head as he moves to the far side of the car.

"You got a haircut," I say over the top of the car.

"Yeah. Rhett did it. Why, does it look bad?"

"No, I like the military style on you. Makes you even hotter." His face contorts as if the comment was ridiculous. "What?"

He rolls his eyes. "Nothing."

"Why do you always have your hood up?" I ask when we're inside the car.

"I feel like if I can't see others, then they can't see me. Sounds weird saying it out loud."

"No, it doesn't. Everyone has their way of coping. If it helps, then that's all that matters."

Before starting up the canyon, we stop and get takeout—burgers and fries—and eat them in the car.

"Do you have a flashlight?" Knox asks when we reach the edge of town.

"I have one on my phone."

"It's a good idea to keep a flashlight in your car in case you get stranded and your phone dies. I'm surprised you don't have one in that post-apocalyptic backpack of yours." His humor catches me off guard—as it usually does—leaving a smile as I drive us to parts unknown.

CHAPTER 31

SERENA

I drive the windy road up through the mountains. When I'm near the top of the canyon, Knox directs me to turn onto a dirt road. The sky is loaded with white puffy clouds edged in vibrant pink. It's stunning.

"Just pull over here," he tells me when we come to a clearing. "It's a short hike to where I want to take you."

My phone buzzes with a new text as I turn off the ignition. Pulling it from my back pocket, I see it's from Rowan, apologizing again.

I text back: *It's fine.*

For the most part, it is. She wasn't being malicious, just her usual self—spouting off before thinking.

I return the phone to my back pocket and climb out of the car. "How do you know about this place?" I follow behind Knox when he starts walking. "Without a car, it wouldn't be easy to get to."

"It's not hard, either," he says, navigating the rocky terrain. "Walking doesn't take as much time as people think. Most people are just lazy."

"Ouch," I respond to the insult while watching my feet. There isn't a trail so much as an open space with low, scraggly brush that we have to maneuver around.

"I didn't mean *you*, and maybe lazy isn't the right word. More like busy. It's quicker and easier to drive than to walk." He changes direction and starts making our way down the mountain on a trail he picked up.

"Fair. I'm surprised you would be out exploring with your struggle to leave your apartment. Sorry." I cringe. "That came out wrong. I guess I'm just trying to understand you better."

"It's fine. I'm not easily offended. Most days, I force myself to go out. I'm afraid if I don't, someday, I might not be able to leave at all. On the days I'm feeling confident, I take the bus, usually in the evening, and explore. That's how I found this place. There's a bus stop before we turned off the main road, and there are loads of hiking trails in this area."

Deeper in the forest, the tall pines block out most of the remaining light, making it difficult to see. I whip out my phone and use the flashlight, shining it slightly ahead of Knox's feet. "Is it challenging for you to meet me after work?"

"It's not easy, but hopefully, the more I do it, the less anxiety it will cause. It's the new stuff that can really put me over the edge—the unknowns—but also being around too many people. It's just the way my brain works."

"I get it. You've learned to navigate your limitations around work and school. Seriously, give yourself more credit."

The trail veers left, leading us along the side of the mountain. I silently take in the night, enjoying the peaceful surroundings on this gorgeous evening. It's nice the way we can enjoy the silence together.

Knox stops at the base of a large rocky outcrop. "We'll have to climb a bit. Are you okay with that?"

I'm glad I'm still wearing my grippy shoes from work. "Sure. No problem." I was so excited about seeing Knox, I forgot to exchange them for my street shoes.

"Give me your phone," he says. "I'll light your way, then climb up after you."

"Sure." I don't really need the added light. There's still enough left in the sky, especially now that we're out of the dense trees, but I hand over my phone anyway and start the up. When I was little, my parents used to call me their little monkey. If there were rocks to climb anywhere near a hiking trail, I was scaling them.

"You've done this before," he says, sounding impressed.

A proud smirk forms on my lips. "Yeah. I've been bouldering since I was a kid."

When I make it to the top, I ask him if he wants to hand me the phone so I can light his way, but he tells me he can still see. He scales the rocky surface effortlessly—his strength and height making all the difference in reaching the top quickly.

Stuffing my phone in my back pocket, I take in the view. The rocky surface is roughly twelve feet by twelve, jutting out from the side of the mountain. Far below us, the town spreads out in a breathtaking display of shimmering lights. "Incredible."

"This is one of my favorite spots. Plus, look up."

Even with a dusting of light left in the sky, there are enough stars to be wowed. Knox slides in behind me and locks his arms around my waist. I place my hands over his and lean my head back against his chest, taking it all in. The silence. The view. The feeling of being wrapped in Knox's warmth. There is no place I'd rather be.

"I wish I could remember you as a little boy and the times we spent together. Do you remember much?"

"Some. You were tiny compared to me, so I remember being cautious when we played together." He pauses a beat. "I was envious of your sandbox and all the toys you had—shovels, buckets, trucks, and bulldozers." His thumb rubs softly back and forth under the hem of my shirt, sending a zing of electricity across my skin. "We played hide-and-seek a lot. You were easy to find because you always hid in the last place I did. I remember thinking it was cute. And you always looked so impressed when I found you, like I was your hero or something."

Gushing at the image of little Knox, I turn in his arms and plant a gentle kiss on his mouth. The more he shares, the more confident I am that being with him is the right choice. "Tell me more."

"You liked to play with your dolls. And sometimes your mom or dad, depending on who was around, would play catch with me. I loved it when they did that."

"I didn't play with dolls." I glare at him indignantly.

"Yes. You did. But mostly, you liked to bury them in the sand and dig them up again."

"That's morbid." I laugh. "What else?"

He hesitates as if trying to recall, then the corner of his mouth curls up on one side. "When I came over to play, you'd run up to me and grab my hand, pulling me toward whatever you were doing—outside stuff, coloring, painting, Lego building, puzzles. You were always excited to see me and treated me like I was part of the family. You made me feel wanted. Your parents did too."

Emotions well up, prickling my nose. I reach up, take his head in my hands, and gently pull his face down within inches of mine. "No one should have to grow up the way you did," I whisper, my voice cracking with emotion. "You *are* wanted. You are special, kind, protective, and I'm grateful you're back in my life." There's doubt in his expression, and it makes my heart hurt. "If I'd been a little older, I would *never* have forgotten you. And if we ever lose touch again, know that, this time, you *will* be missed."

Tenderness and wonder replace disbelief as he studies my face. "I think you've always been a missing piece of me. I just didn't know until I found you again. And now that I have..." His gaze intensifies, locking with mine. "I'll do anything it takes not to lose you." When he dips his head and our lips meet, a rush of emotion so sweet floods my system, filling every inch of my soul.

Kissing him back, I hope he can feel how much his words mean to me—how worthy he is of every ounce of love in this world. His hands glide up the back of my shirt as he deepens the kiss. When they trail over the long, ugly scar that runs the length of my right side, I flinch. "That tickles," I say, stepping away. It doesn't really, I'm just self-conscious of anyone touching it.

"How did you get this?" He lifts the side of my shirt. "I didn't notice it the last time, we, uh..."

I shove my shirt back down. "Made out?"

He clears his throat. "Yeah. How did you get it?"

I wrap my arms around my waist, suddenly feeling the need to protect myself. "You don't talk about *your* scars," I deflect.

"This one"—he points to the one that dissects his eyebrow—"is from the kid who attacked Annie." He traces the scar on his jaw. "This is from one of my mother's boyfriends when I defended her from a beating." He taps the scar cutting through his nose and lip. "My last foster father." Showing his battered knuckles, he adds, "And these are from standing up to every asshole who's ever come after me."

"Your foster father hit you?"

"He put me in the hospital," Knox says with little emotion.

"Seriously? I hope they put him in jail."

"Yeah, he got some time, but more importantly, he won't be fostering any more kids, *ever*."

"That's awful. Can't they weed people like that out?"

"The system doesn't always work the way it should. It's overwhelmed—the politics are corrupt."

"Maybe someday you can help."

"I'm not in any shape to take on the entire U.S. foster system," he scoffs.

"You never know. You could start with your community and go from there."

"It won't help. People smarter and richer than me have tried and failed."

"You know it took Thomas Edison one thousand failed attempts before he successfully invented the lightbulb?"

"Has anyone ever told you that you have a real talent for deflecting questions you don't want to answer?" he rumbles out a short laugh, then shrugs a shoulder. "It's fine, though. I get not wanting to share the bad shit."

Yeah, but he's shared a lot of his with me. I feel a little guilty not reciprocating. "My story is nothing compared to yours. I'm not sure why I don't like talking about it. Maybe the privacy of family drama." I shrug, then tilt my head back, taking in the starry sky overhead. "On the way home from soccer practice, my dad lost control of the car when a woman veered into our lane. We crashed into a huge oak—the impact being on my side. My father had just come from a business meeting and had been drinking. An ambulance rushed me to the ER with broken ribs, a concussion, and the jagged cut down my side was the worst of it. I was in intensive care for several days from the blood loss. The good news is, I survived and my dad never touched another drop of alcohol. The bad news is, I lost him in that crash. Maybe not his life, but the bond for sure. Our relationship died that day."

"I'm sorry that happened to you, but don't think your story is any less important than mine. It's all shit that has to be dealt with. And it was, *is*, a hell of a lot more than just family drama."

"I guess." Suddenly feeling sorry for myself, I drop my forehead to his chest.

He bumps my chin up so that I'm looking at him. "Why aren't you and your dad close anymore?"

"After the crash. He checked out—emotionally, physically— he just wasn't there anymore. Then, like I mentioned before, he cheated on my mom and moved on. I have twin half-brothers. They're two. I did the math. He got the woman pregnant when he was still with my mom."

His arms circle my body and pull me tight against him. "I can't begin to know what's going on inside your dad's head, but he's a fucking idiot, whatever his reasons are." He squeezes tight, then releases me. "We should get going. We both need to get up early tomorrow." Walking to the edge of the rocks, he looks over. "Damn, it's dark tonight."

"How do you usually get down?"

"I use a headlamp."

An image of a ginormous Knox the explorer wearing a little headlamp has me chuckling to myself.

"What's so funny?"

"You are one surprise after another."

CHAPTER 32

KNOX

Heading back to my place, her story stays with me. I'd always seen her dad as the ideal father. Now, combining his drunken carelessness with his cheating and abandonment, the image of the man I looked up to crumbles into dust.

When we arrive at my apartment, we decide on popcorn and a movie in my bed. Movies have always been a way for me to reset my mood. But sitting beside her like this—so chill and everyday—it's fucking surreal.

We must have dozed off because I'm woken by another ugly nightmare. Rolling on to my back, I stare up at the ceiling. *I'm so over this.*

"Is everything okay?" Serena's voice rasps. Her fingers splaying over my upper arm.

"Yeah. Sorry." I slide an arm beneath her and pull her into my side. Having her here after a nightmare is like seeing a rainbow after a thunderstorm.

That's some flowery thinking, Knox.

She reaches over to my nightstand for her phone and checks the time. "I need to get home." She texts something and sets it back down. "Just a little longer, though." Turning on her side, she snuggles her back against my front, wiggling her body against sensitive areas I'd rather not wake. But the dream flashes back, dousing me like a cold splash of water, keeping that part of me respectful.

As the silence between us stretches on and her breathing becomes a slow, steady rhythm, I wonder if she's fallen back to sleep.

"Who's the demon in your dreams?" she says sleepily, turning in my arms to face me.

"You should probably get going. It's late."

"Who always gives me crap for deflecting?" she asks, her tone sarcastic.

"Not crap necessarily," I stall. *Can't we be free of this darkness for a little while longer—maybe forever?*

"Tell me?" Sliding her hand under my shirt, her fingers brush up and down my side, leaving goosebumps in their wake.

Man, I don't want to do this now, especially with how good her touch feels. But keeping it from her isn't right either.

"His name is Fletcher." How do I describe what he was to me without making myself look just as twisted as he is?

"Is that all I'm going to get, or is there more?"

"Can't that be enough?" I don't know why I say this. I know it isn't, but this shit isn't easy.

"A little more information would be nice, but it's okay if you're not ready to share it." She kisses the exposed part at the base of my neck just above my t-shirt.

Even the soft touch of her lips isn't enough to wipe away the fear that's tearing through me. If I tell her about the monster, I'll have to tell her everything, and I risk losing her. We've only known each other for a short time, but if she walks away now, I'm afraid the barely held-together pieces of myself will crumble into nothing. And there's no way to give her part without the whole.

She deserves to know.

I take a deep, shaky breath, preparing myself. "The nightmares are like... haunted memories, and they're all twisted up into these terrifying situations I can never get away from. They aren't always about Fletcher—sometimes they're about my father, but they almost always involve my mother."

"Was Fletcher the foster parent who beat you up?"

"No. He was a friend of my mother's she met after moving to Denver. He was always nice and looked out for me—food, clothes... sometimes he would take me for ice cream or to a sporting event. After Mom's third stint in jail, things seemed better. I got a job, hoping if I pitched in, she wouldn't let guys use her for money, and the drugs would stop. But in less than a year, she overdosed. At the next foster home, I was a total mess, lashing out, especially at the father. That's how I landed in the hospital. When Fletcher found out, he visited and told me that because I was sixteen, I could emancipate from the system and live on my own. He helped with all of it, gave me a job, and I never asked any questions."

Her big, thoughtful eyes remain on mine while she absorbs everything I've told her. God, I feel like I'm about to kick a kitten.

I search for the right words, hoping she'll understand, maybe even give me a chance regardless. "At first, I was an errands guy, picking up food, dry cleaning, and driving him around. Fletcher got me an apartment, gave me money, and signed me up at a gym that offered mixed-martial arts training. Being grateful can make you blind, but I didn't learn that until it was too late."

I watch her brow crease in the center like she knows something bad is about to come.

"When I turned eighteen, things shifted. Due to my size and fighting skills, Fletcher kept me by his side most of the time. I had a meanness about me that made people think twice about messing with him. That's how I discovered his real profession—drugs. By then, I was hooked on the life and riding high on anything his guys handed me." I internally wince at the admission. I hate weakness. Admitting my own to Serena is scraping me raw, but I know she won't let me stop now. I can see it by the cautiously determined expression on her face—like she needs to know it all.

"The alcohol and drugs made me feel invincible. No more fears. No more nightmares. No more anxiety. But it got to the point that no amount of numbing could clear the horrific images I was witnessing. His control. His brutality. It was beyond disturbing. One night, I talked to him about getting out. He asked if I had a plan for the future. When I said no, he asked me to wait a little longer—said he was going legit. I'm not sure why I stayed." I shrug. "Loyalty? Probably. He got me out of the foster care system."

Needing reassurance that she's still with me, but terrified to tell her the rest, I smooth a hand over her mane of red hair and pull her in for a kiss. But I guess it's like ripping off a bandage—better to get it over with all at once. I brush my lips over hers one last time and continue.

"One night, we were out celebrating. I can't remember what because I was wasted. A guy got in Fletcher's face at a club, accusing him of a dirty deal. We took it outside. The man went for Fletcher with a knife, and I... intervened. When they pulled me off him, the guy was covered in blood and wasn't moving. Fletcher checked for a pulse and told me he was dead. Told me not to worry, that he would take care of it, but I should lie low for a little while."

Serena sits up, her expression wary. *It's over between us. I can feel it.*

"Anyway, I freaked out, went to my apartment, took all the money I'd hoarded, and ran. Ever since that night, I've been looking over my shoulder. No one gets out of that life without consequences—not with everything I witnessed. Fletcher could track me down at any time. That's why I didn't want you anywhere near me. That, with everything else... I'm not good for you."

She places a hand over my heart. "Don't say that."

Confused by her kindness, I sit up abruptly, facing her. "Didn't you hear me? I killed a man."

"Give me a minute." She scoots to the side of the bed and stands. Moving to the window, she stares into the darkness with arms wrapped around her middle. "It wasn't intentional."

In a swift move, I swing my legs over the side of the bed and drop my feet to the floor. "Serena, for fuck's sake, that was barely three years ago."

She whirls on me. "Don't yell at me."

Idiot. You're making it worse. I hold up a hand. "You're right. I'm sorry."

"A lifetime can pass in that amount of time." She gazes at me with so much purpose, my heart trips over itself. "You are *not* that person anymore. If you were, you wouldn't be trying to protect me."

"No way in fucking hell I deserve you."

"I just..." Her focus drifts to the floor as if lost in a deep thought. "This is a lot to take in." She blinks, expression shifting, her eyes lift and narrow onto mine. "And stop doing that—putting yourself down. You deserve everything that was taken from you—security, love, affection—all the things the rest of us take for granted. Don't you get that?"

She's stunning in her fury. "I get the concept, but *feeling* worthy is something else altogether." Regardless of the self-loathing brewing inside me, I push off the bed and take her hand. Not sure if the timing's right, but I need to feel her. Touch her. Connect. So, I wrap my arms around her.

"Is what happened with Fletcher the cause of your anxiety? The reason you have trouble leaving the house?"

She hasn't let go of me. The relief gives me hope and the strength to continue. "I don't know. I guess. Maybe that mixed with all the other crap from my past."

"Please don't take this the wrong way, but have you ever talked to anyone? A counselor or a psychiatrist?"

Releasing her, I sit on the bed and pull her between my legs. "A psychiatrist—a lady Rhett built a house for. I saw her once a week in the beginning, now every other month. She gave me anxiety meds—one I take daily, and one I take for public outings. But I don't like taking it unless I absolutely need to. I want my mind clear, but sometimes I have no choice, like when I go to school to take exams."

Something painful flashes in her eyes. "I came up to you that day... I grabbed your arm. I'm so sorry. I didn't know."

"It's okay. How could you?"

She throws her head back and groans. "And I thought Rowan was the insensitive one."

"Don't." I drape my arms around her legs. "You're not insensitive. Just the opposite."

Setting her hands on my shoulders, she bobs her head as if she hears me but isn't sure she agrees. "One last question. Wouldn't Fletcher have tracked you down already if he wanted to?"

My head falls forward, resting against her stomach briefly before meeting her eyes again. "Yes and no. Rhett helped me legally change my name, which will make it harder, but if he's motivated, he'll find me eventually. It might have been safer to go somewhere I've never lived before in case my mom mentioned us living here, but this place always felt safe to me. And it was a quick decision coming here. I never planned on staying, but then I met Rhett."

"So, Knox isn't your real name?"

"No, it's my middle name. Gabriel Knox Westing." Just thinking of my first name makes me cringe. It's tied to sixteen years of shitty memories. "Mom said she named me after an angel. She must have been really into them at the time—always had figurines around. Anyway, Rhett let me use his last name. Thought it might be safer, you know, harder for Fletcher to find me. So, I became Knox Barstow."

Her fingers play with the hair at the back of my neck. "So, Rhett knows all of this, and he's okay with it?"

"Struggled at first, but yeah."

She bites the corner of her bottom lip and pulls it out through her teeth. "It sounds like Fletcher was a big-time dealer. Why would he care if you bugged out? It's not like you would turn him in. That would only implicate yourself."

"Like I said before, no one walks away from that life. Also, when I got out of the hospital, he told me we were family, and family watched each other's backs. He said he would never let anyone hurt me, and no matter where I was, he would find me. I'm not sure what all that was about, but it stuck with me. He's the kind of person who will give you a big warm smile while stabbing a blade into your back—you can't trust him."

"Thanks for telling me all this." Her tone is even, not giving her true thoughts. "It means a lot."

"And?" I need her to end this torture.

"What happened was an accident. Bad things happen to good people. Did you know it was a rabbi who coined that term? Harold Kushner, I think, was his name."

"Uhhh..." *Where does she get this stuff?*

She taps the side of her head. "Can't help it. I've got too much shit up here." She climbs onto my lap, straddling me. "Do you want to go to prom with me?"

Gripping her hips, I bark out a laugh. "What the fuck?"

"Do. You. Want to go. To prom with me? It's like next weekend, but—"

"*Hell* no. Where did *that* even come from?"

"Trying to lighten the mood. Don't worry, I won't make you go. *I'm* not."

"Ohhh-kay? Sooo, we're good?"

"I don't like who you were forced to become or the things you did, but I understand how and why. And like I said, that's not who you are anymore. So, yeah. We're good." She presses a quick kiss on my mouth. "Instead of going to prom, maybe we could get dressed up, have dinner, and watch a movie here. You know... to make it up to me."

"Dinner and movie, yes. Dressing up, no."

"Fine," she says with a grin and presses herself up against me. "Clothing is optional."

CHAPTER 33

SERENA

I smile to myself, lost in the memories of last night—the stars, his vulnerability, all the kisses, the warmth and affection. But above all, it was his honesty that drew me closer to him. Sure, hearing about his experience made me pause and worry that Rowan might be right, that Knox was just another disaster waiting to happen. But the more I put all the pieces of him together, I realize the present far outweighs the mistakes in his past.

A deep yawn takes me back to reality. The lack of sleep was worth it, but I'm having trouble focusing in school today. And that C on my AP English exam was kind of a surprise. If I'm going to make valedictorian, I need to—wait. Why does it matter? I have my scholarship. As far as impressing my father? He doesn't have a clue, and sure-as-shit doesn't care one way or the other. Why am I putting so much pressure on myself, missing out on the fun of my senior year, for a title that will soon be forgotten? I don't need to prove anything. I know I'm smart.

The sudden realization brings on a sense of freedom. Man, that feels good. I inhale a deep, cleansing breath and exhale an indescribable calmness. Life is about balance, about finding joy in the small moments and the people who truly matter. Mom's been telling me this forever—and in their own way, my friends as well. It just took Knox and a little sleep deprivation to allow it all to sink in.

As I snag a coffee from the vending machine on my way to the library for my lunch break, another realization dawns on me... I really should take Saturdays off. Mom's right—again. On top of everything else, I'm overdoing it with work. I've been stressing because I don't want to ask my dad for money. But I'll be working over the summer break, anyway, and if I have to work part-time while I'm in school, then that's the way it is.

I won't get to see Knox as much, though. I don't like that.

Well, a lot can happen between now and then, so—

My phone vibrates on the table. I flip it over, expecting a text from Rowan or Tish. I haven't talked to them since yesterday's lunchroom fiasco.

555-233-8620: How's your day going?

Me: Who is this?

555-233-8620: Knox

I contain myself from jumping out of the chair and giving a good, solid fist pump. This is awesome! I can't believe he got a phone. I sit back down and quickly add him to my contacts.

"What's with the big smile?" Tish asks, coming to my table with Rowan behind her.

When has Rowan ever trailed anybody?

"Nothing." I turn my phone over, hiding the screen. "What's going on?" My tone is harsh, but I'm still pissed from the other day.

"Not much. Is it alright if we sit?" Tish asks cautiously.

"Yeah. Sure."

After they're settled across from me, Tish nudges Rowan, who grips her hands in front of her and blurts, "I feel horrible. I was hurt that you didn't tell us about Knox. I didn't mean to say what I did. It just came out."

"I get it, but you threw me under the bus, Row, then just sat there and let him attack me."

"It all happened so fast, and then you were gone."

"Bullshit. You don't stay silent for anything. Last time he tried to sit with us, you about tore his head off."

"None of us handled it right," Tish says.

"That's why we kept texting you after it happened," Rowan interjects. "We were trying to make sure you were okay, but you weren't responding. I even drove by your house—late—but your car wasn't there. Where were you?"

"It doesn't matter." Now isn't the time to tell them I was with Knox. "Why were you all suddenly fine with Hayden again? You all could've given me a heads-up."

Tish gives a frustrated shake of her head. "We weren't okay with it. Hayden sitting down took us all by surprise, especially after what happened the last time. Then Rowan makes that comment, Hayden reacts, and it's chaos. You missed it, but we all ripped into him. The guys especially—they're with him the most and are tired of his shit. I mean... crap."

"It's okay," Rowan says. "You're almost eighteen. You can swear if you want to." Tish sticks her tongue out in response, and I can't help the laugh that bubbles out. "Why didn't you tell us about Knox?"

"Because it's... complicated, and I didn't want you hassling me about being with him so soon after Hayden. Which you already did." I glare at Rowan. "*And* you called him mean and scary, which he isn't, by the way. I never expected things to progress the way they did, but I followed him after the fight, and I don't know, the rest just happened." My phone vibrates. I lift it, taking a peek, then smile while lowering it.

"Is that him?" Tish asks.

I nod my response, itching to text him back, but don't want to do it with my friends still here.

"So, what's his story, then?" Rowan asks. "He may not be mean and scary, but he's definitely big, ugly, and intimidating as hell. I don't get it."

"Oh my god, Rowan," Tish jumps to my defense.

"Stuck up much?" I bite back. "He's not ugly. He's..." I watch as she arches a brow. She's antagonizing me on purpose. "Wow... insensitive *and* shallow. You are such a bitch."

"I know," she laughs, waving me off. "So, what's he like?"

"After that? I ain't saying shit."

When we've been friends as long as we have, it's hard to stay mad. I give them limited details. Just enough that they won't worry he's some crazed lunatic. And by the end of the lunch period, our friendship is back on track.

After the last bell, I open my locker and stare at the books inside, trying to decide which ones I'll need when Hayden leans on the locker next to mine.

"I'm sorry about the other day," he says, surprising me. "I don't like the idea of you with that guy."

I pull out my physics book and shut my locker. "Just stay away from me, Hayden, okay? That's all I ask."

"I shouldn't have broken up with you." Catching a whiff of

alcohol as he leans in and brushes my cheek with the backs of his finger, I smack his hand away. *He's drinking at school now?*

His eyebrows pinch together. "Don't be like that. I want to get back together."

"Are you kidding me? Not a chance." I slam my locker closed and walk away.

"I was just trying to make you jealous," he says, catching up to me. "She didn't mean anything." He grips my arm, stopping me. "You did, Serena. You still do."

"You need help, Hayden." I focus on his hand, his fingers digging in. "Let go. You're hurting me."

He quickly drops his hold. "Sorry."

I take off again, needing to get away, but he's by my side in seconds. His stride easily matching my own. "I messed up, okay? I knew I was losing you, and I got desperate. I thought if you saw me with other girls, you would remember what you were missing."

I stop and gawk at him. "Are you serious right now? Do you know how twisted that sounds?" Not to mention there was no forethought involved. He was drunk as shit.

"I—no. I'm sorry. You were good for me. You helped me stay focused on what was important. Now..." He gives a small shrug, looking at the ground.

"Don't put that on me. You are responsible for your own choices."

"Are you sleeping with him?"

"Goodbye, Hayden." I turn and walk away. This time, he lets me go.

I can't believe he tried to guilt me back into a relationship. *After everything he did to me... is he insane?*

How did it even get to this point?

Doesn't matter. He's not my problem anymore.

By the time I get to work, I can barely keep my eyes open. Not that I regret the late night. The only thing keeping me going is knowing Knox will be waiting for me when I'm done.

So far, I've helped a couple of new residents get settled. I visited Stuart, but he was sleeping. I folded a mountain of towels, visited with The Ladies, stopped by Stuart's again—still asleep. Thankfully, seven o'clock finally rolls around, and after making my way to the employee locker room, I change and grab my backpack.

Knox is waiting for me in his usual spot. After a hug and kiss that vibrates to my toes, I get a wild idea and hope to get him on board. "Do you think you could come inside for a minute? I want you to meet my friends, Bertha and Agnes."

He runs a hand through his close-cropped hair, knocking his hood off. "Serena," he starts, his tone giving away his sense of unease.

"They're playing dominoes in the common room. I just left them. No one else is there. You'll like them. I promise." He shakes his head, looking unsure. "What's the worst that could happen?"

"I have a panic attack and embarrass the crap out of both of us."

"You said that you like to push yourself when you're feeling confident, right? You made it here, didn't you?" He eyes me dubiously. "We can say a quick hi and leave." I pick up his hand and wait.

"Just to say hi?"

"Yep. In and out, unless you want to stay."

"I won't."

"I've got you." I lift our joined hands. "If it gets to be too much, give my hand a hard squeeze and we're out of there, no questions asked. I promise."

"Fuck, Serena."

"Do you trust me?"

He takes a moment. I can tell he's focusing on his breathing and wondering if I've pushed him too far. "Yeah. I trust you."

CHAPTER 34

SERENA

After everything he's gone through, the power of that statement hits me surprisingly hard. But I won't let him down. I wish I would have given The Ladies a heads-up, though. Especially Bertha. Rowan's filter sucks, but Bertha's was fried long ago.

I push the front door open. Jessica at the front desk waves hello with a puzzled smile, clearly surprised to see me back so soon. Keeping Knox's hand in mine, I return the greeting and then lead us down the hall to the common room. That's when I notice the slight tremor. "Are you sure?" I slow our progression.

"Say hi and leave. I can do this." The self-affirming mantra has me questioning the intelligence of this idea. Knox will stop me if he needs to. He's been dealing with this long enough to know his boundaries.

Bertha and Agnes are deeply focused on their game when we walk up. "Hi. I'm sorry to interrupt, but I wanted you to meet someone. This is my friend, Knox."

They both look up and smile. "I'm Bertha. This old bat across from me is Agnes."

"Who are you calling an old bat?" she returns.

"I call it like I see it."

Agnes ignores the rebuttal. "It's nice to meet you, Knox."

"You too," Knox responds, still holding my hand. No signal yet—if anything, his grip has loosened.

"You ever play dominoes?" Bertha asks.

"No, ma'am."

Bertha winks at me. "I like this one. He's got manners. Well, have a seat and I'll teach you. The game is a lot better with four."

"Maybe another time," I say. "I haven't eaten and still have homework."

"She studies too hard, doesn't she, Knox?" Agnes says as she flips over the tiles. "What do you say, honey? One game? It's super easy the way we play. It *needs* to be with our ancient brains. All you have to do is match the ends together to make a train"—she demonstrates, lining a couple up—"and whoever uses all their dominoes first wins."

"Have a seat, Knox." Bertha pats the chair to her left. "I'm getting a kink in my neck looking up at you."

His eyes move to mine. He knows he has an out. "Okay," he says, surprising me, and sits where he's directed.

"Just one game," I say, sitting across from him. "You won't like me when I'm hangry."

Bertha snorts. "Is that what they call it these days? Well, then you need to quit starving yourself."

"Funny," I retort.

With Knox out of reach, I worry he won't be able to communicate when he's had too much. He seems fine but I also know how good he is at hiding his anxiety. *He'll leave if he has to,* I remind myself.

His gaze finds mine and he winks at me. I feel my mouth drop. That small action sends a burst of joy zipping through my veins.

"Close your mouth, dear," Agnes says. "Or Bertha will stick her finger in it. You know how she gets."

Man, these two.

"Shut it," Betha snaps. "I would do *no* such thing." She leans into Knox conspiratorially. "She's always been jealous I got the better room." Then she cackles. Knox's face breaks out in a wide grin, dimples flashing. I think my heart just fell at his feet.

We end up playing three games before Bertha tells me I better go and eat because my growling stomach is becoming too much of a distraction.

"You come back and see us, honey," Agnes says as Knox and I stand.

"Please do. Agnes doesn't cheat with you around." Bertha cracks a smile. "Come here, boy, and give me a hug." He crouches and bends to her level, hugging the frail old woman gently. When they pull apart, she reaches up and pats his cheek with an affection in her eyes I've never seen before. "I hope to see you again." She takes his hand, holding it firmly in both of hers as she looks up at him intently. "You are good for my Serena, you hear?"

His gaze meets mine in a way I can't read. "Yes, ma'am."

"Alright then." She releases him.

As soon as we're outside, I ask, "Was it okay?"

"It was fun." His tone gives nothing away.

"Are you saying that because it's true, or because you're trying to appease me?"

"It wasn't easy, but it wasn't hard either."

"I'm sorry we couldn't sit next to each other so you could signal me."

He stops, pulls me into an embrace, and plants a sweet kiss on my mouth. "Don't be sorry. They were a lot of fun. I can see why you like working there."

"On a scale of one to ten on the anxiety scale, where were you?"

"Stop worrying." He pulls his hood over his head.

"It would help me to understand."

Picking up my hand, he starts walking us toward my car. "It was a seven when we went in and a three when we came out."

"Standing outside of the building waiting for me?"

"A five."

"When you came to my house that first time?"

"Serena," he warns.

"I need to know."

"Nine."

We stop at my car. "What happens when you reach ten?" With my research, I have a pretty good idea.

He stares at his shoes. I don't think he's going to answer, but then he says, "My chest gets so tight that I can barely breathe, and I pass out."

I don't need to ask him if it's happened before. I can see it in his expression. In the car, I ask, "Why do you think your anxiety dropped after we sat down?"

He shrugs. "Maybe for the same reason I've always been okay around Rhett. Maybe their age isn't a threat... I'm not sure."

"You haven't met cranky old Jasper," I laugh. "That man is scary when he doesn't get his Jell-O for dessert."

He leans the short distance to touch his lips to mine. "Why don't we go and raid Rhett's refrigerator?"

"I like the way you think."

In the kitchen, surrounded by the comforting scent of leftovers, Rhett's eyes spark with pride when Knox tells him about our time with The Ladies.

By dessert, Rhett is clearly exhausted. "I'm heading off to bed, kids." He stands and gives my shoulder a squeeze. "It was great seeing you again. Drop by any time. I like the company."

"Since when?" Knox retorts, stone-faced.

"Since you smartened up and brought Serena back for a visit." He ruffles Knox's hair. "Night, you two."

"Night," we say in unison just as my phone rings. Jumping up, I dig it out of my backpack only to return it.

"I don't mind if you need to take that."

"It's my father." He gives me a look like *yeah, so answer it.* "I don't want to deal with him right now."

"What if it's important?"

"Fine," I respond, irritated at my father's intrusion. Swiping my finger across the screen, I answer. "Hello?"

"Serena, I finally reached you. It appears we've been playing phone tag."

"Uh-huh." Is he being sarcastic? Because, I haven't called him. "What's up?" My words come out sharp—a clear signal I want this conversation over with.

"Oh..." he draws out and pauses, sounding confused by my tone. "Your mother mentioned you were going to CU in the fall, and I talked with Katie. Well, I was wondering if you would like to live here with us?"

After all this time, he wants me to be a part of his life? Anger coils in my stomach.

"Hello?" he questions the silence.

"Thanks, but I'm good. I'm already set up to live in the dorms."

"Oh, okay." The disappointment is evident in his voice. "I hope we'll get to see you more once school starts."

"I only live thirty minutes away now, *Dad*. We could have seen each other plenty, but you've had other priorities."

"Serena. It's not like that."

"Oh, really? How is it then?"

"That's uncalled for."

"I disagree. Look, I'm with a friend. I have to go."

"Okay... sure. We can talk more another time."

I hang up. *So, now he's ready?* He's ignored me all these years, and what? He's ready for the AA's twelfth step to make amends?

"Are you okay?" Knox asks.

"Can we go to your place?" I need to move before I explode and make a fool of myself.

"Yeah."

Knox takes my hand and leads me out the back door, through the gate, and up the stairs while my thoughts rage. Once inside the apartment, I drop my backpack on the floor with a loud *thud*.

"He never talks to me." I throw my hands in the air. "And suddenly, he's inviting me to live with his family while I'm at school? What the hell?"

"Wouldn't that save you some money?" he asks slowly like he's unsure if questioning me is such a good idea.

"That's not the point." I begin to pace. "And to answer your question, no. My housing is covered as part of my scholarship. Why the sudden change?"

Knox doesn't answer. Just watches me with one hand squeezing the other in his lap. Realizing me losing my shit is making him uncomfortable, I wrap my arms around myself as if to contain all the anger that wants to explode out of my body.

"All I'm saying is that he can't just weasel his way back into my life and think everything's going to be fine. He avoided me after the crash. I don't think I mentioned that. He barely came to see me in the hospital. How twisted is that?" I shake my head at myself. I shouldn't be unloading on Knox this way.

"Maybe he felt guilty," he says cautiously. "And couldn't face you."

"It shouldn't have been about him."

"No... it shouldn't, but maybe he's realizing what he lost and is trying to make it right. People change. He called, didn't he? Offered you a place with his family? That has to count for something."

"I don't care what his intentions are or what his reasoning is. You of all people know how cruel indifference is," I snap. When his eyes hit the floor, I immediately want to slap myself for throwing his past in his face.

"I do, but I also know what it's like to regret choices and end up on the wrong side of where you want to be." With a hesitant tilt of his head, he peers at me through his pale lashes. "People change," he says again as if to drive the point home. "That's what you led *me* to believe."

I move to stand in front of him. "I understand the connection you're trying to make, but this is different. You were a scared kid making bad decisions. He was an adult. *Is* an adult."

He reaches for my hand and pulls me between his thighs. "Mistakes don't have an age limit."

I pick up the hem of his t-shirt and twist it around my fingers. "No. I guess not." I release the shirt and slide my hands up his chest and around his neck. "But aren't adults supposed to be the responsible ones?"

"*Supposed* to be." He encircles my waist with his arms and kisses my cheek, then the corner of my mouth, making me want to smile, but I'm still too pissed off to let it happen. Damn my father for ruining my night. "It's okay to be angry, but at some point, you have to let the bitterness go. It's toxic. I should know. I'm a nuclear fallout." He takes both of my hands in his and holds them to his chest. "I hate to see you hurt." His lips press softly against mine before retreating.

"That helps." I lift a hand and tap my lips. "Do it again." Everything about him elevates my world to a whole new level of good.

One side of his mouth inches up into a grin. "Is that your avoidance behavior talking?"

Even his smile, as small as it is, melts my anger, replacing it with deep affection and an enticing sensation I want to explore further. "No. It's your skills that are distracting me."

"Oh, yeah?" He lands another kiss, sweet and promising. "How?"

"Well, this." I kiss the corner of his upturned mouth. "But most of all, this." I lay a hand over his heart.

There's a moment of silence, one beat, then two, three, four. Suddenly, he scoops me up under my arms and strides out of the kitchen. I burst into laughter at the unexpected move, swinging my legs up and wrapping them tightly around his waist. My hands find their way behind his neck as I lean in, planting loud, smacking kisses beneath his ear.

CHAPTER 35

KNOX

I must be out of my mind.

Reaching the edge of the mattress, I drop a knee and place her in the center. She doesn't let go. Her legs and arms stay securely wrapped around me, playfully keeping us connected. *Shit. I didn't think this through.* All I know is that I want her in any way she'll have me. Sudden terror hits me.

What if she wants it all?

We've been close before, each time building to a level that never found release, but when her mouth finds mine, the fears disappear. A simple kiss becomes a frenzy of who can reach more skin, then clothes are coming off in rapid succession. My brain driven one hundred percent by a need I've only recently realized I was capable of.

The feel of her... all those soft curves.

Now, with only our underwear left on and her fingers slowly trailing down my stomach, my fear springs back to life. When she grips the hardness between my legs, a lightning bolt of mental garbage strikes me right through the center of my chest, causing me to break the kiss.

No, no, no. Not now.

I raise myself onto my forearms to get some distance and gaze down at her. A shy, sweet smile plays across her face, but it falters when her eyes lift to meet mine. She releases her hold on me.

"Are you okay?" she asks. The concern in her eyes torturing me.

My head drops into the crook of her neck. Why does it have to be this difficult? "I'm nervous." Fuck, this is embarrassing. I lift my head but can't meet her eyes. "Excited. Obviously." I wiggle my hips between her legs. "But being with someone I care about is... new to me."

"We don't have to do this if you're not ready."

I groan. "It's not that simple, and I'm not sure how to explain it without making myself look bad."

"It's okay. We can just talk."

She's almost naked underneath me. I'm not sure if I can concentrate.

No. The internal baggage rolling around in my head has other ideas. I don't have a choice.

"You can trust me, remember?" she says.

I did tell her that. When I try to move off her, she locks her legs around my waist and holds me in place. "Please don't leave."

"Let me just readjust." Still resting on my forearms, I keep my upper body over hers and shift the lower half to the bed. When I get settled, I trace the line of skin under her collarbone with my thumb. I need a moment to gather my thoughts. This isn't something I've ever talked about.

"There were always girls hanging around when I worked for

Fletcher. I'm not sure what their deal was, but they liked to get me wound up. Thing was, their touch always made my skin crawl. Fletcher's guys were always bragging about... you know." I drop my eyes. "They liked the attention. I thought there was something wrong with me. And as shitty as their hands on me felt, my body would respond anyway, and they'd take it as an invitation for more. By that point, I was too drunk, high, or embarrassed to stop." Usually, all three. "I'd feel like shit afterward, but..." I shake my head against the shame that's so easy to drown in. I can't believe I'm telling her this shit.

"That must have been an awful situation to be in—to be toyed with that way. You were what, sixteen, seventeen?"

"Yeah."

"I don't know what a male teenager's perception of sex is, but from what I understand, your hormones are kind of in control. And with the drugs and alcohol, you wouldn't have been thinking clearly. The regret you felt after is understandable, but you're a good guy, Knox, and you have a big heart."

"You sure about that?" She's too accepting. "I used those girls to get my fucking rocks off. I didn't want to, but I did it anyway." *But it was more than that.* I think, disgusted with myself. I desperately wanted to feel a connection. And if I closed my eyes, I could pretend like they actually cared. When it was all over, I hated myself. That's why being with Serena is so hard. I'm terrified of feeling that way with her. It would be devastating.

No. This is different.

She is different.

"You are more than your past, and that big heart may be buried under a life that, so far, hasn't been kind, but it's there. I see it in your protectiveness and in the way you share vulnerable parts of yourself that are difficult to talk about. I can feel it in the way you touch me." She brushes her lips against mine. "The way you kiss me." She strokes my upper arms with her hands. "Do you like it when I touch you?"

"God, yes," I groan. But is it enough, or will I hate myself when it's over?

Her hands fall to my hips. "Then come back to me."

There's a split-second pause before she guides me to her and the last layer of clothing is removed between gentle kisses.

The heat of her bare skin against mine...

This feels different in every way possible, but please, please don't let me fuck this up.

She stares up at me with warmth and affection in her eyes. No one has ever looked at me like that except Serena.

One beat, two, three...

Our lips collide in the middle of our shared space and all my negative thoughts go quiet. There's nothing but need as I'm taken over by the thrill of exploring every part of her. To make her feel the way she makes me feel. The intensity. It's overwhelming.

I didn't know.

Why did it take me so long to find her?

Every sensation...

We're frenzied, then slow and gentle. The way she smells, tastes, feels. Time disappears. Life outside of this space ceases to exist. And when I feel myself explode, shattering into a million pieces, I think this must be what heaven feels like.

Breathing hard, I lift my head from her neck and kiss her forehead, cheek, nose, and finally, her lips. Every touch bringing all those scattered parts of myself back together, leaving me feeling stronger and more whole than I ever have before.

CHAPTER 36

SERENA

We move and adjust our bodies to a more comfortable position. For me, that's my cheek resting on Knox's bare chest and a leg draped over his broad thighs.

The first time I had sex, I felt instant regret, but this was like discovering how it was truly meant to be.

I've never felt such an overwhelming sense of being valued… desired. And not in a superficial way, where the goal is all about the endgame.

No, this went beyond the need for physical satisfaction. This was about acceptance—something I think we both crave but don't trust easily.

"Was that okay?" The deep tenor of his words vibrates against my ear.

I should have anticipated how my silence would affect him. Lifting my head, our eyes meet across his chest and a huge smile blooms on my face. "It's not like I have a lot of experience in this area, but I would describe it as earth-shattering."

He frowns. "Don't make fun of me."

"I'm not!" My head pops up. My eyes fixing on his. "I don't know how to talk about this kind of stuff without turning beet red, so I'll rephrase by saying it meant everything to me." An understatement, but he nods with a hint of a smile. "And I'd like to do it again—you know..." I give him a playful nudge. "Just to make sure it wasn't a one-off."

A deep laugh rumbles in his chest as he runs a hand up the side of my leg and kisses my nose. "Thank you."

This sweet, beautiful human being. "No. Thank *you*." I beam up at him.

After Knox explained the sexual trauma he experienced as a teenager, I was worried being together would be too difficult for him. I can't imagine what it must have been like to be stuck in those situations he didn't really want to be in.

My fingertips trace lazy circles on his stomach, then trail up to his chest and the numbers tattooed over his heart. "Where do these coordinates lead?"

He covers my hand with his, flattening it over his heart. "Home."

I lift my gaze. "I don't understand."

"It's the coordinates to the only place I've ever felt safe." He hesitates. "Your house." Taking a deep breath, his eyes find mine with a vulnerability that squeezes my heart. "You. You are my home."

Not only has he laid himself bare, but the fortress he built to protect himself lies in ruins at my feet. With a tender smile, I stretch up so our faces are only inches away and give him something more valuable than a response—a kiss that says more than words ever could.

As the world fades into insignificance, I feel a tear slide down my cheek. It's not from sadness, but from an overwhelming sense of rightness, and the knowledge that the connection we share runs deeper than I could have ever imagined.

After saying goodnight and coming home, I light my Knox candle, then lie on my side, staring at the flame. I only removed myself from his bed out of respect for my mother. Otherwise, I'm not sure I would have ever left. The world be damned.

"You are my home." I'm still reeling from the mind-altering statement. Never in my wildest dreams would those words have come out of his mouth. It was a gift—the tattoo, his declaration, and the intimacy before and after. It's a memory I will cherish for the rest of my life.

The flame wavers, flickering upward in an almost hypnotic motion. The scent of Knox surrounds me as my eyes drift closed. Vivid images of his body, strong and beautiful, play like a powerfully romantic movie until there is nothing at all.

CHAPTER 37

SERENA

Tonight is our grad-class barbecue. It isn't a school-sponsored event, rather a cherished Saturday night tradition held two weeks before final exams. I couldn't bail on my friends since I didn't end up going to prom.

Knox and I had a memorable night of our own. No prom dress needed—or any clothes for that matter.

I can't help but be amazed by how everything has unfolded. Even with all its twists and turns and bruising bumps, I wouldn't change a single thing about it.

Quitting work on Saturdays was one of the smartest decisions I've made. We see each other every day, but having those uninterrupted weekends together is priceless.

We haven't talked about what will happen when I leave for college, but I know I don't want this to end. I love spending time with him. We explore the mountains, read, watch movies, listen to podcasts, talk about any and every topic imaginable. It's easy. It's perfect.

Tish and I are at Rowan's house getting ready. Since she has the biggest bedroom and a private bathroom, it's been our place to get ready ever since we started going out and caring about our appearances.

"Hey, can I wear this shirt?" I ask from inside Rowan's walk-in closet.

Rowan peeks her head around the doorway. "Yeah, sure. Pick out whatever. You know you don't have to ask."

"Thanks."

Coming up beside me, she swiftly browses through her selection of shirts and selects one. "But this one would complement your hair color better." I trade the shirt in my hand for the one she offers and quickly slip it on. "Is Knox coming tonight?" she asks with a playful smirk. "I'd like to officially meet the guy who's stolen my best friend away from me."

"He did not *steal me*, and no, he isn't."

"Why not?"

Knox has been consistently pushing his boundaries, finding new comfort levels all the time, so it only felt right to invite him. I know he won't come, but I wanted him to know he was welcome in every part of my life.

"He has an exam on Monday he needs to study for." The lie is easier than the truth of Knox not wanting anyone to know his struggles.

"Okay." She nods her head in agreement. "But I want to meet him soon. I'd like to get to know him. I was a bitch to him when we met."

"I want to meet him too," Tish calls out from the bathroom mirror where I left her layering foundation on her face.

"You will," I return loud enough for her to hear. I'm not sure how I'll swing it, but all I can do is try.

The barbeque is held in an open field on someone's property not far from town. When we arrive, the first person I notice is Hayden—his voice obnoxiously booming over the music. He's over by the fire with his new girlfriend tucked under his arm. It's hard to tell who's holding who up, being that they're both obviously wasted.

My friends and I walk past a picnic table of junk food, skirt the bonfire, avoiding Hayden, and find the rest of our group at the keg. Rowan throws her arms around Darius's neck and gives him a quick steamy kiss. "Pour me a beer," she demands.

"On it! Serena?"

"Yes, please."

Darius passes a large red cup to Rowan, picks up the tap, and starts filling one for me. "Tish, you want one?"

She cuddles up under Kai's arm. "Nope. I'm the designated driver."

Looking around, it seems to be a social free-for-all with no barriers between cliques. Jocks dance with the punk-rock kids. Stoners are talking with some of the student council members. With years and years of social segregation, it's fascinating to watch the scene as it plays out in front of us. The only downer is that Hayden keeps shooting eye daggers at me. *Seriously, dude. Knock it off!*

I feel like we've been here forever. It's only midnight, but I'm ready to go home. Rowan and Tish have been missing since they left for the bathroom half an hour ago, and the crackling warmth of the fire is making it near impossible to keep my eyes open. It's not surprising given the late night Knox and I had.

I'm smiling at the memory of a shirtless, rock-hard body in

the kitchen making us pancakes at one in the morning, when a heavy arm drapes over my shoulder, jolting me from my thoughts.

"Hey, beautiful," Hayden slurs. "You're looking fine, as usual."

Annoyed, I try to lift his arm away and tell him to back off. Instead, he leans in farther, burying his nose into my neck. "You smell good."

"Seriously? Get off me, Hayden." Again, I attempt to free myself, but he's leaning his full weight into me, making it difficult. I scan the area for Rowan and Tish, but they're nowhere in sight. Darius and Kai are nearby, but far enough away that I'd have to cause a scene to get their attention.

Well, shit.

"You know," Hayden says. "I thought I'd miss you more than I do, but a good fuck goes a long way."

He said what now?

"I know exactly what you mean," I smirk, finding an opening and twisting out of his hold. Having lost his support, he stumbles forward.

"You fucking slut," he hisses. Righting himself, he steps close and grips my jaw painfully, his eyes attempting to focus on my face.

I should be scared, but somehow, I'm just pissed. I yank my face from his hold. "Darius!" I holler, not caring who hears me anymore. When he turns around, I yell, "Get your boy away from me before his balls get knocked up into his throat."

Darius hustles over and takes Hayden's arm. "Hey, man. Let's go and get you another beer."

"That's the last thing he needs," I snap.

Hayden shoves Darius away and comes at me. Snaking an

arm around my body, he pulls me up against him. "I'm not done talking to you yet."

"Hayden. Stop." A hint of fear twists in my gut. "This isn't you, okay? You're drunk." I push against his chest, but at the same time, his other arm encircles my body, locking me in place.

"You'll spread your legs for him, but not me?"

I try lifting my knee in retaliation, but our bodies are too close, and his grip is too tight to wiggle free. Kai has joined us now, and both he and Darius are trying to talk him down and pull him away from me.

"Come on, baby. I deserve a piece," Hayden says, ignoring them both, his warm breath reeking of alcohol.

I turn my head as he tries to kiss me. "Get. Off. Me!" I holler, squirming and shoving in an attempt to free myself.

"You have two seconds to let her go," comes a cold, deep, familiar voice.

My head snaps sideways. Knox is standing two feet away with a lethal look in his eyes. "Hayden. Let me go. Now!" Trying to break free, I wiggle and twist some more, not wanting this to turn into any more of a shitshow than it already is.

"She's good at sucking cock, isn't she?" Hayden sneers right before he releases me and charges after Knox.

In a blink, Knox has him on the ground, a knee pressed into his stomach, throwing jackhammer punches. By the time any of us register what's happened, Hayden's face is covered in blood.

Now I'm screaming at Knox to stop while four guys attempt to drag him off. Knox is relentless, delivering several strong kicks to Hayden's upper body while finally being pulled out of reach.

Hayden doesn't move or make a sound. Terrified, I rush to his side and check for a pulse. When I feel it, I grip his shoulder. "Hayden, can you hear me?" No response. "Someone call 911," I shout to the crowd, then glance at Knox, witnessing the exact moment the blanket of rage pulls from his eyes and he sees the aftermath of what he's done.

I can't worry about him now. Hayden needs to make it through this or I could lose Knox forever. Taking off my jacket, I gently place it behind Hayden's battered head. I don't want him choking on his own blood. "Hayden? An ambulance is on its way." I don't care how much of a fuck-whit he is—he doesn't deserve to die.

When I look up again, Knox is gone. The background noise is a buzzing chatter. "Did you see that? Who was that guy? Is Hayden alive? Should we take him to the hospital? I called an ambulance. Should we call the police?"

Fear burst through me. *Please. No police. Don't make me turn Knox in.*

Hayden's body jerks, mumbled words I don't recognize come out of his mouth. "Don't move," I tell him. "Help is on the way." He passes out again, but I continue to reassure him until the paramedics reach us. I give a brief explanation to the EMTs, then move out of their way.

With my arms gripping my middle, I watch the horrific scene in front of me. I can't believe this is happening. Rowan and Tish appear next to me, each wrapping an arm around my waist as the medical team does their job.

As soon as they lift Hayden into the back of the ambulance, my fears turn toward Knox. "We have to find Knox," I say to my friends as I pick up each of their hands with my own.

Rowan yanks her grasp from mine. "Are you crazy? Did you see what he just did?"

My hands are back around my middle—my body shaking

from the trauma of everything that just happened. "He was protecting me."

"Protecting you?" she sputters. "He's a homicidal lunatic!"

I think about his mother, about Annie, his abusive foster parents, and all the things that went into making him protective of the people he cares about. "You don't understand," I say, feeling panic-stricken as the desperate need to make sure he's okay takes over.

"No, I don't understand," she says. "And I'm not sure if you do either. I don't give a shit *what* he thought he was doing, or what his issues are," she rages. "I am not bringing you to him."

"Rowan, calm down," Tish says. "This isn't helping. Serena, we're just concerned."

"Where were you?" I snap at both of them. "Did either of you see what Hayden was doing to me?"

"That doesn't justify—" Rowan says, but I cut her off.

"He wouldn't let go. He was hurting me, and no one was helping. Knox shouldn't have lost it the way he did, but he was protecting *me* the way no one ever protected him. The way"—I throw my arms in a circle, including Darius and Kai, who just walked up—"the way none of you did. And not just tonight. At school and at the party where Knox had to step in that first time."

No one says a word. Suddenly, I'm exhausted and turn to Tish. "Please take me home." Then I walk away.

As Tish unlocks the door, Rowan is the first to speak up. "Are you hurt?"

"I'll probably have bruises, and I feel sick to my stomach, but I'll be fine."

As I slide into the passenger's seat, all I can think about is getting home so I can jump in my car and check on Knox.

"I'm sorry." Rowan grips my shoulder from the back seat. "For everything, but we're here for you now."

"Anything you need." Tish glances over.

Their words barely register, drowned out by the overwhelming torrent of fear consuming my heart.

As soon as Rowan and Tish drop me off, I walk inside the house and wait by the window for them to leave. Mom is asleep. I should probably tell her what's going on, but she'll ask too many questions, and I'm afraid she'll try to stop me from seeing Knox. I have to make sure he's okay and tell him that Hayden is alive. He needs to know he's not the monster he thinks he is. I don't want him to do anything stupid.

Like run away.

CHAPTER 38

KNOX

Fuck, fuck, fuck! Her friends could have handled it if I'd just waited a little longer. But I couldn't stand there and watch as she struggled to free herself.

One minute, I was pissed at the sight of his arm around her shoulder, the next minute, I lost my fucking mind. After the first punch was thrown, nothing else existed. I didn't see the red covering his face. I didn't hear Serena's pleas for me to stop, or the screaming from everyone watching. And when it was all over, and I was standing next to his lifeless form, it was Denver all over again.

I fucking ran.

I'm a long way from home, but taking a bus isn't an option. My legs are lead beneath my body as I run, but I continue to push myself. I need to lock myself behind my door and never come out.

An image of Serena looking up at me from Hayden's body...

the fear in her eyes... I stumble toward a patch of bushes and lose everything in my stomach. I never wanted her to see that part of me. I'm almost twenty fucking years old! You'd think I'd have better control by now.

Needing the safety of my apartment, I straighten and force my legs to move—one step, two, three—berating myself with each movement as I urge my legs to move faster. *Get home. Get home and disappear.*

My clothes are soaked in sweat. I can't feel my legs anymore and I'm near ready to pass out when I round the corner and see Serena's car already parked next to the garage. Freezing in my tracks, I try to hide the sound of me sucking in air past scalding, constricted lungs. Then, slowly, as quietly as I can, I backtrack, taking myself around the other side of the garage.

Crouching down, I drop my head. With one hand on the ground for support, I start counting backward in my head from a hundred.

My fingers slide over the tattooed coordinates on my chest, clutching at them. But they're just ink, useless now that I've lost my sanctuary—the one place, the one person who ever made me feel whole.

For an hour, I wait as Serena alternates between sitting on the top step and pounding on the door, begging and threatening me to open up and talk to her. Of all the possible reactions, her concern shreds me the most. How can she still care about me after what I did? Can she not see the evil inside me for what it is?

At one point, I hear her say Hayden is alive and she thinks he's going to be okay. I am torn between being thankful and thinking he got off easy.

I'm definitely a sick fuck.

When her voice turns tear-filled, it cuts me deep and bleeds me out. I'm about to step out of my hiding spot and go to her when I hear the creaking of steps as she makes her way down. When her engine starts, then fades down the alley, I make my way up to the apartment, my body growing heavier with every step I take.

Once inside, I lock the door behind me. I'm freezing from being out in the cool air with sweat-soaked clothes.

What time is it?

I see my phone sitting on the counter and pick it up. There are five calls and twelve texts from Serena, all words of concern. It's too much, all of it. Shivering, I slide my back down the wall until I hit the floor, then pull my knees to my chest.

How long will it take for the police to come knocking?

With the crowd of people witnessing what I did, there's no chance I'm getting away with this. Golden Boy will be pressing charges for sure.

Not that it matters. I would do it again in a heartbeat. No way I'm standing by and watching someone get brutalized—especially not Serena.

I wake up in the dark sometime later, lying on the floor, my neck and back seized from the awkward position I settled into. I stare at my hand stretched out in front of me. It's covered in dried blood, swollen to twice its size, and as numb as the arm attached to it.

The thought of moving seems like too much of an effort, but I know I need to—my mouth is grossly dry, and my bladder close to exploding. Exhaling heavily, I use my good hand to push myself to a seated position.

As soon as I'm vertical, all the blood rushes down my arm, needling its way into the bad one. It throbs like a motherfucker.

Rising to my feet, I sway a bit before finding my balance, then make my way to the kitchen for some water.

After using the bathroom and gently washing Hayden's dried blood off my hands, I return to the kitchen for another drink and check the time. Four in the morning. It's Sunday, and thankfully, I don't have to work. The thought of leaving the house has panic reaching up and gripping its steely fingers around my throat.

No, no, no. This can't happen. If I can't work, I'm completely screwed.

Just breathe.

Crouching down, the focus shifts to controlling my breath. *In for four, hold, out for four, hold.* Serena fills my thoughts—big fucking mistake. Every good memory I have is of her, and now, instead of bringing me peace, it reeks of pain and heartache.

"What's the fucking point?" I explode, my non-injured hand punching the floor after every word.

Sitting back on my heels, I clench my throbbing hands in my lap. Anything to drown out the torment raging inside my head.

Serena will be questioned. Thoughts of her having to go through that makes me hate myself even more.

Did she lie about knowing me? Maybe she left before the cops questioned her.

Is that why they haven't come yet?

I don't want her to get into trouble because of me.

Standing up, I walk to the bed and lie down with my head at the foot, then stare out the windows at the night sky until the anger fades and a crushing sadness takes over.

I think I prefer the anger.

After staring into the darkness for what feels like hours, reality begins to sink in.

If I don't do something to help my hands, it won't matter if I can get my ass out the door to work—they'll be useless. And that's assuming, by some miracle, I'm not thrown in jail.

I maneuver to the edge of the bed until my feet land with a *thud* on the floor, then lift myself against the heavy weight that's pressing on my shoulders. I'm even more lightheaded now, stumbling my way to the fridge and bracing myself on the counter as I go.

When I grip the freezer door, the pain that shoots through me just about knocks me to my knees. Puffing out several breaths to amp myself up, I force my least-injured fingers around the handle. "Fuck!" I holler when I grip and pull.

Once the door is open, I take out two bags of frozen peas I use for sore muscles, then use my shoulder to bump the door closed. I throw the bags on the counter, then rest the backs of my hands on them, sucking in a sharp breath at the instant bite of pain.

In small movements, I open and close my fingers. I don't think anything is broken. A small miracle in the midst of my hell.

CHAPTER 39

KNOX

A loud noise jolts me awake. My heart races, pounding against my ribs as I squint at the fading light in the sky. *Is it early morning or evening?*

Three sharp bangs hit the door and I'm jumping out of bed, instantly regretting the quick action as I stumble forward, lightheaded again. My eyes blink and adjust through the silver flecks flashing across my vision, while knots of unease clog my throat in anticipation of the shitstorm ahead.

Will the panic come when the police take me in? Will I pass out on the way to the cruiser? Maybe I'll fall down the stairs, break my neck, and escape the ordeal altogether.

"Who is it?" I shout, sweat already trickling down my back.

"You okay?" Rhett's voice muffles through the door. "You didn't come to dinner, and Serena's car isn't here, so *that's* not the reason."

I press my forehead against the doorframe. A reprieve from total disaster, but for how much longer?

"I'm sick," I tell him, thinking fast. "I better not open up."

"Okay. Do you need anything? Want me to bring you some food?"

"No. I'm not hungry, but thank you," I say, suddenly overwhelmed with gratitude that someone is looking out for me.

"Well, I'll leave you be then. I take it you won't be coming to work tomorrow?"

My skin prickles with apprehension. "No, it may be a couple of days." *What if it's forever?*

"Feel better. I'll check on you tomorrow."

"You don't have to. I'll be fine." He'll bully me into opening the door. I don't want him to see how broken I am. He found me at my lowest. I can't let him see me there again.

"I said I'll check on you, and that's what I'm going to do."

"Okay." I feel the corner of my mouth edge up slightly. *Pushy bastard.* "'Night, Rhett."

"'Night, boy."

The affectionate nickname he uses fills up some of the emptiness inside. I touch the screen on my phone to check the time, but it's dead. The stove clock tells me it's eight-thirty. *Shit. I slept all day.* I'm tempted to charge my phone, but why torture myself? Serena needs to take my silence as a hint and let me go.

I'm not sure how many days passed before Rhett uses his key and finds me lying in bed on my side, staring at the wall. "You look like hell, son. Come on over and have some of this soup I made you." My eyes follow him as he sets a large bowl on the kitchen island.

When I don't move, he comes and sits next to me, resting the back of his hand on my forehead. "No fever. You want to tell me what's going on? I'm pretty sure that vacant stare has nothing to do with being sick, and everything to do with those battered hands. They look horrible."

My response is to slide them under my pillow, out of sight.

When the silence stretches between us, he heaves out a sigh. "Look at me, son." When I don't, he says it again, more forcefully. Slowly, my eyes lift to his. "What the hell is going on with you?" When I let my eyes drop again, he says, "Oh, no, you don't! Talk to me, damn it."

I just want to be left alone.

"Is Serena okay?" I hear the fear in his voice.

At the sound of her name, the wall behind Rhett becomes blurry as hot tears fill my eyes. I quickly turn my face into the pillow, wiping them away. I never cry.

"Okay, okay," he soothes. "I'm here, but I can't help if you don't tell me what happened."

I can't find the words. They would only disappoint him, anyway.

"Son, you need to let it out before it eats you alive, you hear me? Whatever it is. Just tell me."

With my emotions barely in check, I roll onto my back and rest my hands on my stomach. "He was hurting Serena again."

"Who was?" Rhett demands, shooting up from his relaxed position.

"Hayden, her ex-boyfriend. I couldn't control myself. I... I could have killed him. I didn't but—"

"Are the police involved?" he interrupts, alarm in his voice.

"Not yet, but I've been expecting them."

He sighs. "You're not the first man to see red when someone

they care about is being hurt. Look at me." I stare up into thoughtful eyes—bright and full of purpose. "That doesn't make you a monster. That makes you human."

As the words sink in, the knot of guilt in my chest loosens slightly.

"Rage is a scary thing. It can take over for different reasons—sometimes good, sometimes bad. Now, when someone you *love* is brutalized—" My eyes snap to his. "Don't look so shocked. You love that girl. It's plain as day. Well, maybe not to you, but I'm thinking you don't have much experience with the notion, being as how you were raised."

My heart feels like it's being squeezed in a vise—the idea too painful to consider.

"We've already had words about that situation in Denver. No point going over old ground, but I *will* say that I'm proud of you for not running this time. Although, holing yourself up here until the consequences come callin' isn't too bright. You don't need to deal with this alone, you hear me? It ain't healthy."

Rhett pats my arm affectionately. "Now, listen here. You've become a fine young man, and I'm proud to stand by your side, helping anyway possible."

I choke back a sob at Rhett's unwavering support and stare at the ceiling, sucking in a deep breath, trying to gain back control.

"Now, now," he comforts. "You're going to be okay. Have you talked to Serena since it happened?" I shake my head, unable to speak over the tightness burning in my throat. "I didn't think so. You wear that guilt around your neck like a noose. You don't take it off, you're liable to choke. Talk to her. I'm sure she's scared and hurting too."

I clear my throat. "I can't."

"And why the hell not?"

"I'm no good for her. It's better that our relationship ends here."

"There you go again, knocking yourself down, thinking it's easier than fighting for what you want. *Tell* me I'm wrong."

Not having the energy to argue, I shrug.

"You're just scared. Scared she'll leave, change her mind, or not love you back. Love is scary. Damn, right it is." He emphasizes with a nod. "Scary for the best of us, let alone someone with *your* past. Trust is hard, too... but you trust me, right?"

"Yeah." More than anyone I've ever known.

"Then don't be afraid to extend it to another person, especially one as worthy as that girl."

I do, but fear and doubt are buried deep, and after what happened, won't cut loose. But it isn't just that. "What if we fight and I get so angry I lose control? Being alone might be the best thing. I've been doing okay so far."

"Have you?"

"Well enough."

"That's a matter of opinion, and mine says it's horseshit. She's good for you. I saw you coming out of that protective shell of yours." Rhett stands up. "Now, it's time to get out of that damn bed and take a shower. You stink to high heaven. And please, for the love of all that's holy, eat something. You look half-starved. Reminds me of the first day I found you up here, almost frozen to death. When was the last time you ate?"

"I don't remember."

"Your mind will be clearer once you get some food in your belly." He walks to the door and rests a hand on the knob. "Now, can I expect you at work tomorrow?"

I brace myself for the rush of panic at the idea of leaving the apartment. When it doesn't come, relief washes over me. The talk helped. I lift my hands and examine them. "I'm not sure if I can."

"Let's get them X-rayed so we know what we're dealing with."

I shake my head. "I can't." There's no way I could handle being closed in around that many people I don't know. Not right now.

"You will," he says forcefully. "Don't fight me on this. You know I'll win."

Prickling fear claws its way across my body. He's right, though. We should find out. And as much as I hate to do it, I'll have to take my anxiety medicine. "Okay."

"Good boy. Now, get up. You need to eat."

Inching myself to the side of the bed, I stand up. As I do, a wave of dizziness crashes over me. My hand shoots forward, landing on the wall in front of me for support as my vision starts to dim and the edges fade to black. But the severe pain in my hand has me recoiling.

"Damn it, Knox." Rhett rushes to my side, gripping my arm as my body sways. "Sit back down. You're too big for me to hold up if those tree-trunk legs of yours give out."

I do as he says, then drop my head between my knees until my eyes clear and I feel more stable. The hand I used as a brace is now throbbing beyond belief. *Shit. Maybe it is broken.*

"You need to stop torturing yourself and eat, you hear me?" Even as his words bite with anger, I know he's only concerned.

"Yes, sir." After a few minutes, I stand again, even slower this time, and let Rhett guide me to the kitchen island. The room is spinning, but it stops a few seconds after I sit on a stool.

Rhett uncovers the soup in front of me and goes to scrounge up a spoon. When the incredible smell reaches my nose, my stomach grumbles in hunger. He sets the utensil next to the bowl. Since it's too painful to grip with my right hand, I try with my left. Thankfully, it's bearable.

The moment the soup hits my tongue and the warmth trails down my throat, settling in my stomach, tears prick my eyes. *Get it fucking together, Knox!*

"This is so good. Thanks, Rhett," I say without looking up.

He pats me on the back. "You bet." I take another bite, then another. "When you're feeling strong enough, take a shower, then I'll take you to the emergency room for those X-rays."

"Yes, sir."

"Stop that 'sir' nonsense. You know I hate it." He moves to the door. "You'll come and find me when you're ready?"

"Yup."

"Will you be okay on your own? Or... do you need me to help you?"

He sounds just as put off by the idea of helping me shower as I am. "No. I can manage. I'll get ready as quickly as I can. I know it's getting late."

"Take your time. I don't want you hurting yourself worse." He opens the front door.

"I know it's not my place, but call Serena. I'm sure she's worried sick."

When I don't respond, he says, "Stubborn as a mule." And shuts the door behind him.

CHAPTER 40

SERENA

Walking into AP calculus, I take a seat at my desk. Lately, my concentration has been crap. Saying goodbye to becoming valedictorian seems inevitable now. I'd nearly convinced myself it didn't matter, but it's been a goal since freshman year. It's harder to let go than I thought. And considering how that history test went yesterday... I'm sure my chances are already gone.

It's been an agonizing six days since the class barbeque, and I can honestly say, I've never experienced this kind of misery before. When my father exited my life, I struggled, but it was a gradual process, shifting slowly from denial toward acceptance. But with Knox, it's a direct stab to the heart. I've called, texted, and stopped by. Each day he ignores me, it feels like the blade jabbed in my heart is twisting and driving the pain in deeper.

If I could just get him to open the door...

Desperation grips my chest. If he'd just see me, talk to me...

he'd know I'm not mad, that I don't blame him for his actions. He was protecting me.

What if I talked to Rhett? Would he help me?

I could wait by his truck first thing in the morning. Knox would be on his way to work. There's no way he could ignore me.

Maybe that's what I should do. I mean, this can't be the end. Not after everything we've shared. A loud noise breaks me from my thoughts. A girl toward the front of the class picks her toppled book off the floor while the teacher, still pointing at a whiteboard full of equations, gives her an irritated look.

I glance down at my notebook, which is completely blank. I am so screwed.

Hayden is waiting by my locker after the last bell. I stop as soon as I see him, ready to turn around, but his swollen, bruised eyes lock onto mine. Even though I'm shaking with adrenaline at the idea of a confrontation, I can't back down. "What do you want?" I attempt to keep my voice controlled when I reach him.

"I just wanted to apologize."

"Not interested." I turn the dial on my lock, willing him away.

"I talked to my parents." My fingers pause. "They wanted me to press charges against—what's his name again, Knox?" My eyes dart to his, fear swirling in my gut. "They would have forced my hand if I didn't tell them everything—well, almost everything. After Darius and Kai told me what I did, I decided to keep out the worst part. And I don't blame the guy. If roles were reversed, I would have kicked my ass too." The corner of his mouth lifts and drops. "They've set me up in a program."

Completing the combination, I pull the lock open. "That's

good." The need to find out more pulls at me, but the tension of being near him outweighs the desire for answers.

"Could we... maybe talk again once I get my shit sorted out? See where it goes?"

Is he seriously trying to get back together? Anger flairs past the uneasiness. "Hayden—"

He quickly raises a hand. "Don't answer that." Leaning down, he kisses my cheek, then pauses near my ear. "Thanks for listening."

My hands fly up between us and I shove him back. "Stay out of my space, Hayden."

His face falls. "Wow. I *really* fucked up."

"More than you know."

He nods his head in acknowledgement and steps around me. Instantly, I breathe a sigh of relief.

"Hey," Hayden calls out. When my head snaps in his direction, he's walking backward down the busy hallway. "I heard you and Knox aren't together anymore. I'm sorry if I ruined your chances with him, but also, kind of not." With a sheepish half-smile, he shrugs a shoulder, then pivots and disappears into the swarm of students.

Prick.

I get what I need and slam my locker closed. He's getting off way too easy, but at least he's not pressing charges. It's a small consolation, but it's something.

What did I ever see in him?

If I'd just listened to my gut and ended things when I knew Hayden and I were done, Knox wouldn't be in this situation, and maybe we'd still be happy.

I shake my head at how stupid I've been.

Never again.

Before driving out of the school parking lot, I shoot Knox a text, hoping the news of Hayden not pressing charges will prompt him to text back.

I sit in my car a full five minutes, waiting for a response. But it never comes.

By the time I pull up to the nursing home, Knox still hasn't responded. Maybe he lost or broke his phone in the fight. Or maybe I just never knew him at all. Whatever the reason, my stomach hurts all the time and I'm barely sleeping. Thankfully, it's Friday and I don't have to work tomorrow. The emotional weight on top of exams coming up, I'm wiped. I can barely make it out of bed most mornings.

He has to know how much his avoidance is affecting me, right?

Does he just need more time?

Is it over between us?

I don't want it to be. Maybe I'm a fool, but the bond we have... it's messy, yeah. Complicated, sure. But when we're together, he brings out all my best parts. I feel respected, adored.

He's changed so much in the short time we've been together. Not just in his confidence, but in the way his personality has come alive. He's funny—in a dry sense of humor way. He's intelligent, thoughtful, affectionate. Easy to be around.

No. I can't let it end. It's worth fighting for, and I refuse to sit back and let his fear and insecurity destroy it.

I park my car at work. Motivated with new purpose, this is the last place I want to be. As soon as I enter the building, the receptionist tells me Joan wants to talk to me. *Great. What now?*

The Witch looks up from her desk when I walk in. "Oh, Serena. Thanks for coming in. Shut the door and have a seat."

I run through everything I might have done wrong, but I come up blank. "Is everything okay?"

"I wanted you to hear it from me. I'm sorry to report that Stuart passed away last night."

Her words deliver an emotional sucker-punch, instantly knocking the life out of me.

No, no, no. Not this, not now. As my heart cracks further down the middle, Joan fades into a wavy blur of tears.

"He went peacefully in his sleep. I knew this would be hard on you, so I wanted to give you privacy when you found out. I'm sorry, Serena. I know how much you cared for him." She hands me a tissue.

"Thank you." I manage to get past the massive lump blocking my throat. This is part of the job, but Stuart was special to me, like Agnes and Bertha. I thought I had more time.

This hurts. *Really, really* hurts.

"I understand if you want to give yourself a day or two to grieve."

My mind races over everything. Over nothing. "I'd like to see Bertha and Agnes before I go. Do they know?"

"Yes, they know, and it's okay for you to see them as long as you can control your emotions. This is still a professional establishment, and as an employee, you must maintain the appropriate decorum."

"Right." I understand professionalism, but could she not show a hint of compassion?

I stand up on shaky legs and leave the office on the way to the bathroom. When I see the storage room door, I let myself in, needing a moment of privacy the bathroom or the employee locker room can't give me.

Tucking myself into a back corner, I slide my back down the

wall, pull my legs up, and curl myself into a ball. With my head buried into my knees, the tears fall as I sob uncontrollably.

Stuart's death on top of everything else... it's too much. I should have visited him more. I didn't even get to say goodbye. The thought only adds to the misery that has been pulling me into a deep, dark space over the past week, drowning me.

A passing cart with a squeaky wheel startles me. The last thing I need is to be hauled into Joan's office for another lecture on employee decorum. I take a deep, shuddering breath and reach up beside me to grab a roll of toilet paper off the shelf. The stack tilts, then rains down on top of me.

Perfect.

I unwrap a roll, wipe my eyes, and blow my nose, then force myself to stand. Cracking the door open, I check to see if the hall is clear. Seeing that it is, I quickly make my way to the restroom and slip inside. At the sink, I wash my face with cold water, then move to one of the stalls and wait for the puffy redness to subside. I need to see Agnes and Bertha. For me, but also for them. I know they'll be worried about me.

When I feel like enough time has passed, I unlock the door and study my reflection in the mirror. Nope, I can't go out there like this. My face is covered with raised red blotches, and against my ridiculously pale skin, I look diseased. Maybe it's better if I hold off the visit with The Ladies until tomorrow. I don't want to lose my job because I can't control my emotions.

I hurry past several people to the employee locker room, which, thankfully, is empty. I change out of my scrubs, grab my stuff, and leave through a side exit. When I get to my car, I text Knox and tell him that Stuart passed away and that I really need him. If using my pain gets him to talk to me, I don't care—not anymore.

He couldn't possibly ignore me this time. He's not that heartless.

A wave of regret washes over me the moment I hit send. Having him reply out of pity would suck. But him not replying at all would be even worse.

I wait in my car, hoping for a quick response, but I don't get one. Even as the knife in my heart twists in deeper, I give him the benefit of the doubt and go through every possible excuse I can think of. Deep down, I know.

I've lost him for good.

My devastation is complete.

My vision is blurry from new tears, my brain muddled, and still, I can't stop needing to see him. Neither can I stop the overpowering desire to make this right. So, I let my annihilation take over and drive to see Rhett.

It's early evening when I park in front of his house and climb the porch steps. After knocking, I stare off into the yard, feeling drained and wrung out.

Just as I'm thinking he's probably not home from work yet, the door whips open, startling me.

"Serena? What's wrong?" Rhett looks me over.

"I'm sorry. I know I shouldn't be here." The words sound strangled as I fight not to cry.

"Come in." He steps back, inviting me forward. "Are you hurt? Did something happen?"

As soon as I'm in the house, the words spill. "Have you talked to Knox? He won't... speak to me. Do you know if he's okay?"

With a small shake of his head, he drops his eyes to the floor. "Mostly," he says with a resigned sigh.

I shouldn't be putting Rhett on the spot, pumping him for

information like this, but I'm glad I'm here. It makes me feel closer to Knox. "Sorry again for showing up like this. I didn't know what else to do. So, he didn't leave town?"

"No."

Relief that he didn't run washes over me. "Okay... that's good."

"But all this"—he gestures with concern, acknowledging my emotional state— "is because of Knox?"

"Not all of it. I lost someone today." Once again, the hurt steamrolls me and the tears fall.

Rhett pats my back awkwardly. "I'm so sorry to hear about someone dying so young."

"It." *Hiccup.* "Was." *Sniff.* "Stuart." *Cough.* "He is... *was* from the nursing home I work at."

"Awe, hell. I'm so sorry." He takes me by the arm and gently leads me to a big, overstuffed, dark-brown couch. "I'll go and get you a glass of water."

"I shouldn't be here bothering you. I feel so stupid, showing up here."

"Don't you dare feel bad for reaching out," he says, walking away. I hear water running in the kitchen, then he's back, handing me a glass, a box of tissues, and sitting beside me. "As far as Knox, it's not my business to speak for him, but I *can* say his demons have a tight hold on him right now. Be patient, but also don't let him push you away—don't give up."

I wasn't going to, but then Stuart... and he couldn't be bothered to text me back.

After wiping my eyes and dripping nose, I take a drink of water. "Did he tell you what happened?"

"He did."

"That's good. I was afraid he was dealing with this all by himself. I feel better knowing he talked to you."

"You're a good girl, Serena. Give him time. Now..." He pats my hand. "I took some fresh blueberry muffins out of the oven right before you stopped by. How about you come share some with a lonely old man?"

I'm reminded of Stuart, and the painful realization that he had no family by his side when it mattered most hits me full force. I grab another tissue, briefly cover my eyes, and take a deep breath, trying to gain some control, then say, "I'm so glad you and Knox have each other."

"That makes two of us. Come on into the kitchen," he says, his voice gentle as he stands. "Do you want tea or some coffee?"

Lifting myself off the couch, I take hold of my glass and box of tissues. "No, thank you. Water is fine." My arms and legs feel like they're made of cooked spaghetti as I trail behind him.

I'm physically and mentally wiped, but as I sit at the table, picking at my blueberry muffin while telling Rhett about Stuart, some of the heaviness lifts from my chest. It's not the same as talking to Agnes and Bertha, but it helps.

After the visit, I drive around to the back and park between Rhett's truck and the garage. Knox still hasn't texted me back. *Is he so wrapped up in torment that no one else matters?*

Rhett's words repeat in my head: "Give him time."

I've given him plenty of time, I shout in my head. I'm breaking apart, and he doesn't even care. He has no right to cut me off without a word. I know he's hurting, but so am I.

Once again, that panicked feeling of needing answers grips me uncomfortably. *Screw it.*

Climbing out of the car, I make my way up the steps to his place. I knock on the door, getting more anxious the longer it remains closed until I'm banging my fist against it. "Open the door, Knox! I'm not going to stop until you answer."

Rhett said not to give up. This is me not giving up.

When the door opens a crack, a sense of triumph and relief almost puts me to my knees. I breathe easy for the first time since the fight until I see his gaunt face and dark circles below glassy blue eyes. "Knox?"

I take a step forward, reaching for him, but he holds up a hand. "Don't," he warns sharply.

"Okay." I step away. *He's not ready.* As much as I hurt right now, I can't make this solely about me, right? I'm just grateful he opened the door.

To both Knox and my surprise, the door opens wider. "Aren't you going to introduce your girlfriend to your ol' dad?"

"Dad?" I question, my brow furrowed. Knox tries to shut the door, but the man blocks it.

"Oh, come on now, Gabriel. Don't be like that. She's a pretty young thing. You okay, honey? You look like you've been crying."

"Shut the hell up," Knox snaps, shooting him a lethal glare before turning to me. "Serena, *leave.* You can't be here right now."

"You said your father was dead." The man standing next to him looks nothing like Knox. He opens his mouth to respond, but the man behind him cuts him off.

"Well, my beautiful girl, as you can see, I'm very much alive. Why don't you come in and join us?"

"She's leaving," Knox growls. Shoving the man back, he steps outside and shuts the door behind him. "Now's not a good time," he says, his words flat and emotionless. *After everything, that's all I get?* "I don't know why my father is here, but it isn't safe."

Right now, safety is the least of my concerns. "Have you read any of my texts?"

"My phone's dead, and I'm not interested in recharging it."

What? Why not? And why won't he look at me?

His jaw clenches. "I need you to go."

"You don't have to protect me. I know all about your past, remember?" When I reach out to take his hand, he flinches away with an expression close to revulsion. "What did I do wrong? I don't understand. If this is about the fight, it's okay. I understand. What we have..."

"Is what?" he asks. "So special that you let Hayden kiss you?" He looks me over like something dead in the street.

What? My gut clenches from the impact of his statement, but it's nothing compared to the hatred I see in his eyes. I feel like I'm going to be sick. "What are you talking about?"

"I was at school today." His voice strains with controlled anger. "I saw you with that—that loser. I couldn't believe you were talking to him, and then you *fucking* let him kiss you." His gaze sharpens, cold and accusing. "He's an abusive drunk, and you just forgave him? Let him touch you?"

"It wasn't like that, he—"

"I don't want to hear it," he cuts me off. "It's *over*. I don't want any part of this. I went through that shit with my mother, and there's no way I'm going through it with you."

"But he was just—"

"How long have you been playing me?"

"I haven't. Knox." I lift my hand and drop it. "Don't do this. *Please.*"

He reaches behind him and grips the doorknob. "Hear what I'm saying, Serena, and hear it clearly. Don't text me. Don't call me. And don't *ever* come back here." He turns the knob, steps in, and slams the door behind him without a backward glance.

I stare at the closed door, shaking all over. *I don't—what happened? Oh, god.* I double over, feeling gut-punched and sick. Tears blur my vision as I gasp for air. *He thinks I'm back with Hayden?*

There's yelling from inside the apartment, but I rush down the stairs as fast as my legs will carry me. I'm going to throw up.

When I reach the bottom, I lean forward and rest my hands on my knees, taking deep breaths against the nausea. He didn't let me explain. The way he looked at me... I would *never*.

How could he think I would want Hayden back in my life?

How can he think so little of me?

When the urge to puke subsides into queasiness, I let myself in the car, start the engine, and drive blindly to my house. Feeling rejected, humiliated, and confused, I want nothing more than to climb under my covers and never resurface again.

CHAPTER 41

KNOX

My father was right. She'd been crying, and seeing the pain my words caused cut me, but not as deep as watching her cozy up to her ex today. It's like every bad thing he did to her never happened. And after what I did to protect her?

But it's more than that. The moment my father knocked on my door twenty minutes ago, I knew I had to shield her from whatever shitstorm was about to rain down. Seeing her with her ex today just made it that much easier. I still can't believe she played me. I feel like such a fool.

"You shouldn't treat her like that, Gabriel. She's an innocent. I can tell."

"Shut the hell up." My hands clench into fists at my side, but I ignore the pain. "Don't think about her. Don't talk about her, or I'll—"

"You'll what? Kick my ass?" He smirks. "Do what you always wanted to do before but never could?"

"Don't tempt me, you lowlife piece of shit." My chest heaves with rage. He's right. I'd like nothing more than to make him pay for all the pain he caused me and my mom, but right now, I just want him out of here.

A sudden realization hits me like a roundhouse kick to the gut. "How did you find me?" If *he* could track me down, then Fletcher already has. Panic spikes my system into fight-or-flight mode. *Fuck.* I scream in my head.

"Well, *Knoxy*," he screws with the name just to piss me off. "I have a very talented friend who hacked into the Department of Motor Vehicles. You were easy to find. Did you know there are only two people in all of Colorado with the middle name Knox, and only twenty-five with the first name? And here you are in the same town you were born in. Were you *trying* to hide?" he chuckles like I'm an idiot.

My knuckles crack as I squeeze my throbbing hands tighter. Fight mode, it is. "Why are you here?" I grind out as anger mixes with the fear that's spreading through my body like a noxious plague.

"I owe a lot of dangerous people money and—"

"And you expect me to do what, exactly?"

"Well, I asked myself, 'Who do I know that might help me out?' I thought since we were family, you'd be my best bet. I need money to get out of the country and disappear."

"You should have just stayed dead."

Why hasn't Fletcher made his move? I wipe the icy sweat from my forehead with the sleeve of my sweatshirt while the rest trickles down my back. No one around me is safe anymore.

"I tried to, but, well... it's a complicated story. Best you don't know the details. Hey. You're not looking too good. Are you okay?"

Ignoring his question, I walk to the kitchen and fill a glass with water—my mouth uncomfortably dry. "How much will it take to get you out of my space?"

"Five grand should do it."

As soon as my father is gone, I'm leaving town to figure out my next step. The thought of having to abandon my home permanently adds another layer to my misery. "Fine. Then you'll leave?"

"Sure, son," he says, glancing around my apartment.

"Don't call me that! You lost that right the first time you hit me."

"Fair enough. But in my defense, I wasn't in a good place back then."

"And now you are?" I bite back.

"I'm not beating on little kids, *that's* for damn sure."

"Just women?" I sneer. "How does someone do that, anyway? Beat up people who can't defend themselves. Does it make you feel better? Give you power? Did you even care about me at all?"

"Hey, now." His expression turns hard. "That's enough! I've made some mistakes, but your mother was a mess."

"And *you're* the reason," I holler, taking a step toward him.

He holds up his hands, making me stop. "You can't pin your mother's shit on me."

"Fucking right, I can. You're the sperm donor who got the girl pregnant, decided to play house, and when *that* didn't work out, drank yourself into a stupor and beat the hell out of us, and for what?"

"Gabriel, I—"

"Stop calling me that!"

"It's your *damn* name."

"Stop." I close my eyes, begging for calm. "I'll have your money for you on Monday as soon as the bank opens, and then I want you gone, permanently." Ignoring the pain, I jam my fists into my pockets. The X-rays didn't show any broken bones—a fuckin' miracle. "I'm out of here, and I don't want to see you until then. Got it? If I do, you can forget it."

"What, no Christmases together?" he jokes.

Blind with rage, I whirl on him, and in two steps, I have him by the throat, my face inches from his. "I found her. Did you know that? I came home from school and found her lying naked in her own vomit after she'd overdosed."

"I'm sorry," he chokes the words against my grip. "But that was on her."

Feeling his fingers pry at my hold, the red haze clears enough for awareness to seep in, and my hand falls away. I turn, my hand searing with pain as he gasps for air behind me.

"I screwed up and made bad choices when I was younger." He coughs. "Hell, I've been running ever since, but she made her own choices, too. You just got caught in the middle."

It takes all my willpower not to unleash as much damage on him as I possibly can. Best thing for me to do is get out of here, but words need to be said. "If you'd been a decent person, she wouldn't have taken me and ran. I wouldn't have suffered at the hands of the men she prostituted herself to for her next fix, or the shitty foster parents I was sent to."

He doesn't show an ounce of remorse. He's incapable of getting it.

Grabbing my wallet and keys, I slip on my shoes and exit the apartment, slamming the door behind me.

I reach the bottom of the steps, wanting to punch or kick something. Anything to release this need to do permanent damage. *What am I going to tell Rhett?* I can't tell him my father is here. He might try to force me to go to the police. They still haven't come to talk to me about the fight, but they will. Adding this will only make things worse.

I can't lie to him either. I need to trust that he'll allow me to handle this my way.

Letting myself into the garage, I set my stuff down, then sit heavily on the weight bench and drop my head. This is so messed up.

I'm glad things ended with Serena the way they did. Seeing her tonight was a painful reminder of what we'd started and why, and how foolish I was to believe I could have any of it. But past that, at least she'll be safe.

I stand up and pace, then pick up a wrench and throw it as hard as I can against the far wall.

I need to do something with this pent-up rage before something bad happens.

My hands are fucked, so weights are out.

Fine. I'll run until my fucking legs fall off. There's no way I'm going to Rhett wound up like this. I need a clear head and need to be in control.

CHAPTER 42

SERENA

Sitting in the car outside my house, I grip the steering wheel, too broken to go inside. I don't remember the drive, only the desperate need for answers and the cold disdain in Knox's eyes that followed.

When he answered the door, I thought we'd finally get a chance to talk things through. Nothing could have prepared me for the accusations he hurled at me.

How can he believe I would want Hayden back? The thought brings on fresh tears.

My phone rings. "Hello," I answer in a rush, thinking it's Knox calling to explain or apologize.

"Serena?" my father asks. "Are you okay? You sound distressed."

"Now's not a good time," I say, fighting against the devastation I don't want him to hear.

"Is there anything I can do to help?"

I've waited for an inkling of words that show he cares. Hearing it now nearly shatters the defenses I built to protect myself from years of indifference. "No. It's fine. Things are just— never mind." I can't deal with this now. "I'll be fine. Can I call you later?"

"That's two 'fines' and you sound anything but. Where's your mother?"

"I'm on my way inside now."

"Okay. Good. Hey, I know I haven't been there for you the way I should have, but I do love you." *No. Please. Not now.* "If I could go back and fix things, I would, but I can't. I can only do better from here on. That's what I wanted to say the last time I called. Will you let me do that?"

With my shield obliterated, my throat seizes up with emotion and I can't get any words out.

"Serena?" I still can't speak. "Tell me who hurt you so I can make them pay." There's a hint of humor in his tone. It's so out of character, an involuntary laugh escapes, and the tension in my throat loosens enough to speak.

"No one, but..." I swallow hard. "Thank you." The sentiment of protection feels really good right now.

"Will you please call me tomorrow so we can talk more? I'm available all day."

"Okay." Remembering that Mom stuffed a package of tissue in my glove box, I reach over to retrieve it.

"I love you, Serena."

I want so much to say it back, but I can't. I don't trust him. Not yet. "I'll talk to you tomorrow," I say instead.

Despite the unseasonably warm temperature, shivers rack my body as I climb out of the car and walk toward the house, each step heavy with exhaustion.

"Serena, you're home early. What's wrong?" Mom asks, her arms wide, as soon as I enter the house. "Your dad just called. Are you sick?"

I throw myself at her, breaking apart all over again. She's always here when I need her most. And as she holds me tight, remaining silent, my gratitude deepens into profound relief because she always knows exactly what I need.

"Come and sit," she says after the worst has passed. When I nod, she steadies me with an arm around my waist and leads me over to the couch. Once I'm settled beside her, legs bent over her lap, she prompts, "Now, tell me everything."

Mom holds me tight in her arms as I unleash the day from hell, leaving nothing of myself behind but a heap of misery, snot, and tears. "I don't"—*hiccup*—"understand."

She reaches over and pulls several tissues out of the box on the end table and hands them to me. "He saw you and Hayden together. He's hurt. Given his past, I'm sure he has trust issues, and with his father rising from the dead, he probably wasn't thinking clearly." She gives me a squeeze. "I bet he regrets everything he said to you."

"I wish, but no. He meant every word. You should have seen his face. He was furious. And I didn't *do* anything."

"Give him time."

Her support catches me off guard. She's been pretty vocal about her disapproval of me dating Knox. "Maybe." But I know the truth. Between the fight with Hayden, his father, and the betrayal he thinks he saw, I'll be waiting forever.

If only Knox asked about my interaction with Hayden instead of assuming the worst... I lift my legs from her lap and scoot to the end of the couch. "Why are guys such assholes?"

"They aren't *all* assholes. Maybe experiencing the bad ones first will help you appreciate the good ones when they come along."

"I thought I found a good one, then he ripped my heart out and stomped all over it. He destroyed it without a second thought, just like my father did."

"Those are two very different situations."

"They both abandoned me when I needed them the most."

"Okay... that's similar."

"I wasn't enough." I despise the defeated tone of my voice.

"Baby, that's *their* problem. Not yours. And *their* loss. Having said that, your dad loves you. He just needs to get his head out of his ass and figure his shit out," she laughs, giving my foot an affectionate squeeze.

"Did you know that children raised in a home without their biological father are seven percent less likely to graduate from high school? Eleven percent more likely to smoke. Seventy-one percent more likely to have committed a crime, and twenty percent more likely to have used hard drugs?"

"Be that as it may, put that brilliant mind of yours to rest. Labeling never helps anyone. Now. Why don't you give your friends a call? Let them know what's going on with Stuart and Knox. Let them be there for you."

"I don't have the energy to go through it all again right now. I'm going to sleep for a bit, then maybe call them later." Deep down, I know I won't. They'll both be sad to hear about Stuart. But Knox? Tish will be supportive like always, but Rowan will let it be known she was right about him from the start. I just can't take that right now.

"You should eat something first."

"I can't. My stomach hurts." I stand.

"Okay. I'm here if you need me. Have faith. Everything will work out."

As I trudge up the stairs, I wonder if I can pull the covers over my head and hide from the world until it all "works out."

Sitting on the edge of my bed, I fall backward, feeling like I've been blindsided by a Denver Broncos linebacker—my mind stuttering over what the hell just happened. And when the lingering scent of the Knox candle reaches me, it's like being tackled all over again. I lift my head and stare at the offender, aching with the words Knox belted me with.

Why did I think my relationship with him was different? Rowan saw it. Tish probably did too, but was too nice to say anything. Every guy I've dated was extremely flawed in some way. And in every relationship, I'd come to my senses and break things off before I could get hurt, but with Knox, I never saw it coming —not like this.

As a whiff of the candle reaches me again, I sit up, grab the wax-filled jar, and move to the window. I slide it open—grateful for once that the screen is missing—and hurl it into the backyard as hard as I can. The muffled *thud* when it lands gives me a small sense of satisfaction—very small—but it's something.

CHAPTER 43

SERENA

It's been several days since Stuart died and Knox trampled my heart. Today, we're holding a small memorial for Stuart at the retirement home. No family came forward to claim him, so I wanted to do something to recognize his life. *Everyone* should be acknowledged for their existence. Thankfully, Bertha and Agnes helped me put it together, because in my mental state, I wouldn't have been able to do it alone.

Rowan wraps an arm around my shoulder. "I'm so sorry, Serena. I wish I'd met Stuart."

Tish squeezes my hand from the other side. "Me too."

"Thank you both for coming."

Rowan leans toward me, covers her mouth, and whispers, "You know that Bertha woman is kind of harsh."

I bark out a single laugh, realizing suddenly how similar their personalities are.

"What?" She gazes at me, eyes darting back and forth between me and Tish like *what did I miss?*

"Yeah. She *can* be a bit abrasive, but she has a big heart. Be right back." I leave my friends and walk to the front of the room.

I hate giving speeches. Especially right now when I'm feeling so low. Since my mental apocalypse, I've been a zombie, stumbling through my days, doing my best to put one foot in front of the other. My friends have been incredibly supportive. And despite my fears, Rowan never hit me with the smug I-told-you-so look or threw any of her warnings in my face. They've stuck by me, both at school and home, helping me study. With finals starting on Monday, I honestly don't think I would've even opened a book if it wasn't for them.

When I reach the front of the room, I begin. "Hey, everyone. Thank you all for coming."

Sharing the pieces of Stuart's life he gifted me with felt right. The nurses who spent so much time with him rounded out who Stuart was, making the event that much more meaningful.

After the service, Rowan and Tish took me out for ice cream. The camaraderie, mixed with creamy sweetness, was the cure-all I needed for my blues—at least temporarily.

It's around seven when I say goodbye to my friends and make my way to the car. I love this time of day—golden hour—when all the colors pop. As I take in the vibrant oranges, reds, pinks, and yellows, I think of Stuart and hope that wherever he is, he'll be able to enjoy this kind of beauty forever.

Approaching my car, it hits me. I've parked in the exact same spot as the night I followed Knox home. Being this close to him sends a bolt of anxious energy racing through my body and lands uncomfortably in the pit of my stomach. All that ice cream doesn't feel so good anymore.

I shouldn't care what he thinks about me and Hayden, but I can't accept the blame for something I didn't do. If he'd just hear me out, maybe I could handle his decision to break things off.

Without overthinking it, I drive to his place and park. I'm sure this is a really bad idea, especially if his father is still there, but I need him to listen to me. I won't be able to move on until he does.

At the bottom of the steps, a loud crash from Rhett's house startles me. "Get the hell out!" I hear him yell.

"Rhett?" I call out in response, already pushing through the back gate. Rushing up the steps of the deck, I reach the sliding back door and open it. "Hey, Rhett? It's Serena." There's no response, and he's not in the kitchen. "Are you okay?" Making my way into the living room, I find him slumped against the wall. I rush to his side and crouch down. "What happened? Did you fall?"

He raises his head, blood streaming from a gash above his eye. His eyes, clouded and unfocused, find mine. "Run!" he rasps.

"Oh, don't be so dramatic," a deep voice drawls from behind me. "She's safe... for now."

Dropping to one knee, I turn my body toward the voice. The man is wearing a cocky grin like he's enjoying himself. "Hello, my name's Fletcher. I'm a friend of Gabriel's."

Who's Gabriel?

It takes a couple of seconds for my memory to catch up. Gabriel is Knox's childhood name. And I'd bet, this average-looking man in a suit jacket, pressed shirt, and jeans is the nightmare from his dreams.

"Can you sit up?" I ask, taking Rhett's elbow and helping him sit upright against the wall.

"Oh, he's fine. Or he will be if he tells me where Gabriel is.

Excuse me... I mean Knox." I glance up briefly as he shakes his head. "That's going to be hard to get used to."

"I'll get you a rag." I move to stand, my legs feeling shaky.

"Now, hold on," Fletcher says. "Stay where you are."

"He needs something to stop the bleeding."

"Rest easy. Once *one* of you cooperates, we'll be on our way." A giant of a man steps out from the hallway and stands behind Fletcher, feet planted wide apart, hands clasped in front of him. The muscle. "Where's your boyfriend? He seems to have disappeared on me."

Disappeared? So, he's known where Knox has been all this time?

How did he know we were together? Did Rhett say something?

"So?" Fletcher says. "Where is he?"

"If he's not at his apartment, I don't have a clue." *Not that I'd tell him if I did.* "We had a fight, and I haven't seen him since Friday."

"The boy always did have a wicked temper. How about you give him a call and tell him to get himself over here so he and I can talk." Fletcher gives a lazy flick of his wrist. "Change of plans." His eyes drop to Rhett. "Since even *I* can't stomach seeing an old man get roughed up, we'll try this another way." He nods his enforcer in my direction. "Let's go for a little ride instead." The man takes three very large steps covering the ground between us and grips my arm.

"Get your hand off me." I yank against his hold, but the man only grips harder. "Ow!" I cry out.

"I'll call Knox," Rhett says, sounding panicked. "That's what you want, right?" He fights to stand on wobbly legs. "There's no need to take the girl."

"You had your chance, and thanks to Serena stopping by, Knox will give me *exactly* what I want, *and* without argument." Fletcher snaps his fingers and motions his man toward the door.

"Let me get Rhett settled," I say, digging my heels in. "He can't even stand up." This is ridiculous. They can't really think I'll go with them.

"Keep going," he tells his man, who yanks me toward the door. "You'll be fine. Right, Rhett? You wouldn't want us to have to take this beautiful girl by force, now, would you?"

Wait. What? "I'm not going with you!" I lift my chin defiantly, attempting to hold my ground.

"Don't you hurt her!" Rhett fires back.

"Yes, yes. I know," Fletcher says dismissively as I'm marched against my will toward the front door. "I've heard all the threats before."

This can't be happening. My eyes dart left then right, looking for something to grab to defend myself, but there's nothing within reach.

"Call the boy after we leave," Fletcher says over his shoulder to Rhett. "Tell him I'll be in touch. Oh..." Fletcher pauses his stride and pivots back, snapping his fingers in sudden realization. "And if you or Gabriel call the cops, James will dispose of Miss Serena here. He's quick and efficient that way. Do you understand?"

"What!" My throat goes dry.

"I get the idea," Rhett says, his voice filled with frustrated helplessness.

"B-but Knox's phone isn't working." Knox's description of Fletcher was limited, but it was enough that my instinct for survival has fear pumping through my veins. "What if he can't be reached?"

"I'm sure this nice gentleman will know how to track him down. Once Gabriel hears you're in my company, he will make himself readily available. Trust me."

"So, you're just going to kidnap me?" I sputter, still trying to reconcile that this is actually happening.

"No." He stops in the doorway and faces me. "You're keeping me company in the interest of motivation. It's smart business. And if you so much as make a peep outside to draw attention to yourself, I will have James snap your neck like a twig and be gone before anyone knows what happened." The bodyguard grips the back of my neck and squeezes with a jerk for emphasis.

Fletcher's eyes roam my face. "You sure are a pretty young thing. I can see why Gabriel is attracted to you." He lifts a hand to caress my cheek with the back of his fingers.

Without thinking, my hand lashes out, making a loud *crack* against the side of his face. My eyes go wide at the realization of what I've done.

James cranks my arm unnaturally behind my back, causing me to yelp in pain.

"Let her go," Rhett bellows. Out of the corner of my eye, I see him take a step toward us.

"Stay where you are, old man," Fletcher snaps, holding up a hand. "So that fiery redheaded temper isn't a myth, after all?" He rubs at the spot, already turning noticeably pink. "I like a bit of fire, but if you do that again?" he sneers, gripping a fistful of my hair and yanking my head backward. "I'll hit back. You got that? Fair's, fair."

Tears sting my eyes as the roots of my hair burn in pain. *You idiot. You're making it worse.*

Fletcher looks me over in disgust. "I hate tears almost as much as begging."

You're not supposed to show a bully fear, right? You're supposed to stand your ground. Rowan's badassery pops into my head. "I'm not crying," I snap. "You're tearing my hair out." *I'm losing my mind. I must be, talking to him like that.*

He releases me with a derisive snort, then nods to James, signaling our departure. "Not a word, Serena," he says, stepping out the front door.

CHAPTER 44

SERENA

James has a tight grip on my arm as we head down the sidewalk to a big black SUV. Reaching it, he swings the door open and nudges me inside, but my legs are wobbly with adrenaline and I miss a step. Quick hands grip my waist and guide me in. I cringe at the touch, wanting to smack his hands away, but manage to stop myself.

When Fletcher slides in behind me, I scoot as far away from him as possible. I don't want him anywhere near me. "James. The mountain house, if you please."

"Yes, sir," the burly man says before shutting Fletcher's door.

My eyes dart to the door next to me. I need to get away. Once he starts the car and the locks engage, I'm screwed.

Can I get out before Fletcher grabs hold?

I watch as James rounds the front of the car. *He's big, but is he fast?* The moment he slides into his seat, I yank the door open.

Before I can step out, Fletcher snatches the back of my shirt, yanking me back. "Let me go!" Panic overrides my judgment, and I lash out, punching and kicking wildly.

Wham. The impact of his slap blindsides me. "You stupid bitch!" Fletcher barks. A burning pain radiates across my cheek and stars burst my vision. Reaching past me, he shuts the door. "What did I tell you I'd do if you hit me again?" He grips my shoulders and shakes me so hard my head snaps back.

Don't cry, don't cry.

"Damn it!" He releases me with a shove. "James!" Fletcher snaps. "Hit the fucking safety locks and get us the hell out of here." Something is pulled from my back pocket. "You won't be needing this."

My phone. The plan was to leave Knox a voice message explaining things about Hayden if he didn't answer his door.

That seems like a lifetime ago as I sit here drowning in fear. Will I ever see my mother again, my friends—my dad? I never got a chance to talk to him. I didn't have the strength after what Knox did to me. Now I may never get the opportunity again. Every instinct screams at me to crumble under the weight of this nightmare, but I can't. I need to stay strong.

As I stare out the window on the drive through the city, I debate whether channeling my inner Rowan was such a good idea.

All I know is I'm scared shitless right now.

Shouldn't I *try* to keep some kind of upper hand?

Fletcher probably thrives on fear, and showing it will only fuel his need for control—or whatever his kink is.

But if I push too far... I touch the side of my face that's throbbing with a burning heat.

Masking one of Rowan's best you-aren't-worth-my-time glares and turn to him. "Whatever you're trying to accomplish by taking me won't work. I told you. Knox and I aren't together anymore. He won't give a crap."

"You're wrong. *Knox* has a big heart, and it will be his downfall. I tried to bring him up strong. You have to be able to survive in this harsh world, but I failed."

Knox does have a big heart, and angry or not, he would never abandon me if I were in trouble. "What do you want, anyway?" I cross over my chest, letting my inner Rowan fly while my heart rate skyrockets.

"His so-called *father* owes me a lot of money. Leo was seen at Gabriel's place. As I said, with you in my care, I'll get what I want without any hassle."

"Is that what you call this… care?" I snap, angry for real this time.

"You're still breathing, aren't you?" he barks out a surprised laugh, assessing me with new interest. "James. I *like* this lil' spitfire. Shit, for a girl, you really got a pair."

I catch James as he looks at his boss in the rearview mirror, then at me, and raises his eyebrows like *you better watch yourself.*

His warning is a surprise, considering his actions so far.

We've started up the canyon. How would Fletcher know Knox's father was at his place? He couldn't possibly have had someone watching him all this time, could he?

Fifteen to twenty minutes tick by before we turn off onto a gravel road. My speedy heart rate has settled, leaving me exhausted as I mentally take note of our drive. There are lots of houses up here nestled in the forest—some close to the road, some buried at the end of long driveways.

"Don't bother trying to keep track of where we are," Fletcher says. "You won't be escaping, and when this is all over, you'll be back to whatever it is you do."

"So, you're just going to let me go when you get what you want?" I ask, my voice tinged with disbelief.

"*Of course,*" he says, looking shocked that I would suggest otherwise, then gives me a chilling smile like this is all a game—one he never loses.

"Aren't you afraid I'll turn you in?"

"Darlin', as far as everyone knows, I'm still on vacation in Barcelona. I'm a respectable businessman with valuable connections. I'll be fine. I always am."

This is good news, right? As long as he gets what he wants, I should be safe.

Just don't lose your shit on him again.

After several more turns, we make a left down a long, winding driveway with potholes that have us bouncing high in our seats.

"James, see that this road is grated. If this gets much worse, it won't be usable."

"Yes, sir."

We pull up in front of a large, stylish, two-story log cabin. I'm not sure what I was expecting, but this wasn't it. Definitely something shabby and more sinister, not a place glowing with warmth, inviting me in.

Fletcher pats the top of my leg. "It's a great place." The glare I send him for the touch has him sitting back with an amused smile. "You'll like it—very picturesque—and no neighbors for miles. That's why I bought it. Haven't had a chance to get up here in a while. I'm looking forward to it. James, the house is stocked?"

"As requested, sir."

"Excellent." He turns to me as James exits the car. "Good help is hard to find. Gabriel was my number one. Great kid, hard worker, but"—he makes a tipping motion to his lips—"the kid could drink, and like his mother," he says with a sigh, "cared for drugs a little too much. Great for control, but bad for business. Then he went and almost killed a guy." James opens Fletcher's door.

"Almost?"

"Gabriel has a conscience, you see, and had ideas of leaving my organization. When he beat a man near to death, it seemed like a great opportunity to keep him under my thumb—you know, make him think he was indebted to me. Backfired, though. The dumbass ran."

Why would he tell me this?

All this time, Knox's been controlled by guilt for something he never did. He'll be relieved once he learns he's in the clear. Hopefully, Fletcher is telling the truth, and I'll get the opportunity to tell him.

As he steps out of the car, James opens my door and holds out a hand, which I ignore. A blast of crisp mountain air hits me the moment I get out. I left my jacket in my car, and the t-shirt I'm wearing does nothing to ward off the evening chill. The sun hasn't even set yet. But this time of year, at this altitude, where the sun doesn't reach over the trees late in the day, it's near freezing.

"Will you escort Serena into the house?" Fletcher asks James. "I don't feel like getting attacked again. That's what I pay *you* for." He chuckles at his humor.

"Yes, sir," James says to Fletcher's retreating form, then turns his gaze to me. "You coming peacefully? Or am I throwing you over my shoulder?" The brief grin tugs at the corner of his mouth.

"I'll walk," I grumble.

He gestures for me to proceed. Wrapping my arms around myself for warmth, I make my way up the path to the house. James may be a little wider, but Knox is definitely taller. For some stupid reason, I take comfort in that.

The ground is uneven, and with zero support from my flats, I stumble. "Careful." James takes a hold of my upper arm—his gentleness surprising me.

The moment we're in the door, Fletcher asks, "You want anything? A beer, Coke, maybe some water?" He moves into a gleaming stainless-steel kitchen with white cabinets and light-colored granite countertops. From what I can see, the house is a mixture of modern and rustic chic. It has large, open concept, vaulted ceilings, and a massive fireplace in the far wall.

"Water, please." My mouth is bone dry, and being difficult won't help me in any way.

"James?"

"I'm fine, sir." He's moved to the fireplace and starts filling it with paper and logs.

Fletcher hands me a plastic bottle of water. I twist the cap and chug it back. The wetness against my dry mouth is a welcomed relief.

Fletcher walks over to James and talks to him in hushed tones. He isn't a big man, not compared to James, but he's well-built like he takes care of himself. Weirdly, if I saw him on the street, I would think he was a good-looking older man—a nice man—not some evil, dickhead drug dealer.

My phone rings in Fletcher's hand. *It's Knox*, I think as a tidal wave of hope washes over me. *Everything will be okay now. He'll fix this.*

"Is this your mom?" Fletcher walks toward me, facing the screen out for me to see.

When the picture of Mom and me shows on my display, my newfound relief crumbles and a more intense fear rises. One where my mother gets caught up and hurt in all this. "Yes," I say, forcing my voice to remain level, determined to hold on to my tough-girl act.

Fletcher declines the call, then holds the phone up to my face to unlock it. "Let's send her a text, shall we?" He rapidly types out a message, speaking each word as he goes. "Sorry, Mom. Just in the middle of something. We'll talk soon. Is everything okay?"

My mind struggles to grasp the reality of this situation as I stand in front of Fletcher, waiting for my mother's response. Several pounding heartbeats later, there's an alert that she's texted back.

"Everything is fine. She's just wondering where you are." His fingers move deftly once again, composing a follow-up response.

Panic washes over me. "My mother isn't dumb. She's going to know something is up. Let me text her." I'll say whatever it take to keep her from getting involved.

He smiles. "Don't worry your pretty little head. I'll text her that you and *Knox* made up, and you're staying at his house tonight."

"She'll never believe you. She knows I wouldn't spend the night. She's uncomfortable with it. Let me text her."

"And alert her to your situation? No way. What's your best friend's name?"

"Rowan, why?"

He types another text, reading it as he goes. "I'm staying at

Rowan's house. I'm not sure what we're doing tomorrow, but I'll keep in touch." He hits send.

Please let her be exhausted and not read too much into his stupid texts. If he would have let me do it, I would have said we are studying. *Shit. Finals start Monday.*

"Would you like to rest before dinner?"

"Yes." Anything to get away from him.

As I trail after James up the stairs, I worry about what will happen if Knox still hasn't charged his phone. From what Fletcher told me, he has a solid alibi, so if Knox can't be reached, he should let me go, right?

That's what he said he was going to do. So, I should be fine, right?

Besides, he can't keep me past Monday. If I don't show up at school, Mom will call the police.

James flips on a light to a bedroom and tells me he'll be back when dinner is ready. When I enter, he closes the door behind me and a lock clicks into place. *It locks from the outside? What the hell?*

This shit only happens in movies, not to some random person in a small town minding her own business. *Knox warned me.* This was his worst fear. I just never imagined it would actually come true.

At the sight of the large window, I rush over and lift. But it doesn't budge. I release the lock and try again. Nothing. *Is it painted shut?*

I follow around the frame and come across a thick nail jammed into the edges, then several more. The cabin is designed for hostages.

Of course it is.

My body droops in defeat as I walk to the bed. Even if I got myself through the window, I'd probably break something on the two-story drop. And with my flimsy shoes and short-sleeve shirt, I'd freeze to death, searching in the dark for a neighboring house. Besides, most places up here are empty until the summer.

Basically, I'm screwed.

CHAPTER 45

KNOX

Panic shot through my system the moment Rhett's frantic voice echoed through the phone. Hearing he had Serena—the thought of what he might do—I've been racing down the mountain ever since.

Leaving my gear behind was smart. It would have taken too long to pack and would have slowed me down.

He found me.

Rhett said Fletcher would get in touch. I've dealt with him enough to know he always plays by his own twisted rules, so calling him to find out what he's up to could have consequences. Not that I have his number, but I bet he's got Serena's phone by now. The fucker's probably expecting me to call. Hoping, so he can fuck with me.

Why was she at Rhett's place? And why would Fletcher take her? Kidnapping isn't his style—at least it hadn't been. And if he knew where I lived and wanted to get his hands on me, why abduct her? His guys could have easily grabbed me.

Well, not easily.

None of this makes sense.

My father showing up here. That can't be a coincidence.

I stumble on a partially hidden stump, almost eating dirt. Anger bubbles up and I unleash an explosive string of curses into the trees. It's taking forever to get out of these woods, and waiting for Fletcher's call is gutting me. I'm sure he knows it, too. He'll want me frantic, so I'll agree to whatever he asks. He likes his fucking games. I'm so glad I have my phone with me, otherwise... shit. I don't even want to think about it.

With the sun well below the tree line, it's growing darker by the minute. Like the dumbass that I am, I forgot to grab my headlamp when I snagged my wallet.

As soon as my hiking boots hit the pavement, I run full tilt, but these boots are slowing me down. I need to be as close to home as possible when Fletcher calls, but getting there feels like a nightmare—the destination seeming impossible to reach.

The first raindrops hit my body the same moment a set of headlights shine my way. Slowing to a walk, I stick out my thumb, hoping to get picked up, but the car zooms past.

I should have asked Rhett to come get me the moment he called, but in my panic, it didn't cross my mind. Calling him now seems pointless. I'm sure I'll be picked up in the time it would take for him to get here.

I run again until the next car. It passes me by. On and on it goes like this until my phone rings and Serena's name appears on the screen. I slow to a fast walk, then answer.

"You fucking hurt her and I will rip your balls up through

your throat." Talking to him like that is a mistake, but I'm too angry to rein in any kind of control.

"Now is that any way to speak to your old friend?" he chuckles. "We were like family."

Hearing his familiar voice should send me spiraling, but rage and fear for Serena outweighs any reaction Fletcher's voice causes. "Just tell me what you want so we can end this game of yours." Thoughts of Serena's fear flashes through my mind, settling a heaviness of guilt on my chest.

"No game. I need to talk to Leo."

Even dead—allegedly dead—my father is ruining my life. I swear, if Serena gets hurt, his ass is going to jail, followed by Fletcher's. I don't care *what* happens to me. "Didn't know that you knew him. And how the hell did you know he was here?"

"When I discovered your whereabouts, I had hidden cameras installed at your place. After all, what kind of businessman would I be if I couldn't keep track of my own employees?"

"I don't work for you," I snap, but the idea of him watching me spikes a wave of anxiety.

"Yes, you do, and you owe me. This is your payout. Now, where is your dear old dad?"

"He showed up last Friday. Said he needed money."

Fletcher chokes on a laugh. "I highly doubt that."

"Whatever. I gave him five grand to get lost, and he left Monday morning as soon as I got back from the bank." The band that's lived around my chest for too long tightens several notches. This is not going to end well.

"Now, that's unfortunate."

Another car is coming. I step forward, waving a hand. The car swerves a bit and keeps going. *Dick.* "If you've had eyes on me, why wasn't Leo picked up?" I lift the phone away from my mouth as I fight for a full breath. I can't go down this road. I grab a hunk of skin at the sensitive part of my inner thigh and twist as hard as I can.

"It's hard to keep good employees. Time for you to come back. I need someone with your... talents."

The pain helps marginally, but at least I'm able to breathe easier. "Never going to happen. What do you want with him? Never mind. Let me talk to Serena." I just need to hear her voice. I need to know she's okay.

"She's resting at the moment."

"If you hurt her—"

"Hey, it's not my fault she won't eat. Probably upset and all. Understandable. Now... it seems like we have a bit of an issue. You need to find your father and bring him to me."

"How am I supposed to do that?" I snap, anger mixing with panic. "He left four days ago. He could be anywhere."

"That's your problem. And if you go to the police, they will never find your girlfriend. Are we clear?"

I stop as a stab of fear rips through me. "Crystal, just as they'll never find your mangled corpse weighted at the bottom of a very deep lake if anything happens to her. Are *you* clear?"

Fletcher laughs like I've made the king of all jokes. "You really are something special. A chip off the ol' block."

No fucking way. "You think you had a hand in raising me because you hung around my mother and gave me work? I am *nothing* like you." Now would be a good time for diplomacy. Unfortunately, I'm in very short supply at the moment—not that I ever really learned the skill. "Stop the bullshit and let me talk to Serena." I'm not sure I can move again until I hear her voice.

"Temper, temper. You know what happens when you lose control."

"Yeah, and there will be no place you can hide. Remember that."

"Fine. *James*," Fletcher says, sounding like he's on the move. "She's a fighter, that one. Need a second body around when dealing with her." A door opens in the background. "Someone wants to talk to you."

"Hello?" Serena answers, sounding panicked.

Hearing her voice floods my system with welcomed relief. "Are you okay?"

"Knox. I'm in the woods off—"

"That's enough." I imagine the phone being ripped from her hands. "You better get a move on," Fletcher says.

"How about we do this the easy way?" I know I'm grasping, but whatever. "Bring Serena home, and I'll go and find Leo for you. He's a piece of shit. I couldn't care less what happens to him. I want Serena out of this."

"Magnolia Road," Serena yells in the background, but her next words get muffled.

"Ow!" Fletcher's man yells. "She bit me!"

Good going, Serena. Witnessing her spark of fearlessness gives me the strength I need to pull my emotions completely back on track.

"I'm enjoying your girl." Fletcher laughs. "Find him. You know where to reach me. You have twenty-four hours."

"That's crazy. I'm way up in the mountains without a car, and Leo could be in Mexico by now."

"That's *your* problem." The line goes dead.

"Damn it!" I kick a rock and send it skittering down the road, then start running. At that very moment, the sky opens up and unleashes a torrent of rain. *Fucking great.*

I placed a tracker on my father's phone. Predicting bad stuff before it happens is a gift that came from all the shitty things I've experienced. I figured if any of the crap Leo was running from came my way, I wanted to be able to find him. The problem is, he's using a burner phone and could dump it at any time.

I should call the police, or at the very least, Serena's mother, but I don't have time to waste, and both will slow me down with questions, not to mention put Serena at risk. The best I can do is get to my father as soon as possible, make the exchange, and let Fletcher deal with him. If all goes well, I should easily have Serena back by—I check the tracker app, covering my phone as best as I can from the rain. He's six hours away. Double that. Add an hour—hopefully no longer—to get home from here. That's thirteen hours. It's eight now, so I should have her back tomorrow around nine. *If* all goes as planned.

I take a screenshot of his location in case he discards the phone before I get there—even a last known location will be a helpful start. *Fuck, I hope he's there.*

Thirty minutes go by with me trying to thumb down a driver, and I'm soaked. I'm about to call Rhett to come and get me when another set of lights has me frantically waving my arms in the air. This time, the car stops. I feel like crying as the old man opens the door from the inside and asks, "You need some help?"

CHAPTER 46

KNOX

"Are you okay?" I ask, rushing into the house. Rhett wouldn't have let them take her without a fight.

"I'm fine," he says from his favorite chair. "So, that's Fletcher, huh?"

There's a cut above his eye. *Fletcher will pay for that.* "Yep. The piece of shit finally came back to haunt me for real." I quickly fill Rhett in on what Fletcher wants me to do, then say, "I'm sorry for bringing this on you."

"As if any of this is your fault."

No use arguing. "I need your truck."

"Already figured that." He wobbles as he moves to stand.

I place a hand on his shoulder. "You should stay and rest."

He blinks hard and rests his head back on his chair. "Maybe you're right. Keys are where they usually are. How do you plan on bringing your father back if you find him?"

"By any means necessary."

"Don't go all stupid on me. No need to make things worse for yourself." I nod, but I'll do whatever it takes to get Serena back. "On the phone, you explained why you don't want to call the police, but I think it's a mistake, and Serena's mother has a right to know what's going on."

I crouch down in front of him. "I know Fletcher, and all he wants is my father. If I get him, it will be an easy exchange. If police get involved, Serena could get caught in the middle and hurt." Rhett looks torn by his conscience. "Give me the six hours it will take to get to him," I tell him. "If he's not there or something goes wrong, I'll call you, and you can contact the police and Serena's mother."

"Alright. Six hours."

"Fletcher gave me twenty-four. Trust me. I'm securing Serena's safety by giving him exactly what he wants."

"It isn't *you* I don't trust."

"I understand. Can I get you anything before I go?"

"No. You be careful, son."

"I will. I have to ask you for one more thing." I pause, gearing up for a fight. "I need your gun."

"No." His voice is flat and cold.

Fletcher made sure I was trained, but I was the only one in his organization who refused to carry. "I'm not planning on using it. It's insurance in case anything goes wrong. I won't lose Serena because of the screwed-up path my life has taken." Rhett shakes his head, telling me no. "I know where the lockbox and key are. I'll get the gun myself, but I'd rather have your permission."

Rhett narrows his eyes and his lips turn into angry slits. "If you take that gun, don't bother coming back. You got that? You don't carry a gun unless you plan on using it. There's no such thing as insurance, only mistakes and death." He's right. I just feel so helpless right now, and I'm grasping at anything that will give me a sense of control. "How about I come with you?" he says. "You might need help getting your dad to come along peacefully."

"You're a good man. I wouldn't be where I am today without you. That's why I don't want you involved any more than you are, especially if it all goes to shit. If I can't find my father. I'd rather you be here to talk to the police directly."

"Alright. I trust you to do what's right." Rhett clasps my shoulder. The declaration, mixed with affection, rocks me to the core. "You better get going."

The rain has stopped when I step outside. *Thank fuck*. I run up to my apartment, take off the wet flannel, pull on a dry sweatshirt, then grab my phone cord since the phone is only half charged. In the truck, I slide the keys into the ignition and turn.

Nothing happens.

"You've got to be fucking kidding me!" I slam my hand against the steering wheel and try again. Nothing. I jump out of the truck and run for the house. "The battery's dead," I holler as soon as I'm in the back door.

"It's been giving me some trouble lately," Rhett calls out from the living room. "I have a jump box in the garage." His movements are stiff as he walks toward me—his dark skin ashen from the effort.

"Go and sit. Just tell me where to find it, and I'll take care of it?" I growl.

He slides his feet into his shoes. "I have a bump on the head and some bruises, not a severed artery. Stop treating me like an invalid. Now, get out there and lift the hood. I'll grab everything we need."

"What if it doesn't start?"

"It will."

I pinch the bridge of my nose, taking a deep breath in an effort to keep my cool, then follow him out the back door. My head is pounding from stress, fear, and a lack of food, but none of that matters right now.

Rhett comes back carrying a box with jumper cables attached to it. I wait while he hooks it up to the battery. "Give it a try," he says from under the hood. I turn the key and the engine fires up immediately. He lets the hood slam into place and comes around to the driver's side window. "Make sure you let it charge up a while before getting gas. Other than that, you might want to keep it running, just to be sure. You got your license on you?"

"Yup."

"You be careful, ya hear?" Rhett gives me a pointed look. "I don't want anything to happen to you."

"I'll do my best."

His eyes suddenly appear glassy. "And bring Serena home. I like that girl a lot."

"Me too," I force out, the words getting stuck in my throat, then throw the truck in reverse and back out of the driveway.

At a stoplight, I check my phone. My father's location hasn't changed, but that doesn't mean it won't. A satellite view showed it to be a house. If all goes well, I should be back by morning, and maybe this nightmare will finally be over. I know Fletcher will keep his end of the bargain. The question is, once this is over, will he let me walk away, or will I find myself on the run again?

The thought of losing everything that's important to me has my stomach churning, while a low roar of panic simmers just below the surface. *No.* I don't have time for this. I need to get my father, make the exchange, and deal with the fallout after. Getting Serena home safe is all I should be focusing on.

A memory of my father saying he owes a lot of important people money replays in my mind. Fletcher must be one of them. *How did they even meet?* I guess it isn't a huge stretch if my father was selling drugs. Denver, being Fletcher's territory, is only thirty minutes away.

Whatever, it doesn't matter at this point. My father won't come easily and will have to be taken by force. I take mental stock of what I have in the truck. One powerful punch as soon as he opens the door should do it. *If* he opens the door. I'm surprised he hasn't crossed the border already. I guess there's always the possibility his phone is at the house and he isn't.

If he *is* gone, there will be no way I can find him in the next twenty-four hours. I haven't let myself think of that possibility, but now that I have... fear claws its way through my body, and I press down on the accelerator. The engine revving before the truck shoots forward.

Imagining police lights in my rearview mirror if I don't slow down has me easing the pressure on the gas pedal. This helpless feeling is killing me. I want to hit something, scream my head off, but all I can do is drive.

Pressing the radio's seek button, I scan stations until the harsh notes of heavy metal blare through the speakers—violent and broody, exactly the way I feel.

It's midnight when I stop at the gas station. The edginess of not being there yet continues to grate on my nerves. I pay for the gas along with two protein bars, a large bottle of water, an energy drink, and jump back on the highway.

All this driving has given me too much time to think about Serena and how badly I screwed it all up. When I finally charged my phone and read her texts, I wanted to puke. Stuart had died, and I selfishly tore into her, then slammed the door in her face.

I don't know why she was talking to her ex-boyfriend, or why he kissed her cheek, but I should have given her a chance to explain before jumping to every horrid conclusion possible. It's just, seeing them together... the image brings back the swirling haze of rage all over again. I blow out a loud breath and scrub a hand down my face.

Yeah, I jumped to conclusions, but I've gotten used to expecting the worst from people, since that's all I've ever gotten. Rhett being the exception. And If I'm honest with myself, Serena, too, and I've ruined the best thing I've had in my whole miserable life.

I need to get my father and hope she'll forgive me. An image of her devastated expression after I said those horrible things flashes in my mind. There's no good reason for her to talk to me again. On top of accusing her, look what I've gotten her into. But I have to try. She's every bright color, pure sound, honeysuckle sweetness that ever existed. And because of her, I feel freer than I have in my whole miserable life. She gave me that, and I'll do whatever I have to do to get her back.

Several hours later, the GPS directs me to the house. It's not a shithole either, but a cute one-story Victorian. No lights are on, not that I expected any at this early hour. I wish I *could* have brought Rhett. Having him here to at least watch the back door would have been helpful. But I don't, so I guess I'll have to improvise as I go.

I climb out of the truck and open the extended cab door. Rhett built an organization system for easy-to-grab items that we might need on the job. I pull out a spool of rope and use a utility knife to cut it into a useful length, then shove the rope in the back pocket of my jeans. I stare at the knife still in my hands. Nope, just like the gun, it could create more problems than it's worth.

It's still dark out as I take in my surroundings. The sun won't be up for another couple of hours. At the front door, I cover the peephole with my finger and knock.

No one answers, so I knock harder, then harder still.

A light goes on inside the house. The porch light comes on next, blinding me at the same time the front door whips open. A young, petite woman in a bright pink bathrobe whisper-yells, "Will you keep it down? I have a kid sleeping."

"Who is it?" I hear my father's voice from somewhere behind her. Without giving it, or the woman between us, a second thought, I rush past her. Taking several steps forward, I slam my fist into my father's face, knocking him unconscious. After so many years, the action felt even better than I imagined it would.

The woman starts screaming and pounding on my back as I move in to tie Leo's hands behind his back. "Believe me," I tell her. "I'm doing you a favor." Once my father's hands are tied behind his back, I lift his heavy weight up and across my shoulders in a crappy attempt at a fireman's carry.

"I'm calling the police," the woman hollers at me.

"Go ahead," I say, walking toward the exit. "He's a drug dealer, wife-beater, and overall piece of shit." When I reach the door, I glance at her over my shoulder. "He's also my father, who's supposedly been dead for eight years, if that helps." She looks stricken.

A little girl comes out crying, "Mommy."

"Go back to your room, baby," she soothes.

Instead of listening, the little girl clasps her mother's leg and buries half her face in her mother's bathrobe. "What's he doing with Daddy?"

The realization that I have a half-sister slams into me. Something to process later. "Your daddy is hurt," I tell the girl. "I'm helping your mommy by taking him to the hospital. What name is he going by?" I ask the woman.

She looks confused. "Jacob Baxter. I'm Sarah Baxter."

How long has he been married? Whatever. It's all part of another deception he's got going. "Well, his real name is Leo Westing, and if I were you, I'd get as far away from him as possible."

"Please." She grips the sleeve of my hoodie, looking broken. "He's all I have."

I grit my teeth. "Because of Leo, an amazing person is being held hostage by a dangerous man. I'm sorry if you feel he's a loss to you, but I need to go before he wakes up and I have to... restrain him again in front of your child." I'm surprised he's still out. I hope I didn't cause any major damage. Fletcher would be pissed.

She releases me. "Will you bring him back after the—" She pauses, glancing at her daughter. "The hospital?"

I give her props for worrying about her child. She might actually be a decent human being, and that makes her words harder to understand. "Did you not hear what I said? How can you still want him?"

"Please," she begs.

"It's out of my hands. I'm sorry."

I walk out of the house and dump Leo's dead weight into the passenger's seat, then check his pulse in case I caused him to have a heart attack or something.

Thankfully, it's still there.

After buckling him in, I re-tie his hands in front of him, because as much as I want the man to suffer, sitting with them tied behind his back for the next six hours would be torture. I grab the entire spool of rope, tie his feet together, then secure his arms and upper body to the seat until there is no way he can move when he wakes up. Next, I dial Serena's number.

A groggy-sounding Fletcher answers. "I have Leo," I say. "Where are we meeting?"

CHAPTER 47

SERENA

A banging on the door wakes me up. "Fletcher says to get up. Your boy has his father. We need to make the trade."

There is a second of confusion before I remember where I am and why. "Okay. I'll be down soon."

I want to feel relief that I'll be going home, but does Knox really have him, or is this a ploy—a set-up of some kind?

I make quick use of the bathroom and head down the stairs, smelling freshly brewed coffee. "Knox got to Leo fast," I say, fishing for information as I slide onto the stool next to Fletcher at the kitchen island.

"Knox always comes through. The kid was a valuable employee," he says, taking a sip of his coffee.

"So, what's the plan?"

"It should be easy so long as the police weren't called. We'll meet at a rest area on the highway not far from here, make the exchange, and James and I will be on our way. Do you want coffee or something to eat?"

Fletcher is a man used to getting what he wants. Otherwise, he wouldn't be this hospitable. "Coffee would be great with a piece of toast?" I need something to soak up the acid burning in my stomach. I know coffee won't help matters, but I need a clear head.

"Sure. James, give Serena some of those eggs you whipped up. And some toast."

A few minutes later, James dishes up the food and sets a plate in front of me. As I nibble, I wonder how I should prepare for this. I look at the fork in my hand, then at the knife beside my plate. Will they notice if I take it?

A hand lands on my shoulder, making me jump. "Don't touch me." I pull away.

"And I thought we were getting along splendidly," he laughs.

"Sorry." I don't want to get on his bad side. "I'm not a morning person."

He ignores my response and says, "You're nervous. I get that, but do your part and you won't have anything to worry about."

After a quick meal, we get back into the SUV and journey back to the highway, then take it higher up into the mountains. It's no longer than fifteen minutes before we pull off at a rest stop. The place is deserted except for a truck—Rhett's. The tension in my chest begins to unravel. This could all finally be over.

James parks the vehicle in front of a building with a public restroom sign, leaving a three-car width between us and the truck. Knox steps out, circling the back of the truck with his arms lifted and his palms facing outward. I've never felt more grateful to see anyone in my entire life.

I reach to open the door, but Fletcher stops me. "Stay here, be good, and everything will turn out fine." He exits the car.

"Well, well, Gabriel," Fletcher says, the words slightly muffled through the windowpane. "It's good to see you. I swear you've gotten taller—definitely bigger."

"The name is Knox, dickhead." He looks over Fletcher's shoulder at me. "Serena, are you okay?"

"She's fine."

Knox's hand shoots forward, seizing Fletcher by the front of his shirt. "What the fuck happened to her face?" he snarls, his expression contorted with rage.

Shit! I meant to hide the bruise from him. James grabs Knox from behind in a tight chokehold. "Release him!"

"I'm fine," I interject hastily, trying to diffuse the tension that escalated way too fast. I open the door again, but Fletcher kicks it shut with the heel of his foot.

"Knox, I tripped!" I lie easily. At this point, I'd say anything to keep this situation from spiraling out of control. I just want to finish this and go home.

After a tense moment, Knox releases Fletcher. "Let's get this over with," he says with steely determination, but James maintains his hold.

"Let him go," Fletcher orders.

With a quick, fluid movement, James spins Knox around and shoves him toward the truck. Knox shoots a fiery glare over his shoulder before wrenching open the passenger door.

Swiftly untying some of the ropes, he drags Leo—still partially bound—out of the vehicle. "Hey. I'm not sure what you think I did." Leo's excuses to Fletcher start, his words stumbling over each other as he fights to stay upright with his hands and feet still bound. "Seriously, man. What the hell?"

"Knocked him out, did you?" Fletcher ignores Leo's ramblings while eyeing the damage to the man's face.

James reaches past Fletcher and yanks the door open. Seizing my arm, he guides me out, and anchors me to his side, all while my heart hammers violently in my chest. This doesn't feel like the simple exchange Fletcher promised.

"Your move, Fletcher," Knox says, his voice carrying an icy calmness. "I've done what you asked."

There aren't any signs of his crippling anxiety. You'd think in a situation like this, there would be at least a hint of a crack in his demeanor.

"You did. Nice job, by the way."

"I don't want your praise," he snaps. "Let's just get this over with." He looks me over and says, "Are you sure you're okay?"

"I'm fine. I promise."

"She's been well cared for," Fletcher says. "After we get this all settled, there's something we need to discuss."

"Give her to me, and you can go fuck yourself."

"Don't move," a voice commands. Our heads snap in the direction of two men holding guns, approaching from opposite sides of the building. "FBI. Hands where we can see them."

"Stay where you are," James warns, drawing a gun.

My heart leaps into my throat at the weapon positioned in front of me, shifting steadily between the two agents. "Wait a minute." *No, no, no. This can't be happening.* My eyes darting everywhere all at once.

The agents take a step forward. "Sir? Lower your weapon."

In a swift move, James encircles my body with his free arm, pinning my back to his front and pressing the cold barrel of the gun painfully to my head. "Don't fucking move," he growls as terror threatens to buckle my legs.

Knox's foot surges forward, hollering, "No!" as Fletcher scrambles to position himself behind us.

"I said, don't move!" James grits out, jamming the barrel harder against my temple, jarring my head to the side with the force.

Knox freezes. With Leo forgotten, he lifts both hands, his body taut with restrained energy. "Please, just let her go. James. Come on, man. She shouldn't even be here."

"Listen to the young man," the agent on the right says. "Put the gun down."

Sirens sound far off in the distance, but it doesn't lend any relief to the terror coursing through my veins.

"Hey, I'm just an innocent victim in all this," Leo whines.

"Okay, everyone," Fletcher says calmly from behind us. "Let's just take a breath here, and I'll tell you how this is going down. You two jackasses are going to back the hell off because my man here has a twitchy finger when he gets nervous. Knox, get in the car. You're driving us out of here.

I suck in a lungful of air when I realize I'm not breathing.

"You are in no position to make demands," says the agent on the left. "There is no way out of this situation except in custody."

"I beg to differ. You will not risk hurting this pretty young lady, or put young Knox's life in jeopardy. *So*, set your weapons down, call the police off, and then we'll be on our way. When we're at a safe distance, we'll leave these two someplace to contact you. Now, James? Time to go."

"Don't move," the agent says.

James fires at the man's feet. I flinch at the deafening sound. As soon as I do, the gun is shoved back against my head. "Do you really want to call my bluff?" James threatens. "Now, drop your weapons." When they don't move, he hollers, "Now!"

One agent begins to lower his gun, and the other follows. When weapons are on the ground, Fletcher says, "Knox. Get in."

Knox's eyes snap to mine seconds before he rushes to the driver's seat, jumps in, and slams the door closed. Fletcher must be inside because James is pulling me backward and tucking my head so I don't smack it, then shuts the door after us. "Go, go, go!" James yells to Knox.

Since the car was left running, Knox jams it into reverse, and with screeching tires, we jolt back. "Serena—seatbelt," he barks, his focus splitting between the road and the rearview mirror, then hits the gas, hard.

My hands tremble uncontrollably as I hastily grab the seatbelt and struggle to fasten it. Gunshots crack the air, mixing with the sound of tires skidding on loose gravel as we fishtail out of the parking lot.

"They're trying to take out the tires," James yells.

"I know!" Knox hollers back.

Once on the highway, James leans forward from the backseat, straining for a better view of what's up ahead. Knox slams a backhanded fist into his face and yells, "Point a gun at her again and see what happens."

"Knox!" Fletcher's voice booms in the confined space.

James lets out an angry growl and shoves the gun at the base of Knox's head.

"No," I scream.

"Get that *fucking* gun away from my son's head," Fletcher explodes.

Knox's eyes flash in the rearview mirror, a storm of shock and fury. James whips his head toward Fletcher, retracting the gun.

"What the fu—" I start, but Knox slams on the brakes. I'm jerked forward, seatbelt biting into me, while Fletcher and James hurtle forward, smacking hard into the seats in front.

Knox turns with a deadly glare. "What did you just say?"

"Now's not the time," Fletcher says. "As you've experienced, James has a strong instinct for survival. You do *not* want Serena in the crossfire when the FBI catches up." Knox's eyes find mine a second before turning forward. He slams his hand on the top of the steering wheel, then punches the gas once again.

Fletcher is Knox's father? I try to catch Knox's eyes in the mirror, but his focus is on the windy road. The turns are coming fast at this speed. He must be freaking out right now.

I hold the door handle as our bodies sway with every turn, keeping myself against the door as best as I can to avoid contact with James. *Fletcher is right. The guy is like a live wire, waiting to electrocute anyone who gets in his way.*

"Take the left up there." James points to a paved road up ahead.

Knox barely slows before making the turn. I scream without meaning to, fearing we're going to roll, but miraculously, we manage to stay on all four tires.

"How the *hell* did the FBI know where we were?" Fletcher snaps at James as we tear down the new road.

"I don't know. No one has been following us."

"Is there a tracker on the damn car?"

"I check the vehicle every morning."

"Then how!"

The landscape around us blurs into a chaotic mix of green and brown as we take random turns here and there. There is a labyrinth of roads in this part of the mountains, some leading to homes, others farther back into the wilderness.

"Knox, did you contact the fucking police?" Fletcher's voice rises in a panic.

"No way!"

"Cell phones," James mutters to himself. "That's how they tracked us. They couldn't have mobilized this fast otherwise. We need to turn them off. Now!"

"How did they know this was all going down, or where we were making the exchange?" Fletcher thrusts our phones into James's hands. Knox quickly hands his phone over his shoulder. "I used Serena's phone, not mine?"

"I don't know. None of this makes sense." He powers off all the devices. "Even with them off, they can still track us, just not right away." He leans over me and rolls the window down enough to chuck the phones out.

I should be pissed that he tossed my phone, but I'm too overwhelmed to care.

Feeling on the verge of unraveling, I turn and stare out my window. I've been stripped of all control, pushed, pulled, terrorized, and brutalized. Fear and anger swirl in a colossal whirlpool inside my head, but above all, I'm just exhausted.

Knox did everything Fletcher asked. This could have been so simple. If the FBI hadn't interfered, I'd be on my way home with Knox.

"We need to find an empty cabin to hole up in," James says. "Get this vehicle out of sight and plan our next move."

"How will we find anything without a GPS?" Knox asks.

"Dumb luck," James returns.

Out here, a person can live off the grid and disappear easily. Finding a place is going to be tough. People up here like their privacy. The only thing we have going for us is that most of the cabins will be empty this time of year.

James points at the road up ahead. "Take that right turn."

We've been slowly climbing in altitude. It's hard to tell it's early June with all the patches of snow on the road and deep drifts in the trees. Watching the scenery scroll past the window, exhaustion from the standoff settles in, leaving me foggy-brained and a little numb.

"Turn here," James says. "Let's see if we can find something down this way." The snow is deeper. With the rough terrain, we're moving slowly. "Are you in four-wheel drive?"

"For the last several miles," Knox returns.

"There!" James points through the trees. "Stop." Knox hits the brakes and we all look. "I saw a structure through the trees. It's a decent size. I think we should check it out. Sir?"

"Alright. Shut the car off, Knox, and hand James the keys."

"It's going to get cold fast." Knox says, "Serena's not dressed for this temperature."

"None of us are," Fletcher snaps. "I don't want you taking off the moment James leaves the vehicle."

A blast of ice-cold air hits my bare arms when Fletcher opens his door and climbs out. I begin to shiver as James pockets the keys and follows behind him. "I'll move as quickly as I can," James says before Fletcher gets back in the car and shuts the door.

Knox shifts in his seat and fixes a cold, hard stare on his father. "Explain."

CHAPTER 48

KNOX

"You never were one to mince words," Fletcher says. "In the interest of time, I'll give you the condensed version. Before you were born, your father worked for me. As you know, your mother liked to party. One night, after your father passed out, we continued, and a little affair was born. It ended when she got pregnant. She never said it was mine, but the first time I saw you, I was pretty sure. You look a lot like my youngest brother."

"So, you don't *really* know."

"When you were in the hospital after that asshole foster parent beat you up, I bribed a nurse to draw some of your blood, and I had a paternity test done. You're mine."

This just keeps getting worse.

James is back and opens Fletcher's door. "There's a hunting cabin. It's not in great shape, but it's sound."

"We can't leave the vehicle exposed," Fletcher warns. "It's a damn beacon if they send up the search helicopters."

"It's hard to see, but there is a driveway," James says. "Let's get everyone inside. There are shovels on the porch. I'll take Knox and clear enough snow so we can drive the car in and out of sight."

I'd like to unleash hell on Fletcher for multiple reasons, but Serena's vacant stare as she gazes out the window deflates the rage instantly. Her arms are wrapped around her middle, and I can see she's trembling. It's possible she's in shock. She's been through hell, so I wouldn't be surprised. Hopefully, she's just cold. I've at least got my sweatshirt, and I'm still wearing my hiking boots. Serena's just got on a t-shirt and jeans.

When Fletcher climbs out, I ask her again if she's okay.

She nods and swings her door open but hesitates, not getting out. I slide out of my seat and step around her open door to stand in front of her. She's fixated on the deep snow at her feet.

Leaving my t-shirt, I remove my sweatshirt, then quickly pull it over her head. It'll hang to her knees, but will help keep her warm. "I'll carry you," I say when I see her flimsy shoes. Hell, right now, I'd give my left nut to feel her safely tucked against my body.

"I think it would be better if James did that," Fletcher says over the roof of the car. "I don't want you two planning anything."

"Where the hell are we going to go?" I snap.

"Regardless. James," he motions him in our direction.

James rounds the back of the car and makes a move toward Serena. "Don't touch me." She smacks at his hand and backs up into the car.

"Come on, kid. Let's go." He reaches for her again, but she kicks at him. "I said don't touch me!"

It takes every ounce of restraint not to fling James out of her line of sight and pummel him bloody for the way he treated her earlier, but getting her inside and warm is my priority. "Fletcher, let me carry her," I say. "You don't have time for this."

"Fine," he snaps. "James. You lead the way."

"I'm sorry," James tells Serena. "It's nothing personal. I was doing my job."

"I don't want your sorry. I just want to go *home*." The pain in her voice makes my chest ache. She wouldn't be in this situation if it wasn't for me.

James turns from the car, mouth fixed in a hard line, but his eyes tell another story. He's a tool in Fletcher's arsenal, and he handled everything as he should, but he didn't like what he did to Serena. *Interesting.*

She may not let me help her either after the way I treated her the last time we were together. Two seconds after James disappears, Serena bolts from the car and rushes me, throwing her arms around my waist and crying into my chest.

The sound of her distress guts me. "I'm sorry." Cupping her head to hold her close, I press my cheek into her hair. She trembles and sobs harder. "It's okay," I tell her. "I'm here." I remember her next-to-nothing shoes and scoop her up, cradling her against me.

Coming to me this way isn't forgiveness—it's trust—and right now, that's everything.

"Let's go!" Fletcher yells to me, already several yards away.

"Are there any other injuries besides your face?"

"C-cold," her teeth chatter. "A headache. N-nothing more."

A surge of relief rushes through me. "I've got you," I say, pulling her closer. There's so much I need to say to her—to apologize for—but right now, getting her inside is all that matters.

She nestles into my chest with her hands tucked between us. It might be for warmth instead of affection, but I'm thankful that, despite everything, she's comfortable being close to me again.

"Are *y-you* okay?" she asks as I walk toward the cabin.

"I'll be fine." Especially now.

Abruptly, she leans her head away and stares up at me. "You d-didn't kill anyone. In D-Denver. Fletcher s-said so."

What the actual fuck? I stop. "Are you sure?"

"Get in here, now!" Fletcher yells at me from the cabin's porch. "We need to get the vehicle hidden."

"He w-wanted to keep you from l-leaving. That's w-what he told me."

Lost in thought and not focusing on where I'm going, I take a step forward and almost topple us when my foot sinks in deep snow. Serena's arms grip around my neck as she squeaks in fear. "Sorry," I say, sidestepping out of the deepest part of the snowbank and continuing on.

"Not your fault. I'm a l-little jumpy. Did you hear what I s-said? That means you have n-nothing to hide from."

In what kind of conversation would Fletcher share information like that? "I heard you. I'm just not sure how to process it." Everything I was afraid of since running... it's all different. And Fletcher? My father? What the hell do I do with that? Especially right now when all I want to do is strangle him.

"I can understand it's a l-lot to take in. This situation is crazy, huh? What about your anxiety? Like what l-level are you at?"

She should despise me for how I treated her. Yet here she is, worried about me. "No anxiety. I'm just stressed about the situation we're in."

I hear a helicopter in the distance.

"R-really?"

"Yeah." My usual anxiety and panic haven't reared up once since Fletcher called me in the mountains, but I was terrified for Serena, so I'm not sure it's the same. "We need to talk," I tell her.

She looks away from me and sighs out, "I know."

What does she think I'm going to say?

After stepping through the open doorway, I kick the door closed behind us. It's a large one-room cabin with a basic kitchen. There isn't much furniture in the room, just a couch in the center, a small table and two chairs under the window, and a twin-size bed against the far wall.

"We can't light a fire because the choppers will see the smoke," James says as soon as we enter. "Come outside as soon as you can," he says to me, walking past us toward the door.

Fletcher takes a blanket off a small bed against the wall. "You can set her down and wrap her in this."

She locks her arms tighter around my neck. "You have to let me go," I tell her.

It's messed up, isn't it? Finding comfort in her fearful grasp.

"Go and help James," Fletcher barks. "You don't want me intervening."

"Try it and you won't walk out of here," I growl in return.

Serena wiggles to get down. "Go. I'll be fine."

I set her on the couch, slip off her shoes, and rub her feet between my hands. I rip the blanket from Fletcher's grasp, drape it over her, then tuck it underneath, cocooning her in.

"How's that?"

"It's good. Thanks."

I kiss her cheek, then decide to risk it all by capturing her lips with mine. When she leans into the kiss, another coil loosens in my gut.

When I stand, her eyes are mostly closed as she curls into the couch. Taking a step toward Fletcher, I lean in close. "Bother her in any way, and I'll tear you apart. I don't care who the fuck you claim to be."

"Knox!" Serena's voice comes from inside the blanket. "Quit poking the bear."

Not sure why, but her words calm the rage and make me laugh. She's right, though. And the sooner I finish shoveling, the quicker I can get back to her and eliminate at least one fear—the FBI. I don't want a repeat of what happened earlier. It could have gone a lot worse, and I'm not eager for that kind of trouble again. I'm sure Serena isn't either.

Working like demons, it takes fifteen minutes of power shoveling before we can drive the vehicle off the road and into the trees. Luckily for us, aerial surveillance hasn't flown over us yet, but it's getting closer.

James didn't say a word to me the entire time. I'm sure he's still pissed I sucker-punched him. His nose is swollen, and there's bruising under his eyes. I doubt that's the only reason for his silence. None of this has gone as planned.

The man hands me his snow shovel. "Set these back on the porch. I'm going to check out the shed and see if anything useful was left behind, then look for a water source."

I do as he says and head inside. As soon as I'm in the door, Fletcher stands from the table by the window and puts a finger to his lips and points to the couch, signaling me to be quiet.

What the fuck? The self-centered asshole is suddenly concerned about Serena sleeping?

"Do you think the chopper saw the vehicle?" he whispers.

I stare at him, confused by the swift change in mood. "No. They're still a distance away."

He nods as if he's processing the information.

I walk over and check on Serena. She's buried under the covers, fast asleep and looking peaceful. Seeing her that way allows some of the tension coiled in my stomach to relax. I return to Fletcher. "Explain this shit with Leo."

He indicates for me to have a seat at the table with him. As soon as I do, he starts. "Leo created a difficult situation for me before he conveniently disappeared—a debt with the Los Daga cartel, who, several months ago, decided to call in the marker. I've been stalling, trying to figure out how best to proceed, but then your father reappears, much to my surprise."

"Convenient," I deadpan.

"I thought so."

"Why didn't you pay off the debt after Leo's disappearance?" After so many years of fearing this man, it's bizarre having this conversation with him. Who am I kidding? Everything since meeting up with him again has been bizarre.

"It was a huge fucking sum of money, and at the time, the cartel was more interested in favors. I had made valuable associations he wanted in on. When Leo stumbled back onto the grid, I figured I could take care of the two problems at once. It seems to have backfired."

"Seems that way," I say, bitterness dripping from my words.

Several minutes of silence settles between us.

"I hadn't planned to drop the paternal news on you the way I did." He clasps his hands and rests them on the table in front of him.

"Why didn't you tell me when you found out?"

"My head was in a different space."

"That's your excuse for being a shitty human being?"

"Hey. I helped you get *out* of that shitshow."

"By pulling me into another one? I was a messed-up, angry kid. Don't pretend you did it out of the kindness of your heart."

"What can I say? You had useful talents, and I'm a selfish man." He shrugs. "You were fucking it all up, though. Heading down the same destructive path your mother had. That's why when you ran, I decided to let you go. Thought maybe you'd have a better chance on your own."

"How do you figure?"

"The drugs and alcohol wouldn't have been as easily accessible."

"Are you trying to make me believe you have a conscience?"

He chuckles, "Hell no. Far from it."

"Exactly. You fucking let me believe I killed a man just to keep me under your control. I ended up going into hiding, living on the fucking streets."

"It was your choice to run, but I wasn't worried. You've always had good survival instincts. Besides, look where you are now." He has the nerve to smile. "You're finishing school. A carpenter. You got a great girl."

A bitter laugh escapes me. He has no clue about the hell I've lived in—the relentless nightmares, the panic attacks, being held prisoner by my own fears. I've had enough of this reunion. "So, what now?"

He studies me for a moment. "The Feds have Leo, and he'll tell them anything to save his ass. As soon as I can access my accounts, I'll make a wire transfer to my debtor, then disappear." The loud whirring of the helicopter passes over us. Instinctively, we look up.

"What about Serena and me?"

"We'll stay here for a couple of days. Let the initial manhunt move out of the area, then head out and trade the SUV for something else. We'll drop you and Serena off at the first reasonable location we can find, and then disappear." Fletcher nods his head in Serena's direction. "The kid's got fire, and she's strong-willed. She's a good one to have by your side."

James comes in from outside and bangs the snow off his boots at the door—the loud noise a sharp contrast to our whispered conversation.

"You heard the chopper?" James asks. After we nod our response, he moves to the kitchen and starts searching through the cupboards.

"Anything to eat?" Fletcher asks, obviously giving up on the need to be quiet.

I leave them to sort out the food situation and settle down on the floor next to Serena's sleeping form. Watching her squeezes my fucking heart.

After seeing her with Hayden, I let jealousy twist logic in all kinds of stupid angles. Now, I'm just desperate to go back to the way things were, maybe even plan a future together—something I never considered before she stepped back into my life. That's *if* I didn't completely screw it up. She gave me her complete trust, and I threw it back in her face. I cringe at the memory. I really hope she gives me a chance to make it right.

As the helicopter's distant whir cuts through the air, making ultrawide circles above us, I twirl a lock of her hair around my thick finger, feeling its softness.

Watching her eyes move under closed lids, I know I can't go back to the dark place I've been living in most of my life. Not since she brought me into the light. Hell. She *is* the light, and I'll fight with everything I have to be worthy of it.

CHAPTER 49

SERENA

I blink my eyes open to find Knox on the floor with his head resting on my hip. My protector. Even beneath the mustiness of the blanket, the familiar scent clinging to his sweatshirt surrounds me. *God, I've missed him.* The thought instantly depresses me. He hurt me deeper than I ever thought possible, and yet, when he kissed me on this disgusting couch, I melted into the relief of knowing he still cares. Even if it's only a little.

Am I really that needy?

I could blame the chaos of the situation, but I know better. I still want him, and that depresses me even more. Needing someone who can easily throw me away is self-destructive. I've already been through this with my father, and I'd be a fool to allow myself back into that vicious cycle of heartbreak.

I'm dreading what Knox wants to talk to me about. I'm not sure I can handle a polite apology before the final brush off. But if that's what he plans to do, then why did he kiss me?

'*Momentary lack of judgment*'? It has almost been two months since I surprised him at his door and he uttered those words, but it feels like a lifetime ago.

My eyes take in the surroundings. *What's going to happen now?*

At least with Knox here, I'm not as scared as I was. Regardless of everything, I know he'll protect me. He's already proven that.

My mom's got to be freaking out right now. I'm sure she's been filled in on everything that's happened by the police or FBI. I wish I could tell her I'm okay. Hopefully, we'll be out of here soon. I doubt this place has enough food to sustain us for long, anyway.

I hear voices close by, but not from inside the cabin. Fletcher and James must be scheming just outside the front door.

My mouth is incredibly dry, and I have to pee, but I don't want to wake Knox. It's been a stressful thirty-six hours for both of us. I yawn, exhaustion rolling over me once again. I'll close my eyes for a little longer, then wake him.

My nose wrinkles and I twitch as something tickles my face. I swat at the intruder, then crack an eye open. Knox is sitting next to me on the couch with a lock of my hair near my nose, looking mischievous. A very-unlike-Knox expression. "Hey," I say, the word scratchy in my throat.

He releases my hair and holds up a glass of water. "I thought you might be thirsty."

I sit up quickly. Taking the glass out of his hand, I down it. "Thank you." I wipe my mouth with the back of my sleeve.

"How long have I been out?" I glance toward the window. It's almost completely dark outside.

"About three or four hours. Do you always sleep like the dead?"

"Just when I've been traumatized," I joke, but see the pain flash in his eyes. "Don't you dare." I grip his forearm. "None of this is on you."

"Maybe not directly, but I—"

"Stop. Just stop. This has nothing to do with you and everything to do with your father—fathers." I shake my head at the bizarre twist of fate. "You know what I mean."

Knox lifts my hand from his arm and presses it to the familiar coordinates inked over his heart. "I'm glad you're safe."

Home he had whispered on our last night together, and my body aches with the loss. Feeling his heart beat against my palm, I wonder if his action is an absentminded gesture or his way of reminding me—or maybe even himself—what I mean to him. More than likely, it's my hopeless attempt at reading more into this than it is. One way or another, I'm not ready to deal with the emotions that want to pull me back to where we were.

"You should eat."

Not able to think when he touches me, I slide my hand from his and tuck it under the covers. When his expression clouds with concern, it confuses me. He's right. We need to talk, but now isn't the right time. My brain is muddled, and I don't trust myself to say the right things. I don't want any regrets when the situation we're in comes to an end. "Have you talked to Fletcher? When can we leave?"

"When James feels it's safe, we'll head out and switch cars, then Fletcher is going to drop us off in the closest town. They're planning on heading the opposite direction from Cedarvale. As long as nothing gets in our way, we should be home before you know it."

"Is there enough food to last us that long?"

"No. That's the problem. James hunts, but there isn't any gear. He set some snares in the woods, so he might be able to trap something. The good news is, he found a stream not too far away. That's where this water came from." My nose scrunches. *Gross.* "Don't worry. He boiled it. We got lucky. There's a working propane stove."

"Knox." Worry tears through me. "My mom." *What must she be going through?*

"I know." He drops his gaze.

"Can we talk Fletcher into leaving tomorrow? Stick to the back roads."

"Without a GPS, we don't know where any of the roads lead, and there's still a helicopter circling." He tilts his head as if listening. "I haven't heard it in a while, though. They probably called off the search since it's dark."

"Do you trust him? Fletcher?"

"Not really, but there's no reason for him to keep us hostage. We're extra baggage."

"James?" I wonder. His apology threw me. He's a walking contradiction. And unpredictable.

"He seems loyal, but if it came down to his own survival?" he shrugs. "Hard to say." He stands up and holds out a hand. "We saved you some beans. They're going to be cold unless you can wait for me to reheat them."

"Geez, girl," Fletcher says as we near the small table where he and James are sitting. "I was beginning to wonder if you'd *ever* wake up. Knox, get her some food."

James stands, not meeting anyone's eyes. "I'm going to check the snares. Serena, you can have my chair. I'll be back in a bit."

I'm not too sure I want to eat whatever he might catch. I suppose if a person is hungry enough, they'll eat whatever they can find.

CHAPTER 50

SERENA

We all woke up early the next morning, near frozen. The temperature dropped drastically last night. James lit a fire in the potbelly stove after the helicopters stopped circling, but he must have let it die out because it's freezing in here now.

The wind howls past the windows, and it's snowing, hard. A decision is made—we need to leave. It snowed at least six inches last night and doesn't appear to be letting up any time soon. Staying holed up here will be hazardous.

"If we wait much longer, the road could become impassable," James says. "It's your call, sir."

Weather like this is rare in June, but at this altitude, it isn't unheard of. We could easily get a couple of feet of snow that could stick around for several weeks, or it could stop in the next hour and melt a few days later. This time of year, it's a hard call.

"What happens if we're caught?" I direct my question at Fletcher, then look at James. It's been relatively friendly in this small place, but reality is going to hit us out there, and I'm feeling the stress of the potential pitfalls. "I don't want to get caught in the middle if this blows up. Is there a way you could leave us out of it?"

Fletcher picks up the fire-poker and stokes the non-existing fire while we all wait for an answer. After several long minutes, I begin to wonder if he even heard me.

"Knox, did you know I became a legitimate businessman a year after you left?" he sighs and shakes his head. "If that drug lord hadn't called in his marker, none of this would have happened." He sets the wrought-iron poker against the wall. "Now, everything I've built has turned to shit." Fletcher closes his eyes and rubs the spot between his eyebrows with two fingers. "I'm getting too old for this crap." He stands. "Let's head out."

Knox looks worried as he hands me a hunting jacket. I move to take his hoodie off and give it to him, but he stops me.

"Then you should wear the jacket," I say. "I don't need both."

"It won't fit."

"It's freezing out." I pull the sweatshirt over my head, not taking no for an answer. "Take it."

"Thanks."

I crinkle my nose when I slide my arms into the sleeves. It stinks. Under the circumstances, I suppose that's the least of my worries.

"Let's go," James says. "Knox, carry Serena."

Taking quick strides, Knox moves to the couch and grabs the blanket. When he comes back, he wraps it around my body and lifts me into his arms. Instantly, I wonder if this is the last moment we'll have together. As soon as I finish the thought, his eyes find mine.

"Don't even think it," he whispers so only I can hear. "I'm not letting you go this time."

There's so much I need to say, but we're already on the move.

The moment Knox steps outside, the bitter cold bites into my skin. He shuts the door behind us and steps down onto the snowy ground, following a narrow path that's been recently shoveled. I can barely make out Fletcher and James as they head to the SUV. It's snowing hard—the thick, heavy flakes blow sideways.

When we reach the vehicle, Fletcher is already in the passenger seat, and Knox helps me get situated before closing the door. I release a shiver at the sudden warmth. The engine has already been started, and the vehicle cleared of the heavy snow.

The drive back to the main road is a slow, nerve-wracking process, especially with unplowed roads and the blizzard limiting our sight. I have no clue how James is navigating through the swirling chaos. Our drive to the cabin was a maze of turns. With everything looking the same in the whiteout, it will be a miracle if he can find his way.

"I haven't seen any tire tracks," James notes, his focus glued to the nearly invisible road. "It's a good sign."

He must be trying to make us all feel better because there's no way he'd see any with the storm raging around us.

Knox's hand finds mine, his grip a silent reassurance that, no matter what, we're going to be okay. Just as I squeeze his hand back, the glow of headlights pierce through the snow ahead of us.

"Shit," James hisses.

"It might just be a local," Fletcher says.

"Not in this," he returns.

Knox eyes the seatbelt across my chest, and I do the same to him. No one says a word as the car inches closer. The second the SUV passes, we all exhale in a united sigh of relief.

"Fuck!" James shouts, his eyes darting in the rearview mirror. "They're stopping."

Knox and I whip our heads around and see the brake lights, then watch as the vehicle makes a sharp U-turn.

James guns the engine. The surge in speed makes the already lack of visibility near impossible. "I'm not sure how far we are from the main road," he says.

"Slow down!" Knox's grip on my hand tightens to an almost bone-crushing intensity. "This is suicide."

"James. Slow the fuck down!" Fletcher snaps.

"If I can get far enough ahead, we might be able to lose them in the storm. I'll look for a side road."

"You can't expect to find a road when—"

The impact comes out of nowhere, throwing us forward with such brutal force, my body snaps like a whip against the seatbelt. Our world flips over and over with the familiar sickening sounds of shattering glass, crunching metal, and ear-piercing screams. Pain explodes, fierce and blinding, and then nothing.

CHAPTER 51

KNOX

When I come to, the first thing that hits me is the silence. Snow lands with icy pinpricks against my face as I open my eyes. What I see in front of me is total destruction. Our car's flipped on its side. The driver's and part of the passenger's side are crushed in on me. It takes a second to remember the impact. "Serena!"

Her body hangs from the seatbelt above me, limp, lifeless, with glass shards and blood sticking to her face and hair. "Serena!" I call again as a drop of her blood lands on my cheek. *No, no, no.* I attempt to lift my body toward her, but excruciating pain rips through me as a cold sweat breaks out across my body. My legs are trapped behind the twisted remnants of the car.

Reaching up, terrified to touch her and find out she's gone, I slide my fingers along her neck in search of a pulse. *I can't lose her.* Panic like I've never felt engulfs me as my fingers reposition over and over in an attempt to feel proof of life. The moment my fingers sense a faint beat, I sink back to the ground, letting relief wash over me as everything goes dark.

I wake to shouting. Someone in the window above us. "You have to help her," I say, my voice weak. *Can they hear me?* More faces appear. There's a siren, then I black out.

CHAPTER 52

SERENA

Light flickers. A blur of brightness. Intense, unbearable pain. Echoes of voices, distant and urgent. Someone's crying. Everything's too loud. Too bright. And then it all slips away into nothingness.

CHAPTER 53

KNOX

"Let me see her!" I fight against someone's grip on me. "Serena!" I holler, feeling nothing but desperation as my eyes search because my neck won't move. I feel a prick in my arm as bright lights flash by above me. Doors crash open, more movement, and then everything goes fuzzy and disappears.

CHAPTER 54

SERENA

Knox? He's trapped. I can't reach him. He's dead. Knox! I jerk awake.

A hand touches my arm. "You're okay," a soft voice urges. "But I need you to be still."

"Mom?" She comes into view over me. "What happened?" I ask, attempting to look around but can't turn my head. "Where am I?" The sterile smell, the relentless beeping of a monitor, then it clicks. "Where's Knox?" I ask as the sharp edges of panic continue to slice through me. Memories flash—glass shattering, the cruel sound of metal bending and scraping. "We hit something. Knox was with me. Is he okay?" My mother is blurry through the tears. "Why can't I move my neck?"

"You're injured, honey. I know you're scared, but I need you to try to stay calm."

I latch onto her arm. "*Mom*, where is Knox?"

"He's... he's in surgery right now."

Devastation hits like a freight train, shattering me into a million pieces. "I have to see him." I fight against the pain to sit up. The motion makes the aching throb worse, and a sickening wave of dizziness hits my stomach.

"You can't right now." Mom gently presses on my shoulders, easing me back as I try to suck in a breath against an invisible weight of fear pressing down on me. "But as soon as he's out of surgery, we'll see what we can do."

My chest feels so tight. "Do you know if he's going to be okay?" *He has to be. Never seeing him again...*

"I don't have any details yet. Let me get the doctor and tell them you're awake."

"I don't care about the doctor," I holler as desperation takes my breath. "Can you find out what's wrong with him?" I fight to pull air into my lungs as I strangle out the words. "Why is... he in... surgery?"

Mom runs out the door. "Nurse!" she yells.

She's talking to someone outside the door, then hurries back to my side. "You need to breathe, okay?" Her face is strained, her eyes pleading. "I'll check on Knox, but only if you calm down. Please. I can't leave if you're hysterical. Do you understand?"

"Mom. I... can't get air," I gasp.

A nurse hurries in. "You're having a panic attack," Mom says, her voice shaky. "Breathe with me, okay? Focus on my voice and follow my lead. In... one, two, three. Are you with me?" She grips my hand, grounding me. "Listen to me. Focus. Then I can check on Knox. In... one, two, three, hold... and out, one, two, three." I strain against the pressure, my lungs refusing to cooperate. "You've got this. For Knox, okay? Again, breathe in, one, two, three, and four, hold... and out, one, two, three, four. You can do it."

Precious time ticks away—time taking me away from information. "Just go and check." I start to feel woozy, but the crushing weight begins to lift. Mom continues to help me focus on my breathing as an unexpected wave of heavy fatigue seeps in. My eyelids grow heavy. My body feels strangely detached. "Mom?" I question, confusion setting in. "What's wrong with me?"

"The nurse gave you a sedative to help you relax."

"You were going to check... on Knox." My speech is slurred, my mind foggy. "I'm... I'm calm now." *What if they can't wake me up and he dies when I'm asleep?*

"I promise I'll go and check on him as soon as I see that you're settled. I just need to make sure you're resting first, alright?"

She wouldn't lie to me. "Okay," I murmur, feeling every bit of the exhaustion that's been piling on. I fight to keep my eyes open. "I'm good now," I promise. "I don't want to fall asleep."

"Just a little rest," I hear her say.

My body feels as though it's drifting on air, detached from the pain and fear that's rooted me to this bed. Now all I need is Knox.

When I pry my eyes open, my father is sitting in the chair beside me, his chin resting on his chest. "Dad?"

His head snaps up, his eyes—red and weary—take a second to adjust. "Hey, sunshine. How do you feel?"

"My head is fuzzy, and I had the weirdest dreams..." My voice trails off as the harsh reality of the hospital room creeps in. "Knox!" Once again, I'm struggling against the pain to sit up and go to him. "Mom was going to find out how he is. Where is she?"

My father stands and guides me to lie back down. "Please. You need to rest. As far as I know, he's still in surgery. How are you feeling?" Concerned eyes roam my face.

I grip his arm. "Still? How long have I been asleep? Has there been any word?" The weight is back, pressing down on my chest.

"I understand how worried you are. I really do, but if you get hysterical, they'll sedate you again. Don't let it get there, alright? As soon as you calm down, I will explain about Knox."

I shut my eyes, struggling to curb the rising panic. I want to scream—demand answers.

"Your mother is way better at this stuff than I am, but I bet she'd tell you to take some deep breaths." I'm too drained to argue, so I follow his advice. Thanks to the drugs still in my system, calming down is easier this time. "That's better," he says, nodding with relief, clearly convinced I'm not on the edge of freaking out again. "You've been asleep for about four hours. Your mother told me that Knox's surgery is going well."

A small sense of relief washes over me. *Why didn't he just say that to begin with?*

"Are we at the hospital where Mom works?" If she was able to get information on Knox, we must be.

"Yes. It was closest to the crash site."

I close my eyes against the awful sounds echoing through my head.

"Can I get you anything?" he asks, snapping me out of the traumatic memory.

"Some water, please." Every time I swallow, I have to peel my tongue from the roof of my mouth.

Rising, he smooths my hair back from my face and kisses my forehead. The sudden affection startles me. It's been so long. He smiles briefly, then turns away, hastily typing a message on his phone, likely updating Mom.

He fills a cup from a pitcher on the table next to my bed and hands it to me. "Seeing you like this... I feel like I'm reliving that horrific accident all over again. I could have lost you, again." His voice cracks. "I didn't realize how far apart we'd become. It shouldn't take a disaster like this to wake me up."

He scrubs a hand over his face and sits beside me on the bed. "The guilt... if I hadn't been drinking that night, maybe I wouldn't have lost control of the car and hit the tree." His hand, trembling slightly, finds mine. "My weakness... and you paid the price." He shakes his head in disgust. "Sorry. I didn't mean to make this about me. I just want you to know that I am here now, ready to support you through this in any way you need."

When he hands me a tissue, I realize my cheeks are stinging from the salty tears in fresh wounds. The sting jolts me back to Knox. "I appreciate everything you said, and I'm sure I'll process all this later, but I can't think past the need for information. So, please... tell me everything you know about Knox."

He nods in understanding. "I only know the basics, but here is what your mom found out."

CHAPTER 55

KNOX

It's a sharp pain that wakes me. I hear the beeping, then the sensation of someone's hand squeezing mine. *Serena.* My eyes flash open, and there she is. Her beautiful face marred with nasty cuts and bruises—her upper body locked in plastic. "No," I say, my voice raspy as I reach out to touch her. A tangle of tubes and wires shift with my movement.

"It's okay," she says through a watery smile. "We're okay."

"How badly are you hurt?" I try to sit up, but the agony in my ribs leaves me gasping.

"Don't move," she tells me. "You're in ICU. You were in surgery until a couple of hours ago."

"You didn't answer my question." Briefly closing my eyes, I breathe through the discomfort.

"I'm going to be fine." She carefully lifts herself from a wheelchair.

"No, you're not. You're in a fucking wheelchair." Fear squeezes my chest, the pressure making it hard to breathe.

Ignoring my rant, she carefully positions her hands on either side of my body and lowers her lips to mine. The gentle pressure calms me instantly. Closing my eyes, I breathe her in. When she draws back an inch, I exhale an indescribable mix of relief and longing.

"I was afraid I'd never get to do this again," she says, her mouth hovering over mine. "I thought... I thought I lost you."

"I'm sorry. If I could go back..." She leans away—her expression sad and weary. She must be in terrible pain. "Please, sit back down. You shouldn't be out of that chair." She doesn't argue as she eases back into her seat. "I can't believe your parents let you out of their sight, let alone out of bed."

"I didn't give them much of a choice. Mom is outside the door, anxiously waiting to get me back to my room."

"Thank you for being here. If I'd woken up alone, I would have lost my mind wondering if you were okay. Now that I know you are, you should go back and get some rest. But before you do, could you tell me how bad you're hurt so I can stop worrying so damn much?"

"Yes, but don't freak out. It's nothing major. Promise?"

"I'll do my best," I grind out.

"That surly-ass mouth of yours. You have no idea how happy I am to hear it." Her bright smile has me growling in frustration. "I'm sorry," she laughs, resting a hand on my arm. "I shouldn't get you worked up. I'm just so happy you're okay." Her face sobers. "I have two cracked vertebrae in my neck, multiple cracked ribs, and a fractured collarbone. You've seen my face. Head trauma, but they already did a scan. There aren't any edemas. See? I'm going to be fine."

Fine? Every injury hits me like a physical blow. There is nothing *fine* about this.

"Stop it!" she says. "I can see the guilt all over your face. You didn't choose your parents or the disaster that followed. But all that's over now."

Yeah, but is it? What's going to happen once the FBI question me? I try to lift a knee, but nothing happens. Then I try the other. Same thing. "Why can't I feel my legs?" I whip my covers away and suck in a sharp breath.

Serena is on her feet again. "You're going to be okay." She sets a reassuring hand on my chest. "Knox?"

Her voice sounds far away as profound terror engulfs me. I can't take my eyes off the carnage in front of me. "Am I paralyzed?" I manage to get out.

"No. You're not paralyzed." When I continue to stare, she says, "Knox, look at me. You are going to walk again." When I still can't look away, she pulls the covers over my legs, hiding them from view. "All I do know is your prognosis is good. The doctor will have to give you the details."

"But why can't I feel my legs?"

"I'm not sure. Let me go and ask my mom to find someone who can give you answers."

She makes a move toward the door, but I grip her hand before she can pull away. "You'll come back, right, with the nurse or whatever?" For so long, all I wanted was to be alone. Now the idea terrifies me beyond belief.

"Absolutely. Mom will find someone for you. I just have to talk to her, and then I'll come right back. I promise. And Rhett should be here soon. He has been by your side the whole time, but I made him go and eat something while I sat with you."

"Okay, but get back in that damn wheelchair. Better yet, let me call a nurse."

"The nurses are busy and take a while. I can get to my mom faster," she says, halfway to the door before I can object.

"Knox," a male voice wakes me. My lids are lifted, and a bright light shines in my eye.

I flinch away. "What the hell?"

"Sorry about that. I'm Dr. Leahy."

Rhett is sitting on a small couch, Serena in her wheelchair next to him, their obvious concern stressing out my already-frayed nerves from the doctor's jarring wake-up call. I don't even remember falling asleep.

"Your vitals look good," the doctor says.

"Why can't I move my legs?" That's all I want to know. Suddenly, I feel like I'm going to puke.

"You should have some feeling by now." He frowns, lifting the bottom of my blanket to reveal my feet. "Try wiggling your toes." I do as he asks. At the slight movement, I feel intense relief, along with excruciating pain. "Both legs suffered extensive damage. There are multiple screws, plates, and rods holding the bones together, so your legs need to remain immobile until the swelling goes down and we can get you casted. If you don't follow post-surgical protocol, there will be complications, and you may need further surgery. Chances are, you won't be fully weight-bearing for six to eight weeks."

"I can't miss that much work!" I say, sitting up and instantly regretting it.

"*Boy*, hush," Rhett says. "Let the doctor finish." I slowly lower myself back against the pillows. *Fuck, that hurt.*

"After we remove the cast, you'll require extensive physical therapy to maximize your chances for a full recovery. However, even with dedicated rehabilitation, there's a possibility that you may have a residual limp. Fortunately, you have the advantage of youth and a skilled surgeon," he says, a hint of confidence in his cocky grin. "In addition to the internal bruising, you have several fractured ribs. Fortunately, there's no evidence of any punctured organs. You've sustained a transverse fracture of your radius and ulna in your right arm, as well as a hairline fracture on your right collarbone. There's evidence of moderate head trauma, but no bleeding of the brain. I'm sure I don't need to emphasize how fortunate you are."

"How long will I have to stay in the hospital?"

"Expect a month, possibly longer."

"No way. I'll lose my fu—my mind."

"Count your blessings that you're still alive. And trust me, you will be happy for the assistance, if for nothing more than with your bodily functions. Now, I've prescribed painkillers. Once I step out, the nurse will come in and administer the next round."

"I don't want any narcotics."

"Are you certain about that?" he says, raising an eyebrow. When I nod, he responds, "Very well. I'll prescribe anti-inflammatories, instead. However, if at any point you find the pain unbearable and it is hampering your sleep in any way, have a nurse contact me. Sleep is crucial to your healing process."

No way am I staying in this bed for a month. "I have a high pain tolerance," I grit out. "I'll be fine."

"Suit yourself. I'll schedule a follow-up appointment in a week, unless any complications arise," the doctor says and starts writing in my chart.

Realizing I'm being a moody, ungrateful ass, I sigh. "Thank you. For, um, putting me back together."

"It was my pleasure." He closes the folder and tucks it under his arm. "Just make sure you don't undo all my hard work," he says, a genuine smile sneaking past the intense façade.

"I won't." I've been through all this before. Not to this extent, but still...

Rhett is by my side as soon as the doctor leaves. "Don't you worry about a thing. Once you get out of here, you can stay at my place. We'll hire any help you need when I'm at work. And before you fret, insurance pays for it."

"Thank you. For everything."

"Someone's got to have your back. Now, you just focus on getting better. The job will be there when you're all fixed up. In the meantime, get ready to be taken care of. I know you hate being indebted to anyone, but you're going to have to deal with it."

"Yeah, yeah," I grumble with a weak smile. I'm fucking alive, after all.

"Knox." Serena wheels herself over. Rhett steps back so she can get in close to the bed.

Shit. Fear instantly coils in my chest. *There's more.* I can see it all over her face. "What?" *The doctor would have told me everything, right?* My eyes quickly take in her appearance, then land on Rhett. He looks exhausted, but... *did I miss something?*

"Um—" Serena starts.

"What is it?" I cut her off.

"It's Fletcher," she says, gently lifting my hand and cradling it between hers. "I asked if I could be the one to tell you. He didn't make it, and neither did James."

"Oh." A guilty sense of relief takes over.

"Are you okay?" she asks, worry in her eyes.

"I think so." It's a lot to take in on top of everything else. What Fletcher was versus who he came to be... I'm not sure how to feel about the news. And James, he seemed like a decent guy in a really shitty job.

"You two talk," Rhett says. "I'm going to go home and get some sleep. I'll be back tomorrow to check on you." He touches the fingers on my casted arm. "I'm glad you're still with us," he says. "It's been a long time since I've been that scared. Don't do that to me again, you hear?"

"I'll try not to. And thanks. For everything."

"You bet."

Serena and I both watch silently as the door closes behind him, an odd sense of relief washing over me. Fletcher is gone. My nightmare is over. That's some fucked-up thinking. The man lost his life.

"There's one other thing I need to tell you," she says, still holding my hand.

"Can it wait until tomorrow?" I blow out a tense breath. "I don't think I can handle any more bad news."

"No. This is a good thing."

"Okay, but then you should go back and rest. Your parents will have my balls in a vise if your health suddenly goes to shit."

"No. They understand this is the best medicine for both of us right now. Besides, I'll rest easier now that I know you're going to be okay." She smiles at me before continuing. "So, the FBI wants to talk to you—"

My body goes rigid. "I thought you said this was good news," I blurt, not allowing her to finish. *So much for the nightmare being over.*

"It *is* good news because my dad said he'll represent you. After I explained everything to him, he doesn't think you have anything to worry about. See? Good news."

"Serena, I don't have that kind of money."

"He's doing it pro-bono. Like Mom, he remembers you. He wants to help."

"You told him everything?" A jolt of alarm sends my heart racing.

"Everything that was relevant." She stares at me, confusion mixed with concern. "Why? What are you afraid of?"

I didn't kill anyone. The idea hasn't settled in yet. "Nothing. I guess I've been hiding my past for so long. The defensiveness... it's become a part of me." Suddenly, exhaustion has my eyelids drifting closed.

"I'll leave his card next to the phone. Call him tomorrow. You should get some sleep."

She starts to pull away. "Don't go." I tighten my grip on her hand, then realize I sound like a big-ass baby and release her. "Never mind."

With the lightest touch of her free hand, she brushes her fingers up my forearm. "I can stay a little longer."

I close my eyes, soaking up the sensation, but images flash behind my lids—glass and debris, icy flecks burning my skin. Serena hanging by her seatbelt. My eyes pop open as a sudden wave of dizziness turns my stomach.

"Are you okay?"

Seeing her here, feeling her touch... it's the only proof I have that we both survived. But what if I'd lost her? Panic tears through my chest as the sudden need for her to stay intensifies. *Don't go there, Knox.* She's right here.

"Knox?"

I never got to apologize. What if Serena won't give me another chance? When she kissed me earlier, she was worried about me. It didn't mean anything. What if she wants nothing more to do with me? My throat is suddenly choking off my air.

"Knox." She gently shakes me. "Hey. What's wrong? All the blood just drained from your face. Should I get the nurse?"

The heart monitor begins to beep its warning. "No," I say, hating that there is no way to hide my fears from her. "It's—"

She pushes herself out of the wheelchair and sits beside me on the bed. "Knox. Look at me."

"Are we—" My throat is so tight. I swallow hard to try to get my words out.

"It's okay. You're okay," she reassures, pulling our linked hands close to her chest. "I understand what panic feels like. When I thought I lost you—"

"But did I? Did I lose you?" I say, fighting against the suffocating grip taking control.

"What are you talking about? I'm right here."

"I'm so... sorry." The words come out as gasps. "For Stuart... for not letting you explain... about Hayden. For ghosting you. Did... I... lose you?"

Realization flashes in her eyes. "Never." Bending forward, she presses a kiss on my lips. "But I need you to breathe with me. Can you do that?" I nod, fighting the humiliation against the need for air. "Okay. Like this..." Counting, she takes a slow, deep breath, holds, then exhales. This process isn't new to me, but the calmness of her voice makes all the difference.

Her lips touch mine again. "Keep going." As I do, she releases my hands and sets one of hers over my heart. "Remember the image you call home? Well, I'm here. Right in front of you, and I'm not letting you go. Do you hear me?" She holds my gaze. "You are mine, and I am yours. Then and now. Always."

The instant her words sink in, the tightness in my chest releases, and air rushes into my lungs. After several full breaths, I lift her hand from where it lays over my heart and kiss her fingers, then place her palm against my cheek and lean into her touch. "Everything got twisted up in my head after I showed up at the party and lost it. After that, I didn't want you to be around all my shit, and then when I saw you with Hayden, every insecurity and fear I've ever had came crashing down on me. I let it take control. Then my dad—I didn't handle any of it well."

"*Shhh*. You're forgiven." She peppers my bruised and battered face with gentle kisses, then leans back, her eyes unwavering as they meet mine. "Nothing you did was malicious. Even kicking the shit out of Hayden... you were protecting me. It was extreme, but with everything you've been through, I understand the reaction."

"You're letting me off easy," I say, my heart full of regret.

"*Ohhh*, I may have forgiven you, but I'm going to let you suck up to me for a *very* long time." She grins with a shrug.

Amusement washes away some of the guilt. Fighting against the pain, I lean the short distance forward and kiss her. "Promise?" I say against her lips.

"Promise, but let's leave the past where it belongs, okay?"

Pressing back against my pillow, my heart swells with hope and possibility. "That's the best news I've heard today." My eyelids drift closed, exhaustion taking over. "Serena?"

"*Hmm?*"

"I might screw up again, but next time, I'll try not to be a dick about it." Her laugh chimes like soft bells. *Am I already dreaming, or am I hallucinating?* My thoughts blur around the edges, and sleep takes hold, but one sensation remains.

A profound sense of gratefulness.

Because I made it through hell and back and found something worthwhile on the other side.

CHAPTER 56

SERENA

It's been three months since the accident. My exams had to be postponed for several weeks, and needless to say, I didn't receive the honor of valedictorian, but that's okay. I got something better. I got Knox.

Dealing with the aftereffects of this accident hasn't been easy on top of the trauma of my previous accident. I'm not sure how I ever got back into a car. Driving—being in control helps—but more than anything, having Knox and not dealing with this alone has made all the difference.

I'm on my way home from Denver to visit him now. College is awesome, but only getting to see him on weekends is rough. I miss him like crazy. The upside, I'm only thirty minutes away, so when neither of us is too busy, we get together. Sadly, that doesn't happen often enough.

At least he's out of the hospital. As the doctor predicted, Knox spent a month in bed. The inactivity was hard for him, but since he had so much time on his hands, he finished his coursework and graduated high school. Having that to focus on helped him get through. That, and all his visitors. Me, of course, but also Rowan and Tish, along with Rhett, and The Ladies— even my mom. Everyone adding a spark of energy to his otherwise monotonous days.

My GPS follows the pin he dropped. The location is up in the mountains somewhere remote, so I have no idea what he's up to. As far as I know, he's still not allowed to drive.

Rounding the next bend, my adrenaline spikes. I haven't been up here since the accident. Not for any other reason than I haven't had time, but now... damn, this was unexpected.

I consider pulling over to steady my nerves, then decide seeing Knox is exactly what I need to settle me down. That, and I have to keep reminding myself it could have been so much worse. Fletcher and James died. It wasn't easy for Knox or me to cope with the viciousness of their deaths. We've talked a lot about it without really coming to any worthwhile conclusion. Guilt played a factor for both of us, because as twisted as it sounds, Fletcher's death gave Knox his freedom.

"In a quarter-mile, turn left," the GPS lady kindly states.

The psychologist Rhett insisted Knox see, besides his usual psychiatrist, concluded that he has been suffering from post-traumatic stress disorder, stemming from his childhood trauma, heightened by the fear of Fletcher finding him and his guilt of killing a man. With all of that resolved, his anxiety and panic attacks got a lot better—at least more manageable. So, yeah, freedom.

"Turn right."

I'm grateful the FBI dropped their investigation. As it turned out, my dad didn't have to invest too much time in the case. With

Fletcher gone and Knox lacking any useful information regarding his father's recent business dealings, they no longer needed to involve him. Leo, on the other hand, was sentenced to several years in jail for a multitude of reasons—one being that he faked his death and had a "wife" receive a large life insurance payout. She got a cut. He got the rest.

"Go past this left, then turn at the next one."

So far, my dad has kept his promise to me. I've been to dinner at his house quite a bit, and I feel like we're on our way back to a good relationship.

"Turn left." I put on my blinker and do as the nice AI lady insists.

I can't wait to see Knox. We didn't get a chance to see each other last weekend because my twin brothers celebrated their third birthday. It's been fun getting to know the rambunctious duo. They've appointed me their human shield against all things disagreeable, mostly vegetables and getting ready for bed.

"You have arrived."

I slow to a stop. "Arrived where?" I look around, not seeing anything but the deep green of tall pines and the shimmery gold of the aspen leaves. I inch my car a little farther forward and see a navy-blue truck parked a short distance down a dirt driveway. "Huh." That's not Rhett's truck. Looking around, trying to decide what to do next, I see Knox using a cane to support his leg, which is encased in a plastic boot, as he walks toward me.

Nerves instantly squashed, I squeal in delight, shut off the engine, then bolt from the car. "Where are your crutches? Your cast is gone! Should you be walking? You know what the doctor said. You can't—"

Knox steps forward, grips the back of my neck, and plasters

his lips against mine. It feels like eons since we've been this close. I can't help but melt into him.

Will this connection ever get old?

Not with those talented lips.

I groan in displeasure when he breaks the kiss. He's smiling with dimples on full display when he tells me they took the cast off a couple of days ago.

"Why didn't you tell me?"

"I wanted to surprise you." He leans forward, kissing my forehead.

"Did Rhett get a new truck?"

"It's mine."

"You bought a truck?" I beam in surprise.

He grins. "I did."

I look around. "Are we having a picnic or something?"

"No. Sorry. That would have been a good idea. Actually, I needed help deciding where the house should go."

"It's a beautiful spot. Is Rhett letting you design the layout of his next build?"

"Not *his* build. Mine. I bought the land."

"Seriously? Holy crap!" I hug him hard, then step back, surveying my surroundings. "With this location—all these trees—you shouldn't have any trouble selling it when it's done." Building a spec house is a great investment.

"I'm not selling it." He slings an arm over my shoulder. "Which direction do you think will have the best view off the porch?"

I'm so proud of him. He's living his dream. "You're the expert." My head falls easily to his shoulder.

He squeezes me into his side and kisses the top of my head.

"Yeah, but this will be your home, too. I think you should have a say."

My head snaps up and to the side so fast, the muscles in my neck seize with a twinge of pain. "What?" Wincing, I grip the back of my neck. Even after all this time, it still gives me grief.

"Here, let me." He steps behind me and lets his fingers loose on the cramped muscles. "I know you have lots of school left. Hell, I don't even know if you want to live in Cedarvale when it's all done. As long as I'm with you, I'm fine wherever you want to live. In the meantime, I'd like this to be ours. Weekends, holidays, summers. When you finish college, it's up to you. I can sell the house, and buy or build something wherever you want to be."

Warmth fills my heart to the point of bursting. My plan has always been to move away from here, but now... I stare off, taking in the land surrounding us, then spin around to face him. "Did you win the lottery or something?"

"Actually, Fletcher had a large life insurance policy, as well as a trust fund set up when he found out I was his kid. Sorry. I probably should have told you, but I've had my eye on this lot for over a year. Once I dealt with the news from the lawyer, I got the idea to surprise you."

It's difficult to be angry when I see the raw emotions playing across his face. "It's okay." Though I'm surprised he took Fletcher's money.

"I decided to donate the trust to an organization that helps women with children get back on their feet after rehab. I don't want his dirty money." A sense of pride swells in my chest. "The life insurance is what I'll use to build the house. The rest... I'm not sure. We could travel for fun after you graduate. Maybe go to Europe?" He shrugs with a weak smile. "I don't know how well I'll do, but with you by my side, I think I'd like to try."

"You and me exploring the world together?" I grin up at him. "I like that idea."

He picks up both my hands, sucks in a lungful of air, then releases it through his lips. "You bulldozed your way into my life and refused to let me hide." His eyes fix intensely on mine. "You have the kindest heart and the patience of a saint. You never gave up on me. You helped me believe I was worthwhile."

I think my heart just stopped.

"That sounded way more awkward than it did in my head." He drops his head back, then refocuses on me. "I know we've never said the words before. Hell..." He drags a hand through his neatly cropped hair. "I've never said them in my entire life. I always thought they were for novels and suckers, but... I love you, Serena. So, so much. It's been a hard, painful road to get to where we are, but worth it. So... will you help me design our house?" His eyes plead with mine.

I step forward, wrapping my arms tightly around his neck before leaning back, gently placing a hand on his cheek. "I'm not sure words have been invented to describe the way I feel about you. Saying 'I love you' doesn't even begin to cover it, but they'll have to do. I love you, Knox. More than I thought was realistically possible. And yes, I will most definitely design a house with you."

Not wasting a second, Knox's lips collide with mine with an entirely new level of emotion, and I'm instantly lost in the rush. From where we began to where we are now, I never dreamed of being in this moment.

With all his anger and sharp edges, always keeping the world at a distance, I wondered if he was just another mistake. But he isn't a mistake. He's a gift from a woman who, after so many wrongs, got it right.

Named after the angel Gabriel, Knox has become mine. With a pure spirit, unrelenting courage, and a selfless will to protect, he's become the radiant light that fills my heart.

When his lips leave mine and he wraps me in an all-consuming embrace, I can't help but feel an overwhelming sense of gratitude for all the challenges that led us here. They made us who we are. But you know what? They don't define us. Our past, our struggles—they don't get to write our ending.

This is *our* story, and *we* decide what comes next.

———

For bonus content, please sign up for my email here or type in raynayork.com into your browser and receive: deleted scenes, an alternate ending, and the original dream that started it all.

If you enjoyed Every Scar Tells a Story, please consider leaving a review at the store where you purchased it. More than anything else, your words help authors get the exposure we need to create new stories to share with you, our beloved readers.

You can also scan this QR code to listen to the official *Every Scar Tells a Story* Spotify playlist.

AUTHOR'S NOTE

Writing this book was a challenge, both in adopting a dual perspective narrative and in addressing themes that are deeply personal to me. For seven years, I grappled with severe anxiety triggered by a traumatic incident. The journey towards recovery was anything but direct, but I emerged stronger than ever.

During this period, I came across a woman with a tattoo on her forearm that read *Every Scar Tells a Story*. The words struck a powerful chord with me. Although I never intended to use the phrase for a novel, the moment Serena and Knox were created, there was no other title that would fit the characters so perfectly.

We all bear scars, not just the visible ones, but also those invisible wounds that mark our hearts, minds, and souls. Like physical scars, they may fade over time but never vanish completely. I acknowledge that some people bear deeper mental scars than others, ones that time alone cannot heal. However, I've learned that every one, no matter its size or depth, holds significance. They matter. You matter. You're not alone. Although it may seem like no one can help, there are professional, innovative therapies out there that could alleviate some of the pain and suffering. While I'm not an expert, and people's responses to trauma and their paths to recovery can vary widely, I speak from personal experience when I say, *don't give up*. Even the smallest steps can help reclaim some of your power. As for you, remember, the world needs you, scars and all. Let's be kind to ourselves and each other.

XOXOXO
Rayna York

ACKNOWLEDGMENTS

Writing a novel involves so much more than piecing words together. While the creation may seem like a solitary task, bringing the final product to life involves the efforts of many.

I want to express my heartfelt thanks to my author friends, C.L. Walters and Julia Blake, for reading the manuscript in its ugly stages and not judging me. A big shout-out to my beta readers, Laurel Clouston and Laura Stockwell, whose honest feedback was indispensable. I doubt Serena and Knox's story would have been as impactful without their insights.

A huge thank you goes out to all my editors: Marissa Taylor for line editing, Elaine York for copy editing, Lara Wilkinson for proofreading, and finally, Olivia Kirby and my mother who caught those pesky mistakes that slipped through.

To my launch team whose early reviews and social media buzz kick-started the momentum. An immense thank you for lifting my book out of the deep depths of obscurity.

Thank you to my readers for absorbing the pages I so carefully crafted. (this one took forever) Without you, the words wouldn't have a voice. Please stay in touch by signing up for my newsletter at http://www.raynayork.com. I promise not to spam the crap out of you.

And finally, thank you to my family for being my biggest cheerleaders of all.